8/11/2020

RELENTLESS

ALSO BY R. A. SALVATORE

THE LEGEND OF DRIZZT BOOKS

Homeland

Exile

Sojourn

The Crystal Shard

Streams of Silver

The Halfling's Gem

The Legacy

Starless Night

Siege of Darkness

Passage to Dawn

The Silent Blade

The Spine of the World

Sea of Swords

Servant of the Shard

Promise of the Witch King

Road of the Patriarch

The Thousand Orcs

The Lone Drow

The Two Swords

The Orc King

The Pirate King

The Ghost King

Gauntlgrym

Neverwinter

Charon's Claw

The Last Threshold

The Companions

Night of the Hunter

Rise of the King

Vengeance of the Iron Dwarf

Archmage

Maestro

Hero

Timeless

Boundless

SAGA OF THE FIRST KING

The Highwayman

The Ancient

The Dame

TALES OF THE COVEN

Child of a Mad God

Reckoning of Fallen Gods

Song of the Risen God

FORGOTTEN REALMS®

RELENTLESS

A DRIZZT NOVEL

R. A. Salvatore

HARPER Voyager

An Imprint of HarperCollins Publishers

FIRST EDITION

Designed by Paula Russell Szafranski
Maps courtesy of Wizards of the Coast
Frontispiece and opener art © Aleks Melnik / Shutterstock

Library of Congress Cataloging-in-Publication Data has been applied for.

ISBN 978-0-06-268867-5

20 21 22 23 24 LSC 10 9 8 7 6 5 4 3 2 1

This book is for the readers, both those who have wandered this road with me for more than three decades now and those younger than the earlier Drizzt books they're holding in their hands as they join the adventure for the first time.

For me, what a wonderful journey it's been.

And here's to Diane, long-suffering in social isolation with me during these surreal times!

CONTENTS

DRAMATIS PERSONAE

In the past . . . all of them drow.

HOUSE XORLARRIN

Matron Zeerith Xorlarrin: Powerful leader of the city's fourth-ranked house.

Horroodissomoth Xorlarrin: Xorlarrin house wizard and former master of Sorcere, the drow academy for practitioners of the arcane magic.

Kiriy: Priestess of Lolth, daughter of Zeerith and Horroodissomoth.

HOUSE SIMFRAY

Matron Divine Simfray: Ruler of the minor house.

Zaknafein Simfray: Young and powerful champion of House Simfray, with a growing reputation putting him among the greatest warriors in the city. Coveted by ambitious Matron Malice, both for the growth of her house and her personal desires.

HOUSE TR'ARACH

Matron Hauzz: Ruler of the minor house.

Duvon Tr'arach: Son of Matron Hauzz, weapon master of House Tr'arach, determined to prove himself.

Daungelina Tr'arach: Eldest daughter of Matron Hauzz and first priestess of the minor house.

Dab'nay Tr'arach: Daughter of Matron Hauzz, currently studying at Arach-Tinilith, the drow academy for Lolthian priestesses.

HOUSE BAENRE

Matron Mother Yvonnel Baenre: Also known as Yvonnel the Eternal, Matron Mother Baenre is the undisputed leader not only of the First House, but of the entire city. While other families might refer to their matron as "matron mother," all in the city use that title for Yvonnel Baenre. She is the oldest living drow, and has been in a position of great power longer than the longest memory of anyone in the city.

Gromph Baenre: Matron Mother Baenre's oldest child, archmage of Menzoberranzan, the highest-ranking man in the city, and most formidable wizard in the entire Underdark, by many estimations.

Dantrag Baenre: Son of Matron Mother Baenre, weapon master of the great house, considered one of the greatest warriors in the city.

Triel, Quenthel, and Sos'Umptu Baenre: Three of Matron Mother Baenre's daughters, priestesses of Lolth.

OTHER NOTABLES

K'yorl Odran: Matron of House Oblodra, notable for its use of the strange mind magics called psionics.

Jarlaxle: A houseless rogue who began Bregan D'aerthe, a mercenary band quietly serving the needs of many drow houses, but mostly serving their own needs.

Arathis Hune: Drow lieutenant to Jarlaxle and assassin extraordinaire. Taken into the band, as with many of the members, after the fall of his house.

In the present . . . many races.

Drizzt Do'Urden: Born in Menzoberranzan and fled the evil ways of the city. Drow warrior, hero of the north, and Companion of the Hall, along with his four dear friends.

Catti-brie: Human wife of Drizzt, Chosen of the goddess Mielikki, skilled in both arcane and divine magic. Companion of the Hall.

Regis (Spider Parrafin): Halfling husband of Donnola Topolino, leader of the halfling community of Bleeding Vines. Companion of the Hall.

King Bruenor Battlehammer: Eight king of Mithral Hall, tenth king of Mithral Hall, now king of Gauntlgrym, an ancient dwarven city he reclaimed with his dwarven kin. Companion of the Hall. Adoptive father of both Wulfgar and Catti-brie.

Wulfgar: Born to the Tribe of the Elk in Icewind Dale, the giant human was captured by Bruenor in battle and became the adopted son of the dwarf king. Companion of the Hall.

Artemis Entreri: Former nemesis of Drizzt, the human assassin is the drow warrior's near equal or equal in battle. Now he runs with Jarlaxle's Bregan D'aerthe band, and considers Drizzt and the other Companions of the Hall friends.

Guenhwyvar: Magical panther, companion of Drizzt, summoned to his side from the Astral Plane.

Andahar: Drizzt's summoned steed, a magical unicorn. Unlike the living Guenhwyvar, Andahar is a purely magical construct.

Lord Dagult Neverember: Open lord of Waterdeep and lord protector of Neverwinter. A dashing and ambitious human.

Penelope Harpell: The leader of the eccentric wizards known as the Harpells, who oversee the town of Longsaddle from their estate, the Ivy Mansion. Penelope is a powerful wizard, mentoring Catti-brie, and has dated Wulfgar on occasion.

Donnola Topolino: Halfling wife of Regis, and leader of the halfling town of Bleeding Vines. She came from Aglarond, in the distant east, where she once headed a thieves' guild.

Inkeri Margaster: A lady of Waterdeep, the noblewoman is considered the leader of the Waterdhavian House of Margaster.

Alvilda Margaster: Cousin and close associate of Inkeri. Also a noble lady of Waterdeep.

Brevindon Margaster: Inkeri's brother, another Waterdhavian noble.

Grandmaster Kane: A human monk who has transcended his mortal coil and become a being beyond the Material Plane, Kane is the Grandmaster of Flowers of the Monastery of the Yellow Rose in far-off Damara. He is friend and mentor to Drizzt as the drow tries to find peace at last along a turbulent road.

Dahlia Syn'dalay (Dahlia Sin'felle): A tall and beautiful blue-eyed elf, Dahlia strives to surprise as much with her appearance as with her brilliant fighting techniques. Once the lover of Drizzt, she is now the companion of Artemis Entreri, the two finding a better way together than either ever paved alone.

Thibbledorf Pwent: A walking weapon in his spiked and sharp-ridged armor, Pwent is a battle-hardened dwarf whose loyalty is as strong as the aroma emanating from him. He led every seemingly suicidal charge with a cry of "Me King!" and gave his life saving King Bruenor in the bowels of Gauntlgrym. His death was not the end of Pwent, though, for he was slain by a vampire, and now continues as one—a cursed and miserable thing, haunting the lowest tunnels of Gauntlgrym and satisfying his insatiable hunger by feeding on the goblins beyond the dwarven realm.

The Brothers Bouldershoulder, Ivan and Pikel: Ivan Bouldershoulder is a grizzled old veteran of many battles, mundane and magical. He's risen to a position of great trust as a commander in Bruenor's Gauntlgrym guard.

More eccentric and extreme than Ivan, the green-haired Pikel fancies himself a druid, or "doo-dad," and helped Donnola Topolino create wonderful vineyards in Bleeding Vines. His limited and stilted vocabulary only adds to the deceptive innocence of this quite powerful dwarf.

Kimmuriel Oblodra: A powerful drow psionicist, Kimmuriel serves as coleader of Bregan D'aerthe beside Jarlaxle. He is the logical foil to the emotional Jarlaxle, and Jarlaxle knows it.

ETERNAL BEINGS

Lolth, the Lady of Chaos, the Demon Queen of Spiders, the Queen of the Demonweb Pits: The mighty demon Lolth reigns as the most influential goddess of the drow, particularly in the greatest drow city, Menzoberranzan, known as the City of Spiders for the devotion of its inhabitants. True to her name, the Lady of Chaos constantly shocks her followers, keeping her true plans buried beneath the webbing of other more obvious and understandable schemes. Her end goal, above all, is chaos.

Eskavidne and Yiccardaria: Lesser demons known as yochlol, they serve as two of the handmaidens of Lolth. The pair have proven so resourceful and skilled that Lolth gives them great rein in walking the ways of the drow and making a glorious mess of everything.

RELENTLESS

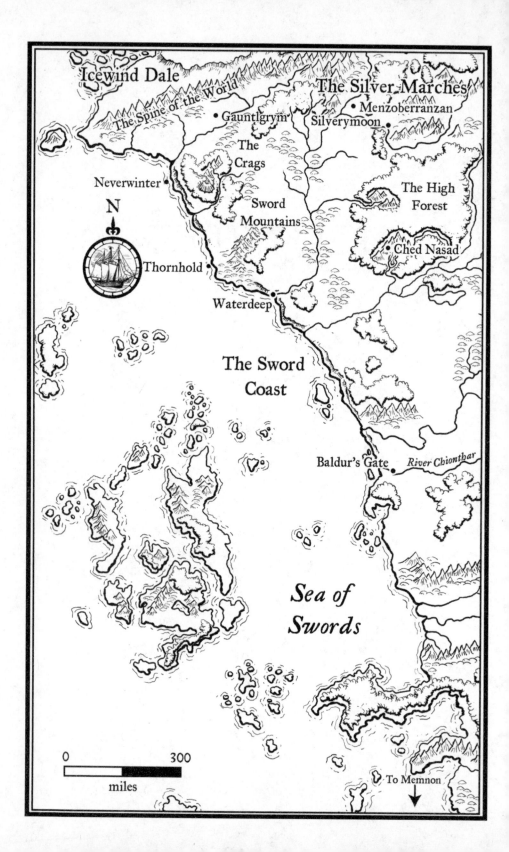

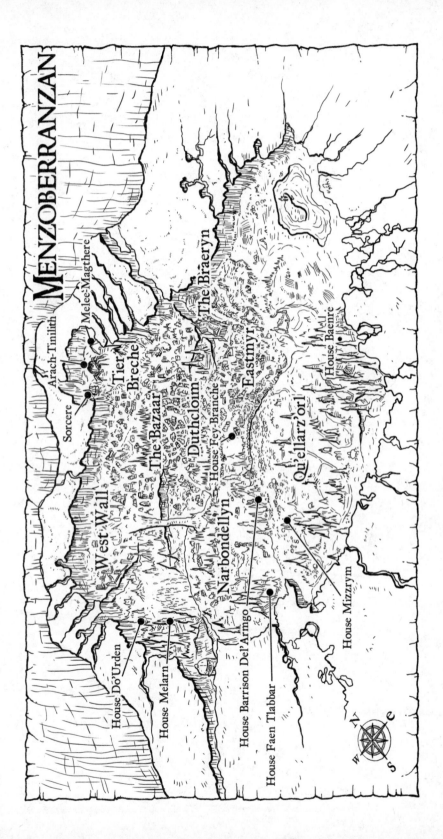

PROLOGUE

B rother Afafrenfere repeatedly told himself not to be taken in by the old man's appearance. He seemed so . . . withered, so frail, a wisp of a human whose shrunken features would have most people guessing him to be over a century old.

They'd be right, although a guess of a century would be about half of the man's actual age.

Afafrenfere spun to the left, rolling fast around and around, keeping away from his opponent. He made it to the weapon rack and pulled forth a long sword, its blade thin and curving. Afafrenfere whirled about, presenting the weapon suddenly, as if he expected the old man to be standing right behind him, ready to strike.

But Kane, Grandmaster of Flowers, remained on the raised circular platform in the center of the large round room. He stood at seeming peace, relaxed and empty-handed. He hadn't chased Afafrenfere after their last open-handed exchange of blows, and neither had he moved to any of the other weapon racks spaced about the curving walls, to answer Afafrenfere's katana.

Brother Afafrenfere stalked back toward the dais, then stepped up to stand across from his opponent, who still did not react. The tip of his sword held steady, pointed right at Kane as the younger monk stalked in, carefully turning his feet and shifting his weight to remain in perfect balance, standing in such a way as to allow him a sudden retreat or to dart out to the side.

"You were doing well with your open palm," Kane said to him in a tone so very soothing.

Magically soothing, Afafrenfere realized only when he noted the dip in his sword tip under his drooping eyelids.

"Bah!" he cried, shaking himself from the fog, and he leaped forward, sword stabbing—but Kane's left arm shot up vertically and slapped out just a bit, backhanding the blade on its side and pushing the stab harmlessly to the left.

Retract and stab!

The same hand came back to center, forearm hitting the blade and pushing it to the old monk's right.

Retract and stab!

The left arm vertically swept another backhand, and brought another near miss. So close! So tempting.

Afafrenfere executed three more sudden and powerful stabs, and each time he thought he had a hit right up until the very moment the blade slid to the side of the Grandmaster of Flowers, close enough to shave him if he had a beard of any length or volume.

Another thrust went for the old monk's gut, and Afafrenfere cleverly added a left-footed kick for Kane's hip.

But now it was Kane's right hand coming across to turn the blade, combined with a sudden movement into a stork-like pose, his right leg snapping up to intercept Afafrenfere's kick. Afafrenfere's foot struck Kane's shin hard, but Kane's bent leg only bent more, absorbing the impact, stealing the sharpness of the blow.

Suddenly vulnerable, Afafrenfere couldn't even wait for his kicking leg to return to the ground, instead pivoting on his right foot, rotating his heel in quickly, pushing forward his kicking leg, and punching out with his left hand.

But Kane's hands were quicker.

His left looped over the angled sword, pushing it out wider as his right hand disengaged the blade and snapped out suddenly, viperlike, striking first, slamming Afafrenfere's ribs just under his left breast. It wasn't a typically sharp strike, crunching at the point of impact, and instead felt more like a sudden, immovable brace, as if Afafrenfere had crashed into a stone wall.

A *moving* stone wall, as Kane's hand kept driving forward, undeniably.

Afafrenfere felt the monk's ki releasing through that strike, shoving him with tremendous force.

He felt as if he should be able to resist that combination of physical and spiritual blows. He was twice this withered old monk's weight. He had to be stronger—much stronger. He had to resist, but he could not.

His left hook came around, but was short of the mark. So very far short of the mark, and only when seeing the pathetic strike—missing by feet, not inches—did Afafrenfere understand that he was flying backward, finally stumbling to a stop but nearly tumbling end-over-end on the lower part of the floor, a dozen feet and more from Grandmaster Kane.

Afafrenfere brought his hands up and out to either side, one clinched tightly about the sword, the other balled into a tight fist. He tightened his jaw, too, and flexed his muscles in a sudden and powerful movement, forcing blood to flow through him with power and the healing power of his own ki. Down came his arms, and the powerful young monk called upon more of his energy pool, physical and spiritual, to enact a sudden and powerful leap, landing in a roll just before Grandmaster Kane.

He came to his feet with a powerful stab, and bore in with kicks, cuts, and punches, a whirling machine of devastation.

Kane picked off every strike, but Afafrenfere moved with such startling power and precision that he felt no counters from the mighty opponent.

Across went the sword, missing (though whether Kane had ducked it or jumped it, Afafrenfere didn't even know, and didn't even care as he executed the sudden, also futile backhand).

He didn't mind the second miss at all, for the backhand was for nothing more than to properly align his blade. As it came back out to the right, Afafrenfere rolled the sword with a flip of his wrist and rolled his arm with a flip of his shoulder, lifting the blade up high with startling suddenness.

Down and across he swung.

Again, he missed.

And again, he *knew* he would miss, even shortening the swing.

For this, too, was a feint, and Afafrenfere continued his follow-through, bringing the sword and his arm down and around, using the momentum in a sudden flip, up and over, ending with the perfect execution of his sword coming around in an overhead swing, second hand joining the first on its long hilt, bringing more weight to the downward stroke, a cut thrumming with lethality.

Even though the blade was blunted for practice, Afafrenfere felt a pang of guilt for the headache he would bring to Kane when the old monk awakened!

But no, his downward chop was met by Kane's arms, uplifted above him in a cross, and as the sword connected—the very moment it connected, the eyeblink of its touching flesh—Kane's arms uncrossed.

Even had the blade been sharp enough to cut stone, the impact with the old monk's arms was too short for any serious bite, and Afafrenfere doubted that any steel in the land would have been strong enough to withstand Kane's scissor.

Out went Kane's arms, out flew the broken half of the sword blade, and before Afafrenfere could even register the movement, Kane's right hand swooped down and in, then shot straight up, wrist cocked, palm up and rising, slamming the sword hilt under Afafrenfere's hands.

Up went Kane's hand, driving, driving, pushing the half sword right from Afafrenfere's grasp and sending it flying.

Afafrenfere went into a desperate flurry, striking and kicking, left and right, up high and down low.

So did Kane, the monastic brothers exchanging a blur of heavy strikes and kicks, too many to count, too many for Afafrenfere to even take note of any individually. He didn't know how he was blocking Kane's barrage just as he didn't know how Kane was blocking his. For he was past his own consciousness then, into a zone of pure reaction, muscle memory overwhelming any notion of planned sequence.

But then a miss—a missed block by Kane! Afafrenfere's right cross straightened. It didn't connect, but he had Kane dodging awkwardly down to his left.

Or so Afafrenfere thought until he jabbed out with his left, for at that moment, he felt Grandmaster Kane's right foot sweeping out and around his own planted right leg, and when Kane's right palm snapped up to intercept, Afafrenfere felt an immovable object there, one that forced him backward over Kane's tripping leg as he extended.

Kane completed his move by driving that blocking palm forward and driving his right leg powerfully back, dumping Afafrenfere to the ground.

A desperate backward roll brought Afafrenfere to his feet, and he was amazed at how quickly he had executed that escape, even though Kane was right there before him, hand flowing in a blur of chops and punches. Working hard and brilliantly, Afafrenfere deflected or absorbed those blows, putting him in what seemed a clench with the grandmaster, the two only a foot apart, their arms interlocked out and down to either side.

Afafrenfere moved to head-butt, but before he even got going, he felt a stunning blow on his face.

A kick.

A kick! *Impossible*, his mind screamed at him. He and Kane were too close! How could Kane possibly have kicked him in the face when they were barely a foot apart?

He didn't believe it. He refused to believe it, even when he was sitting on the ground.

Afafrenfere shook his head, shook the swirling stars out of his eyes, and looked up to find Kane staring down at him, extending a hand to help him back to his feet.

He took the hand and started up, but slumped back down to his bum, then half fell, half rolled down to his side.

Sometime later—he knew not how long—Afafrenfere propped

himself up on his elbow and looked at his opponent, his dear friend, who sat cross-legged before him.

"I thought my forward flip and chop maneuver effective," Afafren-fere said, spitting blood with every word. He had a pretty sizable gash in his lip, he knew, and the ache in his jaw sent waves of sharp fire with each movement.

"It would kill almost any opponent," Kane congratulated.

"Not you."

Kane shrugged. "No."

"Drizzt?" Afafrenfere teased, for the dark elf had taken his place as Kane's private student.

After a moment and a pensive pose, Kane shrugged again, but added no verbal denial.

"If Drizzt and Afafrenfere fought, on whom would Grandmaster Kane place his wager?" Afafrenfere asked.

"Grandmaster Kane wants for nothing, so he has no need of wa-gers," Kane answered.

"Pretend."

"You may not like my answer."

Afafrenfere laughed, then groaned and grabbed at his face. He pinched his bloody nose between his thumb and index finger and pushed it to the side.

That made his teeth hurt, and he suspected a crack in the bone from the bottom of his nose to his gumline.

"If you could defeat me, why would you bother challenging the Mistress of Winter?" Kane asked then, and Afafrenfere looked at him with surprise at the change in topic.

"Mistress Savahn awaits my second challenge?" he asked, a not-subtle reminder that Savahn had defeated Afafrenfere the previous season. The monk tried to keep the eagerness out of his voice. He had been chasing Savahn for a long time now, both before and after his defeat, and had nearly recovered and improved enough to chal-lenge her a second time to become the Master of the East Wind. But Savahn, too, perhaps spurred by Afafrenfere's surge, had trained hard and had climbed to the next rank before Afafrenfere could formally initiate that second challenge. She was now the Mistress of Winter, and Afafrenfere had attained the unclaimed rank of Master of the East Wind without proving himself in training combat against any of the three monks at the Monastery of the Yellow Rose ranked above him: Savahn, the Mistress of Winter; Perrywinkle Shin, the Master of Spring; and Kane, Grandmaster of Flowers.

Kane nodded. For now the rank immediately above Afafrenfere was occupied, and there could be only one. For Afafrenfere to become the Master of Winter, he had to defeat the current Mistress of Winter, Savahn. Then he would have to defend his new title—most likely against a resurgent Savahn or perhaps the rising Master of the West Wind, Halavash, who was, by all accounts, also making great strides in his training (and also rumored to be working quietly with Grandmaster Kane).

"Will Grandmaster Kane bet on *that* fight?"

"No."

"If he did, would he know which to bet upon?"

"Yes."

"If he did, would Grandmaster Kane think it a safe bet?" Afafrenfere pressed.

Kane grinned at that, and answered, "Yes," then started walking away.

"May we both live long enough so that one day I might properly challenge you," Afafrenfere called after him.

Kane stopped and held still for a moment, then slowly turned about. "Brother Afafrenfere, you are my friend. Through you and with you, I and we have accomplished great deeds for the good of the folk. And so I say this, and hope you hear it as my most important lesson of all: this cannot be your goal, to take the title of Grandmaster of Flowers."

"I only wish to challenge you and to defeat you because in that victory I will see my own improvement," Afafrenfere answered.

Kane nodded. "Your own improvement," he agreed. "The competition is within yourself, my friend, the striving for physical and spiritual peace and perfection."

"And yet we challenge each other to measure that improvement."

"What is your goal?" Kane asked.

"You just said it."

"No," Kane replied. "It is not your goal. Never think of it as your goal. It is your *journey*. It is how you make sense of your existence and peace with the tumult of the mortal self and the uncertainty of the ending we all know we must one day face."

"All in the Order of Saint Sollars strive to be as Grandmaster Kane," Afafrenfere said.

"The scribe who undertakes a tome seeking the goal of finishing a tome, pursuing the goal single-mindedly, diminishes the experience of those months of penning, surrenders the joy, emotions, insights, and memories of his journey through the process. So I ask again, what is your goal?"

Afafrenfere stared at him blankly.

"You have no goal," Grandmaster Kane answered his own question. "What is your journey?"

"To learn, to live, to grow, to move toward the truth," Afafrenfere answered.

"The truth?"

"The truth of myself, the truth of all that is around me."

Grandmaster Kane smiled with satisfaction and nodded his approval.

"Do not lose sight of that," Kane warned as he departed, "or you will relinquish the title of Master of Winter very quickly after you have achieved it."

It took Afafrenfere a moment to realize the implications of Kane's last words. The grandmaster, so wise and knowing, fully expected him to defeat Savahn. Overwhelmed, he slumped back onto the floor.

He still had no idea how Kane had kicked him in the face with such force when the two had been practically face-to-face.

Someday, he would understand, he thought, and he put it out of mind. It would come in time or it would not, along the trails and trials of his physical and spiritual journey.

AFAFRENFERE SAT ON A HIGH ROCKY BLUFF, A TIGHT LEDGE after a difficult climb, and one that held great notoriety with the Order of St. Sollars. For from this place, a century and a half before, the great Kane had transcended his physical body and become one with the multiverse.

Afafrenfere had his legs crossed tightly before him, his hands on his knees, palms up, thumb tapping his index finger. His breathing was slow and perfectly steady, the exhale and inhale at exactly the same length.

The monk's mind was deep inside and far without all at once. He had never been more away from his own body, yet had never felt less removed from it.

He felt his goal nearing, felt as if he had at last learned the bonds of his physical limitations, the very glue that gave Afafrenfere form.

He didn't feel the cold bite of the high mountain wind. He didn't hear it in his ears, nor the squawking of the great condors that drifted about on the updrafts of the high mountain.

For the immediate area didn't matter. His focus was inside himself and all about, everywhere, without.

He teased at the glue with his will, felt as if he was weakening the bonds.

He could break them altogether, he was confident, and when he did, he would know eternity. He would transcend his mortal coil. He would become one with everything . . .

Thinking about it interrupted Afafrenfere's needed concentration, though. The memory burned within him, for he had done this before—but with help. Grandmaster Kane had been within him, possessing him, sharing their form. When the great white dragon had reared before them, Kane had broken Afafrenfere's physical bonds, had unglued the multitude of particles that had come together to make the collection, the being known as Afafrenfere.

The beauty of that experience was not easily forgotten, even though it had only been a short journey to the place of everything.

For Kane had reformed him almost immediately, as soon as the dragon's murderous freezing breath had been expended, so that Afafrenfere could then slay the wyrm.

The monk fell back into his meditation, forced himself to patience, and again settled in that place of deep calm, a place both empty of thought and contemplative at the same time. He searched out the bonds once more.

He felt the glue and began to disperse it, to disperse himself.

A hand slapped down on his shoulder, startling him before he could truly begin the process.

Afafrenfere's eyes popped open wide. He felt the wind; he heard the wind. He snapped his head to the side to find Grandmaster Kane standing there, slowly shaking his head.

"You are not ready," Kane told him.

Afafrenfere blinked repeatedly, shocked.

"Come, let us return to the monastery," Kane said, holding out a hand.

Afafrenfere shook his head. "This is not your place, nor your choice, nor your journey!" he blurted.

Kane didn't blink and didn't retract his hand.

"You are the Grandmaster of Flowers, the greatest of the Order of Saint Sollars—ever," Afafrenfere said. "And with all respect, with more respect than I have ever known for another, I tell you again, this is not your place."

"It is my place."

"Because you are the Grandmaster of Flowers?"

"Because I am your friend," Kane said.

"I can do this," the younger monk insisted.

"I know."

"Then . . ."

"But you cannot yet undo this."

Afafrenfere started to reply, but held quiet and just stared.

"You will transcend," Kane explained. "You will become as one with the everything. And you will know harmony and beauty beyond anything you have ever imagined. But that will be the end of Afafrenfere."

"Death?"

"Of this existence, yes."

"And death is the end . . . of everything?"

"I do not know," Kane admitted. "When you first transcend, it is not the end—you know this, too, from our journey together from your body. But the time to return is short—days, not months—and what may come after that period when there is no return, I do not know. For what is after that, we have only faith."

"I have faith. Do you?"

Kane shrugged. "I do not know what I do not know. I do, however, have hope."

"Then I will return quickly, before that point where I cannot . . ."

"No. You will not. You are not ready."

"You do not think me strong enough?" Afafrenfere asked, doing well to keep any anger out of his question. "You think I will not be able . . . ?"

"You will not want to," Kane interrupted. "Your ties to this place are not strong enough for you to consider turning about once you have initiated that journey."

"What does that even mean?"

Kane shrugged. "It means that you are not yet ready to take this step from your mortal coil. Almost, but not yet. There are several ranks before you. Patience, I beg."

"The world is a dangerous place. Perhaps I will lose my chance and will be taken from this world when it is not of my choosing."

Kane shrugged as if that hardly mattered. "Not yet," he said. "As your friend, I beg of you."

Afafrenfere winced at that, both disappointed yet truly flattered to hear such concern from this greatest of monks.

"You came back," he said, because he couldn't think of anything else to say.

"I almost did not," he said quietly, and that startled Afafrenfere. "I almost did not even think to. I was much older than you are now, and much stronger in the ways of our order—though, fear not, my friend, for you, too, will rise to that level of mind-and-body perfection. Of that, I do not doubt. Unless, of course, you follow through with this transcendence, and then you are gone forevermore."

Kane held out his hand once more.

"I wish to make this journey," Afafrenfere said.

"I know. And I know why."

Afafrenfere's gaze went from the hand to Grandmaster Kane's eyes.

"Because of him, Parbid, whom you loved," Kane said. "Because he is there, you hope, waiting, and his embrace you wish again, more than anything."

Afafrenfere's mouth hung open. He tried to shake his head in denial but failed miserably.

"Nothing in the multiverse is more powerful than love, my friend," Kane said, and he smiled, and moved his hand.

Afafrenfere took the offered assistance and unwound his legs, easily rising beside his friend. "Do you think he is there, Grandmaster? Do you think he waits for me?"

Kane shrugged, and Afafrenfere understood that the man had no answer and would not lie to him for the sake of comfort.

"You already said it," Kane did reply. "You have faith. And I have hope."

The two remained quiet for some time as they picked their way along the trail down the mountainside.

"I still do not understand," Afafrenfere admitted when they came in sight of the lights of the Monastery of the Yellow Rose soon after sunset. "You make it sound as if the return to your mortal coil is a great feat of tremendous struggle."

"It is."

The younger monk shrugged. "When we went together beyond this body of mine in the face of the great white dragon, the return seemed so . . ."

". . . easy," Kane finished. "It seemed easy to you because you did not initiate the transcendence, nor were you even aware of the action, and so you had not even begun to hear the music of the heavens or see the beauty of everything before I pulled you back into the being known as Afafrenfere."

"But you did so effortlessly."

"Not as much as you believe, but yes, with each ascent beyond the mortal coil, the barriers to and from the place beyond become . . . thinner. In that instance, the danger to us and to our friends was so immediate that it was a smooth return, I agree. We had to be there, or woe to those we loved."

"But . . ." Afafrenfere said. He seemed to choke on the word and just shook his head.

"You will come to better understand," Kane promised. "Continue your studies. Make of perfection your mind and body. But I warn you, when you think yourself ready—and this could be years from now and I may not still be here to guide you—in that first instance of transcendence . . . Well, it might be your only one, and the utter end of Afafrenfere in this existence."

"So you have said, but why, master?" Afafrenfere pressed. "I know that my work here is not done. If I know that I am not ready to experience the next . . ."

"If there is a *next*," Kane put in.

"If there is a next," Afafrenfere agreed. "If I know these things, then why do you suppose that I will forsake my mortal existence as a man?"

Kane paused and considered that for a moment, then offered a kind smile to the younger monk. "You have made love—the act itself, and to completion, yes?"

Afafrenfere blushed. "Yes, of course."

"Then you know the moment when the body demands continuation, demands release?"

"Master, yes."

"The body will not turn back and the mental and emotional discipline needed to deny that call of ecstasy is enormous. When you transcend, you will know such joy, unrelenting, even building as time, which becomes meaningless, passes, yet the time to find the needed discipline, the denial of pure desire, is short, and failure means that you will be forever removed from this existence."

Afafrenfere just stared at him, jaw hanging open.

"I know not how to put it more clearly or bluntly," the ancient monk answered that blank stare. "You will not want to come back, and so you, as you are known and as you know yourself, will be no more."

Grandmaster Kane waited a few moments as the weight of his words sank in for the visibly shaken Afafrenfere, then asked, "Do you still wish to do this?"

"I do," the younger monk answered, "but perhaps not quite yet."

"When you are ready," said Kane.

"How will I know?"

"When you are not afraid that you will not return. When you believe that you have learned here all that you wish to garner from this existence. It is not about sadness and weariness with life, no. Such a state of mind would make transcending the mortal form impossible. But rather, it is about fullness—such fullness that you know there is little more room in this existence for anything new!"

"That is where you are?"

"That is where I have been for a century and more!"

"Yet you are still here."

Grandmaster Kane shrugged. "Somewhat," he answered cryptically. "Part of me is still here, part of me is removed forevermore."

"Then tell me of the mystery!"

"I cannot. That part of me which knows is not here."

"I don't understand. Then there is something more, even, than transcending the physical form?"

Kane shrugged again, prompting Afafrenfere to restate, "I don't understand."

"You do not need to understand. Not now. Not yet. You have much yet to learn."

"Then tell me, Grandmaster, what do I need to know now?"

"That you will not want to come back. That is all."

PART 1

Shifting Fates and Jarring Perspectives

What place is this that is my world; what dark coil has my spirit embodied? In light, I see my skin as black; in darkness, it glows white in the heat of this rage I cannot dismiss. Would that I had the courage to depart, this place or this life, or to stand openly against the wrongness that is the world of these, my kin. To seek an existence that does not run afoul to that which I believe, and to that which I hold dear faith is truth.

Zaknafein Do'Urden I am called, yet a drow I am not, by choice or by deed. Let them discover this being that I am, then. Let them rain their wrath on these old shoulders already burdened by the hopelessness of Menzoberranzan.

Menzoberranzan, what hell are you?

Zaknafein Do'Urden
Homeland

CHAPTER 1

So Many Moving Parts

She didn't like walking these particular boulevards of Menzoberranzan known as the Braeryn, or Stenchstreets. Here lurked the houseless drow rogues, castoffs and refugees from houses sacked. Here lurked the fallen priestesses and the dangerous bastard children of this house or that, doomed to a life of poverty.

Mostly, at least. For Matron Malice of House Do'Urden also knew that here lurked the members of Bregan D'aerthe, a band of mercenaries that had grown quite powerful and wealthy within the city structure. Rogues, all, but useful rogues to the house matrons who knew how to take advantage of their services.

From Zaknafein, her consort and house weapon master, Malice had contacted Jarlaxle, the leader of Bregan D'aerthe, and received the name of the person she intended to visit this day, the person for whom she was walking the Stenchstreets of Menzoberranzan.

It was quite a sacrifice, and the matron had already made up her mind that this person had better tell her that which she wanted to hear, or she would leave the man dead on the floor of his hovel.

Malice was quite relieved when she at last spotted the house in question. She wasn't afraid of this part of her journey, just disgusted, and wanted to conclude her business and return to her house as soon as possible.

She moved to the door, glanced about for the escorts who were shadowing her, and nodded for them to lock down the area. Then she cast a spell, then a second, both at the door, then added a third and a fourth upon herself to protect from any trickery.

A fifth spell blew open the door, and Matron Malice strode through into the small room beyond, to the shocked expression of the robed man on one side of the table within, and a look of absolute terror on the face of the woman sitting across from him.

"I am not done here!" the man protested.

Malice looked from him to the crystal ball set on a base in the middle of the small, circular table. She could just barely make out the distorted shapes of an image floating within it.

A wave of her hand cleared the ball.

"You are now," she said.

The woman then protested, "I paid well for my time!"

Malice's glare stole her voice at the end of the sentence. The matron took a good look at the woman. She was younger than Malice, but not by much, and though she was shapely and seemed to think herself quite attractive and alluring given the cut of her dress, her face and bare arms showed the scars and bruises of one living in the darkness of the Stenchstreets.

"You wear no house emblem, child," she said. "To which matron do you belong?"

"Why would I tell you?"

"Because if you do not, then I know that you belong to no house, so if I kill you, no one will care."

"Woman!" protested the robed man, and he stood to face the intruder. He was old and withered, wearing more than a few scars on his face, and his threadbare old robes hung loosely on his too-thin shoulders.

"Priestess," she corrected.

"Priestess," he said, his tone a bit less indignant.

"High Priestess," Malice corrected.

"High Priestess," the old drow corrected, voice thinner.

"Matron," Malice corrected, playing her hand openly, and the drow male seemed to shrink.

He cleared his throat. "I am not accustomed to uninvited guests," he said calmly. "You startled me."

"And you, dear," Malice said, turning her gaze on the woman. "Are you ready to boast of a house? Though of course you know that if you name one and are proven a liar, the punishment will grow you eight legs instead of just losing the two you seem to cherish."

The woman shifted at that, pulling down the top fold of her slit dress to better cover her legs.

"You are of no house," Malice said when the clearly terrified woman stuttered over some indecipherable mumble. "Go outside and wait for me," Malice instructed. "Perhaps better things await you in your future." She glanced back at the robed man. "Is that what you saw in the crystal ball for her?"

The drow appeared truly flummoxed.

"It is, yes?" Malice added, throwing the weight of a spell of suggestion behind the question.

"Yes," the man blurted. "Yes, yes, of course. I was about to tell her . . ."

"Go," Malice told the woman, and she wisely scrambled from the chair and darted outside.

Never taking her gaze off the man, Malice walked over to the vacated chair and moved to sit. She glanced at the fabric, though, and the many stains upon it.

A wave of her hand sent it flying aside. A quick incantation produced a floating disk of blue light where the chair had been, and upon that, Matron Malice sat. She motioned to the other chair, but got only a concerned and confused stare in return.

"You are Pau'Kros, once of a house that shall no longer be named?" Malice said.

"I am of House Oblodra."

"No, you're *not*. Not yet, though you hope they will one day take you in. Or should I say, you hope they will not see that you are not truly a master of the magic of the mind, but rather a mundane wizard with one extraordinary gift."

The man cleared his throat, but there was more nervousness than indignity in the sound.

"Sit down, Pau'Kros," Malice ordered. "I am your most important customer."

"How? I do not understand," the man replied awkwardly, but he did take his seat, which seemed to Malice a clear signal of surrender.

"Jarlaxle told me of you," Malice explained.

The old drow man blew a sigh. "He could have arranged . . ."

"I do not need him to arrange anything. I am here, you are here, and I require a service." She shifted on the floating disk and crossed her legs comfortably, wanting to show this fool that she was confident of her ability to obliterate him with a word. "Who am I?" she asked, and she placed her snake-headed scourge on the table, the living serpents writhing and hissing, their fangs dripping deadly venom.

Pau'Kros took a deep breath, then cautiously leaned forward and began mumbling, staring into the crystal ball, which immediately clouded.

"Tell me, seer, who I am, and tell me why I am here," said Malice.

He continued to stare and continued to chant for a long while. Malice couldn't make out many of the words, but she understood the arcane inflection of a mage well enough—which played into what Jarlaxle had told her of the man. This drow, Pau'Kros, had graduated from Sorcere, the drow academy for wizards, and had been well regarded until he had fallen out of favor with the mighty Gromph Baenre, an event coinciding with the utter destruction of his family house. Since that long-ago day, he had made his meager living on the Stenchstreets, telling fortunes, and he had been doing it for so long, according to Jarlaxle, he had actually become quite adept at it.

And more than that, Pau'Kros survived because he knew how to keep the secrets of his clients.

"Matron Do'Urden," he said a few moments later, obvious respect in his voice. "I have heard of you. I am honored that you sought my services."

"Prove you are worth it."

The man licked his lips and cleared his throat and went back to concentrating on the crystal ball. Never averting his gaze, he reached into a pocket and produced a quartet of small bones, which he tossed on the left side of the ball. Then he reached in again and drew forth four more, tossing them to the right side, which drew more hissing threats from the snakes of the scourge.

Despite herself, Malice admired the man's concentration as he glanced left, then right, where he managed to ignore the deadly serpents and focus on his thrown divinatory relics.

"Yes," he said, and a thin smile creased his face. "Yes, great Matron Malice, you are with child."

"I knew that," she stated flatly. She lied. She had only suspected a pregnancy, but that wasn't the most important question here, of course.

"Tell me the sire," she ordered.

Pau'Kros swallowed hard and seemed off-balance, and of course, he should be. Telling a matron she was pregnant was almost always a blessed thing, of course, but telling her that her child was from a man not her preference could get someone horribly murdered, or worse.

"The sire," Malice said again, flatly. "Tell me the father of this child. Look in your ball and name the man. You know of me and so you know my reputation—one proudly earned, I assure you. I can narrow it down to four possibilities. You will tell me which man it is."

The man began to sweat. His pleading to the crystal ball became a bit more uneven and edgy, his nerves sounding clearly with every arcane syllable.

But then he stopped suddenly, staring. For a moment, he seemed confused, but then the grin returned and his expression showed an epiphany.

"I know this man," he said, and Malice realized that he was talking to himself. As she considered that remark, and this location, hope began to swell within her.

"Who is the father?" she demanded.

"He was of House Simfray," the seer dared to reply, for House Simfray was no more and it was not considered wise for someone, particularly a lowly male, to speak the name of that which did not exist.

"Zaknafein," he quickly corrected. "Zaknafein Do'Urden is the fath—"

He fell forward, staring more deeply into the ball, and from the backside, Malice could tell that the images were changing quickly, that the seer was gaining insight and knowledge. She didn't dare interrupt, not then.

A long while later, the seer gave a gasp and fell back in his seat, seeming fully spent, his robes clinging to his emaciated form, his face lathered in sweat.

"Yes, Matron Malice, your hopes are realized," he said confidently.

Malice was impressed, though she wasn't about to show it.

"As with your daughter, Priestess Vierna, this is a child of Zaknafein," the seer told her.

"You know him."

"I knew of him," Pau'Kros admitted. "Though that was many decades ago. I am glad that you are pleased with this news."

"It would not take a seer to see that. Who would not be thrilled at the thought of another daughter sired by the great weapon master?"

Pau'Kros nodded, but his expression turned to one of curiosity. "I did not say it would be a daughter," he remarked.

"You did not have to. Zaknafein is too great a lover and sire to bring forth a mere male," Malice asserted, but seeing Pau'Kros's scowl, added, "You doubt the blessings of Lolth?"

"Of course not," he blurted. "I would not even waste your time to look further to confirm that which you already know!"

Matron Malice didn't rise to leave. She just willed her floating disk toward the door, waved it open, and glided out into the street.

There stood the woman from the table, shifting nervously from foot to foot, wearing a look fluctuating between hopefulness and trepidation.

"What do you want?" Malice growled at her.

"You told me to wait outside for you," the woman replied.

"Are you good at following orders?"

"Yes . . . matron," she said.

"Then you will make a fine slave at my house," said Malice, and she looked to the shadows past the woman and gave a slight nod.

"Yes, Matron . . . What? A slave? I am no—"

Her sentence ended there as a fine sword slid through her, back to front, the tip exiting her flesh just below her left breast, bits of her heart upon it.

"You are no witness, either," Malice told her as she fell down dead.

She and her entourage returned to the West Wall and House Do'Urden.

"YOU DID WELL, THEN," JARLAXLE TOLD PAU'KROS A BIT later, the flamboyant mercenary leader taking a seat at the divining table—though he had long before warned the seer never to try a divination regarding him.

"She killed—"

"Madeflava was dying anyway," Jarlaxle interrupted. "You knew that, she knew that. It is a pity, yes, but it was a better end than the yellow mold growing in her lungs would have offered."

Pau'Kros dropped his old face into his thin hands.

"What is the problem?" Jarlaxle bade him. "You told her what she wanted to know. She left quite happy."

"Happy enough to murder someone," came the sarcastic response.

"An act which no doubt made that one even happier," Jarlaxle replied, with a laugh that sounded quite helpless, because it was.

Pau'Kros sighed and buried his face again.

"She won't kill you, you old fool," Jarlaxle said. "She would have done so already. You told her what she wanted to hear. The worst that will happen is that you will have to suffer her presence again sometime in the future if Zaknafein shoots true once more."

"I told her what she wanted to hear," Pau'Kros agreed. "But I did not tell her all that I saw."

Jarlaxle perked up at that.

"It is not a daughter growing in her belly," the old seer explained. "It is a son."

"You *lied* to her?"

Pau'Kros shook his head vehemently. "She did not even bother to ask. She was so sure. She will not be pleased. Not at all."

"Then it is a son," Jarlaxle said with a shrug, as if it did not matter. "Matron Malice already has two, does she not? Nalfein and Dinin?"

It was Jarlaxle's turn to blow a heavy sigh, one that continued to grow heavier as he played the scenario through. No, indeed, Matron Malice would not be pleased, and even less so in her knowledge that this doomed child was the progeny of Zaknafein.

Jarlaxle took his leave then and made his meandering way to the Oozing Myconid, the finest tavern in the Stenchstreets—particularly since Jarlaxle had purchased a controlling interest in the place some fifty years earlier. He wasn't surprised to find Zaknafein there—his scouts had already reported as much to him, after all. The weapon master sat at his usual table in the back right-hand corner of the common room.

"Ah, what brings you out on this fine night?" Jarlaxle asked as he approached, motioning to the bar for some more drinks.

"Same thing that brings me anywhere," Zaknafein replied. "Wherever I am, I can find happiness in knowing that there are a hundred other places in this city I'd rather not be."

Jarlaxle stared at him for a long moment. "I'm trying to determine if I should be complimented."

"You shouldn't."

That brought a laugh from Jarlaxle. "In any case, it is good to see you again. We went years without so much as a greeting, and what now, the fourth time in the last two tendays?"

"Malice has been extraordinarily wretched of late," Zaknafein replied, and took a long swig of his drink.

Jarlaxle almost said something that would have tipped his hand, but he bit it back.

"The witch is pregnant," Zaknafein declared.

Jarlaxle started in surprise—not from the news, of course, but from how fast the news had traveled. Had Matron Malice even returned to House Do'Urden from her visit with the seer?

Jarlaxle stammered over a response, finally settling on, "Is it yours?"

"Are you hinting that my wife is unfaithful?" Zaknafein said with a scowl.

Jarlaxle laughed, as did Zaknafein when he couldn't hold the angry facade any longer. Matron Malice's sexual excursions remained a matter of public record—and awe—after all.

"I'm almost certain that I'm the father," Zaknafein said.

"Because you're just better than the others?" Jarlaxle teased.

"Quality, yes," Zaknafein replied. "But also the matter of quantity. The witch hasn't let me sleep in weeks. I can always tell when she's getting ready to sack another house."

Jarlaxle nodded. Just as her appetite was well-known, so it was no secret among those in the know that House Do'Urden was setting its sights on House DeVir, and no one was more in the know than Jarlaxle of Bregan D'aerthe.

"You were happier with this news the last time, with the first one," Jarlaxle observed.

Zaknafein held up his free hand helplessly as he took another swallow of his drink.

The new round arrived then, and Jarlaxle took his own and quickly waved the serving man away.

"You do not feel that pride any longer when you look upon Vierna?" he dared to ask. "She seems rather exceptional, as priestesses go."

"Yes and no," Zaknafein admitted. "I could have expected no more from any daughter I sired in the house of Malice Do'Urden than Vierna has offered. I am no fool. I know this, and knew it from the moment I first saw my child, and saw that my child was a girl. I think she has done well, but I'm not going to deny the pain of seeing my child, my daughter, become a devotee of that wretched Lolth."

"What choice did she have?"

"What chance did she have?" Zaknafein corrected. He gave a little resigned chuckle. "It is interesting, and it caught me by surprise,

I admit, this purpose of parenthood, these bonds beyond the expected."

"What do you mean?" Jarlaxle asked, surprised to hear Zaknafein speaking so openly.

"The purpose—all of it," Zaknafein replied. "Of this existence. I mean, on a most basic level, I fear death, and I think that true of everyone but the most addled in their god beliefs. I long for personal immortality, of course. Don't you?"

"I don't know that I'd . . . I mean, that would be a long time, yes?"

"So you lie to yourself that you will one day welcome that last close of your eyes?" Zaknafein snorted. "The Jarlaxle I know will try to talk Death itself out of that bargain."

Jarlaxle lifted his glass in a toast to that thought.

"So yes, I would desire immortality, and hope there is an existence beyond this one," said Zaknafein. "I am surprised, though, to learn that through my children, I find some relief against my fears. They are a form of immortality. I never thought of it like that until the day I first saw Vierna."

"That's a good thing."

"It is a scary thing!" Zaknafein replied. "To see your child, Jarlaxle, is to know vulnerability. Is to know that there is something in the world that leaves you truly vulnerable, that there is this person more important to you than you, and that if anything terrible happened to her, it would be a hundred times more painful than if it had happened to you.

"I fear death. I don't want to die. This I know. But I know, too, that I would throw myself before a spear aimed for my child. Even one who has become a priestess of the Spider Queen!"

"So you are pleased that Matron Malice is again with child?" Jarlaxle asked. "Your child?"

Zaknafein seemed perplexed when faced with the stark question. He gave what seemed a shrug, then finished his drink and slid his chair back from the table.

"I have to be back in the house," he said, rising. "We have much to do."

"Before the war."

"There is no war," Zaknafein protested. "What a silly notion.

House Do'Urden has no ambitions, of course, that would go against the edicts of the city's Ruling Council. But we must prepare ourselves in case something terrible befalls one of the houses ranked above us."

"Of course," Jarlaxle agreed, and he smiled at Zaknafein's reminder of how truly demented the laws of Menzoberranzan were. There was nothing wrong with wiping out a rival house, of course. The only wrong would be getting caught in the act. That, the getting caught, and not the act itself, was what the ruling matrons could not abide.

He watched Zaknafein all the way out of the bar, then sat back and digested the unusually candid conversation with the typically reserved man. He knew that House Do'Urden was mere months from their attack on House DeVir, and so he likely wouldn't see his friend again for many months, perhaps years.

And it was an interesting feeling, noticing how much that saddened him.

That's why he so savored these moments sitting across from Zaknafein, for the man was ever full of surprising depth and insight.

Jarlaxle appreciated that, but it weighed on him now. Zaknafein would sire a boy this time, and since this would be the third son of House Do'Urden, the devout Matron Malice would surely give the child to the Spider Queen, quickly and mercilessly.

Particularly given this conversation, Jarlaxle feared that such an act would utterly devastate his old friend.

MATRON MALICE DIDN'T LIKE THIS PLACE. NOT AT ALL. Too many males haunted the winding corridors and sweeping stairs, or kneeled before the vast shelves of scrolls and old tomes.

And not just any males. These were the most powerful men in Menzoberranzan, including more than a few—notably Archmage Gromph, the eldest son of Matron Mother Baenre herself—who could likely destroy Malice in a fight. Even more disconcerting, Matron Malice did not belong in this place and very few knew she was here, and these potential adversaries, the great drow wizards of Sorcere, could surely dispose of a body!

I am right here, came a soothing voice—no, not a voice, but rather a telepathic message that resonated within her. *It has been arranged. You are here at the suffrage of Archmage Gromph and none would dare move against you.*

Matron Malice hated allowing that wretched Jarlaxle creature and his even more wretched Oblodran psionicist friend into her thoughts, but she couldn't deny that Jarlaxle's magical message was anything but comforting.

The woman winced at that internal admission and concentrated even more fiercely on expelling Jarlaxle from her thoughts. If he was in there talking to her, then he could also be in there feeling her emotions as if they were his own.

She did not want him to recognize her trepidation. She was the Matron of House Do'Urden, a rising and powerful drow house, after all.

Malice came to a strange and narrow wooden door, one that would have seemed more fitting in the tower of an elven wizard in some ancient forest aboveground. Its knotted boards rose to shoulder height, then rounded and curved upward into somewhat of a point. The matron cast a spell of warding, then another of magical detection. Before she finished the second, the door swung inward, revealing a small landing and a dark descending stair.

Be well, Matron Malice, said the voice in her head. *I will await your return.*

He couldn't go down there with her, at least not magically, Malice thought, for this portal was set with a powerful spell of disenchantment.

The woman took a steadying breath and strode forward onto the landing. She grasped the smooth and rounded railing, the unfamiliar touch of wood, surface wood, well burnished. The railing creaked, as did the stairs when she began her descent. Down and around they wound, far below the multitowered structure of Sorcere. She was in blackness, then, so that even with her keen drow vision, she could not see the wall beside her or the stairs before her.

She went on, not even attempting to cast a magical light. She didn't need it. She was a matron of a rising and powerful house, she told herself resolutely. No male would dare strike at her.

She didn't count her steps, but she knew it was more than a hundred later when she spotted a distant light far below. A single candle, it seemed.

Spiderwebs brushed her face, but that neither startled nor scared Matron Malice. Indeed, the presence of spiders comforted her. These were allies of Lolth, the Spider Queen, and Matron Malice was in the favor of the goddess.

She picked up her pace, managing a smile when she felt a spider run off a web and skitter down her cheek.

Lolth was with her.

It occurred to her that the mere presence of these blessed little creatures was an admission of fealty by this mage she had come to visit.

She came off the last step onto a wider floor. It was still dark, but not black, with the candle burning in its sconce on a table set off to the side. As she neared, she noted a chair waiting for her on the right side of table, and a seated figure off to the left, not near the table, but against the natural stone wall a few feet from the setting.

Malice understood. She took her seat.

"Greetings. I am honored," the hunched robed figure said. He kept his head bowed, his great cowl pulled below his face.

"Look at me," Malice ordered, for she was curious. It had been a long time since she had seen this man, looking down at him, straddling him after a torrid tryst.

"No, Matron, it is better that I do not."

"How am I to properly prepare the unguent if I do not even fully understand the depth of the affliction?"

"It is not an affliction," the man said, his voice growing tight with anger.

Malice thought to reiterate her command more forcefully—she was a matron and he a mere male—but she held back. This wizard, Gelroos Hun'ett, was an accomplished master in Sorcere, a powerful wizard, though one who was, apparently, somewhat reckless. His specialty was in creating new spells, combining magical effects to make the whole greater than the sum of the individual dweomers. Many of the spells taught at Sorcere were the result of the work of Gelroos, though anonymously, by order of the archmage.

Such dabbling was not without reward, but also not without great risk, and on one occasion decades before, Gelroos's magical combination had backfired, quite literally, taking the flesh from his face, which was, by all accounts Malice had heard, little more than a mix of bone and green goo.

Now she wanted to see it—even more so because the wizard was clearly uncomfortable showing her. Seeing it would give her an edge here, perhaps, by putting Gelroos into a measure of discomfort, and Matron Malice was never one to forgo a possible advantage.

"Look at me," she ordered. Normally, she would have strengthened such a demand with a magical spell, but such an enchantment would likely have little effect on the formidable wizard. And if she made the magical attempt, he would probably detect it.

"I have that which you seek," Gelroos answered instead, a quite effective deflection. "I have associates at Arach-Tinilith, and what the priestesses have shown me, along with that which I hold here in my own library, informs me that the long-ago rumors you heard were not without merit."

"So it can be done," Malice said, leaning forward. She reminded herself not to give up on viewing this disfigured creature, but that seemed like a distant desire in that moment.

"It can be done and it is not so difficult a task," the mage answered. "I believe that it would be a more popular and common occurrence if it was more widely understood, and of course, if it did not hold dire implications for the child."

"Such as?"

Gelroos shrugged, a weird and unbalanced motion in his heavy robes and with his scrawny shoulders, and did look up then. Matron Malice fell back in her chair in surprise and horror.

Nothing she had heard of his disfigurement could have prepared her for the reality of Gelroos Hun'ett, the Faceless One. The descriptions had been honest, though, for his face was a collage of bone edges, stretched and desiccated skin, lipless and gumless mouth, and a drooping triangular hole where his nose used to be. He didn't seem to have any eyelids, either, appearing like a corpse long decaying, except for the notable splotches of green goo, some looking like the wax refuge of a melted candle, other bits seeming almost foamy and more fluid.

Her last recollection of the man flashed in Malice's thoughts. He had never been overly handsome by drow standards, but pretty enough. But now . . .

"It is an auspicious beginning to life," Gelroos answered.

Malice shook away her surprise. She took a deep breath, which merely gave her a blast of the rotting aroma of the wizard's face, and tried to respond, though she had completely lost the conversation.

"You asked of the implications to the child," he reminded her. "It would be an auspicious beginning."

"Yes. Yes, of course," she stammered. "But is it more than that? Is there a curse? A lasting stain?"

The Faceless One shrugged again. "I have seen nothing to indicate so, but then, most of the children born in the ritual have been sons, third sons, and so . . ."

He let it hang there and Malice needed no explanation. A third son in a drow house was traditionally given to Lolth.

"Perhaps that is the curse of birth magic," Gelroos then added. "The curse to the house that a son was born, not a preferred daughter, and a most deadly curse to the child very soon after."

"Tell me more of it," Malice pressed. "Quickly."

"There are wizards who routinely inflict pain upon themselves in the moments of casting, using that sting to sharpen their focus and thus produce the most powerful spell they can manage."

"This is just about the pain of childbirth?" Malice asked incredulously. Yes, of course it hurt, but that alone couldn't possibly explain the potential power of the birthing magic ritual!

"There is more to birth than pain," Gelroos replied. "It is an experience unlike any other, one that encompasses both the body—both bodies, mother's and child's!—and the mind, heart, and spirit. The corporeal and ethereal. It is a moment of great vulnerability, but also one of great reception, and in that open state, the mother seems to collect all the magical energies about her, almost as if she is bringing the magical energy of those spellcasters around her into her own dweomer."

"How is that possible?"

Gelroos shook his head. "I am a mere male, Matron Malice. I cannot fully understand the experience of giving birth." He lifted up a skinny hand, holding a scroll tube, and moved it across to the woman.

"You have read it?" Malice asked, taking the item.

"There would be no reason," Gelroos said with a wheezing chuckle. "This is one spell that is truly beyond my means. Also, my priestess associates forbade me from even glancing at the spell, and instructed me to relay to you, though they know not your identity, that great secrecy is demanded. Copy nothing of the dweomer. Forget it as you cast it, and speak little of it. Let the rumors swirl, as mystery is no threat."

Malice rolled the scroll tube in her hand, feeling the weight of his words. She had used birth magic before, but only in a minor way and certainly nothing akin to this. Even on that occasion, though, a simple spell of poison to aid her ascent, she had felt possibilities more profound. Joining other priestesses in the ritual? She felt as if she could hardly breathe, as if she was holding in her hand the power of a goddess.

"Clearly," Gelroos continued, "this kind of power could be seen as a threat to the matrons of the Ruling Council. This is no mere dweomer, Matron Malice. Do not underestimate the magical destructive power you will discover in the heightened moments of childbirth. And, I warn you as one who wishes you well, do not seek to exploit or abuse that power beyond our agreement here. The Ruling Council and the priestesses of Arach-Tinilith will be paying attention, and the combined weight of what would fall upon House Do'Urden in the event . . . well . . ."

He left it there with another shrug.

"I MAY NEED YOUR PROTECTION," THE YOUNG MAN, BARELY more than a boy, explained to Jarlaxle, the two sitting in the Oozing Myconid late one quiet night.

"You are the noble son of a ruling house. What could I possibly offer?"

The man, Masoj, sighed and shook his head at the ridiculous remark. Even he, who had rarely been out of his house before being sent to serve his older sibling as a slave in Sorcere at the drow academy, was worldly enough to understand the growing power of Bregan D'aerthe. The band had the complete endorsement and protection of House Baenre!

Even without that, Jarlaxle had created enough quiet alliances and assembled enough firepower to make the band of rogues formidable on its own. Jarlaxle knew it, and knew that Masoj knew it, so his feigned humility could elicit no more than a groan from the young man.

"Why do you think you would need the protection of Bregan D'aerthe?" Jarlaxle asked finally.

"What you ask me to do could get me sacrificed, or turned into a drider."

"Ask? I have asked nothing of you," Jarlaxle reminded. "You came to me with a request and a bag of gold coins."

"And you refused my contract!"

"I told you that such things are better taken care of within a family. Else, one risks war, and wars are messy and costly. But I did not ask you to do anything."

"You hinted that I might find more allies if I succeeded."

"How so?" Jarlaxle asked.

Masoj started to answer, but bit his lip and tried to honestly recount his previous meeting with this most enigmatic drow. When he had gone to Jarlaxle hoping to pay for an assassination, the clever rogue had merely explained that such things were better handled within the house, both for the reason Jarlaxle had just reiterated and also because then the assassin had, in no small way, proven himself worthy of the resulting rise in stature.

Masoj wanted Jarlaxle to do this. He was afraid, rightfully so, for his much older brother was quite powerful in the ways of arcane magic. At one point, powerful enough to be considered a possible future challenger to Gromph Baenre as archmage of the Menzoberranzan. All of that promise had fallen away in the flash of a spell gone horribly, irreversibly wrong.

"I will tell you this much," Jarlaxle said, leaning forward in his seat, his hand coming over the table and sitting there, palm up, fingers beckoning.

"How much?" Masoj asked.

"All of it."

"No."

"Then I leave, and warn you to take great care in your next schemes, and great care in pointing any fingers or words toward me or this place."

"It had better be worth the price," Masoj mumbled, pulling out the small bag of gold and dropping it onto Jarlaxle's still-waiting palm.

"Events are soon to unfold that may show you your opportunity, both to do that which you wish and to get away with it," Jarlaxle replied. "Pay very close heed to the student who serves as your brother's primary assistant." As soon as he finished the sentence, Jarlaxle was up and away, not looking back.

Masoj cocked his head curiously as he watched the mercenary depart. "Alton?" he whispered under his breath.

At first, he felt cheated, but he put that notion aside. Jarlaxle's reputation was not to be dismissed. The rogue's cryptic words were known to move houses to war. The young apprentice, who thought himself a slave, drained his drink and left the Oozing Myconid soon after, determined to pay very close attention indeed.

"WHY WOULD YOU GET INVOLVED IN THIS?" DAB'NAY, THE only priestess—and one of the very few women in Bregan D'aerthe—asked Jarlaxle when the young man had left the tavern.

Jarlaxle dropped the pouch of gold on the bar. "No risk and some coin to show for it," he replied.

"You can have all the coin you want without getting involved in the family squabbles of a ruling house," Dab'nay reminded.

"There may be gain here. The target is surely no friend to us, and if the whelp is successful, I'll know a secret he can ill afford to have whispered. And the whelp will no longer be a whelp, will he? He will be the elderboy of a powerful ruling house."

"Still, that target is no minor player, nor is Matron SiNafay or the house she rules."

"The house that speaks ill of us at every meeting of the Ruling Council?" Jarlaxle reminded.

Dab'nay settled back and spent a while digesting that obvious exaggeration, if not outright lie. House Hun'ett would not dare speak ill of Bregan D'aerthe in the presence of Matron Mother Baenre, and had even dealt with the mercenary band on more than one occasion to mutual benefit.

But then, the priestess had her epiphany. When Jarlaxle referred to "us," he didn't mean Bregan D'aerthe. He meant Zaknafein Do'Urden, and by extension, Jarlaxle, as well. It was no secret that Matron SiNafay was often quite vocal against the quick rise of ambitious Malice Do'Urden and her band, and the rumors were longstanding that Malice's youngest daughter had been sired by SiNafay's patron, and that insatiable Malice had often bedded SiNafay's eldest son before his unfortunate circumstance.

"You can have all the coin you want without getting involved in the family squabbles of a ruling house," Dab'nay repeated, because she was out of other things to say.

"Ah, yes," Jarlaxle agreed, "but it would not be as much fun."

DESPITE THE FINAL WARNING OF THE UGLY FACELESS ONE, Matron Malice was almost giddy with excitement when she returned to House Do'Urden.

She would soon deliver another child of Zaknafein, and now she was confident that House DeVir would be destroyed. Even without the birth magic, she had thought that DeVir was ripe for the picking, and with this added boost, her victory seemed assured—and likely a victory with minimal damage to her own house.

There was only one tempering notion here—or rather, two potential issues, though very related. Despite her earlier bravado, could she really be certain that Zaknafein's progeny would be a daughter? And if it was a boy, she would have no recourse, particularly after utilizing a most sacred spell, which required the blessing of Lolth. A male child, even Zaknafein's child, third boy of the house, would have to be sacrificed.

If it was a daughter, there remained the possibility of a residual curse from the casting of the destructive birth magic. But no, Malice told herself, determined to press on in her insatiable desire to climb the ranks of Menzoberranzan. They didn't know there would be a curse, or if there was, perhaps it wouldn't truly prove to be a curse at all, but possibly a blessing. Her eldest daughter, Briza, was the child of a brutish sire who was part demon or cambion or some grandparent not of this plane of existence, by all rumors, and yet the savage Briza—and even more so, the ultimately savage Uthegentel Armgo—certainly couldn't consider that trait an affliction or curse!

"It will be a daughter, a priestess," Malice whispered to herself. "And she will have the ambition of Matron Malice and the discipline of Zaknafein."

As she smiled, she silently added, *And this one will have the compassion beaten out of her. She will not be like Vierna.*

CHAPTER 2

Expendable

S he is pleased. Quite," Jarlaxle reported to Matron Mother Yvonnel Baenre in the dungeon chapel of the city's First House.

The great Baenre turned to her entourage: her five daughters, three of them high priestesses, a fourth soon to be, and the fifth, young Sos'Umptu, no doubt on her path to be perhaps the greatest of all, for her devotion could not be doubted.

Jarlaxle liked that one, Sos'Umptu. She was the quietest of Matron Mother Baenre's daughters, and least ambitious, despite her obvious skill in her clerical studies.

"You will watch carefully from afar," the great Baenre instructed.

"Oh, I will," answered Bladen'Kerst, the second oldest.

Jarlaxle winced despite himself. He hated and feared that one most of all. She was a hulking thing with wide and strong shoulders, and took particular delight in inflicting pain. Was there anything she had ever done to anyone whom she perceived below her station that was not cruel?

"We will," corrected another—another of whom Jarlaxle carried a great enmity. This was Vendes, the fourth Baenre daughter, who seemed determined to ascend to the rank of high priestess by whipping as many victims as possible to death with her horrid seven-headed scourge, its living serpents writhing at her side as she spoke as if they understood every word and anticipated the taste of blood.

"No, *she* will," Baenre commanded, nodding toward her eldest daughter, Triel. She was the shortest of the group, not even topping five feet, and quite ugly as drow women went. But she was broad and strong.

And calculating, Jarlaxle knew. Triel would succeed Yvonnel Baenre to the throne of the First House . . . if the old witch ever decided to die. That was probably a good thing, to the mercenary's thinking. Triel wasn't blinded by unrelenting sadism, like the other two, nor was she a pampered and privileged nit like Quenthel, the third daughter.

Nor was she blindly, wholly consumed by her love for Lolth like Sos'Umptu.

She would rule, and she would rule the house and the city wisely and with a measured hand—publicly, at least. Thus, she would want Jarlaxle and his growing mercenary band to carry out her dirtier deeds.

Jarlaxle couldn't suppress his nod, considering his possible relationship with this one compared to that of the great and powerful Yvonnel, Yvonnel the Eternal, who had sat as a powerful force in Menzoberranzan, and indeed as the Matron Mother of the city, beyond the memories of the oldest drow. They said she was two thousand years old, many times the life expectancy of a drow.

Jarlaxle believed it.

Yvonnel the Eternal was . . . different.

"I hope High Priestess Triel is not dismayed by what she sees," Matron Mother Baenre said, turning back to Jarlaxle. "You should hope so, as well."

"I took her to the Faceless One, as you instructed me," Jarlaxle replied.

"When will she cast the spell?"

"She will give birth early in the next year."

Matron Mother Baenre looked to Triel, her expression questioning.

"If birth magic is as powerful as they say—" Triel started.

"It is," the Matron Mother interjected.

"Then should we be concerned? Would Matron Malice Do'Urden dare turn her sights to a greater target?"

"She is not suicidal, child," said the Matron Mother. "Do you think any of the Ruling Council would allow for such a thing without extreme retribution?"

Triel nodded and fell silent.

"Leave us," Baenre instructed her. "And you," she told Quenthel. "And back to your studies, child," she told Sos'Umptu.

Jarlaxle shifted nervously, which was no common occurrence for the confident and capable rogue. He hadn't been thrilled when told of the location of this meeting, and was less so now, being in this place with Matron Mother Baenre's two most vicious and sadistic daughters.

For this was the burial chapel for Baenre nobles, and Jarlaxle was surrounded by the graves of those who had gone before, including the tomb of one Doquaio Baenre, resting directly behind the spot where the Matron Mother had chosen to place her magically created seat.

Purposely, of course—everything she did was purposeful.

Jarlaxle had a history with Doquaio—one might even say that Jarlaxle had killed Doquaio, though Jarlaxle had no memory of it, for it all had happened in the first moments of his life.

"The Faceless One has promised his help?" Baenre asked Jarlaxle.

The rogue nodded. "He will clean up the loose ends at Sorcere when House Do'Urden executes the assault."

Matron Mother Baenre shuddered visibly. "A hideous fool," she said, "so consumed by ambition that he melted his own face. I do so hate ambitious men who cannot accept their place."

Jarlaxle didn't try to hide his smile at that, particularly given the positions of Baenre's two openly admitted sons: one the archmage of Menzoberranzan, the other, Dantrag, a superb weapon master considered to be the finest swordsman in Menzoberranzan. Dantrag wanted nothing more than to be appointed as the principal master of Melee-Magthere, the drow academy of physical combat, a position for which he was supremely qualified. But Matron Mother Baenre wouldn't allow it, valuing his presence in the house too much.

To say nothing of his *own* ambition.

"What has the Faceless One told you of the birth magic?" Baenre asked.

Surprised by the question, Jarlaxle shrugged and immediately lifted his guard. If he admitted knowing too much, might Baenre loose Vendes and Bladen'Kerst upon him then and there?

"I only arranged the meeting, as you instructed," he answered. "I never glanced at the scroll."

"Or where he got it?"

"Or . . ." Jarlaxle started, then fumbled over the thought and spent a moment considering the question. He had seen, he realized—and had an idea, at least—of where the Faceless One kept the original.

"He penned it?" Baenre pressed.

"Yes."

"From an original scroll?"

"Yes."

"And now Jarlaxle knows where that original is?"

"Yes . . . no . . . somewhat," the rogue stuttered.

"Good," said the Matron Mother. "You will better discern the location. Nothing more, nothing less."

"Of the original writing?" Jarlaxle asked, completely lost by this unexpected turn in the conversation. If Matron Mother Baenre wanted him to enlist the Faceless One again with such a dweomer, that could be easily enough achieved.

Unless . . .

Jarlaxle cocked his head. "Matron Mother?" he asked leadingly. "Are you . . . ?"

"Be gone, Jarlaxle," she replied. "You bore me. Need I have my daughters here remind you that all that we have said is for no other ears, or all that you have learned is for no one outside this room in the moment that you learned it?"

"No, of course not," the rogue answered, and now he was hiding his smile. For he, he alone among the drow outside of House Baenre, now knew that Matron Mother Baenre was pregnant.

In Menzoberranzan, perhaps more than anywhere else in the world, knowledge was power.

Of course, in Menzoberranzan, knowing things often got one killed, particularly if that informed person was a man.

Jarlaxle left the compound of the First House soon after, mulling it all over. He performed many tasks for Matron Mother Baenre and the others of her family, but this one had kept him off-balance from the very beginning. Even the desire of House Baenre to put their thumb on the scale of power in this inter-house battle had caught him by surprise—more so when he had learned that Baenre wanted to intervene on *behalf* of House Do'Urden.

House Do'Urden was the city's tenth house. The Do'Urdens were no threat to House Baenre, of course, and would almost certainly never be, so why did Baenre care? And particularly, why would she care about House DeVir, the city's fourth house, when that house was widely rumored to be on the decline?

Was House DeVir reversing their fortunes and quietly regrouping, growing too strong for their own good, Jarlaxle wondered. Did the Matron Mother feel the need to take them down?

Jarlaxle suspected he was missing something here, and that bothered him most of all. He survived on information. He hated not knowing something when knowing that something could lead to profitable opportunities.

He sent out couriers as soon as he arrived at the Oozing Myconid, then gathered together some food and tried to enjoy his meal and release the spinning troubles from his mind. It would all make sense soon enough, he assured himself repeatedly.

Dab'nay joined him soon after in answer to one of his summonses. She took her seat tentatively, Jarlaxle noticed, never taking her stare off him.

"Is there a problem?" he asked. "And would you like some food?"

"No and no," she answered. "But I know why you have asked me here, and the subject is beyond my understanding and my freedom to discuss."

"You have never heard of the birth magic ritual?"

"I did not say that."

"Well?"

"It is not a subject to be discussed. Certainly not with a man, and certainly not by a priestess who is not in the favor of Lolth."

"Are you not? The Spider Queen has not abandoned you," Jarlaxle replied. "There are no mercenaries carrying bounties for your murder. Your magical spells do not fail you."

"I was never a high priestess."

"You still receive your magical bounty from Lolth."

Dab'nay replied with a slight nod that seemed more of a shrug. Jarlaxle backed away from the conversation, which normally was not an unusual subject between him and Dab'nay. They both understood the anomaly here: Dab'nay had abandoned any formal house or church structure. She had openly spoken ill of Lolth. There was nothing in her life now to indicate any fealty to Lolth or to the Spider Queen's spokeswoman on the material plane, Matron Mother Baenre.

Yet her spells still came to her, even the more powerful ones that required some acquiescence from the otherworldly handmaidens of Lolth.

She was an instrument of chaos, Jarlaxle had concluded. Lolth liked that, even if the instrument didn't much like Lolth. In a strange way, that gave Jarlaxle a bit more respect for the Spider Queen. She would put her own ego aside, it seemed, and allow Dab'nay to do her work, even if Dab'nay didn't do it in her name.

Pragmatism always impressed Jarlaxle.

And yet Dab'nay would still not betray this particular bit of information.

Jarlaxle's second summons was answered then, when another drow joined them at the table. Exceptionally thin and not tall, the man seemed almost a child in a decorated nightshirt rather than a formidable wizard in appropriate robes.

Jarlaxle knew better than to let appearances deceive him.

"Well met, Hazaufein," he said. "I believe you know my friend here."

"Priestess Dab'nay," the man said in greeting.

"I am glad that you were able to join us," said Jarlaxle.

"A fortunate coincidence, nothing more," the man replied. "I did not expect to hear from you."

"How fares Matron K'yorl?" Jarlaxle eyed Dab'nay when he asked that question, expecting her surprised expression. And indeed, she was suddenly looking at the newcomer with more scrutiny.

Of course she was! For Matron K'yorl Odran was the matriarch of House Oblodra, the city's third house, and the most unusual, and unnerving, house. The Odrans, or Oblodrans, drew their power from psionics, the strange mind magics. They were ranked third, but no one really knew how powerful that family might be, since the magic was so unconventional and not fully understood.

"As vicious as ever," Hazaufein replied.

"How do you know Matron K'yorl?" Dab'nay asked, and Hazaufein turned a startled stare her way.

"I am her elderboy," he answered.

"Have you never been formally introduced to Hazaufein Oblodra?" Jarlaxle remarked, knowing the answer but wanting to see her reaction.

"But you are . . ." Dab'nay stated, then turned to Jarlaxle. "But he is a wizard. He studied at Sorcere when I graduated from Arach-Tinilith."

"It is true," Hazaufein said. "Not all the nobles of my house are proficient in mind magic. And the more traditional wizardry serves as a fine compliment."

"And puts K'yorl's eyes outside of House Oblodra," said Jarlaxle.

"She hardly needs that," Hazaufein said dryly. "She can wear the eyes of anyone she wants, whenever she wants."

That reminder had Jarlaxle shifting a bit in his chair, then adjusting his eyepatch simply to feel the magical item, which protected him from the kind of possession to which Hazaufein had just alluded.

"What do you wish of me?" Hazaufein asked impatiently.

"I am only curious if you have heard any rumors. Of war, perhaps?"

"Why would I be foolish enough to speak openly of any such thing?"

"Because you value my friendship," said Jarlaxle. "You wish to be granted a title of savant at Sorcere. I may be in a position to help you acquire that."

"What is the price?"

"Just the answer to my question."

"There is a rumor that a band of rogues are trying to start a minor house, perhaps by defeating the city's least house," Hazaufein said after a moment of reflection.

"That rumor is ten tendays old, and more, and it is one I started," came the dry reply. "I speak of House DeVir."

"Then you speak alone," Hazaufein sternly replied.

"The name angers you."

"House DeVir is the fourth house. House Oblodra the third. Any such rumors are dangerous."

"More so because House DeVir has quietly allied with House Barrison Del'Armgo," Jarlaxle replied, taking a chance on a hunch here.

"No one allies with Matron Mez'Barris Armgo," the Oblodran wizard answered unconvincingly.

In the uncomfortable silence that followed, Jarlaxle noticed that Hazaufein wasn't even asking him what rumors of House DeVir he might have heard—rumors that would certainly affect House Oblodra. To Jarlaxle, that unasked question might be the most important information of all.

"Is there anything else?" Hazaufein asked.

Jarlaxle shook his head.

"I expect payment."

"Of course. I will speak to Archmage Gromph," Jarlaxle assured him.

Hazaufein abruptly rose and departed the tavern.

Jarlaxle watched him go, then turned to see Dab'nay staring at him, shaking her head, clearly at a loss.

"What?" she asked. "What did I just witness?"

"DeVir is stirring," Jarlaxle told her.

"I thought Do'Urden was stirring."

"They are, but only because House DeVir has done something that has shaken Matron Ginafae DeVir's standing with the Spider Queen."

"You think she meant to move against House Oblodra? Wouldn't that please Lolth, since Matron K'yorl is hardly devout?"

"Yes, you would think that," Jarlaxle replied, a smile curling on his face as it all began to become clear to him. Yes, DeVir had meant to move on House Oblodra, but something had stopped them. Matron Ginafae would not have even considered a move against the strange and strangely powerful third house without the blessing of either Matron Mother Baenre or Mez'Barris Armgo, the unpredictable matron of the audacious second-ranked house.

It had to be Barrison Del'Armgo, the mercenary decided, for that explained why Matron Mother Baenre had taken more than a passing interest in the expected fight, and why she had allowed the intervention of the Faceless One with the coveted and rare birth magic spell.

This probably wasn't even about House DeVir at all to Matron Mother Baenre's thinking, Jarlaxle mused, but rather, a warning to any other houses that might consider allying with the wild and wildly ambitious Armgo family.

"Jarlaxle?" Dab'nay asked, and he realized it was not for the first time.

"Matron Ginafae DeVir is out of favor with the Spider Queen, or soon will be," he replied. "Find out why."

"A mere male should not be speaking of such favor or disfavor where matrons are concerned," Dab'nay replied.

"Mere?" Jarlaxle said with a wry grin. "Why, yes, I would agree with you on the point that no mere male should speak of such things. Need I ask you again?"

His grin proved infectious, and Dab'nay left the table and the tavern wearing a smile of her own.

The intrigue of Menzoberranzan was fun, Jarlaxle knew, and it pleased him whenever one of his mercenary band came to recognize that truth.

It was all a game.

Always dangerous.

Often deadly.

But still a game.

THERE WAS A LIGHTNESS IN JARLAXLE'S STEP A FEW DAYS later, after Dab'nay and some of his other scouts had finally discerned the impetus for the coming war. It seemed that Matron Ginafae DeVir, in her desire to please Matron Mez'Barris Armgo, had overstepped her bounds quite sacrilegiously. Anxious to weaken House Oblodra so that her house could pass it—perhaps even eliminating the strange psionicist house altogether if it came to blows—Ginafae had cast blessings upon a group of deep gnomes, the hated svirfneblin, in order to help them on a quest to eliminate a certain member of House Oblodra's noble family.

It was a reasonable attempt, Jarlaxle thought. Certainly the deep gnomes were not to be given the blessing of Lolth in normal circumstances, but this was House Oblodra, a Menzoberranzan drow family whose devotion to Lolth was always in question. Nobody liked the Oblodrans, since everybody feared them!

A reasonable risk, but apparently, Matron Ginafae had lost her bet. For the gnomes had been destroyed, the Oblodran noble secured, and now House DeVir had shown its hand.

"They are holed up their compound, huddled in fear," Jarlaxle's psionicist friend, Kimmuriel Oblodra, informed him. "Matron Ginafae understands that she has lost the favor of the Spider Queen and so her house is vulnerable. The Armgo forces will not defend her unless she regains that favor, and without that alliance, there are several houses that can likely overcome DeVir."

"Like House Oblodra," Jarlaxle dryly replied.

"We have no interest in inter-house warfare," Kimmuriel replied, as Jarlaxle had expected.

It was true enough, obviously, given the history. This was a strange time in Menzoberranzan, as both the second and third houses had ascended rather swiftly (none ever more swiftly than House Barrison

Del'Armgo, surely), and with minimal battles along the way. Unlike the Do'Urdens and most other climbing houses, these two hadn't clawed their way one battle at a time. When House Barrison Del'Armgo had at long last fully revealed their power, it became clear that only Baenre was greater, and that it would take two, probably three, of the other great houses to combine their strength to have a chance against them.

For the Oblodrans, they had been given the status demanded by Matron K'yorl simply *because* no one had any desire to do battle with them. Their psionics had the Lolthian priestesses wholly unnerved. K'yorl had demanded a high seat on the Ruling Council, and they had given her the third rank, with Matron Mother Baenre and Matron Mez'Barris Armgo leading the vote.

It was a secret deal, Jarlaxle knew, though surely one that would not hold forever. K'yorl would be content with the third rank, and the two greatest houses would be glad for the strange buffer between them and the rest.

But now House DeVir had potentially upset all of that, and so, Jarlaxle knew, Matron Mez'Barris would wash her hands of them. She wasn't about to risk her coveted seat right behind House Baenre for the sake of a house like DeVir, which was too highly ranked in the first place.

"Does your brother even know that he was the target?" Jarlaxle remarked.

"He is not my brother," the impassive Kimmuriel replied, and it was technically true, as Kimmuriel was not the son of Matron K'yorl. He had been taken into the noble family as a son, however, because of his extraordinary intellect and his growing prowess in the art of mind magic.

"Hazaufein is a noble son of House Oblodra, as is Kimmuriel."

"If Matron K'yorl was the rumored sire instead of the obvious mother, no one would believe that heritage."

Jarlaxle laughed, knowing that to be as close to a joke as he would ever hear from this passionless one.

"And now it all makes sense to you," Kimmuriel said—quite astutely, Jarlaxle thought. "Matron Mother Baenre is pleased, Matron

Mez'Barris fearful. Some house will overwhelm House DeVir, and so Matron Mez'Barris's budding alliance will meet a swift end."

Jarlaxle snickered but didn't reply. He thought—not for the first time and certainly not for the last—that someday he would be thrilled to formally induct Kimmuriel into Bregan D'aerthe as a full member, beholden only to the band and not the dangerous Matron K'yorl.

"And how do you know that?" he asked.

Kimmuriel arched a thin white eyebrow. "I know many things."

Indeed he did, Jarlaxle understood. Interrogation was never more fully served than in the act of mental possession. Kimmuriel could thread his thoughts into the mind of another, weaker intellect, with practiced ease.

With that unsettling thought, Jarlaxle adjusted his eyepatch, as he had the previous night when talking to Hazaufein.

It's becoming a bit of a tell, he thought, and promised himself to work on not reaching for the eyepatch every time psionics was discussed.

"What else do you know?"

Kimmuriel stared at him, unblinking.

"The Faceless One?"

"The birth magic," Kimmuriel replied.

"You should show more respect. It is quite powerful."

Kimmuriel snickered, which rarely happened. "It is, I suppose, as near to the mind magic as mundane wizards and priestesses can approach."

Ah, yes, the haughtiness of the Oblodrans, Jarlaxle thought, but did not say.

"Underestimate it at your peril," he did say.

Kimmuriel snickered again.

"I ask, then, if you are so sure of this, why aren't the Oblodrans, or Odrans, or whatever name your house currently wears, sitting atop the Ruling Council?"

"Have you ever watched a lizard race?"

Where was this going? "I have wagered more than the treasury of House Oblodra on such events."

"When they run in the higher tunnels, where the air isn't still, the wise rider keeps his mount behind the shoulder of the lead runners," Kimmuriel explained. "He lets them do the work in breaking the press of the wind until it is time to glide past them."

"Matron Mother Baenre would pay me well for such information," Jarlaxle slyly replied.

"She would, but you won't tell her."

His certainty bothered Jarlaxle, mostly because the mercenary leader knew that Kimmuriel was right.

CHAPTER 3

Seeds

D inin Do'Urden rolled out from under the swirling cloud
of conjured wretchedness, his vision blurry, eyes burning,
throat thick with bile and mucus. He realized immediately
as he executed his second roll, putting him clear of the
conjured cloud, and started to stand that he had chosen the wrong
exit angle.

Magical webbing grabbed at him as he began to rise, clinging and
holding fast.

Nalfein had thrown this second dweomer to the left of the cloud,
while Dinin had expected it on the right.

He tried to pull free, half turned and slashed with his drow
blades—except these were blunted practice swords and not the fine-
edged magical weapons the drow warrior usually carried.

Dinin turned to face his adversary and tugged hard against the
stubborn webs, and indeed, he felt as if he was making progress and
expected to break free.

Not in time, he realized, as Nalfein's waggling fingers completed the next spell, a bolt of lightning leaping out to slam against poor Dinin, throwing him backward. The webs behind him burned in the blast, so he wasn't trapped, at least.

But he was surely stung by the lightning bolt, and he tried to keep his muscles behaving and following his commands, but they—some of them, at least—seemed to have developed minds of their own. His legs trembled and a step forward became a slide to the side, and poor Dinin was down on the ground again, gyrating uncontrollably for a few moments, doing all he could to simply hold on to his twin swords.

He gradually regained control, tasting blood in his mouth from the damage caused by chattering teeth, and threw himself to his feet.

And there stood Nalfein, his next spell ready to launch.

"Yield!" Zaknafein ordered from the side. "The battle is ended."

Nalfein flashed that awful grin, one that bit into the heart of the proud Dinin. He hadn't wanted this fight but had been goaded here by his most powerful Do'Urden sister, Briza. She had taunted him to the point where any refusal on his part would have been more embarrassing even than his defeat.

"So we have a winner," said Zaknafein, and Nalfein crossed his arms over his chest in a gesture of condescension and superiority.

"This time," Zaknafein added, "and I will add, by the flip of a coin."

Nalfein's grin became a frown. "I struck him three times before he got near to me. Had him choking and caught and helpless, and the last strike, the lightning bolt, could have been fatal had this been a true fight and not a sparring match."

"You guessed correctly on the location of the web," said Zaknafein. "Had Dinin come out the other side of your magical cloud of stench . . ."

"He still would have faced the lightning," Nalfein argued.

"Unhindered by the web, though, and so he might have avoided its bite, and where would Nalfein then be?"

"If you think all of my tricks had played out, weapon master, then you are mistaken."

Zaknafein shrugged and let it go, but Dinin did not.

"It is a ridiculous challenge in the first place," he argued. "A wizard strikes from range, a fighter up close. How can a fighter succeed when the wizard knows the battlefield and can strike from afar?"

"You chose to accept the match," Zaknafein reminded him. "It was not one I arranged, nor one I advised you to take."

"My brother is correct," Nalfein said. "In a fair fight, a mere warrior has no chance against a wizard."

As soon as the words left his mouth, the timbre of the very air seemed to change. Nalfein bit off the last word, and Dinin fell perfectly silent, his eyes going wide as he looked from Zaknafein to Nalfein.

For many heartbeats, Zaknafein just smiled. Then he waved Dinin off to the side, walked to the weapon rack across from Nalfein, and took up a pair of swords, waving them easily to test their balance.

"What is this?" Nalfein demanded.

"It is a challenge for you to back up your last proclamation, of course."

"I have already used my spells."

"You are a noble son of a powerful family, a graduate of Sorcere, and one also trained in the arts martial. You have plenty of spells left, of course."

"I . . . I do not wish another challenge this day."

"But you have *found* one, Nalfein. For now I am curious. I am a mere warrior, after all, and you a wizard. If your assertion proves correct, perhaps I will toss aside my swords and go study in Sorcere."

At the side of the room, near the dissipating web and stinking cloud, Dinin snickered.

"Are you ready?" Zaknafein asked.

"No," said Nalfein.

"Yes," said Zaknafein. "Prepare. You may strike first."

Nalfein glanced all around, then closed his eyes only briefly, obviously formulating a series of spells to rain over this more formidable enemy. He exploded into motion, arms waving, chanting his arcane words.

Zaknafein, true to his word, didn't move, standing easily some forty feet away.

A pea of flame appeared in Nalfein's hand. He threw it across the room, then immediately launched into his second spell.

Dinin gasped in shock. A fireball! In a room in House Do'Urden, Nalfein had thrown a fireball!

Zaknafein leaped up and back, spinning as he rose, rose, rose— incredibly so! For he called upon his innate drow powers and his house emblem to enact a levitation spell as he lifted from the floor. He was up more than a dozen feet when the pea of fire dropped and exploded into a magnificent fireball, and when the roiling flames had cleared, there was Zaknafein, tucked up into the top corner where the curving wall of the arena joined with the ceiling, his magical *piwafwi* cloak tight about him.

Perhaps the flames had reached him and bit at him, but if so, he hardly appeared injured as he unwound and turned, planting his feet against that corner, his magical levitation still enacted. He kicked off, gliding down and away from the wall toward Nalfein, and he reached into his drow powers once more, the magic of the race granted by the emanations of the Faezress, and planted a globe of darkness on the floor before Nalfein.

Dinin gasped again when Zak's levitation expired, when he dropped with perfect angle and tucked to land in a roll, one that sent him spinning back to his feet with such force that when he leaped away, such a great leap it proved to be, launching him right over the ten-foot darkness globe.

A lightning bolt cut through the heart of that globe beneath him, harmlessly.

And now the skilled Zaknafein landed with grace once more at the far edge of the darkness globe, rolling to his feet and rushing forward with stunning speed and precision.

Nalfein slashed his own practice sword across to slow the weapon master, and lifted his hand, his fingers arcing with lightning energy. But that electrical slap got nowhere near Zaknafein, who dropped to a slide on his knees, back-bending under the sword swing and the reach of those lightning-crackling fingers.

Across came Zak's left-hand sword on a low backhand, Nalfein fast-stepping to avoid getting tripped up.

Across came Zak's right-hand blade just behind it, on the same level but in a wider arc, and Nalfein escaped the brunt of it only by stumbling backward.

Zaknafein let the swords continue around, using the momentum to spin back up onto his feet, rushing forward as he came around.

Nalfein's shocking grasp swung down at him, but Zak's sword was faster, slapping hard against the wizard's forehand with enough force to draw a yelp of pain. Back fell Nalfein, forward came Zaknafein, his twin swords rolling out and under, then doubly stabbing forward as Nalfein tried to run out of the room in retreat.

The dulled tips of the blades caught the wizard in the armpits, and Zaknafein bore forward and up, lifting poor Nalfein into the air, where two running strides by Zaknafein slammed him into the practice arena's wall.

And there Zak held him, scowling.

"If you wish to make such boasts of the superiority of priestesses, I have to accept it," Zaknafein admitted. "But you speak of professions mostly filled by we, the mere males of Menzoberranzan, and that, when it is just we men, I will not abide. A mere warrior, Nalfein? If I take out your heart and hold it beating before your eyes, will you admit the error of such a claim?"

"Zaknafein," Nalfein said through a pained grimace.

"Will you?"

"I am the elderboy of House Do'Urden!" Nalfein managed to growl out.

"And I am a murderer with little to lose," Zak answered. "Will you admit it?"

"I . . . was . . . wrong," Nalfein said, Zaknafein twisting a blade with each forced word.

Zaknafein retracted and Nalfein dropped to the floor.

"We support each other against them," Zaknafein told him, and turned as he spoke to include Dinin. "We men, we lessers. We have enough enemies here in the City of Spiders without battling each other."

Nalfein didn't respond, other than to grab at his pained armpits and stumble aside, rushing out of the room.

"He will probably run to Matron Malice to cry about the treatment," Dinin said, walking over.

Zak scowled at him, too. "He defeated you," the weapon master reminded.

Dinin stopped, eyes hard.

"How did you let that happen? You foolishly chose to attempt an attack instead of backing out of the cloud. You could have easily exhausted his magical abilities, but you got impatient. I have taught you better than that. Did you think to impress me?"

"I guessed incorrectly," the still upset Dinin argued.

"You shouldn't have guessed at all! He is a wizard."

"A mediocre wizard."

"Who defeated you."

"It is hardly fair to put a melee warrior in an open arena with a caster who can strike at range!"

"True," Zak said, his voice dripping with sarcasm. "What warrior could ever win such a challenge?"

"That is not . . ." Dinin sputtered. "You are . . ."

"I am the weapon master of House Do'Urden," Zaknafein finished. "It is my duty to keep you alive and prepared for all events. I did that, but you failed here, miserably. In a house fight, you would be dead, and I would suffer the wrath of Matron Malice for your impatience and stupidity."

"I am a house noble," Dinin growled back. "Son of a matron."

"An angry one, I see," Zak taunted, and up came his sword suddenly, tapping against the underside of Dinin's chin.

The outraged Dinin fell back, then came forward, swords appearing in his hands, a sudden and brutal attack to repay the insult. His left-hand blade stabbed ahead and was easily guided wide by Zak's already uplifted sword. That was the feint, however, for Dinin's right-hand blade came under and around the hooked swords, a clever move executed with impressive precision, balance, and strength.

But Zaknafein's right-hand blade came up horizontally to lift that stabbing blade, and the weapon master's parrying weapon bent over diagonally so that the lifted sword got pinched between it and the blocking lower sword. Up went Zaknafein's arms, lifting Dinin's arms and swords up high, lifting Dinin up on his tiptoes.

Zaknafein stepped in close and snapped his head forward, driving his forehead into Dinin's nose. As the younger warrior fell back a step, Zaknafein rushed forward, still holding arms and swords up high, and let go of his left-hand blade, leaving it still hanging from the trap of swords above.

The weapon master stepped his left foot across to the right and ahead, then looped it back behind his opponent even as his left hand slammed against Dinin's chest, tripping him backward.

Dinin didn't resist, disengaging his swords from Zaknafein's, landing easily and smoothly, and rolled perfectly over into a crouch, weapons ready for Zak's advance.

But Zaknafein wasn't there.

The weapon master's sword clanged down from on high, sent spinning by Dinin's disengage, since Zak had let it go. Only when it landed, the sharp sound a signal, did Dinin lower his blades.

He knew.

Of course he knew.

Zaknafein had mirrored his movement and was behind him, and that remaining sword whacked the young Do'Urden hard on the back of his head.

"Do better," Zaknafein whispered in Dinin's ear, and he left his defeated opponent there, crouched and pained.

"And put these swords away and tidy up the room," Zaknafein continued as he walked away, tossing his remaining practice weapon to the floor.

"You embarrass me!" Dinin called after him in a threatening tone.

"You embarrass yourself," Zak answered. "I am just a mirror. The ugliness of your weaknesses are yours alone."

"A GREAT PITY THAT WOULD BE," BRIZA DARED TO SOM-
berly reply, and she felt the cold glare of Matron Malice as soon as she

had uttered the sentence. She thought herself foolish, dangerously so, and felt suddenly vulnerable.

"Pity?"

"The sacrifice," Briza stammered. She understood that she should have let it go and allowed her mother to vent her fears without giving them any credence at all. Malice had only mentioned the possibility of her child, Zaknafein's child, being a boy in her remark that it could not happen, that Lolth would not let it happen.

"But it will not happen," Malice said again, biting short every word. "The Spider Queen would not allow it to happen."

"Of course, Matron. It cannot be."

"Then why did you cast your voice with such lament?"

"Because I wish it could be," Briza blurted, hardly thinking it through. She was just trying to say something, anything, to calm her very pregnant mother.

"You *wish?*" Malice retorted, her eyes flashing with anger. "What priestess would wish for a mere boy?"

Briza paused then, unsure. "Zaknafein's boy," she decided. "Zaknafein is a mere man, true, but he has brought great advantage to House Do'Urden. What might . . ."

Malice fell back in her seat and gave a hearty laugh, and Briza exhaled.

"Great advantage and great pleasure," the matron agreed. "Yes, daughter, any child of Zaknafein, boy or girl, could be a boon to House Do'Urden, but it cannot be any child, can it? Most of all, we must hold strong in the favor of the Spider Queen, particularly now as I ask of her this great surge of divine power with which to punish Matron Ginafae for her heresy.

"We know what is necessary to achieve that," Malice continued. "Or what would be necessary if this child of Zaknafein was of the lesser gender. What are we to do? I have already birthed two boys, and both remain alive. The laws of Lolth cannot be questioned."

Briza nodded and kept her head bent, her gaze to the floor.

She left her mother soon after, marveling at Malice's leadership.

Matron Malice hadn't asked her to do anything, yet she understood exactly what her mother wished.

And Briza had an idea of how she might grant that wish.

She found her brother on the front balcony of House Do'Urden, overlooking the city, high up from the floor. House Do'Urden was built into the western wall of the cavern that held Menzoberranzan, this balcony and the one for the house chapel both affording grand views of the magically lit city, stalactites and stalagmites dancing in the colored flames of faerie fire, the giant timeclock pillar of Narbondel glowing softly in the distance. These balconies were also the only way to get into the house's second floor, affording a measure of protection against the mundane shock troops used by most drow houses who could not levitate.

Even though he had the hood of his *piwafwi* pulled up over his head, Briza noted her brother's dour expression as she neared. The set of his jaw gave it away as he stood leaning on the rail, staring out over the city. She noted, too, when he turned to look at her, that he had his head wrapped in a bandage.

"Nalfein did that to you?" she asked, with both surprise and more than a little bit of mocking in her tone.

"Zaknafein."

"I thought you were sparring Nalfein this day in preparation."

"The weapon master had a few lessons to offer us both after that match," Dinin said, practically spitting the words.

"Yes, I've noticed his foul mood of late," Briza said, taking a spot at the balcony beside him and turning her gaze to the city. "It is expected, of course."

"Why? Zaknafein loves the battles—he lives for them!—and this will be the greatest challenge yet by far. You think he is afraid?"

"Afraid?" Briza echoed with a snort. "Of what? Of defeat? Of dying? I think Zaknafein would welcome his own death, so great is his self-loathing."

That drew a curious stare from Dinin, and he silently mouthed, *Self-loathing?*

Briza hid her smile. Like her brother, she knew that, if anything, Zaknafein was too in love with himself, too haughty, and believed himself somehow above the edicts of the priestesses who served the Spider Queen. That truth didn't serve her now, however.

"His mood might be based on fear," Briza added, "but not for himself or for House Do'Urden. We will win, and he knows it. But there is another involved, one whose future is far less certain."

Dinin's expression grew more puzzled still, and Briza resisted the urge to reach out and slug her slow-witted brother. How Dinin had ever survived so long in Menzoberranzan, she would never know, for she didn't consider him clever enough in the webs of drow culture.

"You may have noticed that Matron Malice has grown of late," she said dryly.

"Yes, with Zaknafein's child, it is whispered. So?"

"It is his, this time for sure."

"And the rumors speak of Vierna as his, as well. Perhaps he has others scattered about the city—he was coveted by many for breeding in the distant past, so I have heard."

"This one is different to him, and likely to Matron Malice. This one is surely of his loins and will bring immediate aid to House Do'Urden in the very act of being born. And this one is very possibly in immediate mortal peril."

"Because of the spell?"

"Shh," Briza scolded. "Lower your voice. That is known to the nobles of House Do'Urden alone. But no, not because of that. Think, brother. You more than I should understand."

"Third son," Dinin said after a moment of pause, and both his voice and expression showed that he hadn't thought of that before.

"And so Zaknafein is in a foul mood, and so is Matron Malice, I warn. She will not dare disobey the edicts of the Spider Queen, of course, and particularly not now, when she is asking Lolth for so much in the coming battle. But a male child of Zaknafein would be grand indeed, in her estimation. A most worthy addition to the Do'Urden ranks."

"She would value a girl more," Dinin argued. "Of course she would."

"If it is a girl, then there is no issue. But Matron Malice is coming to believe that it is a son she carries," said Briza. "Still, I think you are wrong there, brother. In this case, given the sire, I think the notion of a boy truly intrigues Matron Malice. Another fighter of Zaknafein's caliber? She could enrich the family simply by renting him out to other matrons once he becomes a man."

"She could do that with Zaknafein now," Dinin said, seeming quite annoyed. "And you misread her, I am sure."

"Take care how you speak to a high priestess," she warned.

"That is exactly my point," Dinin replied. "No matter how great this son might be, he will never be as great as . . . as Briza. But a girl, a daughter of Zaknafein?"

"Like Vierna?" Briza retorted, chortling.

"Neither you nor I are children of Zaknafein."

"And yet I remain far superior to Vierna in every measurable way. Far superior, and that will not change. Matron Malice has no love for Zaknafein—it is simply family business. I fear not at all the possibility that Matron Malice will have another girl, another daughter of Zaknafein. I remain the high priestess of House Do'Urden and next in line to the title of matron. By the time a new child could possibly grow strong enough to challenge me, Matron Malice will likely already be dead, or will have sealed the line of ascension.

"But a boy, Dinin, a son of Zaknafein! That could shake the very foundation of house noble ranking among the men of D'aermon N'a'chezbaernon."

Her use of the formal and ancient name of House Do'Urden focused Dinin's thoughts more clearly. "But you just said that Malice would not go against the edicts of the Spider Queen, surely, in these critical times."

"Malice?" Briza said quietly, threateningly.

"Matron Malice!" the flummoxed warrior corrected.

"Certainly not," Briza said. "But neither would Matron Malice be displeased if one of her other sons found the misfortune to fall in the battle with DeVir."

"Unlikely."

"But not impossible," said Briza, and she turned and walked away, confident her words had resonated.

CHAPTER 4

The Ever-turning Wheel
of Menzoberranzan

D inin was in a foul mood when he exited the lizard corral and the lower level of House Do'Urden, making his way to a spot below the chapel balcony. His mission, the last before the battle, had been successful. He had identified and magically marked the sentient shrieker mushrooms along the House DeVir border wall, and had gone to see the Faceless One, relaying to him the timing of the assassination of the DeVir wizard, Alton, who remained at Sorcere.

With that success, Dinin had returned to the stable in fine spirits, excited for the battle, which would prove the most consequential of his life thus far, he was sure. But inside, the whispers among the lizard handlers had confirmed the secondboy's concerns.

Matron Malice, they now knew, would deliver a son.

The son of Zaknafein, the third son of D'aermon N'a'chezbaernon, and thus, a child to be sacrificed to Lolth. Malice would resent that, Dinin knew. After his talk with Briza, he could not ignore that his mother would greatly lament this precious sacrifice, and he knew her well enough to understand that her resentment would linger for years, decades, and it would be aimed primarily at the two persons responsible for the sacrifice of Zaknafein's son: Dinin and Nalfein.

He had other fears, as well, suspecting that Briza had not come to him unbidden by their mother. And if that were the case, she had likely gone, too, to Nalfein.

Yes, it made sense to him, and it worried him. If Matron Malice lost Nalfein this night, Zaknafein's son, almost certainly a warrior, would grow in the shadow of elderboy Dinin, also a warrior. But if it was Dinin who died this night, then the elderboy would be a wizard, and no rival to the growing secondboy warrior.

There were three possibilities here, none of them ideal, but one, Dinin believed, better than the other two.

He tapped his house emblem and floated from the floor, rising up easily in the shadows of the exposed portions of the compound, then stepping over lightly onto the balcony, releasing the magic.

"Where have you been?" he heard even as he touched down upon the stone. He turned to see Vierna approaching. "You have been gone too long!"

"Be at ease, sister, I had much to do."

"I know what you had to do," an obviously nervous Vierna retorted.

"Do you? Have you ever marked shriekers, sister? Not so easy a task. One step too close and they sound their alarms, and yet you have to be quite close to put the silenced hand-crossbow quarrels into their thick stems. And if you miss, guess what happens?"

"I need not your sarcasm, brother. Not now."

Dinin started to reply, sharply, but he leaned back instead and took full measure of Vierna, allowing her the benefit of his doubt. She was his favorite sister, after all, the closest in age to him and one who did not flaunt her station above him as a woman, a noble daughter, *and* a priestess of Lolth.

"What do you know, Vierna? Pray tell me."

"It will be a boy," Vierna admitted.

"The whispers of that have already reached the stables," Dinin agreed.

Vierna sighed heavily.

"Does it bother you because it is your brother, both sire and dam?" Dinin asked, trying not to taunt Vierna here. "Or is it because of the thought of what must be done, perhaps what Matron Malice will make you do personally?"

"High Priestess Briza will wield the dagger," Vierna said quickly, but the speed of her words could not hide her discomfort.

Dinin did not chuckle but couldn't suppress his grin. He had always known Vierna's heart to be softer than that of the typical drow woman, and much more so than the typical drow priestess, surely. Briza's remarks to him concerning Vierna came flashing to mind. Yes, why would the powerful and vicious Briza ever fear her station as Matron Malice's heir to this one, the weak Vierna? Would compassionate Vierna even have the temperament to be nominated as a high priestess?

"Go take your place," he told Vierna, reminding himself that he had to be kind to her at this time. She was the one assigned to send him magical messages in the fight, after all. "I must report and assemble my battle group."

Vierna took another breath, gave a slight nod, and scurried away, through the archway and down the house's main central corridor.

Dinin gave her a few moments, then started in boldly, down the corridor to the ornate brass door marking the antechamber to the house chapel, the audience hall of the high priestesses.

And this night, the war room of House Do'Urden.

Soon after he had delivered his assurances to Matron Malice and the others, Dinin led his column out of House Do'Urden, sixty drow soldiers and a hundred goblinkin fighters marching close behind him. With the clumsy humanoids waiting back a safe distance, the drow battle group crept into position.

Other battle groups soon arrived, the silent hand codes working up and down the line as the commoner priestesses took their places and found their marks—the marks Dinin had put on the alarm shriekers.

The moments slipped by, seeming like hours to anxious Dinin.

The priestesses on the battlefield finally moved, stepping forth to cast their spells of protection—beginning all at once, as if they had received confirmation that the time was upon them.

The magical waves rolled along the Do'Urden line, bolstering, protecting, silencing.

Dinin rushed out and produced a sheet of shiny metal and a small pinprick magical light source—quite literally a tiny dweomer cast at the inner base of a hollowed pin. He flashed the object three times to signal his brother and Rizzen, the house patron, and their respective brigades.

Then Dinin spun it up into the air, and his own brigade took the signal and stepped forward, hand crossbows firing at the marked shrieker mushrooms, each throwing a dart enchanted by the priestesses with magical silence.

On came the drow warriors, quietly to the wall and over the wall, Dinin at the front. He was the first to encounter a DeVir sentry. The man drew a sword and stabbed at Dinin as he came over the wall, but the blade never got close to the fine warrior, Dinin's superior sword coming up fast to parry, then riposte, a stab that had the DeVir warrior half turning to dodge.

In rushed Dinin between the man and the parapet. Dinin rolled about as he went, turning his back to the man but sending his left-hand blade around and out to block the DeVir's backhand as he, too, pivoted.

In came the DeVir's second blade for the crouching Dinin, almost reaching its target.

Almost.

For Dinin used a blunt tactic instead, bracing himself against the stone parapet and double-kicking out, a move unexpected from a nimble drow swordsman.

A move taught to a select few by Zaknafein, who was without peer among the drow in rather unorthodox fighting styles.

Both feet landed, and the DeVir warrior flew from the ledge, tumbling the twenty feet to the floor of the house courtyard.

Dinin went down right behind, dropping fast and enacting his levitation only at the very end to ease his landing. The other drow, rolling to absorb some of the damage, came up shakily and gingerly on a wounded leg. Without his balance, Dinin overwhelmed him, hitting him with a series of sudden and brutal stabs and slashes.

The DeVir warrior fought well. He blocked almost half of Dinin's strikes.

As he fell over dead, several sudden flashes to the left turned Dinin about in time to see the main gate of House DeVir swinging inward, smoking and sparking from a series of Do'Urden lightning bolts, and then bursting into its own explosions—fireballs, lightning bolts, and even an ice storm—as the DeVir glyphs and wards went off.

The magical barrage amused Dinin, because none of it made a sound. The Do'Urden priestesses had performed well.

Other Do'Urden soldiers came down beside the noble secondboy. Goblins and bugbears rushed in through the breached gate and kept charging across the compound. So fast and so silently had the initial assault come that the main DeVir forces hadn't even yet risen to oppose the attack.

That was critical, Dinin knew, as his confidence in their success began to soar, for House DeVir could put many more fighters on the field than House Do'Urden could muster, and this was DeVir's home turf, with their noble priestesses and matron on the grounds.

Dinin flashed for his forces to keep pressing, fast and hard. *Do not let them breathe! Do not let them form any defense!* his fingers signed to those around him, who quickly echoed the message along the line.

Still, Dinin knew it would not be enough. Not nearly. *Come on,* he mouthed futilely at the silence. Again, heartbeats seemed like hours.

Finally, wonderfully, he felt the reverberations of some powerful magic—so powerful that it made the hair on his arms and neck stand up and left his skin tingling in its passing wake. He glanced down the line to his fellow warriors, who looked confused, then to the one priestess who had come over the wall with the battle group, who was shaking so hard, her mouth hanging open, tears flowing from her eyes, that Dinin thought she might simply fall over. Tears of divine joy, Dinin understood.

This was the birth magic his sisters had been whispering about, he realized, though he really didn't even know what that might mean. Somehow, it seemed, vicious Malice had utilized and transformed the pain and emotions of childbirth into the weight of the ritualistic spell conjured about that unholy table of Lolth.

The warrior looked to the compound before him, almost expecting it to crumble to dust.

Yet nothing seemed to happen, at least not to him.

He had to trust, so he called upon his warriors. They charged the main houses, bugbears and goblins for the main doors, able dark elves levitating to balconies and dropping ropes for their companions.

The doors burst open, and DeVir defenders, mostly goblinkin, charged out to meet the invaders, and in an eyeblink, the front of the Do'Urden line became a tumble of swords and axes, falling bodies and falling limbs.

Dinin grinned as he watched the battle, for the defenders seemed sluggish indeed, their every effort being more than matched by the attackers.

Nalfein's group arrived at the shattered gate, and magic rained in to strengthen the attack, fire and lightning blasting over the joined combatants and stretching back to the house, melting DeVir fodder and more than a few of the Do'Urden slave warriors, as well.

Soon after, Dinin grinned again when he saw lights shining from the narrow windows of the higher chambers.

Zaknafein had penetrated those rooms, he knew, using light bombs to confuse his enemies.

"Ah, the beauty," Dinin whispered, and now he heard his voice, for he was out of the silence.

He waved his drow warriors on, and together they charged into House DeVir.

SOMETIME LATER, HIS BLADE DRIPPING WITH DEVIR BLOOD, half his brigade wounded or dead, Dinin came upon his brother in a lower hall of one of the lesser stalagmite pillars of House DeVir.

"It nears its end," he told Nalfein. "Rizzen is winning through to the top and it is believed that Zaknafein's dark work has been completed."

Appearing so animated that he seemed silly to Dinin, Nalfein nodded and replied, "Two score of House DeVir's soldiers have already turned allegiance to us."

"They see the end. One house serves them as well as another, and in the eyes of commoners, no house is worth dying for. Our task will soon be finished." Dinin noted the movements about him and his brother. Few soldiers were in the area, all pressing to other levels and corridors. He focused on Nalfein, looking for any signs that his brother was about to begin a treacherous spell.

"Too quickly for anyone to take note," Nalfein said, and Dinin found irony in that. "Now Do'Urden, D'aermon N'a'chezbaernon, is the Ninth House of Menzoberranzan, and DeVir be damned!"

"Look out!" Dinin cried suddenly, peering over Nalfein's shoulder.

Nalfein spun at the expected threat, and Dinin struck, and struck true, his fine sword slipping through Nalfein's spine.

"Too quickly for anyone to take note," whispered Dinin, the new elderboy of House Do'Urden.

"NAME THE CHILD!" HIGH PRIESTESS BRIZA DEMANDED, her fingers rolling on the hilt of the ceremonial dagger, its tip hovering above the chest of the newborn, her half brother, who had been lain on the back of the spider idol.

"Drizzt," the exhausted Matron Malice answered. "The child's name is Drizzt!"

Briza began her sacred chant, formally naming the babe before giving it to Lolth, but neither Maya, the youngest of the Do'Urden daughters, nor Vierna heard her, both reaching out to connect with their brothers. Nalfein and Dinin must know the child's name before it was sacrificed, that the whole of the family could partake in the great gift to the Spider Queen.

Drizzt, Vierna heard Dinin respond to her magical message, and she felt a strong emotive surge from him, surprisingly so.

Maya heard nothing from Nalfein, and knew that her magical message had not reached him. Their preparations had been careful and exquisite, the bonding tight between them, but yet, nothing. There could be only one explanation for that.

"Wait!" yelled, drawing horrified looks from both Briza and Malice. "Nalfein is dead. The baby is no longer the third living son."

As a discussion commenced between Maya and Briza, who still seemed eager to kill the newborn, Vierna barely heard it, her focus locked on Maya, her thoughts still on Dinin's strange reaction. Perhaps Nalfein had been killed by a DeVir, but Vierna had her doubts.

"Stay your hand," Matron Malice commanded, ending the argument between Maya and Briza. "Lolth is content; our victory is won. Welcome, then, your brother, the newest member of House Do'Urden."

My full brother, Vierna thought, but certainly did not say. In truth, she wasn't even sure that Zaknafein was her father—she had heard many rumors, but had never received any confirmation. Still, she was grinning now, anxious to see her new brother Drizzt grow.

CHAPTER 5

Hopes, Fears, Vulnerabilities

He was, perhaps, the first—perhaps the only—person within Sorcere who knew that House DeVir had fallen, thanks to a Bregan D'aerthe associate he happened to run into when he was taking the Faceless One's chamber pot out for dumping.

"Happened to . . ."

Masoj passed that thought through his lips a few times, knowing that it was no coincidence. Jarlaxle wanted him to know of the development.

He was never surer of that than when he returned to his duties in his older brother's chambers and Alton DeVir arrived to answer a summons from the powerful master. Masoj knew that a matron had been in to see the Faceless One recently, and that another nobleman had been there earlier that same day.

So, though he was thrown back, Masoj was not really surprised when the Faceless One sent a mighty magical blast at Alton almost as soon as the older DeVir brother entered the chamber, a bolt that shattered the door and tossed poor Alton to the floor.

It didn't kill Alton, though, and the wounded DeVir wisely rolled and scrambled and sprinted out of the room, down the curving stair beyond.

"Clean it up!" the frustrated Faceless One yelled at Masoj, and Gelroos swept out of the room in pursuit of his target.

Masoj nodded and started sweeping, but as soon as Gelroos was out of sight, he moved for the door. He paused and rushed to the side, to an enchanted item he had long admired. Then out he went, in pursuit, following the taunts of the Faceless One.

"Do not run, DeVir. You only lengthen your torment!"

He heard some glass shatter and sighed, knowing he would have yet more to clean, and knowing, too, that glass and blood was a particularly nasty mess. That sound told him exactly where he'd find the two, however, because he knew this suite of rooms in Sorcere better than anyone alive, even Gelroos the Faceless One himself.

"My mirror!" Masoj heard Gelroos cry, confirming his guess. "First my door, and now this, my mirror! Do you know the pains I suffered to acquire such a rare device?"

Masoj had to fight hard to suppress a laugh.

"Why did you not just stand still and let the deed be finished cleanly?" Gelroos demanded, as Masoj came to the side of the room's entrance.

"Why? Why would you want to kill me?" Alton desperately pleaded.

"Because you broke my mirror!"

Masoj slapped a hand over his mouth to shield his snort. What a grand comeback, he thought. He peeked in as the drow continued to banter, then stepped back and slowly, so slowly, pulled back the drawstring and locked it.

When he peered back in, he understood that the conversation was about to end with absolute finality.

"Who?" Alton cried. "What house did this? Or what conspiracy of houses brought down DeVir?"

Masoj paused, wanting to know that answer as well.

"Ah, you should at least be told," Masoj's brother taunted the poor, doomed man. "I suppose it is your right to know before you join your kin in the realm of death."

A dramatic pause had both Alton and Masoj leaning forward with anticipation—or, at least, Alton was trying to, Masoj noted, except that the poor fool was caught in a magical web of sticky filaments.

Not that it mattered.

"But you broke my mirror!" Gelroos howled. "Die stupid, stupid boy! Find your own answers!"

The moment of truth, Masoj knew. He lifted the finely crafted, likely enchanted, two-handed heavy crossbow, leveled it, and, as Gelroos gyrated, gathering the energy of his next, killing, spell, he pulled the trigger.

Gelroos made some deep gurgling, croaking sound, his back arching, arms flying up and wide. Then he fell facedown on the floor, twitching and dying.

"Nice weapon, Faceless One," Masoj noted, rolling it over in his hand. It was obviously magical, and the large quarrel that had just cut through Gelroos's spine was very heavily poisoned—although Masoj was pretty sure that it would have killed the wizard even without that insurance.

As he set the next quarrel in the weapon, the trapped DeVir babbling and pleading, Masoj carefully considered his next move.

What would Jarlaxle do?

He listened to Alton's claims. The easiest thing would be to shoot the idiot, and thus make it appear as if the student and the master had killed each other in a heated exchange of spells and crossbow bolts.

But was the easiest thing always the most beneficial?

What would Jarlaxle do?

ZAKNAFEIN HAD BEEN TOLD THAT VIERNA WAS POSSIBLY his child only long after the girl had come into the world—indeed, soon after her fifth birthday. Even then, for more than a decade, Zaknafein had been led to believe that it was merely a fleeting possibility.

It wasn't until she had gone off to become a priestess of Lolth that Malice had told him the truth that he was almost certainly the father of Vierna.

The timing was deliberate. By that point, Zaknafein knew that the young woman was lost to him, particularly since she was going to embrace the Spider Queen. She was becoming that which Zaknafein hated most of all.

Still, he and Vierna had subsequently developed the closest relationship that Zaknafein knew with any of Malice's female children, indeed with anyone in all of House Do'Urden other than perhaps Dinin. It was a relative standard, however, and a very low bar of measurement. As he considered it, Zak figured that his feelings toward Vierna might stay his hand if he was about to kill her.

Or might not.

This time, though, felt different. This time, Zaknafein entered the quiet side chamber to find Vierna sitting by the cradle, knowing that the child in the cradle, without doubt, was his.

His son.

"Drizzt?" he asked, for that was the name he had been told upon returning from the slaughter at House DeVir.

Vierna nodded and moved back, inviting the weapon master to move up close. She knew, Zak realized.

"Look at his eyes," Vierna told him as he peered at the babe wrapped in soft furs.

So striking! Purple eyes! Such a rarity among the drow, and these were rarer still for the intensity of the coloring, almost as if they were backlit, shining out from the hollows of Drizzt's dark face.

Vierna kept talking, but Zak wasn't listening. He leaned over the cradle and stared, taking in the look and the smell of this baby, his son. A sea of emotions swirled about him, different and distinct, each rising like a wave threatening to break over him and drown him.

Did this, his progeny, afford him some measure of immortality? Was this child lying here before him, his son, his blood, destined to carry on his name and memory long after he had gone? Zaknafein had recently passed his four hundredth birthday, middle-aged for a drow, although all knew that the back half, once a reputation (particularly a grand reputation) had been formed, proved a much more difficult span than the first. How many weapon masters or noble-born fighters or even commoners in the Braeryn wanted to challenge Zaknafein to prove their own worth? Among that number were weapon masters of great skill and strength: Dantrag Baenre of the First House, Uthegentel Armgo of the Second House, along with too many others who would love to have their names spoken as the warrior who defeated Zaknafein.

Every day was a threat, of course. One lapse could spell the end for him, as could one bad decision by the often reckless Matron Malice.

But now Zak had a child, one he knew about from the beginning, one he could help mold, one who would carry on when he was gone. He couldn't deny his pride, his hopes, his soaring heart when looking upon this little one.

Then the flip side of that spinning, sparkling coin hit him, quite unexpectedly and quite forcibly.

Zaknafein took a deep breath to steady himself and had to brace himself on the side of the cradle for several heartbeats.

What would happen to him if this child, this beautiful little creature named Drizzt, was taken from him? What pain might he know if his child, like so many in the city, particularly those with ambitious matrons, found the wrong end of a spear?

Zak glanced back at Vierna, silently chastising himself for never considering such a thing regarding her. He didn't hate her the way he hated her sisters or her mother, but he had never been very close to her. He had never been given the chance.

Now she was a priestess of Lolth, and it disgusted hm. Lolth disgusted him. The way the goddess played her people against each other disgusted him. The sexism of drow society disgusted him. The brutality of the women who raised drow children disgusted him. All of that was almost without exception, even among the matrons who put men into positions of power, like House Barrison Del Armgo, known for its male warriors, and House Xorlarrin, whose powerful wizards were mostly male. Those matrons didn't value men more highly, he believed. No, they simply used what they had for their own craven ambitions.

It was all because of Lolth. And Vierna, perhaps his daughter, had given herself to Lolth. Now was she destined to train Drizzt, this son of Zaknafein, to be another subservient pawn in the grand scheme of the Lady of Chaos?

Zaknafein wondered if there were other drow enclaves somewhere in the wide Underdark, perhaps in the wider world above, where the corrupting influences of the Spider Queen were not ever-present? How he wished he could find such a place and spirit Drizzt off to there.

But not Vierna, he thought, and the notion unsettled him. No, she was likely too far gone, too corrupted.

Zak realized he was wearing all his myriad emotions on his face by Vierna's puzzled stare.

"What is it?" she asked, her eyes roaming his face, studying him carefully.

There were so many things Zak wanted to say to her right then.

Regrets.

Anger.

Apologies.

All of it wanted to come spouting forth, but he couldn't sort where any of it fit, especially in this moment, with his new son looking back at him—a child that had escaped death only by good fortune and the timing of a few heartbeats, from what he had been told.

"It is nothing," Zaknafein replied. "I only hope that this child will grow up to exceed Nalfein, for the glory of Matron Malice and House Do'Urden."

"We all hope that," Vierna said, and she added with a sly grin, reminding Zaknafein of the parentage involved, "And we all expect that, Matron Malice most of all. Much will be asked of this second-boy."

Zaknafein tried not to wince at that, for he understood all too well what such expectations might entail.

"BRILLIANT!" JARLAXLE SAID QUITE UNEXPECTEDLY, MAK-ing the mage sitting across from him glance up, a look of surprise on his face (as much as that melted face could appear surprised, Jarlaxle thought). The young man over by the door had a much stronger reaction, rolling back on his heels, eyes going wide.

Jarlaxle made a mental note to keep a close eye on that one.

"What do you mean?" the mage quietly asked. "I did only as I was told."

"You were told to take the place of Gelroos Hun'ett?" Jarlaxle asked with sarcastic surprise. He eyed the young man over by the doorway again and added, "Your brother, I believe."

"I . . . You speak with the voice of a fool!" the mage retorted. "A reckless fool."

"If you think I fear Alton DeVir, then you are mistaken." Jarlaxle shrugged and chortled. "I did not fear Gelroos Hun'ett, so why would I fear you?"

The Faceless One's eyes rolled in their near-skinless sockets to regard the young apprentice, who slyly stepped back out of the room— but then returned a moment later at the end of a quartet of longswords, two wielded by each of the Bregan D'aerthe associates who had quietly and secretly entered the Faceless One's suite in Sorcere.

The Faceless One sucked in his breath, which made a whistling noise through the many holes in his mouth and throat.

"Before you act, either of you, consider that no one may enter Sorcere without the knowledge and permission of Archmage Gromph," Jarlaxle warned.

"But be at ease," Jarlaxle added, leaning back comfortably in his seat. "He does not know, or if Gromph does know, he doesn't care. I am not accusing you, Alton DeVir, nor judging you in any negative way. Indeed, I above all others tend to salute such resiliency and cleverness, and yes, I do know what Gelroos had planned for you on the night of the fall of House DeVir. Like Archmage Gromph, I do not care for any of that. I care only of that which now is, not what was."

"Perhaps you would do well to understand that which *was* determines that which *is*," said the new Faceless One, formally Alton DeVir, who had obviously burned off his own face after disposing of Gelroos Hun'ett's body. He sat up straighter, trying desperately, Jarlaxle knew, to hold on to some level of danger and mystique. He was trying to command the situation, something Jarlaxle found quite amusing.

"And you think it all resourcefulness, or cleverness, or simply chance?" Jarlaxle asked. "You do not think that Matron Mother Baenre knows of, and allowed, the death of the old wretch? Poor young man, there are so many parts of the world of which you do not know—but I warn you to know this one thing above all, always: you do well to stay in the favor of Matron Mother Baenre."

"As do you?" Alton half growled, half wheezed back at him.

"Always. I am no fool," came the easy reply.

"Yet you come here and threaten me?"

"Of course not. I come here to *advise* you, and advise you wisely. And so I will again. Do not let your anger move you to rash action. House DeVir is dead. Alton lives." He glanced at the other and added, "And Masoj lives. The City of Spiders goes along."

With that, Jarlaxle tipped his wide-brimmed hat and rose, motioning to his minions and following them out of the room, but not without pausing to cast a smile and a nod of admiration in the direction of young Masoj Hun'ett, one designed to let the young man and the mage seated at the table know that he, Jarlaxle, knew much more about what had happened than he should.

So many drow had found similar surprises regarding Jarlaxle, over this secret or that.

Knowledge was power, particularly in Menzoberranzan.

Jarlaxle was undeniably powerful, and growing more so all the time.

CHAPTER 6

Simply by His Presence

Zaknafein's step was lighter than usual that day in the second month of Dalereckoning 1304 as he made his way through House Do'Urden. He hadn't been inside the main chambers in many days, as Malice had been keeping him busy with this task or that.

It had surprised him how much being away had made him miss Drizzt.

Oh, how Zak had rushed through those last tasks thrown at him, including traveling to the island of Donigarten to select a proper rothé for a house celebration meal, and going to Arach-Tinilith to deliver a long paper prepared by Maya Do'Urden explaining the names and preferences—food, drink, sexual, and execution—of the more common handmaidens Lolth had been sending to Menzoberranzan to answer the calls of high priestesses of late.

Zaknafein had been as surprised by this task as the priestess who had opened the door of Arach-Tinilith, a startlement that had fast dissolved into a profound scowl. Men were not very welcomed at

Arach-Tinilith, though a handful of matrons sometimes used men as couriers to the school just to show that they were important enough to thumb their noses at the unspoken rules.

Zaknafein had spent a long two hours inside Arach-Tinilith, snake-headed scourges writhing all about him, angry glares from every priestess who saw him. His reputation preceded him—all in this school knew that the weapon master of House Do'Urden seemed to take special enjoyment in killing priestesses, high priestesses, even matrons.

Yes, Malice had sent him there to dare someone, anyone, to strike at him. He was her bait, her proof that she was too important to anger. He didn't much like being used as such, of course, but as soon as he was dismissed by Sos'Umptu Baenre, one of the more powerful mistresses of Arach-Tinilith, he had sprinted from the place and left behind any ill feelings before his foot touched the cobblestones outside the spider-shaped structure's front door.

Then he had collected the House Do'Urden commoner, sitting outside on the steps of Tier Breche, and together they had run with all speed to the cavern's main exit, where Zak presented his exit pass to the guards. Out into the Underdark they went, silent as death, swift as a descending sword, going to fetch Dinin with all speed, leaving the commoner as Dinin's replacement. Zaknafein had been briefed on the route of Dinin's patrol group, and knew these nearby caverns quite well. Still, it took them three full days to find the patrol, and it would take two more to get back to Menzoberranzan's gate.

Zaknafein pushed Dinin to make it back in a day and a half, answering every complaint from the elderboy with a scowl that brooked no debate.

When Dinin at last came to sort out the reason for the rush, he actually laughed at Zaknafein.

"Drow men don't celebrate birthdays," he reminded.

"He is a boy, not a man."

"He is not a *girl*. He does not matter."

That remark had Zaknafein spinning about to face the elderboy, anger flashing in his red eyes.

"Would you care to say that again?" Zak asked in a low, even voice.

"Do you deny it?"

"He matters to me."

Dinin paused and wisely nodded, and when Zaknafein turned around, muttered, "Would that any of the rest of us had."

That retort had stopped Zaknafein in his tracks. For a moment, he felt regret, guilt. But only for a moment, only until he considered the source, a clear reminder that this one was not being genuine, that this one was never genuine. In this instance, Dinin was trying to gain some minor advantage. The ploy showed Zak just how threatened Dinin must feel by his young brother, a lad who had not even yet passed his seventh birthday.

"I have trained you to the best of my abilities," he replied, not bothering to look back. "If you are still inadequate, that is because of your own limitations, not mine."

"Or perhaps because of the breeding?" Dinin offered, and now Zak did stop and spin about once more. "That is the incitement of this rush, is it not? Tomorrow is Drizzt's seventh birthday."

"Why do you even remember it, if it is not important?"

"Because the other celebration is important, and will be mentioned by Matron Malice, for that is also the seventh anniversary of my ascension to elderboy of House Do'Urden."

Zaknafein had to nod—that anniversary, not Drizzt's birthday, was why he had been sent out to personally select a rothè cow for the family meal. Not Dinin's ascension, of course, but because this was the anniversary of House Do'Urden's move to become the Ninth House of Menzoberranzan.

"A most fortunate coincidence, you will agree?" Dinin asked.

Zaknafein shrugged as if it did not matter, but his nonchalance wasn't buying him anything, he understood from Dinin's grin.

"I hurry because we must be there, and be presentable, in time for the celebration," he said finally.

"The least of the three events, no doubt."

The unending sarcasm of this one! Yet, Zaknafein couldn't argue with any of Dinin's reasoning, and he found that he didn't want to. So he merely laughed and shrugged again.

"You are observant," he said. "Your mind is keen, your thoughts ever-forward. Matron Malice is fortunate to have you as her elderboy. She knows it, too."

Dinin seemed caught off guard by that—of course he was! When had Zaknafein ever complimented him?

"You think I care nothing for you, but that is not true," Zaknafein told him, and with some sincerity. "You are in my charge—I am trusted to prepare you, to ever prepare you . . ."

"Along with every other warrior of House Do'Urden."

"Not nearly to the same level."

"True enough. But it is out of fear of Matron Malice, not love of elderboy Dinin."

"Perhaps a bit," Zaknafein admitted. "But I am not your enemy. I have never been your enemy, and unless you give me reason, I will never be your enemy. I am the one who dismisses the whispers, elderboy."

Zaknafein played those last two lines over in his head now as he trotted through House Do'Urden. He had accomplished much in those tunnels beside Dinin. He had gained a measure of the elderboy's trust, perhaps, but more than that, those last two lines had left Dinin no room to wriggle.

Because "the whispers" was a reference that had struck Dinin profoundly. Zaknafein knew the truth of Nalfein's demise, and Dinin needed Zaknafein to keep dismissing the rumors of that truth.

Yes, Zaknafein didn't have to worry that Dinin might look for advantage at Drizzt's expense.

So he had properly relayed his message to Dinin, and now he was back in House Do'Urden, nearing the chapel, nearing his son.

Happy for the first time in days.

Then he heard the whimper, then the growl, a young boy's groan between tightly clenched teeth.

Zaknafein peeked in, and he sucked in his breath when he saw Drizzt. The boy sat on the side of the room, on the floor, stripped to the waist and with his left hand reaching back over his right shoulder, fingers gingerly touching a new wound there, the two punctures of a viper's strike, dots of blood visible.

That wasn't all. This new wound was surrounded by scars all too familiar to Zaknafein and all males in Menzoberranzan. Scars made by the fangs of the vipers when the priestess struck with her scourge, then dragged it along the victim's back. This latest strike showed no trails of the dragging fangs, but the one beside it surely did.

"It is not so bad," he heard Vierna say, as he moved to the door of the chapel. "Only Silaas bit you and her bite is more pain than damage."

Then her tone changed abruptly. "Quit looking at me!" Vierna demanded, and lifted her scourge threateningly. "Do you want more?"

"Why?" came the boy's answer, one full of innocence and pain and confusion.

Zaknafein noted the movement as Vierna rocked back on her heels.

"You must learn, idiot child," she said. "You must learn your place and hone your abilities. You can do well, for a mere boy, a mere man, in this city. But if you do not learn your place—if you do not hold it strong in your heart, then know that you will suffer a most cruel fate."

"Like being whipped by those wicked vipers?" Drizzt asked, and Zaknafein's eyes widened, his heart caught somewhere between swelling pride and a terrible fear that Drizzt would meet a swift end if he could not learn to curb his own venom!

Vierna snorted. "Hardly. You cannot imagine the pleasure the matron will take in tormenting you, or the end result of her torture. If you are lucky, you will die."

"Do all women take pleasure in such pain?"

The question came from a place of innocence, Zak understood, as did Vierna, apparently, for instead of lifting her whip, she fell farther back upon her heels.

"If I don't teach you, you will be horribly punished," she said at length. "Better me than another."

Zak believed it. He had heard mumblings about and from Vierna about her weanmother status overseeing the growth of Drizzt. She would likely have become a high priestess by now if her studies hadn't been interrupted by the unexpected survival of this child.

Zak snuck in for a better view.

His grimace deepened when those scars came more clearly into view—his boy's back had been truly dug.

But not by Vierna, Zaknafein realized, for the wound showed several parallel sets of scars. Vierna wasn't yet a high priestess—that she carried a snake-headed scourge at all was unusual. Hers had only two writhing snakes.

The one that had made the marks on Drizzt had many more. Zaknafein nodded, recognizing the mark of a certain Do'Urden.

His hand went to his sword pommel, murder in his red eyes. He took a deep breath.

"He earned it, I trust," Zak said lightly, standing straight and walking past the pews openly, as if he hadn't been trying to sneak in or conceal himself at all.

Vierna, clearly uneasy, jumped at the sound of his voice. She spun on Zaknafein, her expression roiling through a series of emotions, ending with a look of superiority, the priestess scowl that Zak knew so well. A look that seemed to say, of course Drizzt had earned it, if for no other reason than his gender.

She couldn't hold it, though, and Zaknafein silently hoped that was because of her lack of conviction. As far as he could tell, in the seven years Vierna had been tutoring Drizzt as his weanmother, she had been far less cruel than most others he had known in such a role.

"His mind wanders," Vierna said to Zak, and scolded Drizzt at the same time, turning her disapproving scowl upon him. She looked up to a statue set in the wall above the boy. "He can reach it. I've seen him float up there to polish the whole of it in one levitation. But his thoughts are elsewhere, always elsewhere."

"I polished it yesterday," Drizzt complained, and Vierna's eyes and nostrils flared.

"And you will polish it again, and now," Zaknafein said, before she could scold him. "It is important. This is your place. The reward is tomorrow, young Do'Urden."

"But the punishment is immediate," Vierna warned, one of the snakes on her scourge hissing, the other slithering up and around her arm.

Sighing, Drizzt gathered up his shirt, beginning his levitation before he had even pulled it over his head, enacting the dweomer so fully with his own innate magical abilities that he didn't even need to wait to touch the house emblem pinned to the garment.

As he floated up, Zak turned to Vierna with a smile.

"*Par tu'o ammea ulu vos jalv del lil orthae'scour lueth jalm del lil belbolcahal,*" Zaknafein said in a singsong manner, an old drow saying usually reserved for girls: "This one seems to need less of the holy lash and more of the cake."

Vierna's nostrils flared again.

He had gone too far, perhaps, Zaknafein understood, and he quickly dismissed himself and moved away, not wanting to make things any worse for Drizzt, certainly.

He went to his own chambers to change from his trail-weathered clothes, then to Matron Malice's palatial suite to announce his return. He was surprised when the female guards led him into the private chambers to find most of the house nobles there beside Malice: Briza, Maya, Patron Rizzen, Dinin.

Zaknafein gauged the mood quickly, and it was not one expected on the eve of a grand celebration.

Almost as soon as he was announced by the guards—who then departed—Priestess Vierna entered the room.

The timing, Zak suspected, was not coincidental.

"I have done all the tasks you assigned me, Matron," Zaknafein said with a bow.

"Not secretly enough," the woman replied, drawing a curious look from Zak, for Malice hadn't mentioned any secrecy to him when she had sent him forth. Indeed, how might one be secret when procuring special rothé from the tenders on the island? How might one be secret when going out among a drow patrol and replacing a noble warrior with a house commoner?

How might one be secret to the other houses of Menzoberranzan when delivering an essay to Arach-Tinilith? Every major house in the city, every middling house in the city, kept eyes on that structure above all others!

"There is too much whispering," Matron Malice announced, standing dramatically and waving her arm out to encompass all the nobles in the room. "There will be no celebration tomorrow. No *bel-bolcahal*."

That brought a series of groans and murmurs from the others, one that seemed a bit too practiced to Zaknafein. Beside him, Vierna shifted uncomfortably, and she wilted beneath his gaze when he more carefully regarded her.

"We cannot have the Ruling Council see us celebrating on the anniversary of House DeVir's demise," Matron Malice went on. "There is too much whispering about complicity at this time, perhaps signaling too much whispering among members of this very house."

Zak noted that her gaze kept lingering on him as she spoke, and it was all he could do to suppress a laugh at the ridiculousness of it all. Everyone in Menzoberranzan knew what had happened to House DeVir.

Everyone.

But then Zak realized that she wasn't talking about whispers regarding House DeVir's fall. No, she was playing one of her games—one aimed at him. She turned to her eldest daughter, the ever-vicious Briza, and nodded.

"He is still in the chapel?" Briza asked, moving swiftly for the door, hand falling to the handle of her six-headed scourge.

Vierna muttered an affirmation.

"What did you do?" Zaknafein quietly demanded of Vierna.

"What did *you* do?" Matron Malice corrected him, sharply. "What did you dare to do?"

"I . . . did nothing," a flummoxed Zak replied.

"The boy will be given to you for training when it is time," Malice said to him. "Until then, he is not your matter, not your student, none of your business. The breaking of a child is the domain of the weanmother alone, except for others I sometimes call into play."

As she finished, the room's door shut hard, Briza departing.

Zaknafein lowered his head, both to appear humble and to hide his building rage.

This wasn't any training technique for Drizzt, he knew, even though his son was about to be whipped severely. No, this was Malice training *him*, reminding him, after all, that he was just a man, a very small man in a matriarchal world.

JARLAXLE WAS STOPPED IN HIS TRACKS WHEN HE WENT into the Oozing Myconid that same night. He had just returned from a private and secret meeting with Mistress Sos'Umptu, where the topic of House Do'Urden and an unexpected visit from Zaknafein (who was known to the Baenres as an old associate of Jarlaxle) had come up. Thus, he was still thinking of his old friend when he returned to his tavern, only to find none other than Zaknafein Do'Urden sitting there at his old corner table along the back wall.

Jarlaxle closed his uncovered eye and stared at the weapon master through the magic of his eyepatch, hardly believing that his friend, whom he had not seen in several years, was sitting at his old table, hunched over his drink, looking so much like the same Zaknafein Simfray who had first come into this place.

The mercenary leader moved to the bar and collected a drink of his own, then waved off unimportant questions from his minions and made his way directly to Zaknafein's table, dropping into a seat across from the weapon master as comfortably as he might slip on his old shoes.

"To old times," he said, lifting his glass in toast.

Zaknafein stared at him cautiously for just a moment, then nodded and lifted his glass, clinking it against Jarlaxle's.

"I am quite pleased—dare I say honored?—that you have returned to my most humble establishment," Jarlaxle said.

"You can say it, but I won't believe it," Zaknafein answered, bringing a wide grin to Jarlaxle's face.

"You see right through me, alas."

"Like a skinny gelatinous cube."

This time, Zak led the toast.

"Yet you remain as opaque as black pudding to me," Jarlaxle said as they clinked glasses again.

"No one who has ever known Jarlaxle would believe such a thing, but that is the charm of your lies. Everyone knows you're lying, but most spend too much time trying to find a purpose in the falsehoods. I know you better than that, Jarlaxle. I know that the charm is the point, nothing more—usually."

"And you can tell the difference and discern those times when there is more?"

"Of course."

"I have heard such things before."

"From who?"

"No one who lived long enough for you to know them, or who died honorably enough for me to tell you about them."

Zaknafein considered that for just a moment, then shrugged and took another drink.

"It is good to see you again," Jarlaxle said after a few moments—moments during which Zaknafein's eyes drifted to the side absently. Something was bothering him.

"I need your help," Zak said, turning his gaze intensely upon the mercenary leader.

Jarlaxle didn't reply.

"I know," Zak said. "I have avoided you for years, and here I am, coming to you when my own situation demands it of me. I understand—"

"You are my friend," Jarlaxle interrupted. "There are not many who I can proclaim possess that label. If you need my help and did not come to me, then I would be offended."

Zaknafein nodded. "Get me out of here."

"Out of?"

"The city. I need you to get me out of the city."

"In hiding? Do you plan to run away from Menzoberranzan?"

"No, no, nothing like that. I would just leave now, but not forever. For the first time, I have a more compelling reason than my own weakness to stay."

"The secondboy," Jarlaxle reasoned, and Zaknafein nodded.

"Then why leave?" the mercenary leader asked.

"For him, the secondboy, my son Drizzt," Zak explained. "Malice uses . . ."

"Matron Malice," Jarlaxle sternly corrected, and when Zak froze in a surprised stare, Jarlaxle couldn't hold the joke and gave a laugh. "Do tell, my friend. What is that vile witch doing now?"

"She uses Drizzt to punish me and control me—by punishing him most severely," Zak explained. "There is little I can do to help him in the next few years—I can barely get near to him, and when I do, Malice often shows me just how foolish I was to interfere with her designs."

"So you would leave the child to Malice for the sake of the child?"

"As foolish as that sounds, I cannot do anything but leave the child to Malice, and in those moments of weakness when I think otherwise, I am fast reminded, at Drizzt's expense."

"It is no small thing that you ask," Jarlaxle said after considering Zak's request for a short while. "Malice will not easily let you go, and woe to Drizzt, I fear, if you just run out."

"Nay, I cannot just run out. I want you to arrange it, and in a manner where Malice cannot refuse."

Jarlaxle sat back and rubbed his face. He had only one extra-Menzoberranzan mission on his docket, and that involved a very complicated and dangerous situation, one that could blow back badly on a house associated with anyone involved on Bregan D'aerthe's side.

Otherwise, this particular mission would fit Zaknafein's wishes perfectly . . .

"What do you know of House Hunzrin?" Jarlaxle asked.

"Hunzrin?" Zak asked with obvious surprise. "The stone heads? I was just on Donigarten, securing a rothé from a daughter of House Hunzrin. A minor house, yes? One no one would mention, except for their stewardship of the fields and cattle of Donigarten."

"Not so minor, and that perception will change," Jarlaxle assured him. "They control most of the city's farms."

"But they are weak."

"In the city, yes, but they have tendrils, ones that must be tended and occasionally clipped. Understand, they are in the favor of Lolth, and more than that, in the favor of the eight houses of the Ruling Council. All eight. Even Oblodra."

"This sounds like an assassination," Zaknafein said. "You ask me to kill someone in exchange for your actions to get me out of the city? Well, if it is a priestess of Lolth, I agree."

"Would that it were that easy!" Jarlaxle replied. "No, this will involve much more than that, both in danger and in cleverness. I hesitate."

"Because I am neither dangerous nor clever?" Zaknafein asked with a snort.

"Oh, you are both, perhaps more than almost any person I have ever known who was not born to great power. But there are implications here beyond you. Implications to House Do'Urden, unless we are very careful."

"We are always very careful."

"I fear that I may have to recount a story about the two of us running across the webbing balconies of Ched Nesad."

"There were three of us," Zaknafein reminded, and Jarlaxle winced at the reference to Arathis Hune, who had once been the mercenary leader's closest ally and principal advisor. "In that, too," Zak continued, "I was careful and clever, and very dangerous. Mortally so."

"Indeed. I'm still working on things—there is much for me to consider, and much groundwork to be laid," Jarlaxle explained. "When can you return to me?"

"It will be tendays, at least, I expect, before I can again sneak out from House Do'Urden."

"Good. I will need that time and perhaps more to properly sort through this possibility."

"And if it is not possible?"

"Then I will find another way to help you remove yourself from Menzoberranzan for an extended . . . respite," Jarlaxle promised.

Zaknafein nodded, then finished his drink with one great gulp and rose from his seat. With only a slight nod to his old friend, the weapon master left the tavern for House Do'Urden.

"You heard?" Jarlaxle asked priestess Dab'nay, who came up to the table as soon as Zaknafein was gone.

"Only the end. You think to involve Zaknafein in our dealings with House Hunzrin? He is closely associated with a prominent house," she warned. "You could well start a war."

"I always profit in war," Jarlaxle glibly replied.

"How great your profit if Zaknafein is killed?" Dab'nay asked. "How great your guilt if he is not but his child is?"

"Not so great," Jarlaxle admitted. "And that is why we must be clever. Can you tell me that you would be distressed to have Zaknafein by your side again when you venture into the wilds of the Underdark?"

Dab'nay's answer came as a smile, one she let linger for several heartbeats before asking, "You think Matron Malice will let him go?"

"That is the easy part," Jarlaxle replied. "What may happen when he is gone is far more challenging."

Hearing his own words as he spoke them sent the mercenary leaning back in contemplation. Did he really want to go this far this early in the solidification of Bregan D'aerthe as a powerful force in Menzoberranzan? By including Zak, he was indeed risking inciting a house war, and one that could be traced back to him. Worse, Jarlaxle knew well that if things went badly out in the tunnels of the Underdark, it was very likely his entire expeditionary team would be obliterated by the Hunzrins.

That would include Zak, no matter his skill.

Was it a chance Jarlaxle was willing to take?

THE PASSING OF THE DAYS WAS INTERMINABLE FOR ZAK-nafein as he went about his duties in House Do'Urden. As far as he knew, Matron Malice hadn't learned of his secret venture out to the Stenchstreets to visit Jarlaxle—or at least, she hadn't punished Drizzt for it and had said nothing to Zak.

Now the weapon master spent his time almost exclusively on the first level, the commoner level, of House Do'Urden, working tirelessly with the house guards in coordinating their watches and perfecting their fighting formations. He only floated up to the second floor on occasional nights, and only then when Malice summoned him to her bed.

He didn't want to do anything to incur the matron's wrath at that time, now that she had a way to truly wound him.

The vulnerability. Yes, that. Zaknafein could never have imagined such a feeling of helplessness and profound emotional pain. He thought of the many hours he had spent with the babe in those first days after the fall of House DeVir, of the bond he'd formed with Drizzt.

Now he suspected that those visits, too, had been granted by Malice for exactly this end. Even though her own heart was blackened by the shadow of Lady Lolth, she understood the vulnerability of parenthood. She considered it a weakness, no doubt, and she had likely suspected all along that Zaknafein was possessed of such weakness.

And she was correct. Zak understood that so clearly now.

For the first time in his life, he was terrified of her. For the first time, he knew that she could truly break him. Always, she could murder him, torture him, even turn him into a drider. Stubborn Zaknafein could accept those risks.

But now . . . now, Malice could do all that to Zak's child.

She could break him.

He was working with a score of warriors out at the lizard stable in the far back end of the first level when the courier rushed in, anxious and out of breath from hustling.

"Zaknafein, Weapon Master!" she gasped when he saw Zak.

Every step she took in her run to Zak thumped in his heart as if someone were beating it with a drumstick.

The young woman skidded to an abrupt stop, nearly crashing into him despite her exceptional drow agility, and thrust a parchment out at him.

"To the throne room with you, at once, by order of Matron Malice!" she blurted.

"I am in the middle of—"

"At once!" the woman yelled at him. "I am to accept no excuse, by order of Matron Malice. There is no excuse! At once!"

Zak pulled the parchment from her hand, reading it as he departed, then throwing it aside when he saw that it was nothing more than a signed note from Malice telling him to appear at once, without a hint of the reason.

He feared he knew the reason. He feared for Drizzt.

He tried very hard to keep his stride solid and assured as he crossed the room toward the dais, where Malice sat, flanked by her three daughters. He took some comfort in the fact that not one of them, not even Briza, seemed happy at that moment, as they surely would have been—particularly Briza—if there was a brutal punishment soon to come.

He focused on Vierna for the last few strides, but her expression was impassive, almost bored.

"You have been rarely seen of late," Malice said to him, as he moved before the stairs to the throne and bowed appropriately.

"I have not left the house."

"You have spent little time among the nobles."

"We have not been to war in seven years," Zak explained. "I fear that those less . . . devout among us have lost their way in any fighting beyond singular combat. These are lessons that must be renewed, and so I—"

"Yes, yes, yes," Malice dismissed the notion. "I am sure that we will be well served by your efforts. But you are the weapon master, and your duties are far beyond moving the pawns into formation."

"I am available to the elderboy or to any of the nobles if they wish private training."

"Enough with your talk of training, you insipid fool," Matron Malice scolded. "You are one of the prime faces of House Do'Urden. Your most important role is to please me, at my whim. Beyond that, you are to present to Menzoberranzan at large, and not just to those within, the strength of our house."

"You would have me go out into the city?"

"Not to the Stenchstreets, if that is what you are hinting," the matron was quick to reply. "No, but there are other opportunities that arise from time to time that I expect you to embrace, and so to shine brilliantly upon the Ninth House of Menzoberranzan."

"At your service, always, great Matron Malice," he said with another bow.

"Such an opportunity has been offered to us this day," Malice explained. "Matron Baenre has sent a note to me of an expedition departing the city very soon, aiming at sacking a fledgling city of filthy svirfneblin. We have gnomes to conquer, and I expect your personal victories to exceed any of the others."

"Of course, Matron Malice," Zak replied, keeping his head bowed, for he was trying to work through this news. Was this Jarlaxle's expedition under cover? Or was there really a deep gnome band nearby that needed to be conquered?

"Arrive at the north gate when Narbondel's light has climbed the height of a single woman. Report to . . ." She paused and read the name on a parchment she held. "Report to city scout Beniago Kurth of the First House, who will lead the group."

Zaknafein quietly breathed a huge sigh of relief. Beniago Kurth was indeed a nobleman of that most powerful house, but he was also one of the most important diplomats and scouts in Jarlaxle's Bregan D'aerthe.

Zaknafein had found his escape.

PART 2

Entrenchment and Enlightenment

I am caught off-balance, and in a way more painful than any disadvantage I've ever known, even in combat. Unlike in combat, I fear that the recovery will prove much more difficult and will take me many tendays, or months, or years, or lifetimes.

If I can ever find my way through to a place of acceptance with my son and those he considers his dearest friends—indeed, those he values more than he values me. That last thought is not a complaint, certainly, for these are the friends he has surrounded himself with for the majority of his life, the companions who have journeyed beside him on many adventures and stood beside him in many fights—legendary battles, from what Jarlaxle has told me.

So there is no jealousy here, nor bitterness about his relationship with these others.

Besides, my current predicament is my own fault. I know this, but admitting it even to myself is painful.

I hear the words coming out of my mouth, the reflexive jokes and jabs, and it is not until I see the expressions coming back at me, and then, sometimes, the angry words, that I realize that I have offended.

I am nearly two hundred years removed from the world of the living. Perhaps it is the different time, but more than that, I am in a place the likes of which I never knew in my former life.

My former life was that of a dark elf, a Lolthian drow. I never lived beyond Menzoberranzan and spent the entirety of my half millennium there, with only the exceptions of missions, all but two exclusively in the Underdark, and almost all either patrolling the perimeter corridors around the cavern that holds my city home, or to other drow cities in the thrall of the Spider Queen, usually Ched Nesad.

I saw a few humans, a few dozen dwarves, and only a handful of elves in that past life, and I did not mistreat them, and encouraged others, as much as I could without forfeiting my life, to similarly show mercy.

I thought that was correct of me, was something to hang a mantle of pride upon. How big of Zaknafein not to torture or murder a dwarf simply for being a dwarf!

I did not recognize my own prejudice, attributing my quieter, honest feelings to the simple matter of "that is the way of things."

It did not even occur to me that in applauding my own kindness, there was, too, an unspoken condescension. Unspoken, but I cannot honestly say unintended. For while I recognized the value of the human or dwarf or elf or halfling or gnome as a person and not as a goblinoid monster—and while I tried, in my brief interactions, to judge that non-drow person by her beliefs and what was in her heart, by her words or behavior—the judgment I expressed was conscious alone.

It wasn't in my heart.

Whether it was simply my upbringing, the community about me, the "way of things" hidden from my determination to prove otherwise, the truth was, I thought that I, as drow, was superior. I couldn't admit it to myself— perhaps I didn't consciously know this truth—but I imposed upon those other races limitations of expectation of their abilities, physical and mental.

I see it now, see it clearly, particularly when confronted with the reality that my son has married a human and that she carries within her womb a child both drow and human!

I recognize within me my own feelings of prejudice, but that does not mean they will be easily expunged.

No. I see that truth every time a prod, a jab, a mock slips past my tongue, one diminishing to the many non-drow around me, or one somehow designed to remind those few drow around me of the "way of things."

Now I know. The "way of things" is the most stubborn and debilitating demon of all.

Zaknafein Do'Urden

CHAPTER 7

THE YEAR OF DWARVENKIND REBORN
DALERECKONING 1488

The Eight Hundred

W e have a gift for you," Yiccardaria the yochlol told Matron Zhindia Melarn, who had camped with her forces in the destroyed halfling village that had been known as Bleeding Vines.

"You seem to need it," giggled Eskavidne, another of the handmaidens of the Spider Queen. The two could not have been more obvious. They had come not in their natural form, which resembled a slumping, half-melted candle of dripping mud, but walking as beautiful drow women—fully and unashamedly naked. To them, so they had explained to Zhindia when she had once complained of their distracting presence, wearing the mantle of a drow was no more than putting on the costume of an animal, so why would they bother with pretty clothes when the form itself was so much more aesthetically pleasing?

"I need it?" the matron asked, skepticism displayed openly on her face. "The dwarves are in their hole with no way out. The halflings are . . ." She paused and swept her hand across, to invite them to look upon the gutted buildings. "Luskan has fallen to Brevindon Margaster, by all accounts, and Port Llast is gutted. I have all but won the north, and so swiftly."

"All but," said Yiccardaria.

"Should we tell Lady Lolth that you refuse her great and generous gift?" Eskavidne added.

"No, of course not," Zhindia blurted.

"Where are your demon hordes?" Yiccardaria asked.

"Down below, fighting in the upper levels of the complex the dwarves call Gauntlgrym, but one that I will soon rename in tribute to the glorious Queen of Spiders."

"The *upper* tunnels," said Eskavidne.

"The dwarves are a stubborn foe," Yiccardaria added. "I have been told by more than one demon lord that a hundred demons are being destroyed for every dwarf falling. Perhaps more than a hundred."

Zhindia Melarn shrugged. "The demons can be replenished. They open their gates to the Abyss and more stream through, even many of the same reconstituted lesser fiends that were destroyed the day before."

"But you have fewer major demons now who can perform such portal magic than you had in the beginning of your adventure," Yiccardaria reminded her.

"Of course. And so I have ordered the major fiends back from the fighting," Zhindia replied. "It is not an easy command to enforce, I admit. They do so love killing."

"Tell us, child, what will you do when the first armies of the humans show up to do battle with you here?" said Yiccardaria. "When the lords of Waterdeep arrive with their thousands and your demon armies remain underground in mortal battle with the dwarves?"

Matron Zhindia's face tightened.

"And when you recall the demons to fight up here, do you think the dwarves will remain in their hole?" Yiccardaria went on. "They are not cowardly."

"Luskan will—"

"Luskan will do nothing to aid you here," Yiccardaria insisted. "The city teeters and will do so for months, if not years. There remain other forces up there more formidable than those of Brevindon."

"The Hosttower," Zhindia muttered.

"Others," said the handmaiden.

"If you speak of Jarlaxle's mercenaries, then go to Menzoberranzan and demand that Matron Mother Baenre leash him and lash him!"

The yochlols both chuckled. "The world is wide up here, Matron Zhindia," said Eskavidne. "There are many forces with which you must contend. You are vulnerable up here, with the demon hordes engaged below."

"But I have the blessing of Lolth, the retrievers—" Zhindia started to argue.

"One of the constructs failed and was destroyed," Yiccardaria interrupted, and the blood drained from Zhindia's face. Yiccardaria stared at her hard, letting her know that she was taking the loss of the retriever personally.

"How can that be?" Zhindia asked, a rare stutter in her voice.

"The other returned to the Abyss, victorious," Eskavidne added, "and so Drizzt Do'Urden is destroyed. And for that, you are rewarded. Your reward is Lady Lolth's gift, unless you are so certain that it is not needed that you refuse it now."

Matron Zhindia verily beamed at the news, elated that she would forever be known as the matron who defeated Lolth's mortal enemy. She heard their words, however, for she quickly replied, "I accept any gift from the Spider Queen, with gratitude and reverence."

The yochlols looked to each other, then stepped back from Zhindia. Each held her hands far out before her, left hand up high, right hand lower. They touched fingers and began to chant, then slowly moved back and apart, sweeping their hands as they let go of each other, trailing lines of black smoke.

They shaped that smoke into a tall and wide doorway, then moved aside, chanting still, as the smoke curled inward, filling the area inside the formed rectangle.

Their chants grew louder, now compelling obedience from within. Through the gate came a huge spider leg, then a second, and a large drider stepped forth, quickly moving to the side.

Then another, and a third after that, and on and on, a hundred driders, another hundred and more, spilling forth, moving around into predetermined formations, filling the whole of the ruined halfling town and more, and the gate pushed out the Melarni drow and the drider escorts they had brought from Menzoberranzan.

"What is this?" Matron Zhindia breathed, barely able to get sound past her quivering lips.

"Lolth does not dismiss the driders from her service when they are killed," said Yiccardaria. "Behold an army of long-dead driders, the heretical drow of millennia lost. Now they are yours, a greater army still."

Zhindia fumbled for words that would not come. Hundreds of driders at her beck and call? She had hoped to come forth and fulfill her destiny to destroy the heretics—a goal that seemed at least half-completed at this point—but now, with this new power given to her, what else might she accomplish?

"The demon army is not permanent," Yiccardaria said, as if reading her mind. "No demonic army ever is on the Material Plane. When they are gone, the north will be captured, but not by you, not for long. No, your allies here will hold Luskan and Port Llast and all the lands of the northern Sword Coast. But your place is not here."

"Gauntlgrym," said Zhindia.

"Think bigger," Eskavidne replied. "Matron Zeerith, now of House Do'Urden, will be happy to strike out and retake the great complex and the magical forge for the children of Lolth, as Gromph Baenre will be reined in by the dominance of your allies in Luskan to choose a side—and he will undoubtedly choose you."

"Menzoberranzan," Matron Zhindia breathed. "I am the destroyer of the prime heretic, and my armies will return Zaknafein to his grave forthwith. Even House Baenre will bow before me when I return to Menzoberranzan with this army at my back."

The yochlols looked at each other and smiled, then stepped through their gate and were gone, the smoky portal diminishing behind them.

When the yochlols disappeared, Charri Hunzrin, the first priestess of the powerful drow house that had allied with House Melarn, moved up tentatively to stand beside Matron Zhindia.

"What was that conversation?" she asked in a halting tone. "From where and how have these driders come?"

"Drizzt Do'Urden is destroyed."

Charri sucked in her breath. "But still, is this?"

"This?" Zhindia replied with a chuckle. "This, my dear High Priestess Charri, is proof that your matron chose wisely in allying with House Melarn.

"This, High Priestess Charri, is victory."

The word hung in the air for a few moments, and Zhindia liked the sound, so she said it again.

"Victory."

"ME QUEEN, BY ME YELLOW BEARD, IT'S GOOD TO SEE YOU well," said Skiddiday Thunderclap Widebelt, a burly dwarf with a beard so badly captured by an ill attempt at braiding that it more resembled a clew of worms thrown across a floor than anything that should be sitting on a living creature's face.

"And to see you, as well, Skid . . . Thunderclap," Queen Mallabritches Battlehammer replied.

The dwarf, who had given himself that middle name and very much preferred others use it, beamed a gap-toothed smile at the lovely queen of Gauntlgrym. "I just thinked that, as ye been up in the fightin' front . . ."

"I been taking me share of hits, as've all up there," she answered. "Ne'er seen so many demon critters altogether. Ne'er not close."

"And they keep coming," Skiddiday murmured, nodding.

"And down here at the low gate?" Mallabritches asked.

"Quiet, me queen."

"Ye seen 'em? Any of 'em?"

"Not a stinkin' drow, me queen."

Mallabritches stepped through the large iron door, then moved to the parapet beside Skiddiday, staring out over the half wall and down the long corridor. "We know they be out there."

"Aye, me queen, I seen 'em in the crystal ball afore King Bruenor sent me down here."

"But nothing?"

The dwarf shook his head.

"What say ye that we go out lookin'?"

"Me queen?"

"Get yer boys together, twenty o' yer best, and let's go have a look."

Skiddiday's eyes widened at that, and he seemed as if he were trying—and failing—to stop his head from shaking.

"Come on, then," Mallabritches told him with a wink. "Yerself can stay if ye're not up for it."

"Never that, me queen!"

"Ye're hesitatin'."

"Me orders put me here, just here, with a door to shut to seal Gauntlgrym."

"Yer orders from King Bruenor, of course."

"Aye, me queen!"

"And who am I?"

"Err, me queen, I mean, ye're me queen. One o' me queens!"

"Aye, I be. So get yer best twenty. We're goin' out."

"Yes, me queen!" Skiddiday replied with great enthusiasm, and he bounded back through the open portal, rushing past the side rooms, shouting for his boys, telling them to stand to.

Mallabritches kept staring down the long hallway, one filled with magical light spells beyond her vision. She wasn't surprised that Skiddiday and the others hadn't seen anything at this gate.

But the drow were out there.

And they were plotting and planning.

HE SAW THE DROW FROM AFAR, NOT DARING TO GET CLOSE despite his incorporeal, gaseous form.

Hundreds of them milled about the Underdark corridors below Gauntlgrym, setting up their chapels and barracks in natural chambers, sending patrols out every which way. Among their ranks were many wizards and even more priestesses, he knew, for Thibbledorf Pwent was no stranger to the emblems and ways of the dark elves.

Those he avoided with care, as the wizards and priestesses could find him even in this form, and likely destroy him.

He returned to the lower entry corridor, floating high up along the corner where the worked stone wall joined the ceiling, just as a troop of dwarves unexpectedly came forth.

Pwent studied them curiously, not beginning to understand why they would leave the defensive position. There were just over a score of dwarves.

Hundreds of drow.

The vampire dwarf grew more concerned, indeed, when he recognized one in particular: Mallabritches. *Queen* Mallabritches.

It took all Pwent could muster to hold himself in that gaseous state, to resist the urge to become corporeal before these dwarves. It wasn't their reaction he feared, but his own.

For the temptation was stronger now, a nagging itch, a constant hunger, and one that grew nearly overwhelming with a simple glance at the beautiful Queen Mallabritches.

Perhaps I'm strong enough now to make her me love fore'er . . .

He felt his form growing more solid, the gas contracting.

She'll be me own queen . . . Bruenor's got another . . .

A silent growl shut out the voices in his head. Pwent forced the gaseous cloud to widen once more.

Ah, but she'd love me, and I'd be givin' her life forevermore!

The wispy cloud that was Thibbledorf Pwent flew off down the corridor, moving far ahead of the dwarven troop, far ahead of the temptation of Queen Mallabritches—and of all the others, for that matter, for Pwent now could look upon no reasoning, living humanoid without the desire to feed, and worse, without the desire to dominate, to enslave, or, now, even to elevate another, several others, perhaps, into the full un-death state of vampirism.

I could make me own clan . . . Clan Pwent . . . nah, Clan Gutbuster! And aye, but what a powerful clan we'd be! We'd save Gauntlgrym, aye! And chase these durned drow back to their hole.

Pwent slipped through a crack in the floor and materialized in a lower, empty corridor. He would have been gasping for breath, he knew, if he still drew breath. Simply overwhelmed, the vampire stalked back and forth along the hallway, trying to sort out rational thought from evil-inspired fantasy, trying to separate conscious desire from the demands of blood and murder that would not let him go.

He didn't know how long had passed when the first sounds of battle came to his ears with his enhanced hearing.

"Queen Mallabritches," he mumbled with alarm.

Before he was conscious of the transformation, the gaseous cloud of Pwent slipped through the ceiling cracks and flew along the upper corridor. Even in that form, he could smell the blood.

The sweet, sweet smell of blood.

He moved as if on the winds of a hurricane, though the air this deep was still. Through the walls, through cracks in the ceiling, through some more walls to cut the corners of long, bending corridors.

He found the dwarves engaged with a force of several drow and a host of goblins and bugbears. He spotted Queen Mallabritches at once, the powerful woman executing a vicious slash with a double-bladed axe, opening the chest of a charging bugbear.

Stopping that charge as surely as if the creature had run into a stone wall.

The bugbear flew, and the bugbear's blood flew, and the latter seemed to Pwent to be moving slowly, every droplet flying distinctly, clear to see—too clear to see.

And the smell flooded into him. A droplet even spattered far enough to pass through the gas cloud.

Pwent could taste it! Coppery. Sticky sweet.

A dwarf went down, tripped up by a goblin, stabbed by a second, with a female drow leaping in to finish the task.

Pwent's rage overruled his vampiric needs.

The cloud swooped and thickened, and Pwent landed on his feet right beside the dwarf, right before the drow, who pulled up in surprise.

Pwent punched his right fist across, hand spike slamming the goblin that had stabbed the fallen dwarf, driving right into the creature's chest. It fell back, sliding off the bloody spike, yelping and gasping its spurting blood.

As the drow retreated, the vampiric battlerager leaped up and back, his powerful legs propelling him high into the air, above the goblin, the one who had initially tripped the dwarf, as it lunged forward in an attempt to stab him in the back. Down crashed Pwent, burying the goblin beneath him, although unfortunately atop the fallen dwarf.

Pwent grabbed the goblin and yanked it aside, rolling to his back and pulling it right over him, then rolling farther to be back on top. There, the dwarf began to shake and shudder, his entire body twitching and rolling, his ridged, sharp armor cutting the goblin apart.

The blood!

But not goblin blood, no! Pwent hated the taste of goblin blood. But here was dwarf blood, right here on the floor before him.

No! his thoughts protested.

"No!" he screamed, and he saw the retreating drow, and he focused on her. His legs began to pump wildly, propelling him forward, slipping in the blood, tripping over the groaning dwarf. He caught his balance by stepping on the stabbed and writhing goblin heavily, planting his boot and leaping away.

The drow's swords came at him in a blur, too fast for him to block. So he didn't try.

He just put his head down and bore forward, blasting the huge spike set atop his helm into the torso of the drow, then pressed on more, driving the lighter and weaker elf backward—back, back, back, to slam into the wall. Pwent thrashed about, like a wolf killing a rabbit. He punched and kneed and kicked long after the drow had stopped moving, then yanked back, extracting his head spike, and watched the drow sink to a sitting position against the wall.

Still alive.

And the smell . . .

Oh, that sweet smell! Pwent dove on her and bit her in the neck.

The sounds of battle receded, replaced by the pumping of the drow woman's heart.

That's all he heard. That's all he cared about.

The blood.

He drank and drank.

"Pwent, by Moradin's beard!" he heard suddenly, sharply, and his eyes popped open. He felt as if a child had just walked in on him making love, but the moment passed equally quickly.

He spun and looked at the speaker, Queen Mallabritches, her face a mask of horror.

Horror.

Revulsion.

Shamed, the vampire scanned the room only briefly enough to discern that the dwarves had won, though several looked wounded. Goblins and bugbears littered the room, along with this one torn drow.

Thibbledorf Pwent never feared an enemy, never feared a fight. But now he ran, and heard Mallabritches calling to her charges as he left, instructing them to gather up the dark elf woman and get her back to Gauntlgrym: "Before the curse can take her."

The curse . . . you are a curse . . . an abomination . . .

The vampire fell against a wall, needing to brace himself with something tangible, else he'd simply collapse. He was surprised by the tears that came to his eyes, thinking that effect had been lost when he stopped drawing breath.

"Me king," he whispered, trying to remember all those old times beside Bruenor, the good times in Mithral Hall, the hunt together for this place, Gauntlgrym. Pwent's last actions had been in defense of King Bruenor, and always had he been ready and willing to give his life for that wonderful, wonderful dwarf.

But now . . . to hear the words of Queen Mallabritches, Bruenor's wife. The words which led to an inescapable conclusion.

He was an abomination, and for all his willpower, all his inner heart and strength, all his loyalty to Bruenor, he knew then beyond all doubt: the curse was stronger. He couldn't control it.

It was only a matter of time before he murdered a dwarf and brought it into un-death beside him.

The wild dwarf vampire gave a profound, feral growl, pushed himself off the wall, and started his run once more, away from the dwarves and toward the drow. When he saw their first ranks, he thought to crash through, to kill as many as he could and keep fighting until a priestess called upon the powers of her wretched demon queen and blasted him into oblivion.

But no, even there he failed. When the first alarms were raised, the vampire within Thibbledorf Pwent would not allow the suicide run. The curse within him overruled his determination, and he became, once more, a cloud of gas, rising up to the ceiling, finding a crack, and disappearing therein.

Sometime later, he became corporeal once more. He slumped down onto the floor, trying to sort it all out, and recited a litany that had become his primary prayer: "Take me home, Moradin. Ye got me caught here twixt me heart and me hunger, and I canno'. I canno'."

It didn't seem like divine guidance to him then, but even as he spoke the words, Thibbledorf Pwent found what seemed to be middle ground.

He decided to shadow the drow, to strike where and when he could do the most damage. Perhaps to somehow relay tactical information about their movements back to the guardians of Gauntlgrym.

Determined now, he became a bat, and with those heightened senses, the vampire was soon enough back near the vast drow force.

"HOW MANY DWARVES WERE KILLED?" MATRON MOTHER Quenthel Baenre asked the drow who had come with reports of the skirmish.

The two young drow women glanced to each other with obvious concern, Quenthel recognized. They were surrounded by the greatest matrons of the greatest houses of Menzoberranzan, the *valsharessi*, who were more queens of the city than mere leaders of individual houses. And the Matron Mother herself was addressing them directly!

"We thought we had one killed," the taller of the pair began.

"We wounded them all," the other, seeming suddenly nervous and alarmed, quickly interjected.

The first looked to her and caught on, clearly. "Yes, Matron Mother, and there were but a few drow there, and only *sargtlin*, along with goblins and bugbears. Even a pathetic battle dwarf can defeat those goblinkin."

"A pathetic battle dwarf?" echoed Quenthel. "Do you know who wielded the axe that cleaved the head of Matron Mother Yvonnel Baenre?"

Both young women shrank back, now completely off-balance.

"Only *sargtlin?*" asked Matron Zeerith Do'Urden. "Why only warriors? Where were the wizards and priestesses?"

"This was a small scouting party, and moving off to the side of the main corridors," Matron Mez'Barris Armgo answered before the couriers could.

"We must not underestimate these dwarves," said Matron Zeerith. "Particularly not now, when we must carefully pick our battles and even more carefully make sure that none of them lead to something unfortunate, and irreversible."

"Let the wizards scout with their magics," Matron Mother Quenthel decided. "Risk no drow, risk no dwarves. And do not let the vicious slaves out there at all. They do nothing to bolster our cause in this time, and everything to destroy it."

The two young women glanced at each other again.

"Go!" Quenthel demanded. "Go and spread my decree and tighten the ranks. There will be no skirmishes at all, unless I deem otherwise."

"You do not truly think that King Bruenor Battlehammer will parlay with us?" Mez'Barris asked after the Matron Mother dismissed the gathering, with only the *valsharessi* and Sos'Umptu Baenre, who was considered among that elite group by most in the city, remaining.

"They are bloodthirsty beasts, little more," offered Matron Byrtyn Fey of House Fey-Branche, a notable ally of House Baenre. Indeed, Byrtyn's daughter, Minolin Fey, was now a high priestess in House Baenre, and was the wife of Gromph and the mother of Yvonnel, Quenthel's expected successor to the title of Matron Mother. It was certainly notable to the other *valsharessi* that Byrtyn, of all of them, had spoken in some contradiction to Matron Mother Quenthel.

Quenthel noted it, too, a reminder that her decisions here could make or break her reign.

"If we must battle our way through the dwarven city, then let us be quick about it," the ever-vicious Mez'Barris Armgo said with a rather wicked chuckle.

"We have been down that deadly road before," Matron Zeerith countered.

"Some of us more than others," retorted Mez'Barris.

Zeerith Xorlarrin Do'Urden narrowed her eyes at the obvious slight. She and her powerful family, once the Third House of Menzoberranzan, had reclaimed the complex standing in their way now, naming it Q'Xorlarrin, as a satellite city to Menzoberranzan. But then King Bruenor had arrived with an army of Delzoun dwarves, and Zeerith's family had been chased away, suffering many losses and much humiliation. Her seat on the Ruling Council had been saved only by Matron Mother Quenthel's rather surprising decision to install the Xorlarrin survivors as replacements to House Do'Urden, with Zeerith becoming the new incarnation of Matron Do'Urden.

"Send forth scouts, many scouts," Matron Mother Quenthel ordered. "Wizard scouts weaving spells of divination. Find us other paths to circumvent. I'll not put my trust in dwarves, of course, nor will I throw an army against fortified dwarven defenses at singular gates that have been hardened against an invasion such as our own."

Quenthel waved away all other questions. She needed to be alone. Something was not right here, was terribly wrong. She knew that within the memories of Yvonnel the Eternal, the blessing she had been given, lay the answers.

But they eluded her. She couldn't put it all together, and the result, she knew without doubt, would be the end.

Of everything.

"THEY ARE A DIABOLICAL ENEMY, WELL SKILLED IN THE ways of cruel murder," Matron Zhindia Melarn told Kyrnill, the first priestess of House Melarn, who had herself once been a matron of a different drow house. Also, there in the vast entry cavern before the walls of Gauntlgrym was Charri Hunzrin.

"Look at their weapons!" Zhindia continued, pointing up with a stalagmite mound to a hollowed-out, fortified bombardment emplacement, the side-slinger catapult cleverly situated so that it could be retracted and loaded under cover of the stalagmite's thick stone, its throwing arm then sweeping out along trenches dug through the mound to deliver devastating missiles to its area of control. "Such vile little beasts!"

"A balor told me that four thousand demons were destroyed in taking this cavern," Charri said.

"They will be replaced," Zhindia assured her.

"Some, but many major fiends met their destruction here, and so were banished to the Abyss for a century."

"They, too, will be replaced, if that is even necessary," Zhindia answered, now with a bit of pique in her voice. "The cavern has fallen, has it not?"

"The dwarves have been chased back within their walls, yes."

"And your mother, Matron Shakti, still has not arrived," said Zhindia. "Do you not realize that her absence makes me believe that the alliance of House Hunzrin is not as complete as she insisted?"

Charri cast a nervous glance Kyrnill's way, but the former matron didn't respond, and tried to pretend, Charri noted, that she hadn't even noticed. "She is trying to bring House Faen Tlabbar into our conspiracy," Charri answered Zhindia.

Zhindia's snort cut her short before she could elaborate.

"Vadalma Tlabbar is a fool and a treacherous scalawag," Zhindia said.

The venom in Zhindia's voice surprised Charri, but the enmity did not. Zhindia had tried hard to bring Matron Vadalma to her cause before she had decided to make an attempt at conquering these surface lands, and then again later on, so Charri had heard, after receiving the retrievers from Lolth's handmaidens. Faen Tlabbar was no minor house in Menzoberranzan, ranked behind only Baenre and Barrison Del'Armgo now, with the disaster that had befallen House Xorlarrin here in Gauntlgrym.

Everyone believed that ranking to be a temporary thing, however, and there was only one way for House Faen Tlabbar to go: down. They could not begin to challenge either of the top two houses, and once Matron Zeerith had fully integrated her powerful family into the remains of House Do'Urden, it was expected that she would soon enough climb back into that third ranking, where she had sat for many years as Matron of House Xorlarrin.

Matron Zhindia took a deep breath. "Look around you," she said, sweeping her arm out left and right.

The other two priestesses followed that gesture, though they needn't have to understand the point of Zhindia's display. The cavern was full of driders, skittering all about the mounds, patrolling every inch to ensure the safety of this most important trio of women, particularly Zhindia, who commanded them.

Charri understood the point completely. House Faen Tlabbar was noted as among the most devout of Menzoberranzan, but Matron Vadalma had once again rebuffed the conspiracy, even though Zhindia had proclaimed that Lolth's blessing was upon this entire expedition. She had demons, after all. She had retrievers—retrievers!—which numbered among the most precious gifts Lolth could give to any of her servants.

And now, delivered again by the handmaidens of the Spider Queen, Zhindia had driders, so many monstrous, huge, and powerful driders.

"Perhaps Matron Shakti will convince her, Matron," Charri offered. "The evidence of Lolth's favor upon you cannot be missed or understated."

Zhindia just snorted and waved her hand dismissively.

She knew that she didn't need House Faen Tlabbar now, Charri understood. Her army was sufficient in finishing her conquest, and the main goal, the destruction of Drizzt Do'Urden, had already been accomplished by one of the retrievers. What penalties might Matron Zhindia exact upon Matron Vadalma when she returned victorious to Menzoberranzan?

"Vadalma will understand her foolishness and cowardice when faced with Lolth's obvious desires," Zhindia said, and Charri noted that Zhindia had excluded the matron's proper title for the second time. "When we return to the City of Spiders with all the land from Luskan to Gauntlgrym under my control, only then will Vadalma understand her errant choice. Perhaps I will grant her another chance to join with me. Perhaps the elation of conquest will put me in a merciful mood."

Charri understood the subtext of these boasts well enough: on the heels of her great and sweeping victory over the dwarves, over Bregan D'aerthe's hold on Luskan, and over the two heretics, Drizzt and Zaknafein, Zhindia meant to openly challenge Matron Mother Baenre for the prime seat at the table of the Ruling Council. Of course she would give Matron Vadalma a chance to again ally with her, and likely Matron Mez'Barris of the second house would be invited, as well.

Because it wasn't likely that Matron Mother Quenthel Baenre would simply step aside, and war with House Baenre was no small matter, even with the blessings of Lolth.

Not for the first time, First Priestess Charri Hunzrin thought this whole expedition and Zhindia's goals utterly absurd, but when she looked around at the hundreds of driders serving Matron Zhindia so obediently, she was reminded why her mother had decided to throw in with House Melarn.

"Malfoosh!" Matron Zhindia shouted, and an enormous drider skidded to a stop, her hard legs scraping the stone. The powerful abomination turned, noted the speaker, and charged with all speed to stand before Matron Zhindia. This one had taken control of all the driders with sheer power. Even Matron Zhindia's own driders were showing deference to this old being brought back from the dead. Zhindia didn't mind that—quite the opposite, for Malfoosh was obedient, eagerly so.

"What word from inside the wall?" Zhindia demanded.

"The demons are hard-pressed," Malfoosh replied, looking down from on high, but with her eyes averted in abject respect.

It seemed so silly to Charri, for this one, with her huge trident, could almost certainly have struck Zhindia dead then and there. But like a fully broken lizard beneath the rider's crop, there was only deference.

"The greater fiends work tirelessly to gate in more soldiers from their abyssal home," Malfoosh went on, "and send them straightaway into the dwarven tunnels to do battle."

"But they are being killed as fast as they are summoned," Kyrnill Melarn dared to say, drawing a sharp look from Zhindia.

"Yes," Malfoosh confirmed. "But the dwarves are not demons. They grow tired, and then they make mistakes. When a minor fiend is killed, it is fast replaced, but when a dwarf is killed, it is simply dead."

"Well stated," Zhindia congratulated the drider, her stern gaze never leaving Kyrnill.

"When Matron Zhindia allows me to take my legions inside the wall, the dwarven defenses will crumble and they will die more quickly," Malfoosh promised.

"You may yet get your wish, mighty Malfoosh," Zhindia said. "I grow impatient. This is the last fortress standing between me and my—our—glorious return to Menzoberranzan."

And then the driders will know battle, indeed, Charri Hunzrin thought, but wisely did not say.

CHAPTER 8

Purgatory or Hell?

You cannot think to go in there!" Regis exclaimed when Dahlia took the reins from him and veered the coach toward a side trail, from the main road known as the Trade Way, a side road that seemed to lead to the ruined keep of Thornhold down at the seashore, a fortress whose wall had just been scaled by a spider the size of a young dragon.

The halfling couldn't get the reins from her, so he leaned forward and grabbed them nearer the team and gave a great tug, abruptly stopping the carriage.

"We have to see what that was!" Dahlia argued, and she reached to move the halfling's meddling hands away, but then grimaced and dropped the reins altogether, clutching her broken arm against her chest and hissing in pain.

"I already know what it was, and that's why I have no desire—" Regis started to argue, but he saw a sudden look of surprise in Dahlia's eyes and stopped, then followed her gaze to the south, along the Trade Way, behind them, where once more the curly-haired little girl, who by all appearances seemed a creepy little demon creature if Regis had ever seen one, was in view, floating after them, smiling that wicked smile. Regis thought it curious, though, for while this little one had the aspects he would expect from a demonic being, or an undead specter, for some reason he couldn't yet comprehend, she wasn't revolting to him.

Still, it concerned him more than a little that the child had chased them all the way from Waterdeep, from House Margaster.

"Go! Just go!" Dahlia cried, and Regis didn't argue this time, snapping the reins, urging the team to leap ahead. He guided them back onto the main road, pushing them to a full gallop as soon as the ground smoothed beneath the carriage.

"The world has gone mad," Dahlia muttered, shaking her head, tears rolling down her cheeks. She looked back, not at the floating demon child, but into the passenger compartment of the coach, where her beloved Artemis Entreri lay, wrapped in a shroud of some unknown material. A death shroud, she was certain, and one that was every so often spitting vicious little wasps.

Now a demon child chasing them, and a gigantic spider climbing a castle wall. It was all too much for her.

Regis dropped a comforting hand on her leg and slowed the team just a bit, for the demon child was not moving swiftly and had already fallen far behind.

"Hold hope," he told her again. "We have nothing else."

"Then we have nothing," Dahlia whispered, and Regis heard, and he couldn't disagree.

"Rumblebelly!" the halfling and Dahlia heard, above the clatter of the rolling coach and the stamp of horses' hooves. Regis slowed the coach but did not dare stop, and turned back in the direction of the call.

"Rumblebelly!" he heard again, and a dwarf crashed out of the brush at the side of the road, a broad fellow with black hair and a beard braided and tied with bits of dung.

"Athrogate," Regis breathed, leaning back and tugging the reins to halt the team.

"What's he doing out here?" Dahlia asked.

"With her," Regis explained, when another figure, a drow woman, stepped onto the road beside the dwarf. "They are the ones who got me to Waterdeep."

Regis didn't try to turn the coach around on the narrow road, so he held the team steady and let the two trot up to them.

"Climb up," Dahlia told the two before they could even exchange greetings. "We've no time to tarry."

"Up or in, eh?" Athrogate asked.

Regis noted that the dwarf was carrying a large sack over one shoulder, and sticking out from it was a pommel, one the halfling knew well. For its end was carved into the likeness of a panther, of Guenhwyvar. Before he could say anything about that, however, he noticed Yvonnel's face crinkle with surprise, then settle into curiosity, as she stared through the window into the carriage's passenger compartment.

Dahlia started to say something, but Regis grabbed her good arm and squeezed, bidding her be silent, for he saw that Yvonnel was then whispering something, as if casting a spell.

The drow woman's face crinkled again with even greater surprise and apparent disgust. "What is this?" she demanded, turning to the two on the driver's bench.

"It is Entreri, trapped within," said Dahlia.

"Dead?"

"No!" Dahlia said, too sharply, and Yvonnel and Athrogate stared at her.

"Then what is it?" Yvonnel asked again, even more insistently.

She knew something they did not, Regis surmised, and she didn't look happy about it.

"What?" she asked again.

"You should ask her," Regis remarked, looking past the drow and down the road, nodding his chin to turn Yvonnel.

There came the little demon child, floating, smiling, always smiling.

"We must go!" Dahlia said, but Yvonnel held up her hand and shook her head.

"Athrogate, take the cocoon out of the carriage," Yvonnel instructed. "Be ready to jump in fast if we must flee."

"We'll not leave him!" Dahlia shouted down at her, but Regis quickly begged her to be silent.

"Hold trust, Dahlia," he said. "Yvonnel is powerful, more than you can imagine. I have seen her banish great demons with but a few words."

Even as she thought to protest, Athrogate did as instructed, laying the shrouded body down at the side of the coach, yelping as a wasp flew out and bit at him.

He slapped it flat, then pulled the stubborn thing from his face and looked at it curiously. "I seen a lot and seen a bee, but now I'm not knowin' what I see," he remarked.

Yvonnel glanced over at him.

"Body's a bug, but face is a people," the dwarf said, holding up the strange creature. He ended with a "Whoa, now," and stepped fast up toward the front of the carriage when the strange demon-like little girl floated up to hover before Yvonnel, close enough for Athrogate to see that her eyes were perfectly white.

"Hello," the child said sweetly. She seemed to study Yvonnel more closely, then smiled even wider and said, "Hello!" with much more enthusiasm.

"I know you," Yvonnel said.

"Oh, you will. Everybody will. One day."

Yvonnel cast a spell, then another, and the little girl hardly seemed to mind, clearly even more tickled by the beautiful drow woman's apparent confusion.

"You cannot see the truth only because you cannot believe the truth," the floating child said.

"How can it be?"

The little girl giggled and shrugged.

"I know you," Yvonnel insisted. "But it cannot be."

"But it is."

"How? Has all the world gone mad?" asked the befuddled drow woman, a powerful priestess and powerful wizard who knew as well as any living mortal the workings of magic and of the planes of existence.

And of things like this little girl—things that should not be given form.

"She did this to him," Dahlia said. She struggled past Regis and jumped down awkwardly, cradling her arm. She reached back for her powerful staff, but Regis grabbed the other end and tugged with all his strength.

"I will destroy you," Dahlia promised the child. "I will send you back to hell!"

"Hell," Yvonnel echoed. "That is her name."

"That is one name," said the little girl. "Heaven."

"Torment!" said Yvonnel.

"Mentor," the girl answered.

"What is this?" Regis demanded, but he went silent when he realized that no one was listening to him.

"Ah, aye," said Athrogate, and he stepped up beside his drow companion. To the girl, he said, "Punishment."

"Reward." The little girl giggled. "There is always another name. A balancing name."

"And you are the judge," said Yvonnel.

"I am the scale," the girl corrected.

"Judgment!" Yvonnel said.

"Justice!" the girl retorted, perfectly mimicking her intensity.

Yvonnel started to say something more, but paused and conceded the point with a nod, and held up her hand to make sure her companions stayed back.

"What is this?" Regis yelled once more.

"I am called Sharon at this time," the girl said.

"Charon, you mean," said Yvonnel.

"That is one name sometimes given, by the people who need to invent names to try to make sense out of that which they cannot understand. But then, of course, so is Sharon."

"The boat-keeper," Athrogate muttered.

"You should not be here," said Yvonnel.

"Dear Yvonnel, I am ever-present, particularly to those who deny my ever-present voice," Sharon replied. "Is that not reason enough?"

"But like this?" Yvonnel's hand swept out before her, taking in the breadth of the floating child. "What is this form you have been given? An unusual circumstance, yes? Perhaps unique?"

Sharon shrugged. "I did not ask for it, I did not will it. It was there, and so . . ." She giggled again.

"You took form when Demogorgon fell," the drow reasoned.

"It is an interesting time. That fiend is a great corrupter, after all. Perhaps I wondered what his absence might mean for those who hear my whispers."

"And what the fall of the barrier of the Faezress might mean."

"That, too."

"An interesting time," Yvonnel agreed, "but it shouldn't interest you. That is not your place, quite definitely not."

"Definitely so! It keenly interests me, of course, and why would it not? This is the time of chaos, and so these are the times that try the soul most especially. What a grand circumstance of revelation."

"Not revelation to you," Yvonnel argued. "How can it be, for the crimes of the heart are ever known to you."

"Ah, but now the criminals can see it themselves." She motioned to the cocoon. "And now I can show them the consequences. Think back, you who have been given the gift of memories older than your form. This time now? It is not so different from how Lolth was given form, millennia ago."

Regis noted Yvonnel rocking back on her heels at that strange remark, and he found himself surprised when the drow began nodding her head, seeming almost as if she didn't want to but could not help herself.

"When Lolth was given form," the drow priestess repeated, and it was clear to all that she was speaking to herself. Then to Sharon, she said, "In an unusual time, can you hear an unusual request?"

"I witness, I do not try."

"You are not judgment?"

Sharon didn't respond, and for once, her smile left her face—although Regis wasn't sure if that was a good thing or a portent of doom.

"Then what is he?" Yvonnel demanded, pointing to the cocooned Entreri.

"He is of his own making, of course."

"Liar!" Dahlia accused, and she jumped forward and brandished her staff threateningly, though the movement had her grimacing in pain. "You did this to him!"

Sharon just looked at her sweetly, and Dahlia fell silent. Dahlia's face began to twist, and she began to chew her lip, and tears came to her eyes. Her strong pose melted into shivers, and in but a few moments, the powerful woman staggered backward, gasping for breath and trying to cry out, her head shaking in horrified denial.

"Did you have to do that?" Yvonnel asked.

"Would you rather that?" Sharon asked, nodding her chin toward the cocoon.

"Did you have to do that, as well?"

The little girl shrugged.

"Give him back," Yvonnel said. "I ask this of you. Give him back, in fairness. His journey is not yet complete. His path had changed—absent . . . you, who should not be here in this manifestation. Can Artemis Entreri not walk the road to the end of his days, perhaps to a destination less harsh?"

"He has walked longer than any human should."

"A most interesting journey, though."

Sharon smiled once more, even giggled, and conceded the point with a nod.

"Do you not see the problem?" Yvonnel asked her. "You are interfering. You should not be here, and simply because you are, you are passing final judgment on that which is not final."

Sharon sighed, and shrugged, and sighed again.

"You know I speak the truth," said Yvonnel. "You have known this truth for a while now—from the beginning, or are you such that you can force all to be true to themselves except for you?"

That brought a laugh from Sharon, one that seemed heartfelt. "Bravo, clever drow. How clever will you be in the end, I wonder?" She smiled and sighed. "Perhaps it is time for me to leave," she agreed, and she glanced to the side, to the cocoon, and issued a sharp puff of breath. Immediately, the cocoon began to dissolve . . . into more stinging wasps.

"No!" Dahlia cried, and took a step that way. She fell back as a second swarm arose, similar to the first but of a different shade. Then she fell back some more, and Athrogate howled and joined her, and Regis jumped off the far side of the bench seat as the two swarms engaged, wasp to wasp, biting and stinging, fighting each other, mutual death in mutual embrace, a wild war of tiny creatures, so evenly matched that the swarms diminished equally.

"See?" Sharon asked, as the last of them dropped to the ground and died. "There is always another name."

On the ground, Artemis Entreri coughed and vomited, jerking over to the side before half sitting, huddling and shaking. Dahlia rushed to him, as did Athrogate.

"It was . . . interesting," Sharon told Yvonnel. The little girl began to float back down the south road, growing less substantial.

Coming around the back of the carriage, Regis was shocked to watch Yvonnel run after her. "Sharon!" she called. "Conscience!"

"Conscience?" the halfling asked, his eyes widening as he began to figure it out.

The girl, growing translucent, stopped and turned.

"Tell me," Yvonnel implored her.

"Tell you?"

"Heaven or hell?" the drow priestess asked. "Can you tell me?"

"For you?" Sharon asked incredulously, starkly shocked—as if the question itself was so out of bounds that it should never be asked of her, Regis thought.

"No," Yvonnel clarified. "For that, I know you cannot. But . . . for all. For all of us. For the world and those who inhabit this world, this place. I ask you, who see most clearly of all, where does it go? Which side of the scale will prove the heavier?"

The girl laughed at her.

"Tell me," Yvonnel begged.

"Tell yourself." And Sharon floated away to nothingness.

Regis ran to Yvonnel, who started suddenly, her head jerking, her gasp great indeed.

"What?" the halfling asked.

Yvonnel didn't answer, for Sharon had told only her, in her head, where that little girl voice had whispered, *The arc of reason bends to heaven. The darkness of a few can force hell.*

"What?" Regis pressed.

A smile grew on Yvonnel's face and she began to nod.

"What? You must!"

"It is a long game, my friend," Yvonnel told him. "A long road. But hold faith, for now I believe that it is one worth traveling."

"What?" Regis asked again, his voice trailing away. "Are you going to tell me what this is all about?"

"You already know."

"What was her name?"

"She has many."

"Conscience?"

Yvonnel looked down at Regis and smiled, then turned and went back to tend to Entreri.

Regis didn't watch her go. He kept his gaze down the south road, where the little girl, Sharon, had faded to nothingness. He stared as if he was still seeing her, and in his mind's eye, he was, replaying the earlier encounters.

He glanced to the side, just for a moment, to see Dahlia, as he considered the very different reactions he and the elf woman had experienced when confronted with the specter of Sharon.

He had been strangely comfortable, but Dahlia, quite the opposite.

He knew enough of Dahlia's past to put things together, and he found himself nodding as he considered Yvonnel's remarks and the exchange.

Yes, he thought, in the weakening of the planar barrier, the hordes of demons had been set free of the Abyss, and so, too, had come this . . . thing. Sharon wasn't a creature, and yet she was an inescapable part of every reasoning creature.

Sharon was conscience given form and substance.

A gasp turned the halfling about to find Artemis Entreri sitting up, his face pallid, his eyes haunted and red, his jaw hanging open, with drool all over his chin and cheek. As Dahlia pulled off Entreri's shirt, Regis lost his breath yet again, for the man's shoulders, chest, belly, everywhere on his torso and his arms, was pocked with small red wounds.

The wasps, Regis realized.

The wasps that had bothered Dahlia but had barely noticed the halfling.

The stinging wasps of conscience.

Truly, Regis didn't know what to think, or how to feel. He had witnessed something beyond his comprehension, and at the same time, something that seemed miraculous. As Yvonnel cast spells of healing over Entreri, the man already seeming much better, it occurred to the halfling that perhaps the cocoon of Sharon might prove to be a great blessing to the man, a warning, grim and painful.

Artemis Entreri was a much better man than he used to be, Regis believed, and maybe, just maybe, this brutal episode would encourage him to even better things ahead.

He could hope so, at least.

Of course, this was all contingent on Yvonnel's suspicion being correct. It was quite possible that this little creature, Sharon, was nothing more than a malevolent, deceitful demon.

In his heart, though, Regis found he didn't believe that.

Despite everything—the chaos, the destruction, the giant spider, the pains of Entreri—Regis had a lightness to his step when he joined the others by the side of the road.

"Come," Yvonnel bid them all. "Thornhold is just ahead, down at the water."

"Oh, don't go there!" Regis warned. "There's a monster."

"A monster spider," Dahlia agreed. "It scaled the wall. We were far down the road, yet saw it, so great was its size."

"Not a spider," Athrogate said. "And, aye, we seen it go over the wall."

"A retriever," Yvonnel explained. "A great demonic construct. There is likely nothing left alive in Thornhold."

"And you still want to go in there?" Regis asked with an eyebrow arched.

"It is almost surely gone," Yvonnel answered.

"Chased Drizzt in there!" Athrogate said, and Regis gasped. "He gived me his stuff for safekeeping, then took the durned thing halfway 'cross the world and over the wall."

"Come," Yvonnel said. "Let us see."

She started off and the others followed, Dahlia helping Entreri to his feet. Once there, though, the man took only a moment to steady himself, then bent and retrieved his weapons and cloak, and moved to follow.

"I'm glad you're okay," Regis said to him as he shambled past.

Entreri looked over at him skeptically, but nodded and continued on his way.

Regis recognized that skepticism and didn't take it as an affront. No, Regis understood the real source, for in truth, Artemis Entreri looked anything but okay.

HE WAS FREE OF THE WASP COCOON, BUT HE WAS NOT.

He still heard their buzz. Felt their tiny feet crawling over him. And though the vicious demon insects were not biting him any longer, he could still feel their stings profoundly.

He looked to Yvonnel, many steps ahead of him and moving determinedly through the rocky ground before the old keep. She might have some answers, he thought.

But did he really need them?

For in the mind of Artemis Entreri, his ghastly experience seemed clear enough. Only one question nagged at him: Was it some form of purgatory, some forced, painful penance, or was it hell?

Eternal hell?

He hoped for the former and feared the latter, but he knew that the choice was correctly delineated. While in there, the insects biting or stinging, or whatever it was that they did to inflict such fire, he could see nothing with his physical eyes, but couldn't unsee the many crimes he had committed. Not every fight and killing had come at him in that seemingly endless loop of atrocity.

No, only the ones he knew to be unjustified.

Unjustified.

That was something that Artemis Entreri had never openly admitted, not to Drizzt, not to Jarlaxle, not to his first love, Calihye, not even to Dahlia.

In the unrelenting anger that had consumed him for most of his life, had he ever really admitted it to himself?

Now he felt as if he could not hide from those instances. Now they weighed heavy in his heart and flickered like a thunderstorm in his mind, flashing between the too-raw memories of unspeakable, unrelenting, undiminishing pain.

Pain he deserved, he knew.

Pain he could only hope would cleanse him of those old, dead events, like fires consuming the rotting husks of used-up trees.

He heard Dahlia talking to him rather insistently at his side and looked over at her.

"You're free now," she was saying. "We found you. We got you. We got you from that place."

Entreri didn't know how to answer, so instead he asked a question: "Limbo, or hell?"

Dahlia looked at him curiously and did not respond.

But she swallowed hard, and Artemis Entreri knew by that, and by her blanching face as the blood drained, that she certainly understood.

CHAPTER 9

The City Lost

She raced through the streets of Luskan. She tried to stay to the shadows, because she knew that danger was all about her. It had all been going so well! The city had settled under its new conquerors, and the streets, though not yet quiet, were beginning to show signs of normalcy. In the tavern, the talk had been light and flowing freely.

But then she had been recognized. She was sure of it. She had noted the look on the face of the man hurriedly leaving.

Despite her fears, Bonnie Charlee didn't run straight to the secret entrance to Illusk, the ruins beneath Luskan. She had to make sure that she was clear of pursuit, that no eyes were on her, before she got to the cemetery near the bridge to Closeguard Isle and the false grave that brought her to the secret descending stairway.

Just as she was beginning to hope she had outrun any pursuers, the woman turned a corner into an alleyway and nearly ran into a pair of gnolls, each fully two feet taller than she.

They weren't part of the pursuit, she hoped, for she had clearly surprised them more than they had surprised her.

She hadn't the time to figure it out.

The woman threw herself into the nearest burly gnoll, her dagger coming out, pommel tight against her ribs as she used her weight to insert the blade deep into the gnoll's belly.

She pulled the dagger out and shoved the wounded creature away, then slashed across as the second tried in vain to draw its sword, scoring a lucky cut across the beast's throat, her arm just getting past the snarling creature's hyena-like face and snapping maw. Down it went, gurgling, but the other was howling, loudly—and was being answered by others not far away!

She ran down the alleyway, zigzagging this way and that when she heard renewed pursuit behind her. She grabbed at any loose items— trash, a broken cart, an empty cask—as she passed, throwing them down behind her to impede the pursuers.

Bonnie Charlee stumbled in surprise as a javelin flew by her head, skipping off the wall of the building to her left. She glanced back as she caught herself against another cask, and her heart sank and she knew she was doomed, for the lane behind her was full of the rampaging humanoids.

She stumbled out the far end of the alley, gripping her right shoulder where another javelin had clipped her. She knew she was about to be killed, or worse, knew they were right behind her. She even cried out as she turned, flashing her small weapon in desperation, and it took her a long moment to decipher the sight before her.

Darkness filled the alleyway. Not the night, but true darkness, magical darkness.

She heard the yells of the gnolls, then the click of crossbows, then fewer howls and more grunts.

The slide of a sword as if against a metal breastplate. A yelp of pain.

One gnoll spilled out of the alley before her, stumbling, bleeding— yes, covered in its own blood.

It jerked weirdly once and again, and it took Bonnie Charlee a few moments to realize the two new wounds were from heavy crossbow bolts.

Before the dying beast fell, a drow rushed out of the darkness, grabbed it, and yanked it back in, his sword going to murderous work before he and his brutish victim disappeared from Bonnie Charlee's astonished gaze.

The drow came back out—his face, at least. "To Illusk now, you fool!" he scolded.

Bonnie Charlee didn't need to be told twice.

"I THINK IT OBVIOUS THAT YOUR TRIP WAS LESS SUCCESS-ful than we had hoped," Kimmuriel Oblodra greeted Bonnie Charlee when she returned to the secret hideaway of Bregan D'aerthe, deep in the ruins beneath the city of Luskan.

"I got some information," the woman replied, her nervousness showing in the sweat on her brow as she stood before the coldly analytical and surpassingly dangerous drow psionicist.

"And now you have become useless to our cause, because you were clearly recognized," Kimmuriel stated.

"Those who recognized her are dead, however," came another voice, another drow, entering the small room of Bregan D'aerthe's co-leader beside a tall, red-haired man, who appeared to be human.

Bonnie Charlee was more comforted by the arrival of Braelin Janquay, a drow scout and a fellow of an easy manner, than of the other person, who she knew to be no human. He was Beniago Kurth, the front for Bregan D'aerthe in the city, not only a drow but a member of the Ruling House of the Underdark city of Menzoberranzan. Beniago had not been threatening to her any more than any of the others, and less so than Kimmuriel, surely, but there was something about him, some easy danger, that had the woman on edge at the mere sight of him.

"You are certain of this?" Kimmuriel asked.

"We had scouts all about," Braelin answered. "It was a gang of ugly gnolls, nothing more, and they're too bloodthirsty to flee and too stupid to know they should flee."

"I agree with his assessment," Beniago added, and he fixed a stern gaze on Bonnie Charlee that had the little hairs on her arms tingling with fear. "She got lucky."

Bonnie Charlee steeled herself against the tall man's withering glare. She decided then not to mention the man in the tavern who she was sure had recognized her.

As soon as she finished that thought, however, Kimmuriel chuckled, and she knew that she had indeed just told him exactly that. The psionicist said nothing, however, and even nodded a bit at the woman.

"Ye asked me to find out some things, eh?" Bonnie Charlee said defiantly, hoping that she was reading Kimmuriel correctly. "And I went, didn't I? Put yer angry eyes away, mate."

That brought a snort from Braelin. "Beniago's only angry because he still looks like a human," the scout said lightheartedly. "Though, between us, clever lady, he was much uglier before the transformation."

Bonnie Charlee returned his smile and was much relieved by Braelin's tone.

"Well, what did you learn?" Beniago asked, ignoring the jibes.

"Not here," said Kimmuriel, and he started out of the room, the other three following.

Bonnie Charlee paid close attention as the four walked the ways of Illusk. The dark elf had built formidable defenses here, and the preparedness and deadliness of their many sentries could not be questioned.

Bonnie Charlee wanted to know them all. If she was captured up above, her knowledge of this place might prove her salvation, and what did she owe the drow, anyway?

"You owe us your life and nothing less," Kimmuriel walked up beside her and whispered in her ear, almost as soon as the question had crossed her mind.

The woman's legs went weak. Wulfgar had warned her so many times about this one, about how he could enter her mind with ease and read her every thought. He had just read her thoughts about the man in the tavern, obviously, and now she had slipped again.

Bonnie Charlee had no way to defend against that!

"No," he whispered, "you don't."

She chewed her lip as Kimmuriel sidled away, taking up the lead once more as he guided them into the deeper recesses of the Bregan D'aerthe position, heading for the room the woman knew best, the room where Wulfgar waited.

The barbarian was not alone but with priestess Dab'nay, one of the very few women Bonnie Charlee had seen in the drow band. Dab'nay glanced at Kimmuriel and gave a nod, then launched into the chant of a divine spell, a dweomer of healing, obviously, for Wulfgar took it in with the satisfied expression of an old codger sitting on a dock inhaling a cloud of fine pipe-weed smoke.

"Shall I take my leave?" Dab'nay asked.

"No need," Kimmuriel replied. He turned to Bonnie Charlee. "Tell them what you have learned."

Bonnie Charlee paused before she began, noting the exact words of Kimmuriel. Yes, tell *them*, for Kimmuriel already knew it, all of it, perhaps more of it than Bonnie Charlee herself could recall consciously.

She wished she was back at sea, bouncing on the waves in pursuit of a merchant galley.

"They're all behind the new high captain," the woman said, clearing her head of those far-off dreams. "All the ships. Rethnor, Baram . . ."

"Baram is no surprise," Beniago said. "Every high captain of Ship Baram has been willing to move whatever way looks safest for Ship Baram. Likely that one was opening wide his doors for the invaders before they even got into port."

"All of them," Bonnie Charlee said. "High Captain Brevindon's taken yer seat, Beniago. Ship Kurth's now Ship Margaster."

"A Waterdhavian noble family," Kimmuriel noted.

"Taking Luskan out in the open?" asked Braelin Janquay. "That seems foolhardy."

"Or confident," Beniago added.

"That is a common way of thinking among thieves and insurgents," Kimmuriel explained. "When you steal what you want, claim it loudly, and dare anyone to do something to take it away."

"A dare I'd take," Wulfgar remarked.

"The city's all fallin' in line behind him," Bonnie Charlee went on. "Even the gnolls that came in with Brevindon's fleet're given free run o' the city."

"Why?" Wulfgar asked, climbing to his feet and stretching the stiffness and pain out of his shoulders. "Why would they do that? Brevindon led the attack and slaughtered many, sure. Yet half of Luskan or more seems to have surrendered without a fight. Why?"

"Because he don't have dark skin," Bonnie Charlee answered bluntly, before the others could. That drew long stares from the drow in the room, but ones more of curiosity than animosity.

"It seems that my disguise did not fool them, then," Beniago agreed with a laugh. "A human in the captain's chair in appearance, but still they knew that the power behind Luskan these last years has been drow in origin. Now they have a human Waterdhavian lord to call high captain, someone who looks like most of them, someone they think grand and beautiful."

"Such primitive emotions are the trough of despots," Kimmuriel said.

"So, Brevindon's taken Closeguard Isle and Ship Kurth as his home, the other ships have rallied behind him, and Gromph won't let the Hosttower do anything against him," said Braelin Janquay. "Is that it, then? Is it time for Bregan D'aerthe to move on?"

All eyes went to Kimmuriel, the undisputed leader of the band with Jarlaxle nowhere to be found.

"No," Kimmuriel answered. "No. Let them settle in and grow comfortable for a bit longer, then we strike, and often. The facade of strength is impressive unless one understands the weakness behind it. A leader assuming control as Brevindon Margaster has done has also created great enmity with many powerful people who haven't the courage to confront him. So we will make him mortal, figuratively and literally, and let the support for his marauders be shown as the true facade."

"But the option behind Brevindon will remain . . . us," Braelin argued.

"Or him," Kimmuriel answered, motioning toward Wulfgar.

"You ask me to be a puppet ruler for Bregan D'aerthe?" the proud barbarian retorted as soon as the shock wore off.

"I ask you to help us rid Luskan of this demon-backed invasion," Kimmuriel answered. "In fact, I insist upon it."

"Aye. And I've agreed to that part. But I've no desire to rule a city."

"You won't."

"Or to pretend to rule a city," Wulfgar clarified, in a determined tone that brooked no debate.

We will find a path to satisfy both our needs, the barbarian heard in his head, and he tried to keep his expression unchanged, with no hint of the revulsion inspired by Kimmuriel's telepathic intrusion evident.

"Get out and go south," Kimmuriel instructed Braelin. "Relate the news of Luskan and learn the events and status of Gauntlgrym. Stay underground and through the tunnels until you are well out of the city. Take this." He handed Braelin a small whistle set on a silver chain. "And take with you any others you deem necessary to facilitate the mission."

Braelin stared at the strange whistle for a moment, nodding, which let Kimmuriel know that the man recognized it—and why should he not? For Jarlaxle had long worn a similar whistle about his neck. He looped the chain over his head and looked up. "Any I deem necessary? Priestess Dab'nay?"

Kimmuriel considered it for a moment, then replied, "No. Not her. She remains here. I may have need of her."

"Should I be honored?" Dab'nay asked lightly, with a hint of jest, a hint of sarcasm.

Kimmuriel was having none of it and showed her as much with his cold expression. "Honored?" he answered. "No. Perhaps you should be afraid."

Dab'nay started to respond but held back.

"I am to go all the way to Gauntlgrym?" Braelin Janquay asked, obviously trying to change the subject.

"If you must," Kimmuriel replied. "But take great care, and if you encounter something unexpected, then use the whistle." He paused for just a heartbeat. "Something unexpected and dramatic," he clarified.

"Do not waste my time unless you are certain that your call will not prove to be a waste of my time."

"Couldn't you just go to Gauntlgrym and be back in short order?" Wulfgar asked Kimmuriel.

"Do not pretend to understand that which you do not," the psionicist was quick to respond. "There are costs to every action and I have more pressing needs for my powers than to run as courier between the cities."

"And here?" Beniago asked, and Kimmuriel knew from his tone that he was simply trying to change the subject before it got out of hand, intercepting a likely rude retort from the often crass barbarian. "Are we to stay hidden below, or should we commence with some actions to make Brevindon's reign less than simple?"

"Like?" Kimmuriel asked.

"There are lots of dead gnolls in an alley," Beniago said with a wry grin. "Seems a promising beginning for a resistance."

"What is the strongest ship other than Brevindon's Ship Kurth?" Kimmuriel asked. "Rethnor?"

"Easily."

"Nibble at them," the psionicist instructed. "Wound them, but only a bit, around the edges, and make it look like the new Ship Margaster's doing. Then go—"

"To Ship Baram and make them realize that Ship Margaster will eliminate any and all competitors," Beniago interrupted.

Kimmuriel smiled and nodded.

Soon after, Wulfgar somehow found himself alone in the room with Kimmuriel, something he never much enjoyed.

"As we discussed when first the city fell," Kimmuriel told him, "if all goes well, you may get one strike. That is your only chance."

"And if all doesn't go well?"

"Then you are almost certainly a dead man."

"My only chance," Wulfgar echoed, emphasizing Kimmuriel's use of a singular pronoun. "*I* am almost certainly a dead man. What of Kimmuriel?" he asked, just because he wanted to hear the drow's derisive snort.

Whatever happened here in Luskan, Wulfgar understood clearly that the stakes were higher for him than for this strange drow, and likely higher than for any of Jarlaxle's mercenary band.

Bregan D'aerthe always seemed to play things that way.

"One more thing for you to consider as we await our opportunity," said Kimmuriel. "Your friend, this pirate woman, Bonnie Charlee."

"What of her?" Wulfgar asked with a shrug, and he was surprised by how much he privately cared.

"She was recognized in the city, but she chose not to share that. You should make it very clear to her that if she even thinks of betraying us, I will know, and if I know—again—then she will find a worse fate than any creature of your surface world could ever inflict upon her."

"Even a mere thought?" Wulfgar asked. "People have many thoughts that they will not act upon. Would any friend remain a friend if he looked into the mind of a companion at the wrong moment?"

"I can separate whimsy from true threat. Whimsy, I accept. To a point."

"You can't just keep your opinions to yourself. Is that why Kimmuriel has no friends?"

"You speak as if that is a bad thing," Kimmuriel replied, and left the room.

Wulfgar blew out a long sigh, thinking that he would indeed have a long talk with Bonnie Charlee. As much as he hated many of the drow, and Kimmuriel in particular, he understood that he and Bonnie Charlee had to throw in with Bregan D'aerthe fully if they were to have any chance of surviving this nightmare. Only Kimmuriel, or Jarlaxle if he returned, had any hope of getting Gromph to open the portals to Gauntlgrym, and without that, Wulfgar had little expectation that he would ever see his friends again.

For he was fairly certain of what Braelin and the others would find in the south: a land no doubt brimming with powerful enemies and monsters far beyond him.

Yes, he needed to speak with Bonnie Charlee, and immediately. Again, Wulfgar had to pause and consider how much he cared about whether or not this woman survived. He wasn't in love with her or anything like that, he told himself stubbornly, dismissing the notion before even entertaining it.

But she had proven a loyal companion and that seemed a virtue in scarce supply in the City of Sails.

"LOLTH IS WITH HER," GROMPH REPLIED, WHEN THE PSIONI-cist cornered him in his extradimensional mansion within the Host-tower of the Arcane later that same day. "Matron Zhindia Melarn would not have come this far, would not be commanding such an array of demons and vagabonds, without the blessing of Lolth."

"Many with the blessing of Lolth have lost before," Kimmuriel replied. "Even in Menzoberranzan."

"And if those victors were not also in the blessing of Lolth, what happened to them, I wonder?" Gromph replied.

"Why are you afraid?"

"Why are you not?"

The simple question set Kimmuriel back on his heels a bit, which was highly unusual.

"And why do you care so much?" Gromph pressed.

"I work with Bregan D'aerthe."

"Bregan D'aerthe will survive. You can be gone from the city, from this part of the world, if needed, in short order. Jarlaxle survived the centuries because none are better at navigating such a web than he. I expect he hopes as much for the man he named as a co-leader of his coveted band."

Kimmuriel hardly heard the words, shaking his head through it all.

"Look at yourself!" Gromph scolded. "You care. Kimmuriel Oblodra—and how remarkable that any Oblodra or Odran cares! Have you gone soft, then? Have you abandoned your sole goal in life, to find the One Eternal Truth along with those tentacle waggling il-lithids?"

Kimmuriel wanted to deny his words, to deny him, but his responses sounded without conviction.

"Have you become enamored of the flesh, Kimmuriel?" Gromph asked more seriously. "Have you found within your emotionless mind a bit of love for that which we mere mortals covet?"

"You have felt the power of the hive mind unleashed," the psionicist reminded him, for Gromph had been with him when they had channeled the awesome psionic power of the entire illithid collective into the weapon Yvonnel had made of Drizzt in order to destroy Demogorgon.

"And it was glorious," the former archmage admitted. "I hope to find it again, but to do so, I know that I have to live long enough to be worthy of it. And living long enough, I expect, means staying on the right side of Lady Lolth's anger. Matron Zhindia came here with the full blessing of Lolth. Of that, I am sure. Two retrievers, Kimmuriel! Two! When have you ever heard of such a thing?"

He had a point, one that was hard for Kimmuriel to ignore. Retrievers were a great gift from the lower planes, a magnificent construct rarely created because of the effort and cost. Kimmuriel did care, deeply, about the outcome of all this, but his concern wasn't based on any love or desire.

No, Kimmuriel was angry, outraged even.

That silent confession struck him hard. When had he ever let his anger overrule his sensibilities? Even when Matron Mother Yvonnel Baenre had dropped his home, his family, his mother, into the Clawrift, obliterating all that was House Oblodra, Kimmuriel had tempered his rage beneath his good judgment. He had fully joined with Jarlaxle, with Bregan D'aerthe, which served as a strong ally of that same Matron Mother Baenre!

Many times he had thought of revenge, and many times he had put those desires aside, exacting what little punishment he might secretly inflict upon the Baenres whenever he could, but never anything risky. It had always been more of an amusement, a little bit of whimsy, than anything important.

Now, though, he burned with anger. Now he wanted Brevindon taken down in no uncertain terms, the demon within the Margaster crushed before him. He had told himself that his plan, dangerous but possible, was for the good of Bregan D'aerthe, and there was perhaps enough truth in that for him to continue the self-deception.

Not at this moment, though. At this moment, Kimmuriel realized there was much more here, much more personal anger driving him. He wasn't certain why. He was missing something, he thought, some element right there before him that he had not connected, a memory deep in his mind, a hint he had heard elsewhere . . . something.

"If you do not renew the flow of magic to Gauntlgrym and the primordial, the beast will escape and lay waste to the region," he said to Gromph one last time.

"And if I do as you ask, I will be picking sides, and that side will not be the one favored by Lolth."

"Jarlaxle is in there, in Gauntlgrym, as far as I can discern."

"Then Jarlaxle will have to be clever, or Jarlaxle will be dead."

Kimmuriel stood and stared for a while longer, but he really couldn't do anything, he understood. He was more powerful than Gromph in psionics, but if he tried to use any to convince Gromph, he would be facing off against one of the most powerful wizards in the world.

He wanted to satisfy his anger, but he didn't want to make it go away by dying.

He returned to Illusk and the secret drow enclave. Gromph would not be swayed.

CHAPTER 10

Web Weaving

T he surface," the excited drow scout reported when he returned to his commanders.

The strange-looking warrior standing beside High Priestess Minolin Fey Baenre gave a grating and guttural, almost feral, growl. He was large and muscular, particularly for a drow man, with his white hair spiked like the plume of a war crown along the middle of his otherwise shaved pate. A mithral ring hung from his nose, gold pins had been shoved through his cheeks, and he had painted garish white rings about his eyes.

For all his outlandish eccentricities, though, no one glancing upon this warrior would think him anything but formidable. He wore black plate mail, fitted perfectly, and carried a magnificent trident in one hand, with a net awaiting his grasp on his right hip.

"He is trying too hard to be Uthegentel," the priestess Saribel Xorlarrin Do'Urden whispered to her wizard brother, Ravel, nodding her chin toward the unusual warrior, Malagdorl Armgo.

"Warriors try too hard at everything," Ravel replied. "That is why they usually and thankfully die young."

Malagdorl looked over at the siblings then and growled again, and Ravel winked at him, drawing a slap from Saribel. "Fool," she whispered. Then, shielding one hand and using her fingers to sign at him in the silent drow code, she added, *He is Matron Mez'Barris's favored grandson. She sees her beloved, lost Uthegentel, in Malagdorl.*

She sees her lover in her grandson? Ravel silently responded, his face crinkling in disgust.

"Not like that," Saribel reflexively replied, but in truth, she wasn't so sure of her claim. In the silent code, she added, *Look at his hands. He even wears Matron Mez'Barris's gloves, making him even stronger.*

"Did you see anyone to kill?" Malagdorl asked the scout as he stepped a bit in front of the Baenre high priestess. "Elves?"

"Know your place," Minolin Fey scolded, shifting to stand a bit ahead of the uppity male. To the scout, she added, "You may answer."

"There was only silence," he said. "We have found nothing alive. Not a bird, not an . . . elf."

Malagdorl growled.

Ravel snorted and flashed, *I hope the ugly fool dies quickly. Perhaps I'll aid the first elf we see.*

Saribel elbowed him. *Do not discount the great honor Matron Mother Baenre bestowed upon us by ranking us as under-commanders of the scouting group, with only her own high priestess and the weapon master of the second house above us.*

Interesting. Two spells for us to become the commanders, said Ravel's fingers. *One if I aim cleverly.*

Saribel tried not to giggle at her irascible brother's incessant joking—at least, she hoped it was just that, but she knew that with Ravel, she could never be certain. She led the way to join the other leaders of the party.

"We go out to see what we might learn under the land that has no ceiling," Minolin Fey Baenre told the assembled group. "Spread the word among your underlings."

Malagdorl and the four under-commanders all nodded their assent. When Ravel turned to go, Saribel took him by the arm and held him back, directing his gaze to the other two who shared their rank in this group, Kelfain Mizzrym and Kron Tlabbar. It did not escape Saribel's notice that these latter two under-commanders were the patrons of their respective houses, the third- and fourth-ranked in the city, nor that both of those houses had been bitter rivals of House Xorlarrin, an enmity that had not likely ebbed now that Matron Zeerith and her family had assumed the surname of Do'Urden. The Xorlarrins had stood as the city's third house before abdicating their seat at the Ruling Council in order to strike out and claim this very area as a satellite city for Menzoberranzan. Much had changed for House Xorlarrin after the disaster within Gauntlgrym, when the Delzoun dwarves had pushed them out, but Saribel doubted that those changes, including the elimination of House Xorlarrin altogether and the reincorporation of House Do'Urden, though lower in the rank than Xorlarrin had been, had done much to lessen the rivalries.

Now on this grand march of Menzoberranzan, considered the most important one of the era by Matron Mother Quenthel Baenre, the matrons of those third and fourth houses were hedging their bets, clearly. They had sent the patrons, two men eminently replaceable, instead of their more valuable house wizards or weapon masters or high priestesses. The matrons of Houses Mizzrym and Faen Tlabbar had kept their true power close at hand, back within the safety of the main battle group.

What did it mean Saribel wondered. Anything? Matron Mez'Barris Armgo, no friend of either the Xorlarrins or the Baenres, had sent her valued weapon master—but Saribel had considered that a reflection of Mez'Barris's desire to see Malagdorl elevated to rival the legend of Uthegentel. Matron Mez'Barris could never see her grandson to such glory if she shielded him from dangerous missions, and so she would not protect him—nor did Mez'Barris herself need the protection of Malagdorl, surely, with the vast resources of House Barrison Del'Armgo surrounding her.

Matron Mother Baenre had sent a high priestess, but she had little choice if she wanted to ensure complete control of the scouting party. And it was merely Minolin Fey, after all, who had joined House Baenre only because she had married Gromph and birthed a very important daughter.

A daughter who was likely in this very region working against them all, Saribel thought. She kept that dangerous notion very private.

Still, she could not shake the feeling that this was an odd collection on an odd expedition, whatever it might be. Matron Mother Quenthel Baenre was pulling the strings here, but did anyone know what the puppeteer had planned?

"We are not to engage," Minolin Fey was saying when the priestess turned her attention back to the parlay. "We are not to strike at anything we see, not human, not dwarf, not even elf. And surely, neither drow nor demon, unless we are attacked. We are here to learn, not to fight. You have all been warned."

It seemed to Saribel that Minolin Fey was aiming that warning of patience and temperance at one person in particular, and if anyone needed such a warning, it was Malagdorl Armgo.

Twilight had fallen across the land by the time the full scouting party had reached the entrance to the surface world. That was a good thing, as few among the ranks had ever seen the surface, and the eyes of a drow did not easily adapt to the glare of the fiery orb that haunted the overworld of Toril through half of each day.

They moved into their traveling formations with exceptional precision, for even though these hunters had come from a myriad of drow houses and few had ever fought beside the particular drow forming about them, the children of Menzoberranzan shared martial training and knew their place in a small group, and knew the place of their small group in the larger formation.

Silent as shadows, they filtered through the deepening gloom, leapfrogging the point position in systematic order, some climbing trees as easily as squirrels to gain a wider view of the area before them. They moved north for a short while before turning back to the west, then slowed as one when a treetop scout reported activity a short distance ahead.

Drow hands flashed signals to cover and defend when the lead scouts came rushing back to signal the approach of some unknown entities.

On first glance of the large shadows moving through the trees far ahead, Saribel thought them a horde of demons, but as they neared, as the rhythm of their scrabbling legs took on a familiar pattern, she—and those around her—came to know the truth.

She glanced over at Minolin Fey, who crouched with Malagdorl behind a low berm to her right. The Baenre priestess flashed the name: *Driders!*

Saribel wasn't surprised. Matron Zhindia Melarn was up here, and it was well known that she kept many driders in her house (and that she quite enjoyed inflicting that ultimate punishment on heretics).

The identification moved through the drow ranks, but before no more than half had seen the signals, the opposition force became evident, a host of the giant half-spider, half-drow creatures pushing through the underbrush, revealing themselves fearlessly in all their horrid glory.

Whether the apparent leader, a gigantic brute with fiery red eyes and weblike braids in her long hair, knew the identity of those before her or not wasn't clear, but she acted as one would expect of a drider: she hurled a heavy spear at the berm. It skipped off the top, between the two leaders, only narrowly missing both.

Minolin Fey reacted with her voice, commanding the beast to halt, but Malagdorl, predictably, wasn't satisfied with that.

"With me!" he roared, coming up over the berm. A second spear flew at him from farther to his right, but he spun around it deftly, completing the circle in a straight charge at the gigantic central drider.

Clicks of drow hand crossbows sounded, a swarm of darts striking out.

Apparently caught up in the excitement of the moment, Ravel jumped up and began a spell, but Saribel jumped up beside him and slapped his motioning hands aside.

She and Minolin Fey began shouting then, at driders and at their own drow, calling a halt to the fight.

"Dare you desecrate gifts to Lolth?" Saribel yelled at her fellow drow, for the drider abominations were considered exactly that.

"Dare you challenge the priestesses of Lolth?" Minolin Fey yelled at the driders.

Most of the would-be combatants, both drider and drow, eased back, but not Malagdorl and not the behemoth before him.

In charged the drow weapon master and up reared the drider, her front two chitinous legs kicking at him. The drider matched the drow's trident with a larger one of her own, and thrust down powerfully as she dove forward in pursuit, as Malagdorl fell back from the kicking legs.

Malagdorl took a wide-handed grip on his black trident and presented it diagonally before and above him, catching the descending trident between the tines. It seemed ridiculous to Saribel and the other onlookers, who expected the drow to be crushed beneath the powerful press of the much larger and obviously well-leveraged drider, but to her astonishment, and to the gasps of many others, the weapon master of House Barrison Del'Armgo caught that descending trident and the full weight of the monster coming down behind it, and held them there.

With a roar of utter defiance and denial, Malagdorl spun to his right and forward, turning the drider's trident above him and not releasing it until he was too far under the beast for her to bring the weapon to bear.

Like a spider, the drider jumped, straight up, barely avoiding Malagdorl's attempt to impale her abdomen.

She landed to the side, turning in her short flight, spinning her trident back to the ready, and rushing at the drow even as it landed.

And fierce Malagdorl did not shy away, charging back in eagerly.

A ball of flame appeared in the air before the approaching combatants, roiling for just an eyeblink before shooting down a line of divine fire, causing both drider and drow to skid to an abrupt stop.

Minolin Fey came over the berm fearlessly, striding forward with long and determined steps, her robes, those fitting a high priestess of good standing and the grace of Lady Lolth, flowing around her. Saribel's jaw dropped open in surprise—she had known this woman when she was Minolin Fey Branche, first priestess of House Fey-Branche, which was widely considered the least of the ruling houses and not even as strong as most of the houses ranked from ninth to twentieth. Only the long and storied history of House Fey-Branche, along with a tight alliance with House Baenre, had kept Matron Byrtyn Fey on the Ruling Council. That Minolin Fey, the one Saribel had known, the one whose only claim to station was as Matron Byrtyn's eldest daughter, had been the butt of many jokes among the other women aspiring to attain the rank of high priestess.

But this Minolin Fey, Minolin Fey Baenre, seemed much more self-assured, indeed, and much more powerful in every action.

What a wonder to be a member of the Baenre nobles, Saribel thought, with more than a bit of envy. She grabbed her brother by the arm and tugged him behind her as she hustled to catch up to Minolin Fey, determined that House Do'Urden—nay! House Xorlarrin!—would be properly represented!

"Who are you, abomination who dares to attack a disciple of Lady Lolth?" Minolin Fey demanded.

"We did not know," the drider croaked, easing away a bit, clearly intimidated.

"Who are you?"

"I am Malfoosh!"

"Malfoosh?"

"Yes, priestess," she replied.

"What kind of name is that?" Minolin Fey demanded.

At that moment, Kron Tlabbar ran up to Minolin Fey and whispered something in her ear, and the drow priestess seemed to sway for just a moment before composing herself. Saribel cast a questioning glance at the patron of House Faen Tlabbar, but the man just shook his head and stepped back.

"Malfoosh of what house?" Minolin Fey asked, a question that set Saribel back on her heels. These were obviously Zhindia's driders, were they not? "I do not know the drider Malfoosh among Matron Zhindia's troop."

Saribel didn't understand. Why would Minolin Fey know *any* of the driders of the Melarni? Why would she bother to hear their names?

"What house?" Minolin Fey insisted.

The drider's face twisted as if she was in pain. "It was long ago . . ." the abomination started to reply, then halted, shaking her head.

"It . . . wasn't . . . Malfoosh then, priestess. Mal'a'voselle . . . I think."

"Mal'a'voselle?"

"Lady, priestess, I do not know."

"Mal'a'voselle of what house?"

"House Amvas Tol!" the drider said, summoning some pride.

Minolin Fey turned a confused look to Saribel, who could only shrug, for she had never heard of such a house in Menzoberranzan.

"It was a long time ago, priestess," the drider explained. "In the time of the birth of the City of Spiders. My house did not survive."

Saribel and Minolin Fey exchanged another confused look, but Saribel nodded her acceptance of the claim. Mal'a'voselle was an almost unheard-of drow name now, but long ago, it was much more common. Still, driders did not live for millennia.

"Why are you here?" Minolin Fey demanded.

"I do not know why the great Queen of Spiders released us back into this world, priestess."

"You were in the Abyss?" Saribel asked, then bit it back and bowed to Minolin Fey for speaking out of turn. The Baenre priestess didn't seem concerned, however, for that was the obvious question.

"Serving, yes. We all were."

"But why then have you come? Why are you here, Malfoosh?" Minolin Fey reiterated.

"We are tasked with clearing the wood and the hills of all enemies."

"And we are your enemies?" the Baenre priestess asked with obvious incredulity.

"We did not know, priestess. We did not expect to see children of Lady Lolth. Who are you and why have you come? I must tell my matron, Zhindia."

Saribel swallowed hard at the mention of the matron of House

Melarn, and for a moment, she thought they might be in big trouble here.

"We are of Bregan D'aerthe," Minolin Fey lied.

"Bregan D'aerthe? I know not this house."

"It is not a house, but a scouting band available to all the matrons of Menzoberranzan," Minolin Fey explained. "We collect information and give it to the Ruling Council."

The drider seemed perplexed, but in the end simply shrugged.

"We have heard of trouble in the area and have come to see if the dwarves are exterminated, that Q'Xorlarrin can be given back to Matron Zeerith, as it should be," said Minolin Fey.

Saribel smiled at that, surprised by the Baenre priestess's mental quickness and at the tribute she had just given to her beloved Matron Zeerith. She looked to her brother, who was nodding, obviously impressed.

"Q'Xorlarrin? Of this, too, I know nothing."

"It does not matter," Minolin Fey assured the abomination.

"You should come and speak with—" Malfoosh began.

"We cannot," Minolin Fey interrupted with a snort. "We have much to do. What do you know of the dwarves?"

"They fight stubbornly, but the demons are upon them. They cannot hold for long."

"Good. Now go back to Matron Zhindia and tell her that many are watching her with interest."

The drider had no choice but to comply. To disobey a drow priestess was something that had long ago been beaten out of poor Mal'a'voselle, probably long before she had been turned into a tormented abomination.

To Saribel's surprise, as the driders fell back and she turned toward Minolin Fey, the Baenre priestess waved to her to be silent, then hustled her along, moving with the entire band back for the tunnels that would take them to the main drow force. It wasn't until they were well underground before Minolin Fey explained herself.

"Hundreds of them," she said, and Saribel's eyes widened.

"Hundreds of driders?" Ravel asked.

"Many hundreds," Kron Tlabbar replied. "They were all about us, flanked north and south. Huge bands of the abominations, all superbly armed."

"Sent from the Abyss to serve Matron Zhindia," said Minolin Fey, her voice thick with dread. "Released to her cause by Lady Lolth."

Why are we opposing her? Saribel thought, but wisely did not say— not to a Baenre priestess, at least!

"YOU SHOULD HAVE DESTROYED THEM! ALL OF THEM," MAtron Mez'Barris Armgo told the returning scout commanders.

"I tried, Matron," Malagdorl insisted, casting an angry side glance at Minolin Fey. "I was prevented from killing the abominable leader."

"Silence, child," ordered Matron Mother Quenthel Baenre, not taking her sharp gaze from Mez'Barris's adored grandson, not even to offer a glance to Matron Mez'Barris. "You are here only because I allow you to be here, and in this place, in this impromptu convening of the Ruling Council, it is not your place to speak."

Malagdorl moved as if to argue.

"At all," the Matron Mother warned. She turned to Minolin Fey, but then moved her gaze over priestess Saribel.

"There were hundreds of them," Saribel said, aiming the remark as much at Malagdorl as in response to the matron mother.

"Driders from another age," explained Minolin Fey. "Malfoosh, who was Mal'a'voselle Amvas Tol—"

Quenthel silenced her with an upraised hand. The matron mother closed her eyes then, and shut out the many whispered conversations occurring among the other matrons all about her. They were concerned, of course, and why would they not be?

Matron Mother Quenthel, who had been given the gift of Yvonnel's own memories, fell into that dark place in her mind now, considering the name. She smiled as her thoughts flew back across the centuries, across the millennia, to the fledgling days of the City of Spiders. Oh, what a grand time, full of chaos but full of hope!

"The weapon master of House Amvas Tol," she said, and all conversation stopped, and all waited with bated breath.

"A woman," Saribel said before she could stop herself.

Quenthel and the others stared at her, but the matron mother nodded, and Saribel took it as a signal that she should finish the thought.

"Mal'a'voselle," she said quietly.

"Women were often weapon masters in the early days," Matron Mother Quenthel explained to them. "We are the stronger sex, of course, and Lolth's divine gifts of magic were not then fully bestowed upon us. It was a different time.

"She was much like your own Uthegentel, Matron Mez'Barris," Quenthel went on. "A great and powerful warrior, fearless and clever, if I recall correctly. She would have had a promising future, had it not been for the sins of Matron Dunna'da Amvas. Alas, Mal'a'voselle was given as a gift to Lady Lolth right before the heretical weeping matron's wet eyes."

She looked at Mez'Barris and smiled widely, then turned about, letting all the others see that grin before finally settling it on Malagdorl, whom she knew was becoming a bit of a troublemaker. "Mal'a'voselle was given over into abomination by my mother, Matron Mother Yvonnel, as one of her first acts after accepting the rule of the city by edict of the Spider Queen. She made of Mal'a'voselle Amvas Tol a drider. Oftentimes it is a waste, particularly with promising but headstrong young women."

Quenthel's smile only widened as Malagdorl shrank back.

"Hundreds of driders?" Matron Zeerith asked. "Driders returned from the arms of Lolth herself? If this is true, must we assume that Matron Zhindia is in the highest graces of the Spider Queen?"

"If this is true, we must reconsider everything," Matron Mez'Barris stated flatly. "We could join with Matron Zhindia and finish what she has started, returning Q'Xorlarrin to Matron Zeerith and subsequently properly rewarding Matron Zhindia for her foresight."

"Properly rewarding?" the matron mother echoed sarcastically.

"Zhindia would demand the title of matron mother if all that you assume is true."

"And any who sought to oppose that would fall from Lolth's favor and so would be an enemy of us all," Mez'Barris returned, a clear threat.

But Quenthel only smiled again, even snorted as if the whole thing was an absurd proposition.

"Be at ease, Matron," she answered Mez'Barris's tightened face. To Minolin Fey, she asked, "Do they know who you are, or under what banner you march?"

The priestess withered under the glare of the matrons. "I . . . I . . ." she stuttered, trying to find her way to best answer.

"You are a Baenre, dear," the matron mother said. "You were sent to lead the group because of that fact. You did well to hold back the impetuous Malagdorl—you likely saved the entire party, to say nothing of his family's reputation, and thus returned to serve proper warning. Speak freely. Do the driders know your banner?"

"No," Minolin Fey replied, straightening herself and forcing strength into her voice. "I told the drider who called herself Malfoosh that we were of Bregan D'aerthe, scouting the land after reports of conflict."

That caught all the matrons by surprise and incited many whispers, some nods, a couple of gasps, but most importantly, a wide smile from Matron Mother Quenthel.

"Clever," Quenthel replied. "Now Matron Zhindia will be chasing ghosts."

"What do you know, Matron Mother?" Mez'Barris demanded.

"Matron Zhindia is no friend to Jarlaxle's band," Quenthel explained. "She hates them above all others for what they did to her house and family. She herself was killed—albeit briefly—by Drizzt Do'Urden, and her favorite child, Yazhin, was murdered by Jarlaxle's other associate, the human, and in such a way that she could not be restored to life. Jarlaxle was with them in that raid, you remember. Matron Zhindia will not forgive that. Not ever. She will be quick to believe the story woven by High Priestess Minolin Fey Baenre, because she desperately wants it to be true."

Mez'Barris nodded, unable to argue the logic.

"Well done, Minolin Fey Baenre," Matron Mother Quenthel said, emphasizing that surname, making it clear that Minolin Fey's quick thinking had brought them advantage—advantage that might have been naught but disaster if Matron Mez'Barris's grandson had taken the lead and started a war.

"In any case, Matron Zhindia will know of us soon enough," Matron Zeerith put in, verbally and physically separating Mez'Barris and Quenthel by gliding her magical disk in between them. "We should plot our next march."

"Send only your finest scouts," Matron Mother Quenthel told Minolin Fey. "Only the finest, and with them means to magically return to us if they become compromised. I'll not have Matron Zhindia know of our arrival for as long as we can keep the secret."

"Even if she is in the grace of Lolth?" Mez'Barris asked.

"Yes," Quenthel answered without hesitation.

"My scouts will tell you all regarding the lands above and about Gauntlgrym," Minolin assured them.

"Q'Xorlarrin," corrected Matron Zeerith. She turned a stern gaze upon Matron Mother Quenthel. "If Matron Zhindia is in the good graces of the Spider Queen, if Lolth herself sanctions and aids in the march of House Melarn to turn this demon force against our enemies, why is there any doubt remaining, or any hesitation? My wizards will open the deep door and we should sweep through the dwarves, reclaiming Q'Xorlarrin for Menzoberranzan and snatching it right out from under Matron Zhindia's grasp, that we might share in her glory. The dwarven forces are in the upper chambers battling demons. We can push through and take the place beneath them before they even realize that which has come against them."

"We will talk" was all that Quenthel would return, and she looked from Zeerith to Mez'Barris repeatedly, measuring them. "Just we two."

Mez'Barris's expression had brightened at Zeerith's remarks, but then darkened, Quenthel noted, and expectedly so. Having the two powerful matrons conversing in private was not something the Matron of House Armgo would want.

Particularly since it was obvious to all that she, Mez'Barris, would be the topic of that private conversation.

"BREGAN D'AERTHE?" MATRON ZHINDIA MELARN SAID, her voice a husky whisper, as if she were afraid that letting her voice get out of control would send her entire being out of control.

"It is a scouting band," the drider began.

"I know what it is, you idiot," Zhindia snapped, and Malfoosh sucked in her breath. As she let it out, it was accompanied by a low hum that seemed a growl.

"The priestess said Bregan D'aerthe," the drider insisted.

"Where are they?"

Malfoosh shrugged. "They left."

"You let them leave? You did not even follow them?"

"I am not to question the words of a priestess, Matron Zhindia."

"My orders are above hers!"

"Of course, but I had no orders from Matron Zhindia when I encountered the drow."

"I told you to clear the forest."

"Of drow? That is a different matter, Matron Zhindia," Malfoosh reminded. "I, we, are driders, serving penance for crimes against Lady Lolth. We cannot strike at the children of Lolth."

"Unless I tell you to do so."

"Yes, by your precise words, Matron. But you had not told us to do so."

Zhindia threw up her arms and issued a frustrated growl of her own. "Bregan D'aerthe is not allied with our cause. They oppose us in Luskan even now, you idiots."

"Who was this priestess?" asked First Priestess Kyrnill Melarn.

"She did not offer her name, lady," said Malfoosh. "Nor did the other priestess standing with her."

"Two priestesses?" Kyrnill pressed.

"At least. There were others wearing the robes among those many in the ranks."

"Other women?" Zhindia said, catching on and following the reasoning.

"Yes, and men, and a warrior of great strength who battled me trident to trident until the priestess stood us down."

"Zaknafei—" Kyrnill started to remark, but she paused.

"A trident?" Zhindia asked. "Tell me more about him, every detail."

Malfoosh did as instructed, then was dismissed, leaving Zhindia alone with Kyrnill and Charri Hunzrin.

"That had to be Malagdorl Armgo," Kyrnill said.

"They have sent a scouting party to look in on us and determine our progress," Charri said.

"Just a scouting party?" Matron Zhindia asked, walking out a few steps and staring toward the east, where the encounter had taken place. "A scouting party all the way from Menzoberranzan with the weapon master of the city's second house? I cannot imagine that Matron Mez'Barris would put her cherished Malagdorl at such a risk as that."

"Then what?" asked Charri.

"They see that our victory is at hand, perhaps," said Zhindia. "They have rushed to steal my glory." She spun about to look sharply at the other two women.

"It will not be so."

"REIN IN YOUR AMBITIONS AT THIS TIME," MATRON Mother Quenthel told Matron Zeerith when they were alone soon after the gathering with the scouting party. "We know not how this will play."

"We know not?" old Zeerith scoffed. "An army of driders? Hundreds? A horde of demons continually gating in more monsters daily from the Abyss? The dwarves are doomed, the city of Luskan has already fallen. It is as you predicted back before we departed Menzoberranzan: Matron Zhindia will win."

"If she is to win, then we must be a large part of it," Quenthel replied.

"Indeed! So let us beat her to the prize, and take the Great Forge of Gauntlgrym and depose King Bruenor with all haste and with no mercy."

But Quenthel Baenre shook her head. "*If* she is to win."

"How can she not?" Zeerith asked.

Quenthel was beginning to sort for those exact answers but wasn't ready to explain further.

"What is there then to know?" asked Zeerith.

"Everything. When all seems plain and clear, it cannot be. Have you not served Lolth, the Lady of Chaos, long enough to realize that? Do not be blinded by your ambition to return to Gauntlgrym. That will not happen. Our position on the surface in any case is too compromised now. The lords of all the lands have no doubt turned their eyes to the northern reaches of the Sword Coast, with demons roaming free and Luskan in flames."

"The flames will quiet quickly, and few have ever looked to Luskan for stability, and fewer still, by all of our scouting, have formed any real alliances with King Bruenor."

Quenthel didn't disagree. "It does not matter," she replied. "We cannot be planning the return of Q'Xorlarrin at this time, whatever the outcome of Matron Zhindia's war or our march. No matter how the will of Lolth plays out, neither of us can even think of sending your family back here. The dust will be long in settling here and, more importantly, in Menzoberranzan."

"You mean that you will need me there in Menzoberranzan to support you against the rise of House Melarn," Zeerith stated flatly. "Matron Mez'Barris won't stand with you, of course, not if she believes Matron Zhindia in the highest graces of Lolth and sees a chance, at long, long last, to be rid of subjugation at the hands of House Baenre."

"Subjugation? A curious word. Is it a notion Matron Zeerith, whom I have rescued from shame and defeat, shares?"

The old Zeerith wasn't often shaken, or at least never showed it, but at that moment, she nearly tumbled off her floating disk, her jaw hanging open.

"Of course not," Quenthel said, taking the pressure off Zeerith. "You have ever been wise enough to see House Baenre as a benefit, and as the house that rewards its allies. You would do well to remember that with every word going forward in this transitional time. No more mention of Q'Xorlarrin. Even if King Bruenor Battlehammer and all of his dwarves are obliterated, even if Gauntlgrym is emptied of all living things and the Great Forge remains there for the taking, Q'Xorlarrin is not to be mentioned."

"Surely you would not leave such a treasure unused?"

"Surely," Quenthel replied. "And surely the magical movement of wizards, of which you possess many of the finest, will be critical in our using it without drawing attention."

"And without weakening your order in Menzoberranzan," Zeerith added.

Quenthel nodded.

"So I will remain at House Do'Urden, and you will secretly use my wizards to bring smiths to the Forge of Gauntlgrym?"

"And you will be well rewarded," Quenthel promised.

"I wish to be elevated within the Ruling Council. I want my place back, and with an eye, always an eye, to becoming the penultimate house of Menzoberranzan."

Quenthel gave only a slight nod in reply.

"Assure me that House Xorlarrin will not be taken for granted when the victory here is secured and House Baenre holds its position," Zeerith demanded.

Quenthel paused, forcing herself to remain tactful in the face of a demand from another matron. "House Do'Urden," she corrected, "until I determine otherwise."

"Of course," Zeerith agreed, but not without a clench of her jaw, as if the name itself insulted her.

"We will see how it plays, but your house remains my most important ally," said Quenthel. "I assure you that I will not forget, should it come to that."

"Can there be any doubt?"

"We worship Lolth, the Lady of Chaos, dear Matron Zeerith. There is always doubt."

Matron Zeerith Do'Urden gave a helpless snort at that, then willed her magical disk out of the extradimensional chamber the matron mother was using as her audience hall. No sooner had Zeerith departed than First Priestess Sos'Umptu and Quenthel's daughter Myrineyl entered through another magical portal.

"I do not trust her," Myrineyl said. "Her ambition is greater than her loyalty."

"Then she is a fine matron," Sos'Umptu said.

"Her daughter, the priestess Saribel, would be more easily persuaded and held in thrall," Myrineyl said bluntly. "Matron Zeerith is old and too endeared to . . ." She stopped and cast an awkward glance at her mother.

"To Matron Mother Yvonnel the Eternal," Quenthel finished for her.

Myrineyl sucked in her breath.

"It is good and honest reasoning," said Quenthel, calming the woman. "But do not speak of such things yet." Her tone made it clear that she wasn't scolding Myrineyl as much as warning her not to get too far ahead of herself.

Depending on how things up here fell, Quenthel knew that Zeerith might have to be replaced. She hoped it wouldn't come to that, but she reminded herself often that Zeerith was old, very old, and though she remained an ally of House Baenre, her real loyalty was indeed to Matron Mother Yvonnel. And no matter how Matron Zeerith tried to parse her words, ever were they filled with a level of condescension toward Yvonnel's daughters. Zeerith had known Quenthel and Sos'Umptu since their youngest days—indeed, she had been Sos'Umptu's first tutor.

"At least Matron Vadalma Tlabbar will not abandon us, no matter the outcome here," Sos'Umptu said. "She rebuffed Matron Zhindia on this very quest, and thus does she know that ever-vicious Matron Zhindia will show her no mercy if she claims victory."

"Nor will House Fey-Branche abandon us," Myrineyl added. "Matron Byrtyn knows that without House Baenre, her seat on the Ruling

Council would be given to another—almost surely to House Hunzrin if Matron Zhindia—"

"Do you think they matter?" Matron Mother Quenthel cut her short. "Either of them? If Matron Zhindia leaves here as the ultimate victor, she will find powerful allies, including Matron Mez'Barris."

"Matron Zeerith is no friend to the Melarni, or to the Armgos," said Myrineyl.

"But both Matrons Zeerith and Mez'Barris understand well that their ambitions are forever stunted as long as House Baenre rules," Sos'Umptu said.

"And that has been the truth since the days when Menzoberranzan was very young, and Baenre's reign will not end when I am Matron Mother," Quenthel declared.

The other two nodded.

"Matron Zhindia cannot win here," Quenthel decided.

"Then we take the dwarven stronghold before she can get through?" asked Myrineyl.

"Maybe not," the matron mother replied, thinking aloud, falling into the memories of Yvonnel the Eternal once more to find some answers.

"An army of driders, gifted from the Abyss?" Sos'Umptu replied doubtfully. "Two retrievers given to her by the handmaidens of Lolth?"

"Do you think you know the will of Lolth?" Matron Mother Quenthel asked slyly.

That gave Sos'Umptu pause, but Myrineyl, so much less experienced, asked, "Isn't it obvious?"

With a look to the matron mother, which elicited a nod from Quenthel, Sos'Umptu offered to young Myrineyl the most basic understanding of the truth of the Lolthian drow: "The only thing that is ever obvious from the Demon Queen of Spiders is, that which is obvious is not."

CHAPTER 11

Around the Edges of Darkness

The large gate of Thornhold was opened just a bit and was stuck, but there was still a wide enough gap for the companions to slip through one at a time.

"The spider broke the gate," Regis reasoned from the bend in the great hinge, for what else might have done such damage? "It's still in here," he warned. "I don't want to see that thing up close."

"None of us do," Yvonnel told him, but she was looking more at Entreri as she spoke.

When he glanced at the assassin, Regis understood Yvonnel's apparent concern, for the man was wobbling with every step, muttering under his breath, and seeming as if he might fall over at any moment.

"It is, or was, a retriever, as I have told you," Yvonnel went on. "If it remains, then its focus is solely on Drizzt Do'Urden. It is no threat to us unless we get between it and Drizzt. For the sake of your friend, I hope it is still in there, still hunting."

"And then we kill it?" Regis asked.

Yvonnel snorted at that preposterous thought. "In that case, we try to find Drizzt first, and we help him get far ahead of the monster." She blew out a long sigh. "I should have done that on the road when we met up with him, but I hadn't the spells prepared. Nor would it have been a safe prospect, as the retriever would go for him, wherever I put him, and would destroy everything in its path even if it had to cut a trench across half of Toril."

"Sounds lovely," Dahlia muttered. She skipped over to Entreri and bolstered him.

Yvonnel nodded and led the way, fearlessly going through the narrow opening into the courtyard. She peeked her head back out. "The spider is gone."

"In the building," Athrogate offered. "The tunnels here're bigger than ye think."

Yvonnel, her face grim, shook her head, and when the others came through, they understood, for there in the middle of the courtyard was a huge, bubbling mass of black ooze, the now too familiar remains of a demon's departure from this plane of existence.

Not a sound beyond their own footsteps followed the friends to that bubbling goo. The place was dead, the silence profound. They just knew it.

A closer look at the demonic detritus confirmed Yvonnel's claims, for the scar was decidedly spider-shaped, with the eight legs distinctly visible. In front of the beastly remains, the ground was torn, as if hit by a ray of some sort, and there were clearly footprints—humanoid footprints, bare feet—leading *into* it. And there, too, the tattered remains of clothing and boots the friends knew well.

"Drizzt," Regis mumbled, his voice breaking.

"Is he dead, then?" Dahlia asked, and she too seemed shaky.

Quietly, tears rolled down the halfling's cheeks. Athrogate looked stunned, his earlier grief seemingly multiplied by the thought of Drizzt's departure. And Artemis—still shaken from his tortuous cocoon—bowed his head as he put his arm around Dahlia.

Yvonnel realized then how profoundly this rogue dark elf had touched so many people—so many disparate people, with different values and core beliefs. Even Artemis Entreri! It hadn't mattered whether they were openly goodly and kind folks, like Regis, or those with far more sinister backgrounds, or those, like Athrogate, caught somewhere in the middle. All of them wobbled now, and Regis fell to his knees and buried his face in his hands.

The connection to this drow went beyond mere friendship, Yvonnel recognized, and understood, because what Drizzt had given to them over the years could not be measured so simply as that—indeed, the word "friend" seemed empty in the face of this. What Drizzt had given them was universal, and across races—halfling, elf, human, dwarf, and drow, too, she knew, for in watching Regis fighting bravely and failing against his overwhelming pain, Yvonnel saw the foreshadowing of Jarl-axle's response. Above all else, Drizzt had given to those around him honesty and heart, and he had tried, ever tried, to do what he believed was right.

The legacy of that touched Yvonnel profoundly in that moment, and she, too, who hardly knew the unusual drow ranger, choked back tears, overwhelmed by the display of true loss playing out before her, particularly that of Regis, the gentle halfling who had faced Sharon with a smile.

Her heart was warmed by it all, for this seemed a display of justice to her—honest grief, generous grief, offered without any expectation of personal gain.

She thought Menzoberranzan a cold and heartless place indeed.

"It's a big place," Athrogate said again, shaking himself with a bit of hope. He stepped over and hoisted Regis back onto his feet. "Come on then, Rumblebelly. We're not givin' up, and find your faith in Drizzt, what. I ain't seein' no blood, and ain't for doubting that durned elf. Not what we do. We fight. We fight until we can'no' fight no more."

"Don't be the fool," Dahlia scolded, too harshly, Yvonnel thought.

"Ready to turn and cry and run at first sign, are ye?"

"He's gone."

"Y'ain't knowing any such thing!"

"Then why did the retriever leave?" Dahlia asked.

"Might be that the drow killed it to death in battle!" Athrogate insisted.

"A retriever?" Yvonnel asked gently, shaking her head.

"Don't ye never doubt the boy," Athrogate said. "Seen him kill bigger'n that."

Regis perked up at that. He took a deep breath, sniffled once to clear his nose, and squared his shoulders.

"Go and look, then," Yvonnel told the two. "Call out if you find anything." She tried to be encouraging, for these dearest of friends to Drizzt deserved no less, but she heard her own voice and understood the unmistakable thickness of the resignation there.

Athrogate and Regis started for the blasted door of the keep. Dahlia, after helping Entreri sit down on the ground, rushed to join them.

"You have had better tendays," Yvonnel said to Entreri, walking over to join him.

"Just pain," he said. "The whole time I was in there, and lingering now. I couldn't get used to it. Unspeakable pain, unrelenting and undiminishing."

Yvonnel nodded and put a hand on his shoulder.

"Take my dagger and thrust it into my heart," he asked her. "Draw out my soul itself, send me to oblivion, I beg, for if that is what eternity has planned for me, I would rather be nothingness."

"You think your book written."

"I just read it. It doesn't end well."

"It doesn't have to be that way, Artemis Entreri," Yvonnel assured him. "Those were only the chapters you've already lived. There are pages still yet to be filled."

"What do you know?" he asked doubtfully.

"I know that if your fate was sealed, if your story fully told, Sharon would have had no reason to let you return."

"Maybe just to torment me more with the knowledge of what was to come."

"No, that is not her calling. Even though she was out of place these last days, such meaningless teasing is not her role in the multiverse."

"Her role?"

"Her role within the heart of every reasoning being. She is the facilitator of judgment, but not the judge. There is no enjoyment for her either way, the good or the bad. There is no preference."

"Then who is the judge?" Entreri asked. "Some god I never acknowledged? Some great superior being who makes of us pawns in his own strange game?"

"You are your own judge," Yvonnel explained, "in places within your heart, soul, and memory where you cannot hide. You know this. Above all others, in those dark and private places, you know what you deserve."

Entreri's snort was caught somewhere between derision and resignation. "Did Drizzt deserve his fate?" he asked.

"We don't know what fate that is."

"Don't we?" Entreri asked, nodding toward the spider-shaped goo.

"In the afterlife," Yvonnel replied. "Are we speaking of divine justice or of the foibles of mortal beings? I doubt they are much the same. Every day, many get things they do not deserve, good and bad. Every day. A thousand times every day."

She paused and spent a few moments just studying the man. He had been through so much—his pain was obvious. His face was scrunched up in a mask of anger, but there were tears in his eyes as well.

"You cared for him," she said.

"It's complicated."

"Is it? Or do you make it complicated to cover your own . . . ego?"

Entreri looked up at her, his expression dismissive, but only for a moment. "Looking at Drizzt was like looking into a mirror, but one with different lighting. His skin was dark, mine light. But his soul . . ." He paused and laughed helplessly. "He once said, so I was told, that in looking at me, at what I had become, he feared that it was what he might have become. There are no cocoons of stinging wasps awaiting Drizzt Do'Urden, I am sure."

"And is that why you lament your history?"

"No," he answered sharply before she had even finished the sentence. "No," he repeated more softly. "I regret a lot, but because of what I have done to others, my own fate be damned . . . if it is damned."

"Well, then, perhaps, Artemis Entreri, Drizzt showed you what you hoped to become, in some ways, at least."

She patted him on the shoulder and stood up, turning about. She closed her eyes and cast a spell of detection, seeking the radiations of magic. She was surprised when she did indeed sense something of interest, and she followed the feeling into the keep.

The place, too, felt dead to her, and she saw down one hall the bodies of slain dwarves. Broken walls and widened doorways showed her that Drizzt had led the retriever into this complex, forcing the demon construct to do some of the cleansing that was much needed here.

She heard the voices of her friends down a different hall, moving away from her, but nothing seemed amiss. She went back fully into her spell and it guided her to a wall, which at first confused her. When she got very close, she noted a crack in the stone and managed to wriggle her finger in, feeling about and then pulling out a silver chain upon which was set a whistle shaped like a unicorn.

"Andahar," she said, and for the first time she too found her voice cracking. Even in his last moments, Drizzt had thought of another, of this magical mount, and so he had stowed his chain out of the way.

She started to pocket it, but changed her mind when she heard the others approaching, and instead put it back into the crevice.

"For you when you return, Drizzt Do'Urden," she whispered, though she knew that to be all but impossible.

She went back outside to Entreri and waited for the others to arrive.

"Nothing," Athrogate said.

"There's a lower level," Dahlia added, casting a glare at the dwarf. "*He* would not go down there, nor would he allow us to."

"Shut yer face, girl," Athrogate said.

"Drizzt might be down there," Regis argued.

"He is not," Yvonnel said with finality. "I have used my magic. Drizzt is not here. He is gone."

"Just . . . gone?" Athrogate said.

"Taken to the Abyss?" Dahlia asked.

"Then we go to the Abyss and get him," Athrogate said.

"Aye!" Regis agreed.

Yvonnel held up her hand to silence them all. She looked at Regis, at his eagerness to run to the Abyss in pursuit of his lost friend. She doubted she could dissuade him, even if she could properly relate the hopelessness of such a venture. He needed this, she realized. He needed to feel like he was doing something, anything, to try to bring back that rogue drow.

Yvonnel had thought she had a good measure of Drizzt's impact, but now she understood she had underestimated him, even though she had known there was something special about him, about the honest life he had lived. She wondered if anyone would ever so lament her passing, would ever wear a mask of determination and pain as she saw now on the face of Regis.

"In time," she said at length. "We will learn what we may, and enlist the proper and powerful allies. I have been there to the Abyss, or have memories of my namesake's ventures in the swirling smoke, at least. It is not a place one goes with any hope of returning."

"But you have been there," Regis argued. "Or your namesake had, as you just said."

"As the guest of a demon queen, not as her enemy."

"You think Lolth herself has taken Drizzt?"

"It would take a being near her equal to grant a retriever—nay, two retrievers."

"We're not going to get him back," Dahlia whispered.

"Maybe you're not, but I am," Regis snapped at her, an uncharacteristic edge to his voice.

Dahlia returned a hard glare, while Entreri and Athrogate expressed pity for the despondent halfling.

"I'm right, though," Dahlia said. "We're not going to get him back."

They all turned to Yvonnel for some response.

She wanted to offer the one they needed to hear—three of them, at least, for she could not quite gauge Dahlia. She was surprised at how much she wanted to do that. But in the end, she found she couldn't deceive them, and she knew the truth.

"No," she agreed. "We're not."

"GROMPH WILL NOT ANSWER," PENELOPE HARPELL TOLD Catti-brie.

The younger woman sighed, her concern mounting. Her belly was large now, the child very active as her pregnancy neared its end. She wanted to find Drizzt more than anything in the world, to be with her husband, her baby's father, when she gave birth to their child.

Our child.

But where was he? For all Catti-brie's magical attempts, for all the messages Penelope had dispatched, for all the efforts of the other Harpells—truly her friends—she had no word at all of Drizzt.

"Gromph Baenre has an answer, though," Catti-brie reasoned. "The gates are not working, and that almost certainly comes right from the roots of the Hosttower of the Arcane."

"Or Mithral Hall itself," Penelope said, wincing in anticipation that her words would surely worry Catti-brie.

"Have you sent a message to the dwarves?"

"That is more difficult. Our scrying has shown us that the area about Mithral Hall is overrun. Demon hordes and drow."

"Is not Luskan also overrun?" Catti-brie reminded her. "The fleet . . ."

"The Hosttower is distinct and very receptive to magical messages," Penelope replied. "The dwarves are deep in their hole, and likely engaged in fierce battle."

"We need to open the gateways," Catti-brie said determinedly. "And we need, most of all, to learn if their collapse portends something more dire. And we must be fast in our research, for if the Hosttower has weakened its magical energy to Gauntlgrym, the primordial might shake itself free once more. The last time that happened, Neverwinter City was obliterated."

"I will go to Gromph," Penelope announced.

"You don't even know if the Hosttower remains intact, or under his control."

"Someone has to find out."

Catti-brie took Penelope by the arm. "I can'no' lose you," she quietly said. "I know not what I've already lost."

"Old Kipper will take me there, and we'll both have spells ready to remove ourselves quickly, if necessary. I promise."

Catti-brie nodded and let go of Penelope's arm—and Penelope swung about to wrap the very pregnant woman in a tight hug. "I'll find Drizzt," she whispered in Catti-brie's ear. "I promise."

Catti-brie flashed her a smile when she pulled back and turned for the door, but it was a strained one to be sure. She was here, preparing to give birth, and it seemed as if all the world about her had gone crazy.

She had never felt so helpless in her life, not even when she had been a prisoner of Artemis Entreri those many years before, being dragged across Faerun in pursuit of Regis.

She held that memory close now, a vivid reminder that she and her friends, the Companions of the Hall, had been battling long odds—and winning—for a very, very long time.

"BY THE GODS," REGIS MUTTERED, LYING ATOP AN EM-bankment along with his four companions. Below them, a formation of huge driders, perhaps a hundred strong, crossed a wide field. The friends had been traveling for nearly a tenday, a difficult journey both emotionally and, especially for Artemis Entreri, physically. Yvonnel had done much to aid in their progress, with not just spells of healing and spells to provide nourishment, but also spells to propel them on their way. Though not with teleportation or anything of that sort. She wanted them all to digest the new reality fully, and she also wanted to get a good understand of the disposition of the lands between Thornhold and Gauntlgrym.

"Lots o' demons," said Athrogate.

"Those aren't demons," Yvonnel corrected. "The demons, I suspect, are inside Gauntlgrym. This is the vanguard of the drow force."

"I thought driders were rare," said Dahlia.

"So did I," Yvonnel replied. "I have no answers for this."

"How about the big answer to the big question?" asked Athrogate. "Like, how're we meanin' to get to them doors?"

He nodded out across the field, but none had to follow that

movement to know what he meant. Beyond the field lay some trees, and beyond that wood the ruined, and now clearly occupied, halfling village of Bleeding Vines. To the right, south of the village, stood the empty tram station, the exit and entrance tunnels to Gauntlgrym evident along the side of the rising mountain.

"Getting to them won't do us any good if we're marching down into a horde of demons," Regis remarked.

"Not seein' a better way," said the dwarf.

"You have nothing, lady?" the halfling asked Yvonnel.

"I have something," she replied, "but I had hoped to gather more information before using it."

She rolled onto her back then and began whispering, too low for any of the others to make out the words. They started to understand when her magical scouts, crystal-like birds, began to fly in, perching on her chest and whispering into her ears, one by one. It went on for a long while, when finally an exasperated Yvonnel sat up.

"The land about us is all lost," she announced.

"Yeah, we seen that," said Athrogate. "Don't take a bird to know."

"All about us," the drow woman clarified. "Here to Luskan, all of the coast, all of the Crags. Port Llast labors under the crack of gnoll whips."

"Gnolls?" Athrogate snorted. "We should go kill 'em all to death, just because they're gnolls."

"Demons are about the village before us, but mostly the major fiends," Yvonnel went on. "I expect that the lesser monsters are below, likely among the higher levels of Gauntlgrym. King Bruenor is sorely pressed, if not already conquered."

"So what do we do?" Regis asked.

Yvonnel shook her head, mulling it over.

"We go in," said Athrogate.

"And if there is no refuge within?" Dahlia asked. "If it is all demons and drow?"

"Then we go right through and out the other side," Yvonnel announced. "Come now, down the hill." She stood up and paced down the embankment, the others following, Athrogate bolstering Entreri, who was still a bit unsteady on his swollen legs.

"Join hands," Yvonnel instructed them. "Artemis Entreri to me."

"We goin' to run again?" Athrogate asked, for the few times they had done this in the last days Yvonnel had cast a dweomer to speed them on their way.

Artemis Entreri groaned. These speeding travels were draining his limited strength.

"This is different," Yvonnel promised, mostly to the battered man. She took up his hand. "Athrogate, take his other hand. Then you, Regis, then Dahlia. No matter what happens, do not let go. Any of you."

"Or we trip and fall?" asked the dwarf, who errantly believed he had heard this speech before.

"Or you will become substantial in the midst of a thousand fiends, and not I, nor even your god, could save you," said Yvonnel, and as soon as the living chain was formed, she began spellcasting.

"What're—" Athrogate started.

"Just shut up and hold on," Dahlia told him. "For our sake and your own, hold on."

Dahlia's voice thinned as she spoke, became insubstantial, became as the wind in the ears of her companions.

For soon they were the wind and little more, a cloud of swirling vapors. Curiously, Regis still felt the grip of Dahlia and of Athrogate, though he had no hand that he could determine. But they were joined, locked, and he was glad of it as the cloud began to drift, then move with purpose to Yvonnel's tug—a pull both physical, somehow, and telepathic. All as one, they swept up over the embankment and down to the field. Regis had to strain to hold focus when Yvonnel took them right across the formation of driders, weaving through the abominations as if they were no more than a cloud, and indeed, they weren't. Still, more than one drider took note of their passing, though none showed any understanding of what this strange fog might be.

This is what it's like when a ghost passes by, the halfling thought. *A chill breeze.*

Into Bleeding Vines, they passed among drow, and these enemies seemed more aware than the driders had been, several hopping and turning, calling out to priestesses, and Regis saw one, then another, began casting some spell.

Yvonnel moved them more swiftly then, because she was afraid, Regis knew. Could these priestesses pull them out of her wind-walk? Oh, the horror, to be dropped into the middle of this ferocious army!

The halfling relaxed only a bit when they soared into the tunnel, speeding down into the darkness, then, soon after, into the grand entry cavern, the place thick with demons and driders. Regis's heart sank when they crossed to the small pond, then drifted over the pond and into the complex proper, to find the place also teeming with monstrous denizens of the lower planes.

Through the rooms, down the stairs, to the great chamber separating the top levels from the main complex, and down there, too, demons roamed.

The sound of fighting made the halfling's spirits leap as they passed from that huge chamber into the tighter ways leading to the Great Forge. Soon they crossed the battleground, dwarven side-slinger catapults blasting minor demons to pieces, dwarven soldiers holding their ground, beating back the press of the horde.

Then it was all dwarves again, clerics tending to the wounded, reinforcements ready for their turn at the front lines. Beyond that, though, Gauntlgrym, King Bruenor's Gauntlgrym, remained!

They came to a stop in a tunnel with a pair of dwarven sentries, near to the main chambers of the Gauntlgrym leaders, and there, some distance from the two who guarded an ornate door that Regis knew well, Yvonnel released her spell.

The five companions became corporeal in a flash, all but Yvonnel stumbling a bit from the stark transition.

"What ho!" the dwarves yelled, lowering their pikes and readying a charge.

"Be easy, my friends," said Yvonnel. "You know me, a friend of Drizzt and of Jarlaxle."

"And me!" Regis announced, rushing around to put himself between the dwarves and his companions.

"Rumblebelly!" the two dwarves cried in unison.

"Aye," Regis replied. "You must take us to King Bruenor at once. And to Lady Donnola Topolino—please tell me that my wife is safe."

"Aye, Rumblebelly," one of the dwarves replied. "She's as well as any of us, which ain't so well, ye might be guessin'."

Regis of course understood that to be true enough, but his relief was profound. He had just lost Drizzt—he couldn't bear to lose his beloved Donnola, too!

A KNOCK HAD CATTI-BRIE LEAPING UP, OR RATHER, ROLL-ing carefully from her couch and moving as fast as she could manage for her door. She pulled it open, expecting Penelope with news from Luskan, but found instead a tall, thin man dressed in simple light-brown robes.

"Brother Afafrenfere?" she asked, surprised.

"I am formally named as a master now, but yes, good lady." He looked at her very swollen abdomen. "I trust that you are well?"

"I am."

He nodded and smiled warmly, his gaze locked on her belly.

"Can I help you?" she asked, feeling a bit unnerved. "I mean . . . please, do come in."

"Thank you, lady. I am looking for Drizzt. And I beg of you, pardon my surprise and intrigue here. I did not mean . . ."

"Yes, brother, the child is Drizzt's."

Afafrenfere locked eyes with Catti-brie, his jaw hanging open. "He . . . he only mentioned that he could not immediately return with me to the Monastery of the Yellow Rose when last I spoke with him to extend Grandmaster Kane's invitation. I had thought something amiss."

"Well, so it is."

"Hardly amiss!" the monk replied, his arms coming forward as if he wanted to hug Catti-brie but couldn't quite figure out if he should.

She stepped forward and initiated a full hug.

"Oh, but a child of two such heroes will be the grandest . . ." Afafrenfere stuttered, his voice breaking just a bit. "A human and a drow?"

"Half elves are not so uncommon," Catti-brie reminded him.

"But half drow? I have never heard . . ." Afafrenfere said. He shook his head suddenly and quite emphatically, waving his hands as if trying to take back the words, and Catti-brie knew that he had recognized the growing scowl on her face.

"I can only imagine the beauty of this child," Afafrenfere cried, and he surely seemed sincere.

"Fear not, brother, I understand your surprise, and your hesitance," she said generously.

"No, lady, if you think it hesitance, then I have misrepresented that which is in my heart," the monk replied. "This is glorious news, and the child will be wonderful. And beautiful."

"And shunned?"

The monk's eyes widened. "Never!"

Catti-brie smiled to relieve the tension, and in truth, she was just teasing the exuberant Afafrenfere. She knew, certainly so, the trials her half-human, half-drow child would face, and knew, too, that no child born to any Waterdhavian lady or Damaran queen would come into the world with a larger and more wonderful group of supporters to chase away any who could not see past the unusual combination of its heritage.

"May your claim prove true," she said.

"Oh, it shall."

"So, if you've come to entice Drizzt to your monastery, know that I'll not hear of it. And I fear he could not, anyway, for a darkness has come again—or perhaps it is the same darkness, over and over, relentless and destructive."

"No, of course he could not, and word of the growing turmoil in the region has reached us in Damara. But that is not why I've journeyed this far west. I must speak with Drizzt at once."

"He isn't here," Catti-brie admitted. "He is in Gauntlgrym, fighting beside King Bruenor."

She noted the blood draining from Afafrenfere's face.

"What do you know, brother?"

"Perhaps nothing."

"Tell me! Has Gauntlgrym fallen?"

"I have no knowledge of Gauntlgrym, lady, on my word."

"Then what? Why have you come?"

Afafrenfere swallowed hard. "Grandmaster Kane . . ." He paused and seemed to be searching for the proper words. "Grandmaster Kane sensed something. I know not how to describe it. A transcendence of the mortal body. Like death, but not so."

Catti-brie's face screwed up in obvious confusion. As a powerful priestess, she knew of things like plane-walking and astral projection, where a powerful spellcaster could transfer herself to another plane of existence, but she was fairly certain that Afafrenfere was speaking of something else.

"It is almost certainly nothing of concern," the monk said. "I only mention it because it is something that would likely interest Drizzt after his long hours of training with the Grandmaster of Flowers."

"Perhaps Grandmaster Kane thought that the discovery of this sensation of his would tempt Drizzt back to the monastery," Catti-brie offered.

"I am sure that's it," said Afafrenfere.

Catti-brie started to press for more of an explanation, but Penelope Harpell appeared at the opened door, hustling inside. She glanced at Afafrenfere only briefly, with just a slight nod to acknowledge his presence.

"I would speak with you alone," she told Catti-brie.

"Master Afafrenfere has come here in search of Drizzt," Catt-brie replied. "I suspect his road beside us is only now just begun."

Penelope looked at him and offered another nod, then said, her expression grim, "Gromph would not permit me entrance."

"The Hosttower of the Arcane?" Afafrenfere asked.

"His extravagant quarters," she clarified. "His door was closed to me." She turned to Catti-brie. "Your old acquaintances, Lady Avelyere and Lord Parise Ulfbinder, answered my call and took me into Avelyere's chambers to parlay. We spoke only briefly, because Archmage Gromph was not pleased that I had even been allowed into the Hosttower. Not at all. The Hosttower is neutral in this war, by his command."

"Neutral?"

"Yes—it was Gromph who crippled the magical flow of energy and thus shut down the magical portals."

"Then he sides with the invaders," Catti-brie said.

"According to Lord Parise, he claims not to. But the drow who have come to the lands and taken the demon army, and also the fleet that Lord Brevindon Margaster of Waterdeep sailed to Luskan, are very powerful. Gromph made it clear to all the mages within the Hosttower that he—and they if they wanted to remain alive and in their new home—would not go against the invaders. Nor would he allow me to stay, since my presence alone could forfeit his neutral status."

"They court disaster," Catti-brie said. "Woe to them all . . ."

"The invaders are keeping far from the tower. They will not challenge the powers assembled there. They tried once only, and the evidence of the slaughter was thick about the fields surrounding the tower."

"If the drow win across the north, it will only be a matter of time before they fully claim the Hosttower."

Penelope nodded.

"Where is Luskan now, then?" Afafrenfere asked.

"Luskan is under the command of High Captain Brevindon Margaster, it would seem. Fully so, with only the Hosttower allowed some autonomy."

"He took the city that quickly?"

"Luskan's hodgepodge fleet and almost all of her captains are pirates," Penelope explained. "There was fighting for only a bloody night and a day following, but the loyalties of such self-interested people as those in power in Luskan are as changeable as the wind. It would seem that they decided it was better to join with the invaders than to fight them."

"So they simply bent their knees to a new invader?" the monk asked.

"I'd hardly say they bent the knee. But one lord or another . . ." Penelope replied.

"This lord is backed by drow, so it seems, and with demons?"

"And gnolls," Penelope agreed. "The fleet was thick with the wild beasts, and now so are the streets of Luskan. But recognize, too, that the power of Luskan before the attack was also held by drow."

"Jarlaxle and Bregan D'aerthe," Catti-brie explained to the monk.

"Thus, they traded one high captain for another," Penelope said, "and one more wretched, it seems, and so, one who will allow them their piracy and murderous ways with even less restraint. Make no mistake, the largest complaint Parise and Avelyere had heard of Jarlaxle's agent, High Captain Beniago Kurth, was that he was bringing a measure of civility and community to the City of Sails."

Catti-brie nodded and chuckled helplessly, and Afafrenfere looked at her curiously.

"Jarlaxle is no evil person," she explained. "Even King Bruenor approved of Bregan D'aerthe's secret power behind the dark veil of Luskan. Jarlaxle is fierce, but only when he needs to be, and only against those who deserve it. His goal was to use the best interests of the people of Luskan against their traditional behavior."

"To show them a better way," the monk said.

Catti-brie nodded. "Slowly. And with their consent, as they found the ways of trade more lucrative and less . . . mortal than their piracy."

"They think they traded the drow for a Waterdhavian lord, and one wretched enough to accept their lifestyles," said Penelope. "Gromph knows the truth, though. The city will be enslaved soon enough, serving merciless masters—or should I say, Matrons?"

"Damn him," Catti-brie muttered. "Treacherous fool."

"More fearful than malignant, I believe," Penelope said. "From all I could garner from Avelyere and Parise, Gromph is truly afraid of the storm that has come to his front door. Remember, he was once archmage of Menzoberranzan. He understands the power Menzoberranzan has brought to bear. And he feels it most keenly, because he was finding a life he had never been brave enough to even imagine in the grand multidimensional corridors and mansions of the Hosttower of the Arcane."

Catti-brie sighed and waddled wearily to take a seat in a soft chair. "Whatever his reasons, whatever his feelings, we must open those gates," she said.

"We cannot."

"Not from here, perhaps."

"Not from the Hosttower, either. You are in no position to challenge the likes of Gromph Baenre, and we could not begin to bring enough power to bear to convince any within to go against him."

"From Gauntlgrym," Catti-brie explained. "There may be a way to open the portals whether the Hosttower is involved or not. You must get me to Gauntlgrym, posthaste."

Penelope wore a doubtful expression.

"You just teleported to Luskan and back with ease," Catti-brie argued.

"The Hosttower is a prepared destination for such spells," Penelope said. "Both Kipper and I are attuned to the room created for this exact purpose. Neither of us have any real knowledge of Gauntlgrym."

"You have been there!"

"Only once and only briefly, simply to try the portal when it first became active. So, yes, I know the portal room."

"Enough to teleport there."

Penelope paused and offered no agreement. "I saw it only briefly, and saw keenly its low ceiling and cramped walls—certainly it is not a place favorable for such an attempt."

"The gates are similar to a permanent circle, are they not?"

"Are they?"

Catti-brie wanted to answer in the affirmative, but she could not, because she did not know.

"Please, we have to try," Catti-brie pleaded. "If I get to Gauntlgrym, there is much I might be able to do."

"How? The Hosttower controls—"

"The *primordial* is the power," Catti-brie reminded her. "The Hosttower merely harnesses the being. I can speak with it."

"To what end? A primordial is a being that is far beyond our comprehension. Its desires are not ours, and so far removed from ours that you cannot even relate to them."

"We have to try," Catti-brie said again.

"You would risk your child?"

The question rocked Catti-brie.

"Send me," said Afafrenfere.

"I cannot 'send' anyone," said Penelope. "The mage must accompany."

"Then go with me," Afafrenfere said. "If familiarity with the targeted area of your spell is the key for success, then go and familiarize yourself."

"There remains that first journey," Catti-brie reminded the agitated monk.

"Courage is needed," he returned.

"No, he is right," Penelope agreed. "We cannot shy from pursuing any hope, however slight, in desperate times. I will find Kipper. He is much stronger in this magic. We will go to Gauntlgrym together and prepare a circle, then return quickly." She paused, another cloud drifting across her expression. "If we are able, I mean. If the portal room remains free of the demon attackers. We know not if any or if all of Gauntlgrym has fallen."

"Take me, as well," said Afafrenfere. "If we appear in a place of danger, I will protect you while you get us out of there."

"I cannot ask . . ." Catti-brie started to argue, but the monk was hearing none of it.

"You cannot," he said, "because there is nothing to ask of me. This is my choice. Come," he told Penelope, "let us be quick. The crumbling world will not wait for heroes who pause."

CHAPTER 12

The Deep Pool of
Singular Memory

Beniago sat on the front of his desk in Illusk, long and slender arms crossed over his chest. Kimmuriel sat in the corner behind him and to his left, the psionicist insisting on an observational role and giving the meeting over fully to Beniago, who had been high captain for some time and knew the city as well as any in Bregan D'aerthe.

Everyone seated on the benches in front of Beniago was drow, with the exceptions of Wulfgar and Bonnie Charlee. Kimmuriel had insisted on Wulfgar's attendance, and Bonnie Charlee had been filling a valuable role, as she, even after the encounter with the gnolls in the alleyway, could most easily slip about the streets of the city, blending in and spying.

One by one, the scouts had delivered their information, leaving the most important for last: Braelin Janquay. He was tying all the information together, and in a way that seemed to offer little hope for Bregan D'aerthe's continued presence in the City of Sails.

"Their numbers are overwhelming," Braelin continued. "It would seem as if all four of the other high captains have indeed pledged full fealty to Brevindon. Luskan is a city of similar size to Menzoberranzan, and with all four of those ships in alliance with the invaders, we could not hope to defeat them even if every other person in Luskan supported us."

"And few will," added another drow scout.

"It shows the fickleness of humans, short-living and without honor," said Dab'nay.

"What it shows is a city suspicious of change," Wulfgar interjected, suffering the scowls of many others, who had made it very clear they didn't want him, or Bonnie Charlee, in the room. "You offered them change, and they were only just beginning to see it," he told Beniago, and turned as he spoke to make sure that Kimmuriel heard him clearly, as well. "No doubt that change would prove beneficial for all in Luskan in time, but it also meant the weakening of many, particularly the strongest and most vicious. You demanded—perhaps not demanded, but coaxed—that they surrender their lifestyle. Not every pirate murders and steals because he has a future of few options. Some do it simply because they enjoy it. They prefer a life of grand adventure without moral boundaries, even if it means, almost certainly, that they, too, will find a most unpleasant and early death."

"And you label *us* the evil race," Dab'nay said.

"Is Menzoberranzan really any different?" Braelin Janquay asked her. "Do you doubt the joy many priestesses feel when using the scourge?"

"We are far afield of our issue here," Beniago remarked.

"When you retake Luskan, if you do, you would do well to determine the redeemable citizens from the others," Wulfgar finished.

Beniago looked to him, offered a quick nod, then turned back to Braelin.

"Our best hope is the chaos of the gnolls," Braelin went on. "Even Brevindon Margaster cannot fully control them, and their crimes against the folk of Luskan mount."

"And what do we know of Brevindon?" Beniago asked.

"He's a demon in him," Bonnie Charlee answered. "A real one, red-skinned and wicked, and with a swirly sword that'll cut ye in half."

"Aye," Braelin agreed. "That demon, too, may prove to be unwittingly helping us. Brevindon is behaving ferociously, hanging people by the dozen, and soon not a family in Luskan will not know someone who has died at the end of one of his ropes. The people will fear him, the other captains will bow to him, but soon enough, most will hold less love for Brevindon than they ever harbored for us."

"But he's not the only demon in Luskan, and he has a considerable mercenary force that will never betray him, including the gnolls," said Dab'nay.

Others started to respond, but Beniago held up his hand, silencing them as he considered the information—none of which was truly new to anyone in the room.

"Archmage Gromph will not be persuaded," he told them after a long pause, "and there is little we can do without suffering too many losses—Bregan D'aerthe is not a war party. I had hoped to find a role for us under the new leadership in Luskan, but given the power behind Brevindon, which we now know to be Matron Zhindia Melarn, that will never be.

"No, we have to win here, and win soon, while Matron Zhindia remains busy in the south. Continue nibbling on the edges, but let's focus more attention to agitating the gnolls against those most loyal to High Captain Brevindon Margaster. Push him and pressure him to greater cruelty until we can determine the best way to fully strike."

He ended with a look to Kimmuriel, who remained impassive and gave no indication of agreement or disagreement.

THESE WERE THE TIMES WHEN KIMMURIEL OBLODRA WON-
dered if there was such a thing as natural reincarnation, or if, perhaps, the spirit of a sentient being could be injected into an inappropriate corporeal form—both Yvonnel and Quenthel Baenre as possible examples, perhaps. Back in his own "place," Kimmuriel could count his

friends on a single finger—if Jarlaxle even was his friend. Certainly the unusual rogue was the closest to counting as one.

Perhaps Gromph Baenre, perhaps Beniago Kurth, perhaps Braelin Janquay. These were his associates, and with them he had established some measure of trust at least, and with Gromph, he also held a grudging respect, probably more so than Kimmuriel offered any other drow or any member of any other race on Faerun.

But friends? If he had a friend on Toril, it would be Jarlaxle. And yes, he knew, that was stretching the definition.

But here, in this place, nothing was measured in that manner. In this place, Kimmuriel Oblodra didn't exist, other than to be a single colligation in the one being that was the whole of illithid society. Here in the hive mind, his fingers caressing the great pulsing brain, the edifice of connection and oneness, thoughts and memories became interchangeable and mingled. Study in the hive mind was merely a matter of searching what had become your own expansive knowledge and memories rather than hearing or reading the words of a separate being.

Kimmuriel often lamented that he should have been born an illithid.

The hive mind knew this truth within the drow's heart, of course, which explained why he was so welcomed here. One could not easily hide insincerity in this place. One could not easily hide anything from the illithids.

A large part of the individual that was Kimmuriel wanted to just stay here. Let Luskan and Bregan D'aerthe be the concerns of another. He could remain at the hive mind and caress knowledge itself, bask in pure thought, revel in memories as visceral as if he had walked those pathways in the lonely and singular drow form he had been forced to wear.

Arguments came back at him from so many other corners of the hive mind, though. He was unique here, or nearly so. Only this synapse of the hive mind, this being named Kimmuriel, that existed in that drow reality in that world of Faerun, could bring in such expansive experiences and knowledge of that place.

He would be limiting the hive mind and thus limiting himself if he lost the balance between recipient and source.

So he accepted it for the time being and focused his thoughts as he searched.

Demons . . . possession . . . phylactery . . .

The knowledge was extensive, of course, since demons had been milling about existence since the beginning of time itself and, given their potential for destruction and damage, had ever been of concern to the illithid hive mind.

He wasn't learning.

He was remembering, and that was much more powerful and rich.

The memories sorted, the drow lightened his hand from the central brain of the community, ready to remove it and depart.

Be well, be open, he heard in his head, the telepathic voices of so many illithids who had joined with him this day to share their memories. They were one, intimately, in this last moment before the mental unjoining, and so distinct were their communal voices that he could silently and almost instantly thank them, each and every one. He noted most especially Pescatawav, the current most endeared to the central brain, a position that rotated among the hive, and one that Kimmuriel, as an outsider, would never know.

He noted one other, for some reason, as he lifted his hand from the central brain and broke the connection. Something about the way the mind flayer named Ouwoonivisc had imparted the thought struck him . . . differently.

"THIS PLAN WILL NOT SUCCEED," KIMMURIEL TOLD BENI- ago and the others when they gathered again in Illusk. Beniago's scouts and provocateurs had been out and about in the city for a tenday, causing trouble, riling up gnolls, riling up the people of Luskan against the gnolls. Even whispering dire warnings to the ambassadors of the high captains.

There had been some fights but few fatalities, and little progress in weakening the hold of High Captain Brevindon. Indeed, the Waterdhavian noble had now fully staffed and armed Ship Margaster. The whole island was fast becoming a fortress, and that show of strength would keep the pirates, both invader and citizen, in line. And so Kimmuriel was reconsidering, and being pushed toward his more daring conflict.

"Then what is left to us?" Beniago asked. "Does Bregan D'aerthe desert Luskan? Perhaps we leave a minor gang behind to monitor and find ways to bring in some profit, at least. Or should we go back to Gromph and beg him to reconsider his retreat from this fight?"

"Or at least convince him to reopen the portals to Gauntlgrym?" Braelin added. "King Bruenor will not allow the new events in Luskan to stand. If he can at last open the portals to the Silver Marches, he will have three more dwarven armies at his command."

"The gates are closed, and Gromph is too self-serving to reconsider his actions. The retrievers and the sudden gains of the Melarni have convinced him that Lolth is on their side, and he's too wise to invoke the anger of the Spider Queen," Kimmuriel calmly explained.

"But we're not, apparently," Wulfgar dared to say, chuckling—but he was not joined in that mirth by any in the room.

"We have underestimated Brevindon Margaster, or more particularly, this demon Asbeel, who resides within the man," Kimmuriel explained. "He is formidable—they are formidable, and they came here as prepared for the aftermath as they were for the initial victory. Port Llast, too, is in their thrall."

"So we leave," Beniago reasoned.

"No," came Kimmuriel's simple answer.

"Then what?" Beniago and Braelin asked together.

Kimmuriel looked to the side, to Wulfgar, who nodded knowingly.

"We destroy them," the barbarian said. "We send this fiend Asbeel back to the pits of the lower planes, where it belongs."

The looks of the drow commanders lingered on Wulfgar for a bit before shifting back to Kimmuriel, who was still staring at Wulfgar.

"He knows how to do it," Wulfgar told them all.

Kimmuriel almost managed a smile at that. He wished he was as sure as the barbarian on that matter. Something was bothering

Kimmuriel, nagging at him. He felt as if he was missing an important fact. There was a memory floating about just beyond his reach, or several memories that were related somehow in a manner that would give him answers.

"I won't miss this time," Wulfgar promised them all.

You should not have missed last time, Kimmuriel thought but did not say, or project telepathically.

His next thought following that unusual notion—why did he care?—was that he had thought it out of frustration.

But no, he now realized. He had gone to great lengths to protect Wulfgar in that fight on Brevindon Margaster's ship, far out at sea. He had protected the barbarian with a kinetic barrier, giving Wulfgar tremendous power in one swing to reflect all of the energy Kimmuriel's shield had given him. Kimmuriel had done that knowing that Wulfgar, so skilled and powerful, would end the demon within his opponent or would at least shatter Brevindon's physical body. Asbeel was proud and thought himself invincible. His fighting was aggressive, reckless, arrogant.

Wulfgar couldn't miss.

But he had.

How was that possible?

CHAPTER 13

Convergence

They came in with a flash and a puff of smoke, some extra flair old Kipper Harpell had put into his teleportation spells simply for dramatic effect. This time, it almost cost him and those traveling with him dearly, for when they arrived in the small portal room in Gauntlgrym, they found two ranks of battle dwarves with loaded heavy crossbows staring at them, and a side-slinger catapult on the wall, straining to let loose its lethal payload.

"Bows up!" cried Bjarke Lager, the battle group commander, as soon as the smoke had cleared and Catti-brie was fully revealed. Half the dwarves had their weapons there already, having recognized the woman as a true friend of Clan Battlehammer. Every dwarf in Gauntlgrym, every dwarf in Mithral Hall, every dwarf in Citadel Adbar and Citadel Felbarr knew well the adopted daughter of King Bruenor Battlehammer.

"My lady Catti-brie! It is good you have come," Bjarke said, rushing up to the foursome. "But I'm hopin' ye brought a way out if ye're needin' it!"

"Not for needin' it, good master dwarf," the woman replied, so easily slipping into the rhythm and brogue of the dwarves, a way of speaking she had drowned in since her youngest days. It was an unconscious reversion, but a common one and one that brought a smile to her face, for Catti-brie always felt that dwarven brogue, part lyrical, part guttural, was fitting with battle so near. Every word struck like a bolstering slap on the back and conjured images of toasts to great heroes of old who had stood against mighty foes and prevailed. "What I'm needin' is the sight o' me husband and me da."

"Aye, but King Bruenor's a popular one today," Bjarke said.

Catti-brie considered that and looked at him curiously, but didn't press further as the dwarf continued.

"We got to go the secret back ways. Main corridors're full o' fighting. Might be a bit tight with yerself carrying a . . . load."

"Just lead, me friend, and be quick, eh?"

"Eh," Bjarke agreed. "Bruenor'll be in the forge room, or the place what keeps the beast, not to doubt. Come along."

He nodded to the dwarf nearest the right-hand wall, and that fellow hopped over and pressed on specific spots on the seemingly unremarkable stone. A section of the wall dropped away, revealing a narrow but clean and well-worked corridor.

"Pull a torch!" Bjarke called.

"No need," said Penelope Harpell, and with a wave of her hand, she conjured a magical light, placing it on the tip of Bjarke's pointy helm.

"Wizards," the dwarf muttered, and started away. "We see any demon critters and ye be fast in putting out that light."

"Faster than you could douse a torch," Penelope assured him.

"Wizards," Bjarke muttered again.

The six, for a second dwarf took up the rear of the line, rambled along at a fine pace through winding narrow passages. To Catti-brie and the other visitors, the whole of the place seemed a vast maze, with too many turns and forks and intersections of passages that all looked the same, but Bjarke knew exactly where he was going and soon enough had the group at the end of a corridor, facing what seemed like simple stone except for a metal push bar on one side, with a chain hanging beside it.

Bjarke pulled the chain, and they heard a bell on the other side of the door. The dwarf paused for a count of three, then pulled the chain rapidly, once and again. After a brief moment, he pushed on the bar and the door silently swung open into a wide chamber.

A dozen battle dwarves slid their weapons away and watched them enter, as one breaking into a cheer when Catti-brie walked out of the narrow corridor.

Those dwarves parted, nodding and happy, greeting Catti-brie and her companions warmly. Just before they opened the forge room door for the four visitors, they had to pause and take note of another group fast-approaching down a side corridor.

Yvonnel, Dahlia, Entreri, Regis, and Athrogate rushed to join them, all five wearing grim expressions.

"The woods about us are filled with driders," Regis said, rushing up to Catti-brie. "So many, and my friend . . ."

Yvonnel grabbed him by the shoulder and pulled him back, warning him to silence with a scowl. The drow woman then exchanged a rather awkward look with Catti-brie.

"King Bruenor is in the primordial chamber, I am told," Yvonnel explained. "We can relay all the news together at once. The dwarves are gathering Jarlaxle and Zaknafein now to join us."

A hundred questions bounced about Catti-brie's thoughts at that moment, inspired mostly by Yvonnel's tone, and by Regis—something was wrong with Regis. The hairs on the back of Catti-brie's neck stood on end. Yes, something was very wrong here. She saw it on their faces, all of them, particularly the halfling's, for the halfling looked as if he might simply explode.

They went into the forge room and through it to the side corridor leading to the large chamber that held the primordial of fire in a chasm whose walls swirled continually, the great pit capped by water elementals. There they found Bruenor waiting, along with Queen Tannabritches, Ivan and Pikel Bouldershoulder, Lady Donnola Topolino, and the two drow, Zaknafein and Jarlaxle.

"Ah, blessed be Dumathoin," Bruenor said when he saw his very pregnant daughter. "Please be tellin' me that them durned portals're running again."

"Kipper Harpell teleported us in," Catti-brie explained. "No portals."

"And none likely," Penelope Harpell added.

"Bah!" huffed the dwarf king.

"Yvonnel flew us in as a living cloud, through the drow and driders and demons," Regis said.

"Athrogate!" Bruenor cried then, noting his shield dwarf, whom he thought lost at Thornhold. "Ah, but there're stories to be telling!"

"And I'll start with the most important," Yvonnel said grimly. She pulled a sack from around her shoulder. "There is no easy way to say this." She paused and took a deep breath, and those who had come in with her all seemed to hold their breath at the same moment.

Catti-brie's heart fell. She knew. At that moment, that most terrible moment, she knew.

"Drizzt is gone," Yvonnel announced. She laid the sack at the feet of Catti-brie, and when it settled and pitched over a bit, the pommel of a familiar scimitar stabbed out of its opening.

"Gone?" Bruenor demanded. "What're ye meaning, gone?"

"The spider," Regis blurted, running forward because he simply had to. He went straight to his wife, Donnola, and fell into her arms, needing the support.

"He is gone," Yvonnel said again.

"Where's the body?" Bruenor demanded, his voice and ire rising greatly.

"Gone?" Jarlaxle asked.

Yvonnel nodded.

"But not dead," Jarlaxle said.

Yvonnel shrugged.

"It was a retriever," Jarlaxle reminded. "It took him, and thus, he might be held prisoner in the Abyss."

"Then to the Abyss we go!" Zaknafein growled, and Bruenor loudly agreed—as did Artemis Entreri, which surprised most of the others.

Catti-brie wasn't even listening, though. She couldn't hear anything beyond the thrumming of the blood in her ears. She looked to Yvonnel, who seemed the most versed here, and to Jarlaxle, who always seemed to have an answer, but no, they seemed somehow beyond her reach, far away, indistinct.

Like their voices, like all of their voices now, as they bickered and shouted over each other, promising a fight or something . . . something . . .

It was just a mosquito to her, buzzing in her ear. Like that day, that early morning when she and Drizzt were out on the road south of Mithral Hall. That mosquito, yes, and she couldn't quite see it because she couldn't yet open her tired eyes, and she could only hear it, buzzing, buzzing.

Nothing focused for her in that terrible moment except the pommel. So distinct, so familiar.

The pommel.

Drizzt was lost to her.

She didn't know what to do.

So she screamed.

Just screamed. At the top of her lungs, with every ounce of strength she had, she threw out a wall of pure denial, a stream of curses at the gods, at her god, at any god, at divine justice itself, for how could this be?

She just screamed.

And when she had thrown it all out there, her knees wobbled and went out from under her. Down she went, but not far, for Zaknafein, as agile and quick as his son, was there to catch her and support her. Others were fast to the spot as well, Regis with a potion in hand to bolster her, and soon she was up again, apologizing, then feeling stupid for apologizing.

The world spun, and her thoughts spun faster.

She pushed them all away, and when Bruenor, her beloved father, came to hug her, she held out her hands to stop him.

"Don't!"

"Me girl?" the dwarf asked, tears streaming down his cheeks. He started for her again.

"I can'no'," she said, keeping her hands defensively before her. She knew, she just knew, that if anyone touched her to comfort her, she would melt.

She could not do that. Not here. Not now.

She fought through her pain—she had never imagined pain like this before. She let the thoughts swirl—*her child . . . their child . . . Drizzt . . . in his arms*—and swirl some more, like a whirlpool, taking them all down, burying them beneath an ocean of tears.

She always knew this could happen—it was a likelihood of the life they had chosen.

And it *had* happened! To her, to Regis, to Wulfgar, to Bruenor! They had been taken to the afterlife and yet they were back.

But no, not this time, she just knew. She knew the deal Mielikki had given to her when she had kept the four in Iruladoon. That was a special circumstance, the Spellplague, and they were there for Mielikki, not for the desires of mere mortals.

It would not happen again. There would be no second divine intervention—that was the deal. No resurrection.

She stared at the pommel, that beautiful black adamantine hilt fashioned into the likeness of the toothed maw of a hunting cat.

Duty. Responsibility.

She found her focus, but it wavered when she noted all the stares coming at her from those around. The buzzing was gone now. Just silence.

Drizzt was gone.

Duty. Responsibility.

They were all in trouble. She was in trouble. Her child was in mortal danger.

Duty. Responsibility.

But now . . . with their child . . . their child, her child, Drizzt's child, in danger!

The woman growled and pushed away from those standing about her, toward the bag Yvonnel had placed at her feet.

She fished about and found Guenhwyvar first and foremost. Beloved Guenhwyvar, so much more than a magical item, so much more than a companion. Guenhwyvar was family, and Catti-brie decided that she wouldn't let the onyx figurine out of her possession until the day she gave it to her child, to Drizzt's child.

She found next the buckle of the sword belt, a magical construct of her own making, which held within it Taulmaril the Heartseeker, her bow that she had given to Drizzt. She removed it from the belt and slid it into her pouch.

She moved methodically, using her duty to hold herself upright. She had to think about that which she now had to do, and not think about the coming trials and trauma, the reality of life without Drizzt or the possibility of finding some way, any way, to go and get him.

She took out Drizzt's *piwafwi*, the wonderful and finely made cloak that never seemed to show the wear of the road. Jarlaxle had commissioned it for Drizzt. Catti-brie brought it in close and inhaled, smelling Drizzt, burying her face in that scent.

She turned and offered it to Jarlaxle, but he held up his hands and shook his head, declining. ". . . yours," he said, and it was clear he was having trouble speaking in that terrible moment. "Keep it . . . wear it. I beg."

She fished around in the sack a bit more, and found herself growing stronger and more determined. After a few moments, she stood and looked to Yvonnel. "The scrimshaw pendant for Andahar?" she asked.

"Drizzt took it to run from the spider," Athrogate answered before Yvonnel could.

"He wanted to get the beast as far away from the rest of us as possible," Yvonnel added.

Catti-brie nodded, then went to the sack, pulling out the sword belt and the mithral shirt, the bracers Drizzt wore as anklets. She held it all before her, the legacy of her love. On an impulse, she drew his other sword, the scimitar of Vidrinath and Twinkle, joined by Catti-brie in the Forge of Gauntlgrym, presented it powerfully, and told the others, her voice strong and thick with the dwarven brogue, "We're not to lose this war. We're winning. For Drizzt, we're winning. We come too far to let this dream go, demons and driders and drow be durned!"

"Aye and huzzah!" Queen Tannabritches cheered, but the others all looked to the three drow, particularly to Jarlaxle. All except Bruenor, who stood perfectly still, except for his face, which kept grimacing and twisting, low growls coming forth.

He was lost, Catti-brie knew, and that gave her more determination and more strength.

"It is a fair declaration," the rogue mercenary admitted with a shrug. "For Drizzt, then, and huzzah, indeed!"

The others joined in, except for Catti-brie, Bruenor, and one other. She noted Zaknafein, his cheeks twitching, his eyes large and sad, gaze cast down.

She slid Vidrinath away and went to him, directly to him, and matched his stare with her own.

"I am sorry that you never came to truly know your son, or to fully understand the beauty that he gave to us all," she managed to say, her voice breaking several times.

"And that you gave to him," Jarlaxle interjected.

With an appreciative nod to Jarlaxle, Catti-brie cleared her throat and continued. "Here," she said, and gave Zaknafein the bracer and mithral shirt. "Bruenor made this for Drizzt, and these bracers he took from the corpse of Dantrag Baenre."

"I . . ." Zak started to answer, but could get no words out beyond that.

"And these." Catti-brie surprised Zak and everyone else in handing over Drizzt's scimitars. "These are yours now, to wield in the name of Drizzt Do'Urden, your son, who loved you always."

Zaknafein's hands trembled as he took the sword belt.

"However you might feel about me, or about the others around you who are not drow, I trust that you will make good use of these blades in defending all that was dear to Drizzt. And when we win—and we *shall*—you will go as you determine with this part of Drizzt in hand, at least."

"Aye," she heard Bruenor say from the side, and she was glad to know that the dwarf, as good a friend as Drizzt had ever known, as good a father as she could have ever hoped for, agreed with her bold decision.

"Where would you have me go?" Zaknafein asked when he had finally steadied himself.

"Where you will."

"And if I choose to remain here, by your side?" Zak asked, and he looked around at all of them, taking them in one at a time, meeting every gaze. "If I choose to remain beside all of you? Fighting beside you? Learning from you?" He brought his gaze back to stare directly into Catti-brie's eyes as he finished, "Knowing my grandchild as I wished I might have known my son?"

"I would like that," Catti-brie said, her voice somewhat less than a whisper, tears flowing from her blue eyes, and then she welcomed Zaknafein's hug and returned it tenfold, pulling him tight against her, her child, his grandchild, squeezed between them, hugged by both of them.

Regis was there a moment later, then Bruenor, then Jarlaxle.

Catti-brie let herself be swept up in that great hug, in the shared sense of loss.

She remembered then the words of Drizzt and whispered them, more to herself than to the others, "Joy multiplies when it is shared among friends, but grief diminishes with every division."

She opened her eyes then and looked over Zak's shoulder, and noted, curiously, Artemis Entreri.

The man was as shaken as she had ever seen him. Tears streamed down his cheeks as he held Dahlia against his side.

His eyes were locked on Catti-brie, though, and his thoughts, she knew without doubt, were full of sadness and emptiness at the loss of the drow who had been his greatest enemy, his greatest rival, and finally, a model to him of what he might have been and, perhaps, of what he could strive to be.

Catti-brie wanted to tell him, but she could not: hold on to that.

"Hold on to that," she did whisper under her breath, and no one heard but her.

"Hold on to that."

PART 3

Lasting
Ramifications

Are they all like that?

Do all drow children possess such innocence, such simple, untainted smiles that cannot survive the ugliness of our world? Or are you unique, Drizzt Do'Urden?

And if you are so different, what, then, is the cause? The blood, my blood, that courses through your veins? Or the years you spent with your weanmother?

This one is different!

This one is different.

Zaknafein Do'Urden
Homeland

CHAPTER 14

THE YEAR OF THE SHATTERED OAK
DALERECKONING 1313

Making Webs in the Shadows

*Y*ou *know these tunnels?* Beniago's hand movements asked of Zaknafein. The Bregan D'aerthe band had gone silent now, traversing caves far from Menzoberranzan. They had been out for several tendays and, credit to the skill of Beniago and a most exceptional scout, Nav Rayan Dyrr, they had avoided almost all trouble. No small feat in the Underdark.

I do, Zaknafein answered with his fingers.

Then you have been to the City of Shimmering Webs, Beniago's hands replied.

Once, a long time ago.

With Jarlaxle, I presume.

And another, Zak replied. *A brilliant assassin named—*

Arathis Hune, Beniago answered before he could finish.

That set Zaknafein back on his heels. This Baenre knew more than he was letting on, and that likely included the fact that Arathis Hune had met a most unexpected and inconvenient end, not long after the moment when the artery in Arathis Hune's neck had met the sharp edge of the sword Zaknafein now carried on his left hip.

Arathis Hune had been a major force in the mercenary band, second only to Jarlaxle within the hierarchy of Bregan D'aerthe.

I am surprised to witness Zaknafein relating the notion of Arathis Hune as brilliant, signed Beniago.

He was, perhaps, the second most brilliant assassin I have ever known.

Second only to the drow who killed him?

That is usually how it works.

Beniago Kurth nodded in salute to that.

We are going to Ched Nesad? Zaknafein asked.

So it would seem.

Zaknafein slipped back a bit, then, slowing his pace to better take in the images and textures of the corridors around him, using the visual and tactile cues to send his thoughts back to that most thrilling excursion—perhaps the greatest adventure he had known in his life. The three rogues had traveled to the City of Shimmering Webs to parlay with a high priestess, a matron who had allowed her pride to get a bit beyond her earned reputation. She had angered Lolth, so they had been told.

Perhaps that was true, perhaps not, Zaknafein had thought then and still now—for who could really know the will of the chaotic goddess who held these two cities, Menzoberranzan and Ched Nesad, in her thrall?

It didn't matter anyway, of course, for Lolth didn't really care for any single high priestess—or almost any matron, even—enough to demand retribution in this mortal existence. She would surely exact any deserved revenge in the afterlife.

In this particular case, however, the offending matron had done something far more lethal than committing an offense against Lolth.

She had offended Matron Mother Baenre.

A lot of drow had done that over the millennia, Zaknafein was sure, but more sure was Jarlaxle, who had made it quite clear that few had done it twice, and none had ever lived long enough to offend Matron Mother Baenre a third time.

The troupe continued on their silent way for another few days, but then, right in an area that Zaknafein remembered well, a place where he had rescued a band of halfling slaves, the direction shifted dramatically.

The Hunzrin band had veered to the north. Soon after, the scout reported that the Hunzrins were heading back toward Menzoberranzan along a lesser-used series of tunnels and caves.

"They knew they were being followed," Zaknafein said to Beniago.

"I don't think so," Beniago replied. "This particular Hunzrin party left under the utmost secrecy. It is quite possible that they traveled all this way on purpose, just in case they were being watched. We are beyond the range of all but the most powerful diviners now. Their scrying mirrors or pools would not have kept up with the Hunzrins at this point."

"They are being careful indeed, then."

Beniago nodded, and once more Zaknafein got the impression the Baenre fighter knew a lot more than he was letting on.

Zaknafein shrugged off the notion as immaterial. He had known Jarlaxle for centuries and so was used to such things.

"WE ARE NOT BOUND FOR THE CITY OF CHED NESAD, THEN?" the woman asked her hosts.

"You know of Ched Nesad?" Du'Quelve Hunzrin asked.

"Of course," Priestess Iccara replied. "The City of Shimmering Webs. A most worthy tribute to the Spider Queen, do you not agree?"

"I do agree," Du'Quelve replied. She, too, was a priestess of Lolth, hoping to ascend to the rank of high priestess in the next decade or so, and to answer otherwise would have amounted to sacrilege. Not that she had to lie in response to this question, for Du'Quelve was often out of Menzoberranzan in service to Matron Arolina Hunzrin, and many of those journeys had indeed been to Ched Nesad, Menzoberranzan's most favored trading partner.

Not this one, however. Matron Arolina wanted to keep Iccara and her fellow priestess, Bolfae, all to herself. The Hunzrins had come upon the pair on the road to Menzoberranzan, journeying from a place they called the Arach Enclave, which they had claimed as a small but thriving Lolthian drow settlement in the deeper tunnels of the Underdark. For Arolina, for all of House Hunzrin, this place, Arach Enclave, was an entirely new discovery. Perhaps Matron Mother Baenre knew of it, or more likely, perhaps she had forgotten about it, but Matron Arolina was determined to keep the information secret.

A heretofore unknown drow village would make a marvelous trading partner, particularly if the Hunzrins could establish themselves before some other family—or worse, that mercenary band known as Bregan D'aerthe—made inroads.

The timing had been perfect, for this expedition had been planned barely a tenday before the chance meeting with the priestesses Iccara and Bolfae had occurred in some tunnels still well outside Menzoberranzan. All the expedition party had to do was reroute the mission to Ched Nesad, to protect their new interests, and then they could proceed to this most lucrative promise that would very possibly lead them to a more lucrative relationship.

Before Bregan D'aerthe ever knew of the Arach Enclave.

A group of Hunzrins called Priestess Du'Quelve away. As she passed a side corridor, unsurprisingly, Iccara's comrade Bolfae exited that corridor and moved to join her friend.

Bregan D'aerthe is following us, she telepathically communicated to her sister.

Of course they are. Would you expect anything less of Jarlaxle? He knows that the Hunzrins have scored a major dealer in gemstones, one so rich with baubles that it could present a real curb on his insatiable ambitions, Iccara silently replied.

Bolfae muttered some small talk then, in case anyone nearby was wondering why the two were so near to each other without exchanging any words or hand signals. Then, telepathically, she asked, *Do you think he knows of us?*

He knows that two priestesses not of Menzoberranzan have joined with the Hunzrins.

Drow priestesses?

Yes, Iccara responded, but there was no hiding doubts in such tele-pathic communication. *We must assume that to be the case.*

And if it is not?

Iccara laughed at that. *Jarlaxle is no fool. He will take whatever in-formation he gleans straight to Matron Mother Baenre, of course, and she is also no fool. Perhaps this will shine more respect on House Hunzrin. That would be good. Menzoberranzan is such a limiting place. It is time for the Spider Queen to spread her tendrils more ambitiously from the city, and who better to do that than a rising house that typically has more nobles and commoners out in the tunnels of the wild Underdark than in the city proper?*

The same could be said of Jarlaxle and his Bregan D'aerthe band, Bolfae responded.

He is a mere male, so that is irrelevant. Iccara quickly reverted to audible whispers as she noted the approach of Priestess Du'Quelve.

"Good news," the Hunzrin informed them. "The way is mostly clear and we have eyes far ahead. The journey should be swift and easy, and the most recent meeting with our contact shows him ready to deal and rich with a valuable mineral. He has to move the cache, and quickly, else his kin and kind learn of his thievery."

"Why would you trust such a creature?" Bolfae asked bluntly, play-ing her role.

"He's too dull-witted to be an effective liar," Du'Quelve answered. "We know well the place and people involved."

"You have eyes among them?" Iccara asked, though she knew the answer.

"Yes."

"The place?" Bolfae added.

"Blingdenstone," said Du'Quelve. "Is it known to you in the Arach Enclave?"

"No," Iccara lied. "But we know of these ugly little svirfneblin creatures well enough. We keep many as slaves."

Du'Quelve nodded her approval at that, then waved for the priest-esses to follow. Soon after, the Hunzrin party broke camp, moving swiftly and silently along the tunnels of the Underdark, noticed by none.

None except for Nav Rayan Dyrr.

CHAPTER 15

Conspiracy

Gracklstugh?" Beniago asked, more than stated, an older scout named Binnefein, one scarred in a long-ago battle where he had been saved by Zaknafein himself, back in the days when both Binnefein and Zaknafein wore the surname of Simfray.

"Duergar?" Zaknafein asked.

"By the Nine Hells, I hope that's not the case," Beniago answered. "I do so loathe those ugly little dwarves. But if it is so, then spread the word to the others that Duergar are fast to anger and more formidable than is often believed."

"Were we bound for Gracklstugh, the Hunzrins missed the most direct passage," Binnefein explained.

"So we can shortcut the route and arrive ahead of them?" asked Beniago.

The scout considered it for a moment, then shook his head. "I would not recommend such a course. None know the tunnels of this area better than the Hunzrins—except, perhaps, the two newcomer priestesses we've spied among them. If they are avoiding the direct route, there must be a reason."

"If Gracklstugh is even the destination," Zaknafein said.

"True enough," Beniago agreed. "Continue the scouting. Tell Dyrr that I want a new count if he can get close enough to the Hunzrin party."

"Seven men, two priestesses, plus these other two who are not, we believe, Hunzrin. And of course, their slaves, somewhere in the order of a score of bugbear porters and lesser goblinkin."

"Exact count," Beniago clarified.

"They are slaves; the count is fluid," Binnefein reminded him. "Already on at least two occasions since our departure from Menzoberranzan, the Hunzrins have captured and added some goblinkin, and we've found one bugbear dead on the trail, cut by drow blades."

"If only the brutes would accept their place and learn to listen," Beniago said with a sigh. "Keep eyes on them. Very near."

With a half bow, Binnefein rushed away.

"I hope it is Gracklstugh," Beniago said when he and Zaknafein were alone once more.

"You just said the opposite."

"Because I suspect the alternative, and fear it, particularly with Zaknafein in my party."

Zaknafein arched his white eyebrows at that curious response.

"The alternative is a small and hidden gnomish outpost struck out from Blingdenstone," Beniago explained.

"Blingdenstone?"

"A svirfneblin city not far afield of Menzoberranzan. It is no secret among the matrons, but rarely discussed because it is of no importance and poses no threat. If we are bound for that outpost, I expect there may be a fight, and I do not want one with the Hunzrins, and particularly not with two priestesses whose house we do not know among them."

"Particularly with Zaknafein among your ranks," Zaknafein echoed.

"Your feelings about priestesses of Lolth are well known, as are your . . . generosities, to those who are not drow."

Zak considered Beniago's statement and shrugged, unable to deny it. "Deep gnomes? I did not know . . ."

"That's the whole point. Few know, and it is better kept that way. The city of Blingdenstone is but a few miles from Menzoberranzan as the thoqqua tunnels, though it would take a difficult roundabout route to get near to them."

"We are near that city?"

Beniago shook his head. "We are near the outpost. Some gnomes have come out of their fortified home. Perhaps the veins there run thin now, or perhaps they have found more valuable riches—and they must be valuable indeed for the svirfneblin to dare to venture into the open Underdark."

Zaknafein shook his head, at a loss.

"You did not know because there was no need for Matron Malice or anyone else to tell you," Beniago explained.

"I would not expect the matrons to suffer them to live."

"The costs of rooting them out would be great. Svirfneblin are cunning little beasts, and quite adept at rigging entire tunnels to collapse. There is no gain in destroying them, particularly at that hefty price."

Zaknafein considered that for a long while, trying to make some sense of it all. When was gain ever the only motive for the drow to strike out and slaughter anyone who was not drow?

"Svirfneblin are not warlike," Beniago said, as if reading Zak's mind.

"Ah," Zak said, figuring it out. "You do business with them."

"I do nothing," said Beniago.

"Jarlaxle, then."

"Sometimes," the Baenre warrior admitted. "But they are not eager trading partners. If the Hunzrins have made inroads with them, if indeed they have set up some arrangements with one or another of their gem and mineral merchants, then I expect trouble." He looked Zak directly in the eye as he added, "And if there is trouble, I expect Zaknafein to know which side of that trouble he is on."

"What does that mean?" an indignant Zaknafein returned.

"Think of gnomes as halflings," Beniago replied.

Zaknafein didn't miss the reference, particularly given the smarmy tone from the Baenre warrior. Also, they had just come from the cave a couple tendays earlier where the incident had occurred.

"I do not pretend to understand why you would do such a thing for the sake of a few slaves," Beniago bluntly added. "But know this, Zaknafein: if the Hunzrins are indeed heading to Blingdenstone or an outpost of deep gnomes, any mercy you decide upon had better not endanger any of the Bregan D'aerthe soldiers under my command. They have come out here in the wilds of the Underdark trusting me, and I'll not have that threatened by a commoner warrior whose heart is too big for his brain."

"I do what needs to be done," Zaknafein retorted. "And I do it well."

"That is all that is expected of you," Beniago replied. "For some reason I cannot fathom, that is all Jarlaxle expects of you."

"What else is there?"

"Indeed," Beniago said with an eye roll, and he moved away.

Zak's right hand slid down to his hip to clench the hilt of the sword sheathed there. He did not shy from a fight, and was more capable than almost any other in Menzoberranzan at winning one. But now he understood that those around him didn't trust him.

"The halfling slaves from Ched Nesad were no threat," he said to Beniago's back. "They were helpless and caught, and they knew it. There was no fight to be had, just a slaughter."

Beniago turned about. "And Zaknafein did not think that a worthy sport?"

"No," he admitted.

"Why?" Beniago asked. "Why would you put any value at all on the miserable lives of surface-dwellers? Why would you suffer one who does not follow Lolth to live?"

"Does Jarlaxle follow Lolth?" Zaknafein retorted. "Does Bregan D'aerthe? The Oblodran, Kimmuriel, who would prefer the company of illithids? Does Beniago?"

"Take care, Zaknafein. I am the nephew of Matron Mother Baenre, who is as near an avatar of the Spider Queen as might be found in Faerun."

"And your loyalty, Beniago Kurth? To Matron Mother Baenre or to Jarlaxle?"

"Jarlaxle understands and approves of the role I play. It has been many years since you have been a formal part of Bregan D'aerthe. Perhaps it would serve you well to speak less and listen more."

"Perhaps. But I can't listen when you have not answered my question. Does Jarlaxle follow Lolth?"

"He . . . does not fight against her."

"Nor did the halflings."

"Only because they were helpless, as you just said. Do you think if the situation had been reversed, the vile little men would have stayed their blades?"

It was a good question, one for which Zak had no easy answer. He thought that if those halflings had known what was in his heart, then perhaps they would have let him go free, as he did them. He couldn't be sure, though.

"That is what I thought," Beniago said against Zak's silence, and he went on his way.

Zaknafein remained in the small side chamber alone for a long while, fending off the weight of the world. In these moments of uncertainty, it felt to the weapon master as if the tons and tons of stone above him were too heavy suffocating him, trapping him. Nearly three centuries had passed since the incident with Jarlaxle. It had all seemed a minor thing to him back then—Jarlaxle never mentioned it afterward, and indeed, he and Zak had grown closer subsequently.

Clearly, though, Zaknafein's mercy had been seen differently by others in the band, and likely, given that Beniago Kurth had been the one to deliver the revelation, it had been viewed much less favorably in other shadowy corners of Menzoberranzan.

Now he had to be on his guard, that much was clear, and if the fighting started with these svirfneblin gnomes, Zak understood that he would be judged carefully and with a cynical eye.

The weapon master shook his head at the realization.

Any fear of, or longing for, the judgment of the others would not change his actions in any fight. He would do what he had to do to protect himself and his fellow rogues. But if the battle was ended, prisoners taken, he would not now, as he had not then, be a party to murder.

"IT'S SYMVYN," MALTZABLOC RIFFENHAMMER TOLD THE burrow warden. "Got to be."

"Quite a claim, mate," Burrow Warden Belwar Dissengulp replied. "Symvyn's no rogue, and not young enough to be that stupid."

"Not many knew of the arandur," Maltzabloc reminded him.

Belwar considered that honestly. The precious metal was quite rare and much in demand, sought after for the beauty of its refined silver-blue appearance and the resistances such armor provided against lightning and fire and even acid. Blingdenstone was thick still with sparkling gemstones and other metals, but the arandur veins there had long been exhausted. Until a new source had recently been found.

"Cursed arandur," Belwar muttered under his breath, for like platinum and mithral, the precious mineral was known to tempt even the strong. Belwar considered his own climb over his burrow warden brothers to get King Schnicktick to choose him for this dangerous mission, all for arandur. Would he have done that for gold or jewels?

Yes, Belwar had fought hard to lead the expedition to find the vein, and had caught a few fortunate breaks when several more senior burrow wardens had deferred. Which meant that Belwar Dissengulp held a lot of responsibility for the safety of his community here, and his heretofore stellar reputation would take a seriously negative turn if they could not make a go of it.

But Symvyn? Symvyn Rivenstone? There weren't ten svirfnebli in all the kingdom Belwar would have chosen above the clever fellow for such an expedition as this. Symvyn had distinguished himself many times in the tumultuous decades. When an umber hulk had run roughshod over half the kingdom, Symvyn had been the one to get an enchanted quarrel into its backside, allowing the svirfnebli diviners to easily track it the next time it went underground, swimming through the stone to try to catch other gnomes unprepared in another part of the many-chambered city.

Surely Symvyn was not one Belwar would have thought a thief and traitor.

"So you know for certain, or your thinking has led you to Symvyn?" Belwar demanded.

Maltzabloc hesitated. "Few know of the treasure we seek."

"Few know that we know of it," Belwar corrected. "Many wag their tongues when they've a bit of myconid squeezings in them. Aye, many roll their eyes, seeing things that aren't even there, after but a few shots of the potent juice. We told few, aye, but I'd be guessing that all out here know well of the mineral."

Maltzabloc conceded the point with a shrug.

"Can't be Symvyn," Belwar said. "Look harder."

With a nod, the younger gnome bowed and rushed away, leaving Belwar with too many unsettling thoughts. It was dangerous enough just being out here away from Blingdenstone, with its multiple escape tunnels and rooms crafted for ease in summoning earth elementals to help in the defense of the city. The last thing they needed was one of their own cutting deals with the treacherous dark elves, or worse, the duergar, for the gray dwarves could mine almost as well as the svirfnebli, and would probably consider a new vein of arandur worth going to war over. They had never mastered refining the stuff—only the svirfnebli could take the blue-green metal and give it that beautiful silver-blue sheen—but even raw, the metal would bring a fine price.

Even as he went through that thought process, Belwar couldn't find any sense to it. Blingdenstone used the wealth of their trading for all, and no svirfneblin in the city wasn't given a fine life. The best wine, the best food, superb clothing, comfortable bedding—all of it—was provided by King Schnicktick to every one of his subjects. How might one of his comrades out here in the wilds be tempted to steal from the others or, worse, betray them to dark elves or duergar, when they would reap the benefits anyway?

The burrow warden could only sigh. He had seen this before, of course. Every city had moldy mushrooms ruining the barrel, but Belwar had handpicked this adventuring troupe.

It made no sense.

Symvyn? That made less sense, still, but Belwar knew Maltzabloc well and had never known that one to be overly suspicious or conspiracy-minded.

It was all an added weight on the shoulders of Burrow Warden Belwar. He was in command here, out here, in the wilds, surrounded by lethal enemies, and with an important task in hand. That would be difficult enough without betrayals!

With such treachery among this small group, the entire mission seemed impossible.

ZAKNAFEIN CREPT ALONG THE INTERTWINING TUNNELS, one deliberate and slow step at a time. He didn't dare make a sound, didn't dare step hard enough to cause vibrations in the stone. He was well-versed in the region he and the others had entered, and agreed with Beniago's decision to send all off alone.

Two together would alert the burrowers, if any were about, and Zaknafein knew what had created this winding, overlapping, intersecting, and often forking maze.

The smaller holes were those of thoqqua, worms about as long as a drow was tall. They could move through stone as fast as a drow might walk an open chamber. These didn't scare Zak—he knew well that he could dispatch a thoqqua, or several, fairly easily, and thoqqua weren't particularly aggressive unless directly threatened.

The larger tunnels, however, the ones he could walk upright, were not made by thoqqua, obviously. While the wormholes were smooth, the stone melted by the creatures, these larger corridors were rough-edged, chopped and hewn, and not by axes.

No, these had been made by umber hulks, giant and fearsome and formidable. Umber hulks would attack him without hesitation, and Zak had a short list of potential enemies he'd consider more dangerous.

If he encountered one, however, at least he, unlike most other drow, had a fighting chance. That was why Beniago had sent him out ahead instead of the main scouts, neither of whom could possibly stand against such an abomination.

Or perhaps their earlier conversation had convinced Beniago that Zak was expendable.

He took no chances. Every fifth step, he put his ear to the wall, listening for the sounds of an umber hulk or a thoqqua burrowing, noises every drow at the academy was taught well.

He paused before every bend in the winding tunnels, turning all his senses forward with every subsequent inch he moved. He examined every pile of rubble from afar, for the detritus of umber hulk burrowing was most often large enough to conceal a dangerous enemy.

Time and distance had no meaning to him.

Everything was caution and safety in this one spot of ground he inhabited.

If Beniago was impatient, Zaknafein simply didn't care.

His caution paid off. He came up on a bend to the left, the left-hand wall deep in broken stones. As he began to skirt that pile, turning his attention to the tunnel ahead as he became certain the pile itself was safe, he heard a soft whisper.

Up onto the rubble pile he went, carefully picking his steps to avoid upending any loose stones. As he neared the sharper area of the bend, he went down on his belly, crawling to the edge, and peered around. The area ahead was more a chamber than a tunnel, a place where many of the tunnels intersected, and not all at the same level, leaving a multi-tiered Underdark version of a meadow. Enough lichen and glowworms had settled in the place to give it a brighter aspect than many of the tunnels behind him, affording Zaknafein a wider and longer view.

He saw the deep gnome first, a small, skinny-armed but broad-shouldered fellow dressed in gray, wearing a pickaxe on his hip, a thick cloak back over his shoulders, bulging behind him above a large pack.

Across from him, not far, stood a tall drow woman, a priestess, surely, given her wondrous, spider-emblazoned robes. She had her back mostly to Zaknafein, as if he was peering over her right shoulder.

The gnome held something out to her. She took it and brought it in close, then nodded.

"You will get this for me," she said quietly.

"I will get this for you," the gnome responded.

"You will get this for me quickly," she said.

"I will get this for you quickly."

"You will be careful."

"I will be careful."

"But if they find you out, then you will run away, back here, back to me."

"Always to you," the gnome replied.

The stilted conversation had Zak's jaw hanging open, but as he tried to sort it out, something else came to mind.

He had to run down there and join in the conversation.

He started to move, then caught himself.

No, hurry, he told himself, or thought he told himself. *They want to be friends with you. There is great gain to be had here!*

Zaknafein closed his eyes and fought off the compulsion, then opened his eyes just in time to notice something crawling—no, not crawling but flowing—under the rubble across the way.

Every instinct within the warrior told him that something was greatly amiss. The hairs on the back of his neck, on his arms, all stood up, tingling. His muscles tightened.

He couldn't identify why this all was . . . off, but he knew it to be true.

Zaknafein crept back, hopped down from the pile, and ran away.

"JARLAXLE'S BAND WAS WATCHING," BOLFAE TOLD ICCARA, after Iccara's conversation with the deep gnome Symvyn. "You picked well the meeting place."

"Of course," Iccara replied. "I have spent a long while preparing this. I know Jarlaxle well enough. He is clever for a man, and he has no intention of allowing House Hunzrin to threaten his extra-

Menzoberranzan trading partners, particularly not the svirfnebli, and particularly not if they have really found arandur."

"You know him well enough to hate him, you mean."

Iccara shrugged, as if it hardly mattered, and of course, it did not. "The conflict between the two bands, house and rogue, is inevitable. Both seek glory beyond the city and that means crossing over each other's pathways. Better for all that this is settled quickly."

"Better for us that we get to watch it and enjoy it," Bolfae corrected, and Iccara did not argue the point.

"Who will win?" Bolfae asked.

"Who cares?"

"Yvonnel Baenre will care. She favors her lost son and the secret knowledge and power he brings to her."

"True enough, but this will be no fight that carries back to Menzoberranzan," Iccara predicted. "This is a prod, a skirmish, and little more. Although the deep gnome miners may find themselves in the midst of a conflict that is beyond them."

"I hold you in a place of honor to so hold this gnome in your thrall. I had thought them more difficult to dominate."

"Not so difficult, particularly when you tempt them with that which they secretly desire. It is the same with drow."

"Not with the drow watching your meeting then," Bolfae explained.

"Were you close enough to try?"

"I was, and I did. And he rejected the intrusion wholly. He may even have sensed it, I fear."

Iccara nodded. "Jarlaxle selects his minions well, and trains them as if they were nobles in his house. Even the least of them."

"I doubt this was the least of them, in any case. I felt strength of will there as great as I have encountered before."

"Did you discern his name?"

Bolfae shook her head, then straightened and cleared her throat as Priestess Du'Quelve and some others approached.

"Priestess," Iccara greeted her. "It is good that you have come. The gnome traitor gave me this." She held up a small piece of the blue-green mineral. "He has promised me a sizable haul, enough to outfit Matron Arolina in a full suit of arandur armor."

"And enough for me as well?" Du'Quelve asked.

Iccara smiled. "He will come to Menzoberranzan with us, to serve House Hunzrin. He knows the secret of the metal. Your glory will be complete, your ascent to high priestess assured."

Du'Quelve started beaming at that, but fell back a step and looked at Iccara with puzzlement. "How did you . . . ?"

Iccara's smile widened. "I told you, priestess. My sister and I are not of Menzoberranzan, but we did not seek out the Hunzrin traders by accident. We have eyes in the city. We know, and we approve. When Matron Mother Baenre sees Matron Arolina Hunzrin bedecked in a shining suit of beautiful arandur mail, she will want a suit of her own, no doubt."

"What matron mother would not?" Bolfae added.

"And to get one of her own, she will eradicate this gnome band and set her own goblin slaves to mining the ore," Iccara went on. "But all she'll have is the ore. House Hunzrin will have Symvyn in their possession, and the gnome holds the secret of refining. Thus, House Hunzrin will become greatly favored by Matron Mother Baenre, and Matron Arolina will use that to hold an exclusive imprimatur from Matron Mother Baenre to trade with Enclave Arach, as we both desire."

"As we both desire," Du'Quelve agreed. "There is another concern. We have noted spies—"

"It is the mercenary band, of course," Bolfae interrupted her. "Bregan D'aerthe is what you call them, yes? They are of no concern. If they get too close, we will help you destroy them."

Priestess Du'Quelve scoffed at that. "They are in the favor of Matron Mother Baenre."

"Their leader is, yes," said Iccara.

"But the one named Jarlaxle is not here," Bolfae added.

"How do you know this?"

"We already told you, Priestess Du'Quelve," Bolfae replied. "We have eyes in the city. Jarlaxle is known to us, particularly since we are interested in the svirfnebli."

Du'Quelve wore a strange expression as she digested that, looking confused but as if she were trying to make some connections with her bits of information. There were rumors all through Menzoberranzan that someone was dealing with Blingdenstone, both of the visiting priestesses knew, and now, likely, Du'Quelve was beginning to realize that the rumors were true, and that Jarlaxle was almost certainly the one doing the dealing.

"Perhaps it is time House Hunzrin made it clear to Bregan D'aerthe and everyone else in the City of Spiders that they and they alone are the primary source of extra-Menzoberranzan trading," Iccara offered, after giving the Hunzrin priestess a few moments to sort through her puzzlement.

Du'Quelve spent a long while staring at Iccara, and again it was clear she was processing the information and trying to play out all the possibilities. Slowly but surely, she began to nod her agreement.

Iccara and Bolfae glanced at each other.

Let the entertainment begin, Iccara telepathically told her sister.

CHAPTER 16

The Winding Ways of Umber Hulk Corridors

"We should be gone from here," Zak told Beniago when the troupe had regrouped back at the assigned meeting spot.

"Gone? We know the gnomes are about and mining, and now can be fairly certain that House Hunzrin has plans regarding . . ."

Zaknafein was shaking his head through every word, prompting Beniago to pause and stare at him.

"What?"

"They are mining, and yes, House Hunzrin is trying to work with them, or with a traitor among their ranks, at least," Zaknafein explained. "I saw the exchange, a priestess who I think not of House Hunzrin . . ."

"One of the visitors to the Hunzrin troupe, then," said Binnefein, and Zaknafein glanced at his old housemate and nodded.

"He gave her some ore as proof of the find," Zak explained. "Arandur, I expect."

"And you wish us gone from this place?" Beniago asked incredulously. "This is exactly why we are out here."

"And now we know."

"And now we must stop it," Beniago said. "We either stop it by chasing away the Hunzrins, or remove this traitor from the equation. In either case, we ruin their plans. This arrangement cannot stand."

"You do not understand," Zak said. "There is more afoot here than we know. Something . . . strange . . ."

Beniago looked at him curiously. Binnefein moved closer, as did Nav Rayan Dyrr, both leaning in after the atypical uncertainty in Zak's voice.

"There was something strange in the way the gnome echoed every command from the priestess," Zak clarified. "That alone hinted to me that someone or something was in my mind, as well, trying to compel me to go down and join in the exchange."

"To slay the priestess and take the ore as your own?" Nav Rayan Dyrr asked.

"No! Hardly that."

"You always did so enjoy killing priestesses," Binnefein remarked.

"No . . . I mean, yes," said Zak, shaking his head emphatically. "But I didn't want to kill her. I wanted to go down there to join with her and aid her in her endeavors."

All three looked at him with open skepticism.

Zak nodded, accepting and agreeing with their incredulity. "Someone or something was in my mind, trying to compel me, to dominate me."

"Priestesses are demons," Nav Rayan Dyrr remarked.

But Beniago held up his hand to silence Dyrr and forgo any returning quip from Binnefein. "Matron Mother Baenre herself would have a hard time magically enlisting you to her whims," he told Zaknafein.

The weapon master shrugged. "Which is why I have a bad feeling about our endeavor. There is more to this than I saw. More to this than House Hunzrin trying to gain a trading partner among the deep gnomes. More to this than House Hunzrin itself. Of that, I am certain."

Beniago looked to his two other principle scouts. They were a small band here and badly outnumbered by the Hunzrin group, which sported no fewer than four priestesses.

"We know what we came to know," Nav Rayan Dyrr said. "The Hunzrins are trying to work with this splinter svirfneblin mining troupe, and they have some outside help."

"We should let Jarlaxle determine our next steps," Binnefein agreed. "Perhaps his Oblodran friend can determine some of the un-answered questions about these new observations."

"Objections?" Beniago asked, looking to the two scouts, then to Zak.

"I think it best we be gone from this place," Zak said. It hurt him to say it. He didn't want to be back in Menzoberranzan at this time, surely, given the nasty ramifications to his son. But he knew what he felt, and it was obvious to him that their position out here was tenta-tive at best. If someone or something had tried to dominate him, to say nothing of almost succeeding, then that being knew he was out here, and so the Hunzrins likely knew that all of them were out here.

Just as Beniago nodded his agreement, a call from around the cor-ner startled the four. Moments later came the sound of fighting and the goblinoid guttural grunts of bugbears.

Zaknafein had his swords in hand before the others had even begun to register the noise. And as he always did, Zak ran toward the trouble. He came around the corner to see a trio of Bregan D'aerthe warriors about to be overwhelmed by the sheer size and ferocity of a half-dozen bugbears.

He saw his opening and charged in between a pair of fighting drow, his right-hand sword leading with a thrust into the nearest bug-bear's chest, his left-hand blade slashing out wide to drive back the next beast in line as it pressed a drow. Just in time, too, for a second bugbear farther along had tied up that drow's weapons just enough to offer a clear opening to the one Zak had driven back.

"Finish them quickly!" Zak called to his three fighting compan-ions, and it seemed likely, since six bugbears shouldn't prove much of a threat to four superbly armed and trained drow warriors once the element of surprise had been turned back.

Zak accentuated his point by skipping ahead, swords going out left and right to push back the bugbears to either side. The one he had stuck roared and leaped at him, not realizing his speed—who ever realized the speed of Zaknafein until it was too late?

His swords came back in, one high enough to defeat the bug-bear's attempted club attack, the other darting forward, impaling the charging brute right beside the lesser hole Zak had already put into its chest.

It fell away and there were five, but with more coming judging from sounds further along the tunnels, of the shouts of dark elves, the roars of goblins. A bright light flashed from around the corner, orange and flickering, like a flame strike, and Zak understood that the priest-esses were not far afield.

BENIAGO, NAV RAYAN DYRR, AND BINNEFEIN WERE NOT SO inclined as Zaknafein. They knew the odds against them, had a good guess at the strength of the Hunzrin force. The sound of battle in their precarious position did not urge them forward to the fight.

Rather, it sent them fleeing, three together down one corridor, then Nav Rayan Dyrr peeling off at the first intersection, Beniago and Binnefein splitting at the next.

Only Beniago's footsteps slowed as the sounds of fighting receded. He had left Zaknafein behind. Others, too, but Zaknafein . . . That was enough to give him pause.

He knew how Jarlaxle felt about this one. So many thoughts swirled about him, foremost among them that he was a Baenre. Would the Hunzrins dare attack him if he identified himself and surrendered?

He could go back and end this conflict, perhaps, simply by an-nouncing his true name. What house in Menzoberranzan would dare incur the wrath of Matron Mother Yvonnel Baenre?

If he did that, though, his time in Bregan D'aerthe would be at its end, his cover blown to all who would hear the omnipresent rumors.

Which distressed him more: Jarlaxle's anger about the loss of Zaknafein, or Beniago's relegation to once more become a simple minor noble in a house thick with them?

He searched for a third option.

ZAKNAFEIN STABBED AT THE BUGBEAR TO HIS LEFT A third time, then spun about and bore into the one on his right, his right-hand sword rolling figure eights in the air before him, each diagonal slash powerful and demanding attention. The sword moved so quickly, he had the bugbear's eyes following the movement, and so he suddenly flashed that sword back out to the right, then sprang ahead and drove his left-hand sword up under the brute's chin and into its brain before it had refocused its attention back on him instead of the mesmerizing blade.

Behind him, a third bugbear went down. Before him, along the line to the right, one of the drow warriors cut down a fourth. The remaining two stumbled backward and the battle was won, or paused long enough for Zak to glance back for Beniago, Dyrr, and Binnefein.

The weapon master gave a sigh. They weren't coming.

He tried to rally the three standing with him, but two were already running away, and when he looked to the third, he found the fellow standing perfectly still and unblinking. Too still, too frozen.

The two bugbears returned then, with six more in tow.

Zak looked to the young drow, too young even to have completed the academy.

Too young to die, Zak thought.

Zaknafein shrugged and rolled his weapons in his hands.

He charged at the bugbears.

So be it.

Straight up, he would be overwhelmed, he knew, so he started low, diving into a forward roll. He came around and slowed his forward momentum, redirecting it into a leap high into the air, tucking his legs above the down-pointing weapons of the bugbears. He crossed his arms tightly against his chest, sword points out to opposite sides.

He brought them across so suddenly as he neared the bugbear directly before him that it hadn't even begun to lift its weapon when its throat was removed so forcefully its head nearly fell free.

Zaknafein appeared to be pushing right through that brute, but he used his legs expertly to brace against the falling bugbear instead of rolling through it, dropping him to the floor.

One of the nearby bugbears fell for it, but another did not, adjusting its retracted spiked club for a higher swing.

Zak anticipated that possibility, though, and threw his head back—bending—and the club whipped just above him. He tucked and hit the ground and threw himself into another roll, this one to the side, and came back to his feet in a crouch that allowed him to propel himself forward suddenly, so suddenly at the bugbear at the far end of the line, which had turned to intercept him as the first one fell away, thinking he would go right through the line.

Even with its agility, that bugbear had not quite reoriented itself to the swift change in Zak's position, and it was wide open now. Seven separate stabs, left and right alternating, gashed the beast, sending it falling away.

Two down, but four remaining, and when Zak reversed again, throwing himself back the way he had come, he found himself cut off, the remaining quartet spaced about him and now more cautious.

Time was on their side, which Zak knew even more pointedly when a drow priestess arrived at the far tunnel.

"Clay!" came a shout from the tunnel through which Zak had entered the room, a word every member of Bregan D'aerthe knew well.

Zak snapped his eyes shut as not one but a handful of ceramic pellets flew into the room, each specially coated to contain the magical energy contained within, pellets enchanted with powerful and continual dweomers emitting bright light.

When Zak opened his eyes just a moment later, he found the four bugbears shying, covering their eyes, groaning at the sudden brilliant light. The drow priestess, too, had shied, no longer visible in the side corridor.

Zaknafein leaped high and far, passing between the two bugbears on the left, backhanding his swords out to either side to slash hard against skulls and lifted arms. His swords disappeared into their scabbards by the time he landed, running full speed to the magically frozen comrade. He drove his shoulder into that drow's belly, bending the young man over him, scooping him up, and running on.

Down the corridors he went, cutting haphazardly down any side passages that appeared to bring him farther from the enemies. He found one to be a dead end, though, and desperately turned to retreat.

The man he was holding groaned.

Zak lowered him to the floor and slapped him awake, then tugged him along before he could even ask what had happened.

They got back out into the main corridor soon after and sprinted away, finally coming to tunnels they both recognized. At the next fork, Zak nodded to his companion, wished him well, and pushed him toward the right-hand one, while Zak raced down the left.

He hoped he would see this man again one day in Menzoberranzan, but at that moment, Zaknafein wasn't giving either of them very good odds of getting out of this area of the wild Underdark alive.

"WE LOST THREE FOR CERTAIN," BENIAGO TOLD JARLAXLE some days later, back in the offices of Bregan D'aerthe in the Clawrift of Menzoberranzan, beneath House Oblodra. "Three others remain missing."

Jarlaxle stared at him and Binnefein hard.

"Yes, there is no word of Zaknafein," Binnefein admitted.

"He knew," said Beniago. "He warned us that something was amiss, that something more than the Hunzrins were involved here. But alas, his warning came too late."

"No word of him at all?" Jarlaxle asked.

"When last I saw him, he was engaged with a gang of bugbears, a drow priestess coming into the room. I tried to help, but could not remain," Beniago said.

Jarlaxle didn't respond, just sat tapping the tips of his fingers together.

"I thought to demand a truce, to reveal myself as Baenre," Beniago admitted.

"I'm glad you did not," Jarlaxle decided. "For Bregan D'aerthe, it is better that you did not. And better for House Baenre."

"I am tempted to beg Matron Mother Yvonnel to lay waste to House Hunzrin," Beniago said.

Jarlaxle shook his head. "I agree with Zaknafein's assessment. Better to not involve the Baenres until we know more about this Hunzrin scheme. Now, go and learn what you may—ask one of your cousin high priestesses to discern if the Hunzrins have taken Zaknafein as their prisoner. If Matron Malice learns of this, there will be war. Not that that would be a bad thing, I suppose."

Beniago gave a little laugh, clearly relieved that Jarlaxle wasn't holding him responsible for the apparent loss of his friend. He and Binnefein left and returned to the Oozing Myconid in the Stench-streets, where they were overjoyed to find Nav Rayan Dyrr, drinking the ordeal of the Underdark out of his thoughts.

That left only two unaccounted for.

The next day, Beniago was with Jarlaxle when the number went down to one, as the youngest of the expedition returned, shaken but very much unhurt, and with a story of being saved by Zaknafein.

"We parted ways out in the tunnels, as we were trained," he told Jarlaxle and Binnefein.

"And none are better trained than Zaknafein Do'Urden," Jarlaxle said hopefully. His mood improved noticeably after that, his hopes high.

But the days went by without any word of the lone unaccounted-for Bregan D'aerthe associate, perhaps the only drow in the city Jarlaxle considered a friend.

ZAKNAFEIN HATED THE IDEA OF RETURNING TO MEN-zoberranzan. Out alone in the tunnels, more than once was he tempted to just keep running the other way, to strike out and survive as best as he could in a place that was not under the sway of vile Lolth.

In his younger days, perhaps he would have tried, but now, in the end, Zak's roundabout course had him moving inexorably toward Menzoberranzan.

Toward his son.

He entered the city quietly through one of the smaller side gates. These, too, were guarded, but no one asked questions of other dark elves entering. Zak kept his traveling cloak up high and could only hope that he wasn't recognized. He didn't want Malice to know he was back.

For that reason, he avoided the Oozing Myconid—Malice had eyes there often, he knew—and went straight to the Clawrift, moving down the concealed stair and in through the kobold tunnels until he at last arrived at Jarlaxle's private quarters.

"At long last," Jarlaxle greeted him, when Zak walked in. The mercenary leader was trying to play it casual, as if he was not overjoyed to see Zaknafein, and had been expecting him all along, but Zak noted the man's body language, the eagerness pressing his shoulders forward, and understood that for one of the few times in his life, Jarlaxle's posture had betrayed his control.

"Can you explain your delay?" Jarlaxle said. "I would never expect Zaknafein to tarry."

Zak glanced at the other two drow in the room, Beniago and the always annoying Kimmuriel Oblodra.

"It is good to be back," he said.

"You do not believe that," Kimmuriel said, and Zak narrowed his eyes, warning the psionicist to stay out of his head, if he was in there. Zak had never met anyone who made him feel this uncomfortable, including Kimmuriel's psionics-wielding family members and even the matrons of the city.

"It is good to have you back," Jarlaxle replied, and Beniago chirped in with an assenting "Aye."

Zaknafein focused on the Baenre lieutenant. "You thought I would die in that room."

"I did, but I tried to help," Beniago answered.

"I know." He hadn't recognized the voice clearly in the heat of battle, but he had been fairly certain that it was Beniago who had thrown the light bombs, which had likely saved his life.

"When Braelin returned, I was confident you would not be far behind," Beniago said.

"Braelin?"

"The young scout you carried out of there. He returned to us a few days ago."

Zak nodded and was glad.

"Promising young man," Jarlaxle went on. "He was born to commoners, but I find him nobler—certainly more loyal!—than the nobles I know. I found him when he was young and saw something there, so I brought him in. You would know this, Zaknafein, had you bothered to spend more time . . ."

The rogue rambled on, and Zaknafein sighed. Jarlaxle was talking about nothing important not to convince Zaknafein of the worth of this Braelin person, but because he knew Zaknafein was agitated and anxious.

"Enough!" Zak said at length, because Jarlaxle wasn't even beginning to slow in his endless tales. He couldn't miss the smug look on Jarlaxle's face.

"Yes?" Jarlaxle asked sweetly.

"I need to go out from the city again."

"Matron Malice won't agree."

"She doesn't know I'm back."

"Are you certain of this?" Jarlaxle asked.

Before Zak could answer, Kimmuriel said, "He is not sure."

"I'm going to kill him someday," Zak muttered quietly.

"A common sentiment, and one that makes Kimmuriel proud, I am sure," Jarlaxle replied.

"Enough of this, though. I cannot yet return. It is too soon."

"You're not going back to House Do'Urden at this time, no," Jarlaxle agreed. "Not after that disaster in the tunnels. We can't let this stand. The Hunzrins have challenged us, and the treasure is considerable if it really is arandur the gnomes are mining."

"Looked like it to me, though I've only seen it once before in its unrefined form, many decades ago."

"Even if not, I need to answer the Hunzrins, of course."

"What do you intend to do?"

"You told Beniago that you felt someone or something was trying to dominate you telepathically. It makes sense that perhaps this gnome fellow was similarly afflicted. It is not typical of the svirfnebli that they betray their own for the sake of coin or other monetary gain."

"You know a lot about the deep gnomes, do you?"

"I know a lot about everything," Jarlaxle replied. "That's how I stay alive."

"And how you stay surrounded by luxury."

"I live in a cave."

"We both know better."

Jarlaxle shrugged and let it go.

"So, if this gnomish fellow is dominated, mentally enslaved, we have to free him," Jarlaxle explained.

"And how do you plan to do that?"

Jarlaxle smiled at Zak and led the man's gaze to Kimmuriel Oblodra.

"Kimmuriel does love challenges," Jarlaxle said.

"What makes you believe it will be a challenge?" the Oblodran remarked.

Zak sighed again and rubbed his face, hardly thrilled at the idea of wandering back out into the Underdark beside the likes of the strange psionicist. He calmed himself by silently remembering that one day his son would learn of this, and if Drizzt knew of Kimmuriel by then, he would certainly appreciate his father's sacrifice.

CHAPTER 17

Too Far Down the Thoqqua Hole

Priestesses can dominate a victim," Kimmuriel said to Zaknafein, the two of them moving with Jarlaxle along the Underdark tunnels back toward the deep gnome position.

"Not like this," Zak replied, and not for the first time. "I have felt the manipulations of priestesses all my life."

Zak paused for a moment, then added, "Or perhaps it is possible. I admit that I have never battled a priestess in a fair fight, where she had me by surprise or had time to prepare—"

He stopped suddenly and shook his head vigorously, then roared in anger.

"Was it like that?" Kimmuriel asked.

Zaknafein took a step toward the psionicist, his swords coming into his hands.

Jarlaxle was fast to intercept him.

"If he ever does that again . . ." Zak said, pointing one sword over Jarlaxle's shoulder at the distant Kimmuriel.

"It wasn't—" Jarlaxle started to say, but Zak cut him off, his outrage too great to hear anything above the blood pounding in his ears.

"I will kill you," Zak promised. "Do not ever slip into my mind again, because I will kill you!"

"It wasn't him!" Jarlaxle yelled in Zak's face. "He acted on my command."

Before he could think of anything to reply, Zaknafein drove his forehead into Jarlaxle's face, knocking the rogue back two steps. Zak brought his swords in and got slammed brutally, more powerfully than he had ever imagined possible, a wave of energy that scrambled his brain and had his legs shaking wildly, his swords dropping from his hands.

"Enough, enough," he heard Jarlaxle say, but suddenly from far, far away. He saw the stone floor of the corridor coming and thought it would probably hurt.

Surprisingly, though, he didn't feel a thing, at least not until he woke up sometime later, sitting against a wall, Jarlaxle sitting across from him.

"You need to stop that," Jarlaxle told him. "Yes, I told Kimmuriel to do that to you, and yes, I understand the violation involved. Of course I do. Why do you think I wear this eyepatch, after all? We needed to know."

"Was it the same?" Kimmuriel asked from back and to the side.

Zak glared at him.

"Here," Jarlaxle said, reaching behind himself, under his cloak, and bringing forth a finely made bullwhip, one Zaknafein surely recognized.

"You found it," Zak said, his tone changing. The magic in this whip was truly wondrous, its cracking end able to cut a small tear into the plane of fire itself.

"Kimmuriel found it, as a gift to you," Jarlaxle explained.

Zaknafein didn't bother trying to suppress the doubt in his responding expression.

"The Ruling Council had remanded it," Jarlaxle said. "They thought it a weapon too threatening to matrons, and one suitable only to a matron—who, of course, prefer the snake-headed scourges that signify their station. They wanted it put out of the way, probably in no small part because of who it was who had put it to deadly use."

He was speaking of Zak, of course, and the weapon master took the offered whip and rolled it out to get its feel once more. Zaknafein had always enjoyed this type of weapon and knew how to use it expertly—or at least, he once had known the expert handling of a bullwhip. But that, he mused, was more than a century before.

"There, the hurt is mended. Now, Zaknafein, answer Kimmuriel," Jarlaxle demanded. "I brought you out here on your request, I remind you. We three are walking into a potential trap. We need to know."

The reminder of why they were out here, or more specifically, of why *he* was out here, calmed Zak considerably.

"The telepathic intrusion, was it the same?" Kimmuriel demanded again.

Zak considered it carefully for a few moments, then shook his head. "No. This was . . . different. Less demanding. More trick, less pure force. I don't know how to explain it, but with your violation, it didn't seem as . . . evil?"

"Would an illithid seem more evil?" Jarlaxle asked Kimmuriel, who shook his head.

Zaknafein stared hard at the psionicist, who was clearly thinking deeply on the information, and seemed to the weapon master to know more than he was letting on. He didn't trust that one at all.

But he was glad to have the whip back, at least.

THE GNOME CREPT OUT OF THE QUIET CAMP, MOST OF THE miners napping, the cook and the miner assigned to help him busy at their tasks, and Burrow Warden Belwar and that insufferable Maltzabloc nowhere to be found, likely deep inside the new tunnel the industrious miners had dug to inspect the thus far disappointing load of arandur coming from it.

Symvyn paused as he moved into the tunnel past the warded gate, reconsidering his plans here—and not for the first time. "What are you doing, ye damned dumb gnome?" he had asked himself a hundred times.

The first time, perhaps the first ten times, Symvyn had almost thrown up his hands and run to Burrow Warden Belwar with his confession. Every time, though, had come those feelings that he wasn't getting his due, that he was working so hard and so loyally for King Schnicktick and with a title of burrow warden yet to be even hinted at.

But now, for some time, he didn't try to convince himself and justify this. He was simply too far along. *Too far down the thoqqua hole*, as the svirfnebli said of such emotional traps.

He had no choices here now, so it really wasn't a question any longer. Somehow, he had been lured in past the point of no return.

Once he was free of any wards or sentries, the gnome picked up his pace, moving through the tunnels as fast as his short legs would carry him. Perhaps he should have been more cautious, pausing and listening for umber hulks or other potential monsters, but so determined was he to put this distasteful episode behind him that he abandoned caution.

Besides, if anything dangerous was about, wouldn't the drow have taken care of it already?

He saw the drow priestesses—both of them this time, Du'Quelve and Iccara—waiting for him, Du'Quelve pacing nervously, Iccara calmly sitting on a rock, fiddling with her fingernail as if something had gotten stuck under it. He slowed in his approach and glanced to the side, looking to the rock piles in a side tunnel where he had noted some sentient, predatory ooze slithering about during a previous journey here. It seemed clear, but probably wasn't, Symvyn noted, for few things in the Underdark could hide as well as the malleable oozes.

"It is good to see you, clever gnome," Iccara said when Symvyn rushed up to them.

"Where is it?" Priestess Du'Quelve demanded, not hiding her anger.

The gnome fumbled about his belt at his right hip to produce a small pouch, then reached behind, under his cloak, and pulled off two more. He presented the three to the priestesses.

Du'Quelve snatched one and pulled it open, reaching in and pulling forth a small handful of green-and-black ore. She looked to

Iccara, who had taken the other two. "Which is a bag of holding?" she demanded.

Iccara opened each bag and reached in, then shook her head.

"I've no such item," Symvyn told them. "It would be a lot easier if I did!"

"Then where is the rest of my ore?" Du'Quelve demanded.

"I . . . I did my best," Symvyn said, rocking nervously from foot to foot. "The ore's not light, and ye cannot expect me to carry a large sack out of Dun Arandur, as the burrow warden's gone to naming the camp. They're watching, don't doubt. Watching who comes in and who goes out."

"I do not care!" Du'Quelve shouted at him. "You haven't enough here to make a gauntlet."

"A bit at a time," Symvyn said, backing away with every word.

"How much time do you think we have, foolish gnome? Do you expect us to stay out here in the Underdark for tendays while you ferry a handful at a time?"

"Three handfuls," Symvyn said, and he swallowed hard when he saw the look his snide remark invoked on the face of the drow priestess!

"Enough, Priestess Du'Quelve," Iccara said. "The gnome is frightened and not without reason."

Du'Quelve threw up her arms and turned aside, muttering under her breath.

"We do need you to do better," Iccara told Symvyn.

"They count the ore," he replied, pleadingly. "Not exact, but Belwar's knowing how much is there, and so will know how much ain't! They catch me and it's all done here."

"Perhaps he is right," Iccara said.

Du'Quelve spun about, her red eyes wide.

"Perhaps we should change our tactics, then, and not rely on Matron Mother Baenre's reaction to a shining suit of arandur," Iccara explained.

Du'Quelve looked at her curiously for a few heartbeats, then let a smile spread wide as she nodded.

Symvyn watched it all, still not catching on.

"Tell us the location of all the defensive wards," Iccara said to Symvyn.

The gnome felt his face fall as his jaw went slack. "That weren't our deal!"

"This is our new deal," Iccara said insistently.

"That weren't our deal!" Symvyn said again, more loudly, and he found it hard to get the words past his lips, as if his voice suddenly wasn't his own.

"This is our new deal," Iccara said again, this time calmly.

It all came clear to Symvyn then, the answer to his dilemmas, both with the priestesses here and with the dangers of Belwar back in Dun Arandur.

"This is our new deal," Iccara said a third time.

"This is our new deal," Symvyn recited, the statement at first surprising him, but then settling on him as his obvious preference.

He saw Du'Quelve and Iccara exchange smiles then and knew that he had done the right thing.

He was glad to please these new friends who so valued him.

JARLAXLE BENT LOW AND PEERED UNDER THE STONES, watching the ooze as it slipped through a small crack in the wall, disappearing from sight.

"Amazing," he said. He stood and turned and looked to Zaknafein and Kimmuriel.

"There is more afoot here," Kimmuriel warned, echoing Zak's sentiments.

"This . . . thing is gone?" Jarlaxle asked.

"It is confused," answered the psionicist. "It will be confused for a long time. I do not anticipate it will bother us again."

"And if it does, you will be ready?"

Kimmuriel just stared at him.

"Come on, the corner is not far ahead," Zak told them. He started away, but paused and looked back to the stones. "You are sure that thing didn't know we were coming?"

"How certain can I be about an ooze, or whatever it was?" Kimmu-riel replied. "I sensed it. I attacked it. I won."

"But if it somehow signaled ahead to our possible enemies—"

"Why do you even think it is connected to any of that?" Kimmu-riel asked, as if the question was obvious and Zak's conclusions not.

"We think the gnome is dominated. You sensed the creature, ooze, whatever, because of its mental energies. The connection seems evident."

"Only because you dismiss coincidence, which is what I would ex-pect from a warrior."

"I don't believe in coincidence."

"As I just said."

"Whatever the case," Jarlaxle intervened, before it could go any further. "Perhaps this creature is some kind of mind plague and is in-fecting the svirfnebli independent of the Hunzrins. Perhaps it is not connected, and merely came to this place because it sensed other mag-ical or psionic activity. It does not matter—and our time here is short. Let us learn what we may."

Zak and Kimmuriel continued to exchange stares for a bit longer; then Zak turned and moved off, traveling along corridors he recog-nized from his first visit here. His pace was quick, not just because of his familiarity, but because of the formidability of his two companions. He did slow as he neared the rubble he recognized as the pile from which he had witnessed the first gnome and drow encounter, however, for he heard voices up ahead.

The three came to the corner. Jarlaxle peered around, then pulled back and took out a strange-looking, funnel-shaped device. He put the narrow end in his ear and leaned out, the flared end toward the speakers.

Priestess Du'Quelve Hunzrin, his signaled to his companions. His expression changed as he continued to listen, a look of concern com-ing over him.

The gnome is betraying his people fully, he signed. *I think the Hunz-rins mean to attack them.*

Alone? Kimmuriel's hand asked.

He is dominated. Fully, Zak interjected.

Jarlaxle looked to Kimmuriel. *Free him.*

Kimmuriel nodded and took a step toward the corner, but Zaknafein then said, aloud, "We should be gone!"

The other two looked at him in horror, shocked that he would break their silence, but they understood when they followed Zak's gaze back the way they had come, to see a trio of drow warriors and a priestess—a priestess who appeared quite naked—running toward them, though still some distance away.

"Scatter, find your way," Jarlaxle said, and ran off, turning down the nearest side passage, Kimmuriel at his heels.

Zaknafein, though, had a different idea, and instead of following, he went around the bend, full speed, leaping, whip in hand.

The deep gnome cried out in surprise, and the two drow priestesses spun on him, their shock quickly turning to anger and to action, Du'Quelve Hunzrin lifting her scourge, the other waggling her fingers.

Zak raced past the deep gnome, and Du'Quelve moved to intercept him, the living snakes of her three-headed whip lifting and coiling to strike.

But Zak struck first, his bullwhip reaching out tantalizingly toward the scourge and the priestess holding in. A sudden snap of his wrist brought the tip snapping across, and Zak called on the deeper powers of the weapon, drawing a line of fire across the air right before the scourge.

Already in motion, the snakes struck, one, then the second, and two snake heads fell free, severed as they crossed the planar tear.

Priestess Du'Quelve cried out in horror—to a drow priestess, nothing was more sacred than her scourge—and that made Zak smile.

Zaknafein never slowed, though, running by the pair, expecting to be hit hard by some spell of the second priestess. It came as another blast of mental power, an attempt once more to dominate him, to break him immediately to her will.

So much like the first time, and in that moment, Zak was certain that this one and the ooze back there were somehow connected.

He fought through it, staggering a bit, and was quick to throw himself around the next corner—almost running into a pair of Hunzrin soldiers who were waiting for him!

"A NAKED PRIESTESS," JARLAXLE QUIETLY MUTTERED, SUR-prised and shocked by the revelation. For, indeed, he knew what that meant. She was naked because she had been a slithering pile of black ooze only a short while before.

"She," he quipped, for what did gender really mean to such a being? One thing he did know: "she" was a handmaiden of Lolth, a yochlol, and very likely so was the other non-Hunzrin priestess who had come out to deal with the deep gnomes, to dominate this poor fellow.

He sprinted along a fairly straight and even corridor, coming past an opening with a slight turn to ensure that no enemies were hiding within that alcove. He skidded to a stop, noting no enemy but a friend.

Kimmuriel waved him into the alcove, though how the strange drow had ever gotten to this point before him, Jarlaxle could only guess. He seemed to do that a lot regarding Kimmuriel.

"They're not far behind," he whispered.

"Far enough," Kimmuriel replied. "You know the truth now, of course."

"Handmaidens."

"Yochlol, indeed. And two of them, at least. What is this business? Why does Lolth intervene on behalf of House Hunzrin?"

"We don't know that it's Lolth," Jarlaxle replied.

"Two handmaidens," Kimmuriel said dryly, as close to sarcasm as the emotionless drow could manage.

"Two handmaidens who are causing trouble. They do so because they enjoy it," Jarlaxle argued, though his conviction was thin enough for Kimmuriel to notice without even trying to telepathically worm into Jarlaxle's thoughts.

Was House Hunzrin in the favor of the Spider Queen? Was Lolth herself orchestrating this bold move by the Hunzrins, and if so, what did that signal to Bregan D'aerthe?

Jarlaxle didn't like the possibilities here. He had worked for centuries to scrape out some measure of respect and power within the matriarchal society, for himself and for those many drow who associated with Bregan D'aerthe. But they were mostly just men, after all—Jarlaxle could count the number of women in the mercenary band on one hand, with fingers to spare.

Had Lolth finally grown weary of allowing such an elevation of a band of men?

He considered Matron Mother Baenre's reaction, and there, too, he didn't like the possibilities. She would not be happy if Bregan D'aerthe—which was, after all, a willing extension of her power—wound up greatly diminished by the Hunzrin maneuver.

Jarlaxle peered out from the alcove, feeling very uncertain.

We can't let them succeed here, he signed to his companion.

You would risk stifling handmaidens of Lolth? Kimmuriel replied, his hands moving rather awkwardly.

Despite their predicament, Jarlaxle almost laughed aloud at the childlike movements—if fingers could stutter, Kimmuriel's had just done so! Rarely did the psionicist resort to the silent hand code of the drow. Usually, he would simply communicate silently with telepathic messages.

Not with Jarlaxle and his eyepatch, though. And he wasn't about to take it off for ease of conversation, for they knew that more than one psionicist was about, and the others seemed not to be allies.

Jarlaxle considered the question for a bit. "Yes," he whispered. "If they are here on behalf of Lolth, then so be it. The Hunzrins will not win this market."

He peered around the corner again, then pulled back quickly. *They are coming*, his fingers relayed to Kimmuriel.

Kimmuriel extended his hand to Jarlaxle, who looked at it for some moments before finally taking it. He knew what was coming, and he hated it.

Oh, how he hated it.

He heard the voices of the approaching enemies, nearer and nearer, but then they were suddenly far away, and the world about him became a hazy blur. The distinct lines of the glowworms crawling about the corridor caused a distant fuzzy blue-white glow.

Kimmuriel stepped past him, moving into the stone, pulling Jarlaxle right behind.

Small spaces didn't bother Jarlaxle. He had on more than one occasion spent an entire day hiding in his portable hole, a lightless extradimensional compartment. But this wasn't a small space. He and Kimmuriel were moving through solid stone, sliding insubstantially through it.

This wasn't a small space.

This was no space at all.

And no direction at all, to Jarlaxle's sensibilities. Were they even still moving? Now fully within the stone wall, he had no frame of reference, had no visual cue that they weren't simply standing still, and with no resistance, no air movement, no tactile feeling underfoot or anywhere else, Jarlaxle could only hope that this strange friend of his had a better idea of it all than he.

They exited the stone into the same corridor Jarlaxle had just traversed, but now behind the pursuing drow. They became substantial so abruptly that Jarlaxle almost tumbled over.

"I did not expect you would wish a fight," Kimmuriel remarked.

"If there was one, I would have been alone," Jarlaxle replied, and the psionicist didn't disagree.

"I would not battle a handmaiden except in defense," Kimmuriel confirmed. "I am of House Oblodra and would not bring Lolth's disfavor upon my family."

"I wouldn't ask you to."

"Are you not?"

Jarlaxle looked at him, trying to figure out their next move and realizing as the obvious choice came to him that Kimmuriel already had.

"Free the traitor gnome from the grasp of the yochlol," Jarlaxle bade him.

Kimmuriel stared at him.

"Can you?"

Still the psionicist stared, then finally nodded.

Jarlaxle led the way back to the corner.

The Hunzrin priestess was still there, flanked by Hunzrin guards, facing the gnome, who looked perfectly terrified and miserable.

The yochlol priestess who had been beside Du'Quelve, however, was nowhere to be seen.

The two crept nearer, listening to Du'Quelve scolding the gnome.

"It is none of your concern. A band of thieves who will be put down as they deserve. I will have the locations of every ward, every glyph, every guard."

"That was not . . . our . . . deal," the poor gnome replied, his voice faltering, his legs wobbling with weakness as he tried to argue.

Do it! Jarlaxle implored Kimmuriel, snapping the communication off emphatically.

If there are repercussions . . . Kimmuriel warned.

I will assume responsibility, before Matron Mother Baenre herself. I order you to do this in her name.

Jarlaxle could hardly believe he had just said that! If these yochlol were here bestowing the blessing of Lolth on House Hunzrin, he might have well doomed himself and Bregan D'aerthe.

He shook that thought aside and resisted the urge to spit on the ground. What did it matter? If he did nothing, Bregan D'aerthe was surely diminished, perhaps forevermore, doomed by this bold Hunzrin move. Jarlaxle's sanctioned activities would be relegated to the cavern of Menzoberranzan, a place Jarlaxle was coming to view as stifling as the stones he and Kimmuriel had just floated through, and any unsanctioned activities beyond the cavern would as likely get him killed.

Do it! he said again with his fingers.

He watched the svirfneblin then, who suddenly went quiet, cutting short his answer, and so again suffering the berating of Du'Quelve Hunzrin.

The fellow hopped from foot to foot, exactly as before, but his face twitched, his expression shifting, his eyes widening.

Well played, Jarlaxle silently congratulated Kimmuriel. *We will meet again in the Clawrift below your house.*

Jarlaxle tipped his wide-brimmed hat to Kimmuriel, then took the hat from his head and pulled forth a small piece of black cloth.

Kimmuriel nodded and smiled and melted away into the stone.

Now Jarlaxle had to anticipate the coming events, and he didn't like the possibilities. He had to try, at least, but he feared the little fellow surely doomed.

He crept across the corridor, silent as a shadow, then rushed down a side passage, one that he knew ran parallel to the one from which the gnome had come. Some way along, he threw the black cloth, the portable hole, against the wall, and crawled through it into the other corridor, then pulled the hole through behind him, turning it again into a seemingly normal circle of fabric.

Such a wondrous item!

Jarlaxle padded along the tunnel, nearing the confrontation, drawing a wand.

TOO CLOSE TO PUT HIS WHIP TO USE, ZAKNAFEIN HAD TO face three swords and a dagger of his two drow opponents with only a single sword. A lesser warrior, an average drow warrior, would have been overwhelmed or at least driven back into the room with Priestess Du'Quelve.

Not Zaknafein Do'Urden, however. By all that the drow taught at Melee-Magthere, he should have played full defense, dropping the whip, drawing his second sword, and fighting a quick turn-and-retreat technique to buy him some breathing room.

Instead, he blocked the lead sword of the drow to his left, then the stab of the drow to his right with a quick cut and backhand. He dodged the second sword from the left, accepting a stinging clip on his left hip, then ducked the thrown dagger, lifting his sword arm to deflect the spinning weapon before it came around to its point—and again, took a stinging cut, this one on his forearm.

Those two hits, though, gave him a step backward, and when the opponents moved to pursue, they met not the sword of Zak but the whip. In that small space, he expertly set it into motion, snapping it in short order left and right in the air before him. The cracking sounds alone gave his opponents pause, and more than that, the whip left tiny tears before the material and fire planes of existence, with dribs of fire falling from the sky.

He never hit either of the drow before him with the whip—that wasn't the point.

He had their attention, both of them, on the whip and not on Zak's feet.

A subtle turn and set launched Zaknafein forward, a final crack of his whip going forward this time, slicing between the two drow, cracking hard against the floor.

The drow to his left glanced at that last crack of the whip, reacting by stepping out wider. She realized her mistake and swung back, lifting her swords defensively.

Too late.

Zak's sword stabbed above them, clicking off her fine armor and lifting to dig into her collarbone and the side of her neck. She fell back, stumbling, as Zak bulled forward.

He didn't finish the charge, instead stopping short, slashing a wide and powerful backhand that drove through the second woman's single sword, catching her across her chest in the precise moment she was reaching for another dagger. She staggered to her left with a wobbly step, then dropped to one knee, her free hand coming up to her gashed torso.

She looked at Zak and fell facedown.

Zak barely noticed, already sprinting down into the maze of corridors, trying to put as much ground between himself and the Hunzrins as possible.

A short while later, though, he came to a fork in the tunnel, and his thoughts screamed at him to go to the right.

Too much so, he realized, and so he understood, too, that the source of that instinctual compulsion was neither instinctual nor internal.

Someone was trying to manipulate him here, to drive him down that right-hand corridor, to try to slip past him back the other way, and likely with guards down the right-hand corridor waiting to engage.

Zak growled and started right, but skidded to a stop before he had taken his second step. The violation angered him, outraged him.

The violator was to the left.

Zaknafein, too angry and too powerful to be so coerced, went left.

HE SAW THE BACK OF THE DEEP GNOME, HANDS IN THE AIR, pleading with Priestess Du'Quelve Hunzrin. The fellow was trying to twist her away from her desires that he fully betray his people, that he set them up for slaughter, by answering her every demand with a question about what had just happened. "Who is that drow man who ran through here?"

Du'Quelve told him it was none of his affair.

"If the city isn't behind you, how can I offer that which you ask?" the svirfneblin tried to argue.

Du'Quelve signaled to the two warriors flanking her to take him. "You will tell us what we want to know," she warned the gnome. "One way or another."

The poor fellow shrieked and tried to run away, but the guards were right behind, reaching for him, and he couldn't outrun the agile and graceful drow.

A globule flew at the shocked gnome and he ducked, though the aim had been perfect and the rolling, amorphous green blob would have gone over his head anyway. Over his head, but not over the heads of his two pursuers, who were too busy trying to grab the little fellow to see the viscous glob flying at them.

With grunts muffled by a wall of sticky goo, the two stopped in their tracks and tumbled backward, and the goo that seeped between and around them stuck to the stone floor as it had to their faces, holding them fast.

The gnome glanced back, any relief he might have known thrown aside in the piercing ring of another shriek, for behind him, Du'Quelve rolled her hands, head bobbing, lips moving in a magical chant, fiery energy building visibly about her fingers.

The gnome turned and cried out in surprise, for the floor was gone before him and he pitched headlong into nearly complete darkness. He landed hard and rolled about, looking up from the unexpected pit to the glowworms crawling on the ceiling high above.

But the darkness closed around him as the edges of the hole came together, and then there was only darkness, complete and absolute.

It didn't last long, as a blue glow revealed his newest captor, a drow man wearing a ridiculously wide hat.

"Be at ease, Symvyn," Jarlaxle said, speaking the svirfneblin tongue and not the cruder and less precise Undercommon typically used by the reasoning races of the Underdark when conversing interracially—and speaking it with such perfect inflection and dialect that had Symvyn not been staring straight at the drow, he might have thought a burrow warden was addressing him.

"You're safe now and free of the magical domination that led you to this place."

YOU DO UNDERSTAND THAT HOUSE OBLODRA SURVIVES AT *the suffrage of Lady Lolth?* the yochlol asked Kimmuriel. *You are heretics, one and all, and yet K'yorl Odran sits in a place of honor among the Ruling Council of Lolth's city.*

Not heretics, Kimmuriel telepathically responded. *We worship no other goddess.*

Atheism is heresy, as is agnosticism.

We believe in Lolth, of course. Are you not proof of her existence? Are not the magical weavings of the high priestess proof of her existence? Kimmuriel argued.

You play a dangerous game, Odran.

Oblodran, Kimmuriel corrected. *And how so? I am here with Bregan D'aerthe, a band covertly, even overtly, sanctioned by Matron Mother Yvonnel Baenre, as you know well, Handmaiden Bolifaena.*

And I serve Lolth directly, the yochlol, now in the guise of a drow priestess—and one naked at this time, for she had just returned from the form of oozing black goo. *As does my sister, Yiccarda—*

That is not my concern, Kimmuriel said, cutting her short. *I have* no imprimatur to ignore the demands of Jarlaxle, who speaks for Matron Mother Baenre within the movements of Bregan D'aerthe.

Above the commands of a handmaiden? Bolifaena asked, her telepathy conveying a clear sense of outrage.

You did not announce your presence to us, nor did you announce your intentions regarding the minor House Hunzrin to Matron Mother Baenre. Or if you did, she did not think it important enough to dissuade us in our efforts here, Kimmuriel fought back, not giving a bit of ground. I did not know that I was dealing with handmaidens, but even had I known, I am commanded by Matron K'yorl to serve Bregan D'aerthe as I would serve House Oblodra, and thus am I bound. Why did you come here to do this thing?

That is none of your concern, Handmaiden Bolifaena retorted, and Kimmuriel sensed the change in her tone. He had her back on her heels, illusionary though those drow heels might be. The overall disposition of this dastardly intervention will be adjudicated by Lolth alone, so be not so certain of your correctness here. Beyond that, I warn you, if this goes badly for my sister, I will hold Kimmuriel accountable.

Kimmuriel didn't bother to respond to the threat, but neither did he mask his amusement to Bolifaena. He understood handmaidens well enough to realize that she was no match for him. Their greatest powers lay in mental deception and domination, and Kimmuriel was far beyond them in that regard.

Find Jarlaxle and the warrior and call them back, Bolifaena ordered.

Go home, Kimmuriel countered. The traitor svirfneblin is free of you. You have failed. House Hunzrin's bid here is ended.

Bolifaena glared at him through her drow eyes—perhaps she wanted to communicate a bit more, but Kimmuriel shut the conversation down, shut her out of his mind altogether. So she stared. Then she assumed a true yochlol form once more, a half-melted giant candle of mud waving appendages wildly. From there, she diminished to nothingness and was gone.

Kimmuriel considered her last order to him, to go and stop Jarlaxle and Zaknafein.

He thought not.

He turned for Menzoberranzan.

ZAKNAFEIN SPRINTED DOWN THE TUNNEL AND AROUND A bend, not slowing. There she was, the other priestess from the first room, eyes closed, right hand lifted and in a clawing position as she continued her attempt to dominate him telepathically—and from the looks of her, she thought she was succeeding.

So did the man, the Hunzrin guard, standing before her, and he only noticed the charging Zaknafein at the last moment. He gave a shout and lifted his hand crossbow toward Zak.

A cracking whip took the weapon and wrapped his hand in the same flow enough for Zak to tug him before disengaging the weapon.

It wasn't a large tug, just enough to slightly bend the man forward, to slightly alter and lower the angle of his defense. To most, it wouldn't have seemed as much of anything, but to Zaknafein, the opening was huge, and exploited.

His sword took the man in the gut, sending him sprawling aside, grabbing at his belly. He wasn't coming back into the fight any time soon.

"You dare!" the priestess scolded. "Do you know who I am?"

"A dead priestess," Zak replied. "Who you were before that will hardly matter."

"You have doomed yourself!" the priestess roared at him. "Behold, you, a handmaiden of the Goddess of Chaos!" She continued to bluster until Zak cut her short, using his whip as an exclamation point of an answer, reaching it out to its full eight-foot length to snap it across the side of her face. He used the power of the whip, as well, drilling a line of extraplanar fire right through her cheek and into her mouth.

She shrieked and fell back, staggering, a line of blood erupting from the left side of her torn face.

Or *was* it blood?

Zak's confusion about the oozing substance coming from the woman's cheek did not freeze him in place—quite the opposite. He had learned from years of battle that moments of indecision could be fatal, and so his reflexes answered his perplexed thoughts by propelling him ahead.

But then he did skid and stop, when the drow before him was no longer a drow, when the yochlol revealed herself in all her ugly glory, her priestess robes tearing apart as she widened and transformed into the roper-like demonic form.

"Doomed, foolish male," the creature said in a gurgling voice that sounded like the popping bubbles in a heated mud puddle. "I am—"

Zak leaped into the creature, springing fast between the waving appendages, driving his sword deep into the monster's torso. He dodged aside to avoid the vomit of muddy goo, tearing free his sword, then plunging it right back in.

The yochlol shivered and shuddered, flailing its eight appendages, missing with almost every swing, but landing a few heavy blows on the weapon master.

Zak ignored them, accepted them. Again and again he struck, determined to overwhelm the demonic creature with sheer ferocity.

Then it was a drow again, naked now, cheek still showing the tear. The handmaiden leaped backward, then set herself strongly and jabbed a finger at Zaknafein, throwing a powerful psionic attack and command: "Stop!"

And he did, as surely as if he had been hit by a giant-thrown boulder.

The yochlol stood straight and narrowed her red eyes. "I will take you with me," she promised. "Lady Lolth—"

Zak ended his feint—he had felt the telepathic assault, but it had not stopped him!—and whipped her again across the face, then leaped in for the kill.

But she was gone, replaced by a cloud of roiling green smoke and stench, choking Zak and burning his eyes. He knew he had to get out of there, and fast, knew he had to find this demon before it played more tricks.

He stumbled and swallowed the vomit climbing his throat.

He had to get out. He had to get away.

The cloud paced him, surrounding him, suffocating him, and only then did Zak realize the truth: the stinking cloud was not a magical spell. The stinking cloud *was* the handmaiden.

Zaknafein waved his sword wildly, but the gas just swirled about it.

He couldn't escape!

He couldn't hurt it!

He tried to call out and vomited.

He tried to run and stumbled and dropped his sword. He started to reach for it, but changed his mind suddenly and instead straightened and took up the whip in both hands, wildly snapping it back and forth, bringing tears in the material plane with every snap. Lines of fire dripped all about him, and bits of the cloud crackled and sparked, the gas hissing in protest.

His senses failing him, his eyes burning, Zak knew that to inhale was to falter, and so instead he screamed, a long and loud wail of protest and outrage, his whip snapping all the while, the air about him dripping fire.

Then he was joined in his scream by the agonized voice of a yochlol in its drow guise once more. Zak looked at her only momentarily, just long enough to realize that she was lined with sharp burning gashes—the whip's violent work had crossed through her material forms.

She turned to him as if to strike, but Zak had never slowed, and now rolled his whip across instead of back and forth. He didn't snap it this time but let it roll around her neck, once and again.

Zaknafein turned and yanked and leaped away from her, pulling with all his strength. The unwinding whip turned her, pulled her, threw her off-balance, and jerked her from her feet, to flip and roll in midair, spinning about to land hard on her back.

Zak let go of his whip, drew his remaining sheathed sword, then fell over her, plunging the weapon down with both hands into her chest.

The yochlol flailed and screeched. It reverted to its natural form only briefly before melting into a black ooze—and from that, Zaknafein leaped back, fearing for his sword, fearing for his whip, which was under the goo.

But no, this was not a living and battling ooze. This was simply the demonic creature melting from the material plane, back to the smoke of the Abyss where it belonged.

Out of breath, throat burning, eyes burning, Zak sat down heavily on the stone and nearly rolled fully prone.

It took him some time to realize that he was not alone. He turned about to see the Hunzrin man he had gut-stabbed just a few steps behind him.

The man stood straight—or tried to, but could not, his arm still wrapped across his belly. He dropped his sword from his other hand and held it up, pleading for mercy.

Zak just stared at him. He had no breath to reply, had no strength to stand and face the man.

The Hunzrin staggered away, Zaknafein's glare following him every step.

Until he was out of sight.

At which point, Zaknafein slumped to the ground and passed out.

CHAPTER 18

Making Feywine from Rotten Grapes

H e's awake," Zaknafein heard as he struggled to open his eyes. His vision came into focus slowly, revealing a small figure standing over him . . .

A svirfneblin.

Zak's hands went reflexively to his swords, but he relaxed when he found that he still carried them, and when a more familiar figure appeared, towering over the gnome.

Zaknafein sat up, grabbing at his throbbing head, squeezing his eyes closed for just a moment to push the pain away. When he opened the eyes, he found Jarlaxle's hand extended toward him to help him up.

"Noxious gas," Zak mumbled.

"And a fair thump in the head, I expect, given the lump rising beside your left eye," Jarlaxle replied in Undercommon and not drow.

Zak took the hand and pulled himself to his feet, unsteady for only a moment. He looked around at the floor, which was still smoking with dissipated demonic goo.

"It was no drow priestess, I think we can agree," Jarlaxle remarked.

Zak looked about, replaying the fight. He looked at Jarlaxle when he answered, though, wanting to gauge the mercenary's response. "Yochlol."

Zak didn't miss the shadow that passed over Jarlaxle's face. He had expected the answer, Zak realized, but the confirmation swatted him hard.

"The Hunzrins with a yochlol? What does it mean?"

"I do not know," Jarlaxle admitted, the words he most hated saying.

Zaknafein looked past Jarlaxle then, to note a man sitting against the wall farther along—the fellow he had gut-stabbed, he realized. "Did you tend to him?"

"Of course. I give you Intern Vielle."

"Intern Vielle *Hunzrin*," Zak said.

"Not necessarily," Jarlaxle said with a wry grin, one that Zak had seen so many times before. "Can I trust you not to kill him while I bring this gnome home to his burrow warden?"

"Good question."

"He didn't kill you as you lay there," Jarlaxle explained. "He could have."

Zak stared at Jarlaxle, then at the wounded Hunzrin.

"Good," said Jarlaxle, as if that answered that. "I'll return presently, and if not . . . well, run."

Zak nodded, his thoughts still back on his battle with the handmaiden, and on what was left of the demonic creature.

He had destroyed a handmaiden of Lolth—or had done as much as one could against such a creature of the lower planes while on this plane of existence.

He tried not to think of the implications.

"HE'S NOT LYING," SYMVYN INSISTED TO BURROW WARDEN Belwar. "He saved me, and the damned drow fought the other damned drow."

"It amazes me, I tell you, that any o' the damned drow're still alive," Belwar Dissengulp replied. "Their blades are bloody more than their lips are wet."

"But this one saved me, and he wasn't alone," Symvyn insisted.

"Saved you from yourself, you mean."

Symvyn shuffled nervously from foot to foot. "Aye," he admitted.

"Come on, then," Belwar invited him, and led him into the entry foyer of the multichambered cave Belwar had taken as both office and home. In there, the strange drow with the wide-brimmed hat and the uncomfortably easy way about him reclined on a rock, hands behind his head, legs crossed at the ankles, showcasing a remarkable pair of high, hard-soled black boots—more remarkable to Belwar because all the reports of this one's entrance into Dun Arandur spoke of the absolute silence of his movements.

"Do not be too hard on Master Symvyn," the drow said, rolling from the stone to stand. "It was not his choice to betray you. It was never his choice. The enemies who found him coerced him with magic, not with promises of personal enrichment. Surely, you cannot hold poor Master Symvyn responsible for that."

"You're asking me to believe all that happened out front," Belwar replied. "I'm old enough to know that believing a drow is a risky proposition."

"My associate freed him of the magical domination," Jarlaxle said.

"You intervened right when we came to know that Symvyn was the one selling us out to the drow, stealing our ore and selling it."

"He was doing much more than that," Jarlaxle answered, and he looked to Symvyn, who was shaking his head. "Tell him, or I will."

"It is nothing," the clearly nervous gnome said.

"It is everything to . . ." Jarlaxle looked to Belwar. "What did you call it? Dun Arandur?"

"What are you saying?" Belwar asked in low and even tones, then to Symvyn, "What's he saying?"

Symvyn took a long, deep breath. "I don't know how much I gave them," he admitted. "Not much—I wouldn't. They were going to kill me."

"And?"

"I wouldn't do it!"

"He held out, and they were going to make him pay dearly for that, most assuredly," Jarlaxle interjected. "They wanted him to betray you in more than stealing your ore."

"Ain't that enough?" Belwar asked.

"It wasn't his choice," Jarlaxle reiterated. "He was under magical domination, but when they asked for more . . ."

"They wanted our guards and wards, our sentry posts," Symvyn admitted. "When I couldn't get them enough ore, they decided to come in and take it, and kill you all. But I said no."

"He did," Jarlaxle added.

"And they'd've killed me!" Symvyn pleaded.

"No, they wouldn't," Jarlaxle surprised him and Belwar by saying. "They would have tortured you until you told them what they wanted."

"Then killed him," Belwar reasoned, nodding. He put a hand on Symvyn's shoulder comfortingly, his demeanor clearly softening here.

"Probably not," Jarlaxle said, surprising them both again.

"Symvyn knows the secret to refining the arandur, correct?" Jarlaxle asked, then laughed when Burrow Warden Belwar's expression became overtly suspicious.

"It does not matter to me," Jarlaxle said, holding his hands up defensively. "But it should matter to you. I suspect that Symvyn knows because they chose him, and they would need someone with that skill. I tell you now, Burrow Warden Belwar, your charges with whom you should be most diligent and careful in protecting are those who know the secret, because that is as valuable as the ore."

Belwar continued to eye the strange drow skeptically.

"My duty here is done," Jarlaxle announced. "I could not let this hold, for Symvyn's sake, for your sake and that of all Dun Arandur, and, yes, for my own sake. My interests in strengthening my relationship with you here and with Blingdenstone are indeed partly selfish. That I admit openly."

"It's not my place to start any relationship with a drow," Belwar replied evenly.

"Agreed!" Jarlaxle said. He smiled and bowed low then, sweeping off his great hat. He didn't put the distracting chapeau back on as he stood, and pointed to his bald head as he added, "I will speak with King Schnicktick when the time is right. I thank you, most honorable Burrow Warden, and with your permission, I take my leave."

Belwar's jaw drooped and he stared hard at Jarlaxle, the hint of recognition belying his stoic demeanor. "Why am I thinking that you're leaving with or without my permission?"

"I prefer to have it," Jarlaxle replied.

"Yeah," Belwar conceded.

ZAKNAFEIN APPROACHED THE DO'URDEN COMPLEX TEN-tatively. More than once, he glanced to the northwest and the nearest major exit from the cavern of Menzoberranzan. More than once, he thought of just throwing his hands up in defeat and fleeing, running far, far from this place and never looking back.

He let his gaze move farther west, out toward the Braeryn and the Oozing Myconid, wondering if he would ever see the place again.

Jarlaxle had kicked him out of Bregan D'aerthe.

The mercenary leader had told Zak to return to Matron Malice, had taken his refuge, and had even taken back the magical whip.

Zak had wanted to argue, but he couldn't. He had been waiting in the Oozing Myconid, impatiently, when Jarlaxle had returned from his business this day. Zak knew where he had gone, for where else could he have found the answers he needed? He had gone to see Matron Mother Baenre, and she had no doubt warned him to lose no further favor with the Spider Queen.

Zaknafein Do'Urden had killed a handmaiden, and so his time with Bregan D'aerthe had come to an end.

He wondered if his time, period, had come to an end.

He looked to the northwest, the exit. The gate was closed to him, emotionally if not mentally, he realized to his great despair. It was too late. His only refuge had been the moments with Bregan D'aerthe, and now Zaknafein knew—correctly—that years would pass before he even had a chance to speak with Jarlaxle once more. If he lived that long.

He looked to the northwest, the exit, one last time, the weight of finality bowing his shoulders.

Then Zaknafein strengthened and thought of his son, not yet wholly ruined.

Running was not an option.

He went into House Do'Urden, determined only to protect his son from the misery of the Lolthian drow.

"HIS TEMPER RUNS TOO HOT FOR ANY WHO WEAR THE robes of the Spider Queen," Dab'nay Tr'arach said to Jarlaxle when she found him sitting alone at a table in the tavern. "He can't control himself. It drives him to pure rage."

"He hasn't killed you yet."

"I haven't threatened him, or tried to enter his mind with magical domination," she answered.

"You prefer other wiles, I know," Jarlaxle quipped.

Dab'nay laughed. "Zaknafein is a good man. Too good for this life we have made in Menzoberranzan."

Jarlaxle looked up at her, his face suddenly impassive. "Who?"

"Za . . ." she started to repeat before she caught on to Jarlaxle's true meaning here.

Zaknafein was gone, was no more of Bregan D'aerthe, and therefore was no more of Jarlaxle's concern. Dab'nay studied the inscrutable rogue for a long while then, trying to find some hint of what she knew to be true: Jarlaxle was hurting. Zaknafein was as close as he had ever known to being his friend.

"For all of your posturing, my friend," she dared to whisper, bending low. "For all of your achievements and cunning and amazing organization, you remain a prisoner here like all the rest of us. I feel your pain profoundly."

Dab'nay kissed Jarlaxle on the cheek and moved away, glancing back once or twice at the stone-faced mercenary.

He wouldn't give her any indication of agreement, wouldn't show anyone this personal pain—of course not! For in Lolthian drow society, emotional attachment was weakness, and weakness led to disaster and demise.

But Dab'nay had been with the mercenary band for a long time now, though she was more removed now than in years past, spending more time in the Oozing Myconid with another of her fallen house's survivors, Harbondair, even helping him to run the establishment, and using her divine powers to ferret out poison—at least that aimed at those Jarlaxle did not wish dead. She hadn't been involved in the day-to-day excursions and web-weaving of Bregan D'aerthe proper for years, nor had she even heard the name of Zaknafein in months and months until he had arrived to again adventure beside Jarlaxle.

She winced as she considered that, for when she had heard, a part of her hoped that he would be spending more time in the tavern, more time around her. She missed him, missed his touch.

She focused on Jarlaxle's impassive expression and gave a knowing little smile.

He missed Zak more than she. She had missed the weapon master—had felt a thrill when he had come back into the fold of Bregan D'aerthe after so many months away. But it was nothing compared to what Jarlaxle felt for him. In every way but physical, his relationship with Zaknafein was more intimate than hers had ever been. He had done as he had been instructed to do, with no room for interpretation.

And it was wounding him profoundly.

CHAPTER 19

Wandering Wyrm

T he Year of the Wandering Wyrm, Dalereckoning 1317, had been a fine one for Jarlaxle and his band, and now these early months of 1318 were promising more of the same or even better. Bregan D'aerthe was now fully integrated not only into House Baenre's designs, but also among many of the other matrons who sat on the Ruling Council. Even though his business dealings with the svirfneblin of Blingdenstone had not worked out as he had anticipated— King Schnicktick would not sell arandur to him for any reasonable price—House Hunzrin had not recovered from the events those years before, and that blow was more than worth its weight in the ore. Priestess Du'Quelve had not been anointed as a high priestess, and probably never would, and Jarlaxle was glad of that, because she was an adventurous one, who wanted still to turn her eyes outside Menzoberranzan.

Even if there was no such place as Enclave Arach, the entire construct a ruse by a pair of mischievous yochlol.

Du'Quelve had protested, and was no doubt still protesting, that she had acted on behest of a pair of handmaidens. That's what had kept her from complete ruin. Except it was clear that she had not known. Or, if she did, didn't quite understand the full extent of their purpose, seeing how it could lead only to disaster.

In any case, Du'Quelve had been humbled, and Jarlaxle doubted she would ever recover. And more importantly to him, House Hunzrin had been put back in their place, fully so.

Yes, things were well with Bregan D'aerthe, and Jarlaxle was now plotting a time of quiet for the group, building the secret extra-Menzoberranzan networks he could use to fully exploit the (relative) goodwill being offered him and his band.

It helped that the city, too, was fairly quiet, at least as far as the continual backroom whispers typically went. It made sense: the most unruly drow house of any real consequence at this time was Do'Urden, and with her prized son at the academy, even anxious Malice wouldn't be so quick to start trouble.

Of course, with that insatiable priestess, anything was possible.

That thought brought a smile to Jarlaxle's face as he entered the Oozing Myconid that night. The place was bustling, so Jarlaxle went straight for the bar and was met with looks from Dab'nay and Harbondair—he couldn't quite make out their expressions.

As one, they motioned to him with their chins, and when he followed their lead, the smile left Jarlaxle's face, replaced by a slack-jawed look of shock, something not very common with this one.

For there, across the tavern, sat Zaknafein.

Jarlaxle composed himself and looked back to Dab'nay, holding up two fingers. When she nodded, the rogue turned back to his old friend, composed himself once again, and walked over.

"Well, well, the weapon master returns," Jarlaxle greeted him.

Zak didn't look up, staring off the other way. "I hope one of the two you ordered was for me," he said.

"It is if you'll allow me to join you."

"The irony of your words," replied the man who had been kicked out of Bregan D'aerthe.

Jarlaxle took a seat. "So many years," he said. "How long has it been, my friend? Half a decade?"

"More. I've been busy."

"Training your progeny, no doubt. They are already whispering of his excellence at the academy."

"He could defeat half the masters there," Zaknafein said matter-of-factly.

"I've seen you fight. I don't doubt it."

Dab'nay came over then and set the mugs down in front of the two. She patted Zak on the shoulder as she walked away, not saying a thing, and it was pretty obvious to Jarlaxle that she and Zak had already exchanged words.

"What brings you here?"

"Am I not welcome?" Zak asked.

"More than welcome, of course. You drink free for as long as I own the place."

Finally, Zak turned to look at Jarlaxle directly. "I am good enough to sit at your table, yet not enough to serve in your band, then."

"That was a long time ago."

"So, I'm redeemed?" came the response—and how Jarlaxle had missed that sarcasm! Few Lolthian drow would dare, since satire could be purposely misconstrued as heretical words. After generations of living in such anxiety, few drow in Menzoberranzan could even comprehend or play that word game now. Fewer still could play it well, and only Zaknafein had ever challenged Jarlaxle's supremacy in the art of true ironic needling.

"I am sitting with you here in a tavern everyone knows—but no one admits—that I own," Jarlaxle replied. "That is a start, yes?"

Zak lifted his mug in toast to that thought.

"I could use a distraction," the weapon master admitted.

"Would you settle for information?"

"Then the answer is no."

"You destroyed a handmaiden," Jarlaxle bluntly replied. "You knew who it was when you finished the killing."

"Or I would have been killed by the handmaiden."

"If that was its judgment, then . . ." Jarlaxle let his voice trail off there.

"You shrug," Zak chortled. "Would Jarlaxle have surrendered to the whims of a yochlol demon? Had it been you in that corridor, the handmaiden would have been obliterated. What then, Jarlaxle? Would you have relinquished control of Bregan D'aerthe and accepted whatever may come your way?"

"My charm is more considerable than you remember, I see," said the rogue, and he painted on a rakish smile. "I would have convinced the handmaiden otherwise."

"Stop it!" Zak demanded.

Jarlaxle held up his hands, a silent apology for his making light of the damning situation. It was Zak, after all, and not Jarlaxle, who was paying for the issue in the tunnels.

"I will see what I can find out," Jarlaxle promised. "Nothing would please me more than to unwind the events of that day, at least as far as your situation is concerned. So I will look to the Abyss. Perhaps time has healed this wound, or at least, has mitigated the angry fires."

"Or maybe your inquisition will fan those flames to new life," Zak replied.

"I will be clever."

Zak lifted his mug in toast again, a helpless and resigned movement. "To cleverness."

"And other information," Jarlaxle said, leaning in. "I have eyes in Melee-Magthere. As I said, your son is doing well. His skills have already been noticed."

"He is doing well," Zak replied, "which means that he is accepting their indoctrination. That's how they do it. They dig a hole and coax you in, until all light is left far behind. Lie by lie, deed by deed, you dig your own soulless grave."

"You escaped it."

"Did I? I sit here, an unwilling pawn, but a pawn nonetheless."

"If I could give you a priestess to kill, I would," Jarlaxle said.

Zak snapped his gaze up at Jarlaxle, then laughed with the joking rogue despite himself. He lifted his mug yet again, this time with some enthusiasm, and more than a little gratitude. Clever Jarlaxle had joked exactly the right way in that moment to break through Zak's dark clouds.

"We will adventure together again," Jarlaxle promised with as much conviction as he could manage. He didn't really believe it, though, and could tell that Zak didn't, either.

Both of them had to at least pretend they believed it, though.

Without that, they had nothing.

"IS THIS ALL TO SLAKE YOUR LUST?" DAB'NAY ASKED ZAK-nafein, as she lay in his arms one night many months later. Ever since Zak's visit to the Oozing Myconid, he and Dab'nay had resumed their affair—even while Zak had seen Jarlaxle only once or twice and never with more than a passing word.

"My matron is Malice Do'Urden," he replied, stating the obvious.

"Perhaps you grew bored with only one partner."

"For all of her many shortcomings, Matron Malice is hardly boring in matters carnal," Zak replied. "Why would you think my trysts with her involve only one partner?"

Dab'nay gave a helpless laugh. "Her reputation precedes her indeed."

"Her reputation isn't half the truth of that one."

"But still," Dab'nay said, growing serious. "Why are you here? What are we doing here?"

"Perhaps I'm just trying to get back in the graces of Lolth so I can rejoin Bregan D'aerthe," Zak replied. "And perhaps Dab'nay simply cannot resist me."

The woman was already rolling her eyes before Zak confirmed the joke with his second sentence.

"I mean it," she said. "We're here, and yes, I want to be here and this is no complaint! But why? Why am I here? The risk to me is . . ." She paused, shaking her head.

"Is what? Are you afraid that you will fall from the graces of the Spider Queen by sleeping with the man who defeated a handmaiden?"

"Do not admit it," Dab'nay scolded, pulling back from Zak's embrace. "Do not ever admit it, to me or to anyone else."

Zak pulled his arm off her and rolled onto his back, staring up at the few glowworms Dab'nay kept in her bedroom. They wriggled and snaked across the ceiling, almost as if they were trying to form some letters, or words, or answers. Zak laughed at the mere thought of that, considering that the answer to the great dilemma of Lolth might be found in the simplest of life-forms.

Perhaps simplicity was indeed the antidote to the tangled webs of that ultimate witch.

"I don't see it as a risk," Dab'nay said quietly, evenly. She, too, rolled onto her back and offered a heavy sigh. "There is no favor to risk, although I am still confused as to why I am granted divine spells without the favor of Lolth."

"Maybe because you serve her."

Dab'nay rolled up onto her side quickly, scowling at him.

"Would you even know if you were?" Zak asked. "Do any of us, truly? She is the Lady of Chaos—who more than Jarlaxle creates chaos among the children of Lolth?"

Dab'nay's scowl melted as she considered the words. "I find that possibility even worse somehow."

"Because it is a trap without an exit."

Another sigh escaped the woman. "You still haven't answered my first question. Why are you here?"

"Why would you even need to ask?"

"You don't love me, Zaknafein. You cannot. In fact, in some place deep in your heart, I know that you must abhor me."

"The war between our families was a lifetime and more ago," Zak answered. "And neither of us precipitated it anyway, and only did what we had to do to survive, as is the way for almost everyone in this fallen place."

"Not the war!" Dab'nay said. "How could you possibly love me when I am a priestess of she you most reject and despise? A *priestess*! For all of my failings, I gave my oath to Lolth."

Zak shrugged, playing those words around in his thoughts. He couldn't deny the literal truth of them, but those facts meant nothing to him. He imagined a fight between Bregan D'aerthe and House Do'Urden that would lead him into a chamber where Dab'nay cast her spells—he remembered his assault on House DeVir!

But no, he could never attack this one. She was a priestess of Lolth, but she wasn't, not really, not in her heart and not in his.

"We are here because we're safe here, because we understand each other—maybe even better than we understand ourselves," Zak said.

"A horde of driders could burst through that door and kill both heretics at the same time," Dab'nay answered. "Safe?"

"Emotionally," Zak said. He rolled onto his side to face her directly and brought one hand up to gently stroke her soft cheek. "We are here because this is where we don't need to lie."

"About?"

"Everything. Maybe when we're here, as when we're working with Jarlaxle's crew, we have found a refuge from our own lives, which are nothing more than lies."

Zak welcomed the intensity on Dab'nay's face as he said that. She was hearing his every word. This was important to her, as it was to him.

"That's how they do it, isn't it?" he asked.

"Do what?"

"Bring us into their webs. Bring you into the clergy of a goddess who is not in your heart."

Dab'nay's lips moved a bit as if she was trying to formulate a response, but she just shook her head, a signal to Zak to go on. He was extemporizing here, mentally improvising—this was no long-thought-out theory coming from him now. Certainly it was a subject he had often considered, but suddenly, there was clarity.

"They speak a lie and even though we don't believe them, they speak a line of hate—against the elves above or the deep gnomes or another drow house—and even though we don't agree with them, we don't speak out," Zak said. He was considering his own early days at Melee-Magthere, and thinking of his son, his poor son, caught there now. "I wonder how many in the crowd of listeners would agree with us—but no, we will never know. Because we all take the only course open to us, the road that leads away from exclusion and worse."

"The road to life as a drider," Dab'nay agreed.

"The road of self-preservation. And so we nod, perhaps laugh at their terrible mocking jokes at those others we must hate, and even though we do not believe their lies, or even though we see the cruelty in their jokes and threats and venom, we nod, or at best, remain silent. Thus are we complicit. We have followed them into the ditch they are digging, grain by grain, and we become numb to it. The lies and venom become no more than words to our thoughts, mundane, no longer shocking, and without meaning—but only without meaning to our conscious thoughts. For then they dig deeper, they lie louder, they hate more, and this, too, we accept, and now the lesser lies and venom seem reasonable by comparison."

Dab'nay's face screwed up in confusion and she shook her head, and Zak got the distinct impression he was losing her.

It didn't matter, though. He was talking to himself and not to her at this point, as finally he began to unravel a strand of that most awful web.

"And so we begin to lie, and so we become complicit," he realized. "And so the hole deepens around us, walls from which we cannot escape. And then the deeds—we kill for them. Maybe a goblin or a kobold or some other insignificant being. Something *less than*. Something not a person. It matters not. All that matters is that we have struck a blow in support of their deceit, and so we are more complicit still.

"They lie louder, and they hate more. And the lies and hate and deeds that were not lesser become more so—the path is only one way. Deeper. We dig beside them. We are lost in their hole."

Dab'nay's breathing was raspy then, giving Zaknafein a strong feeling that the woman wished she had never asked the seemingly simple question in the first place.

"I see it so clearly now," Zak finished. "I cannot believe that I did not understand it before, or perhaps I was too invested in not admitting my own complicity in this evilness."

He didn't miss that Dab'nay was leaning away from him. He stared into her eyes, shaking his head just a bit, trying to somehow signal to her that it was so plain now, and had been said aloud, and that in and of itself was freeing. So very freeing!

"You say that you wish to get back into Bregan D'aerthe," Dab'nay said finally.

Zak just looked at her curiously.

"Jarlaxle will never allow you reentry with such words as these, spoken openly," Dab'nay explained. "He has too much to lose. He is too close to powers that would utterly destroy anyone who dared speak such blasphemy."

"This isn't about Jarlaxle," Zak replied. "It is about us. We two. This is why we are here, in this place, intertwined. This is the truth and that, in this place, is our freedom. Do you not see it?"

Dab'nay thought on that for a long while, then meekly nodded her head, and Zak wasn't sure he believed her.

He said no more, though, just rolled onto his back once more and lifted one arm over his eyes, wanting no more glowworm-incited introspection. After a while, Dab'nay nestled against him, and the two drifted off into slumber.

They would get together many times over the next few years, but never again would Zaknafein speak of such things to Dab'nay. Eventually, he came to understand that he had unsettled her greatly with his declaration of truth, and as the years wore on, the visits became less frequent.

"DO NOT DO IT," DAB'NAY TOLD JARLAXLE, SURPRISING HIM.

"A decade and a half," Jarlaxle said, for indeed that much time had now passed since Zaknafein's fight with the yochlol. "It was a long time ago."

"A long time to a goblin, a lesser time to us, a speck of time to a handmaiden," Dab'nay said. "I know you miss him. So do I, but he is not worth it to Bregan D'aerthe."

"I would have thought you pleased at the news that I am considering his reinstatement."

"I am. But I'm also not blind to the realities of why he isn't part of Bregan D'aerthe, as you seem to be. Why now?"

"Because his son nears the end of his decade at Melee-Magthere, and young Drizzt has built, by all accounts, a most magnificent reputation for himself."

"Matron Malice will be willing to part with her consort, so you believe," Dab'nay reasoned.

"She will have a lesser need for him. She'll want her son as weapon master as soon as he is able."

"She'll want both as she plots her rise to the Ruling Council," Dab'nay said bluntly.

Jarlaxle shrugged. "He will not be expelled from House Do'Urden, but he'll not be needed as much as he is now."

"Do not do it," Dab'nay told him again. "You don't understand. He is incorrigible. There is no redemption for Zaknafein in the eyes of Lolth, whether or not her handmaiden has forgiven the incident. I don't tell you this lightly, and I wish it were different—how I wish that! But Zaknafein will bring disfavor to us, of the highest order. You cannot control him and he will never, ever accept Lolth or her edicts."

"Nor does Kimmuriel, and he has become an important part of our work," Jarlaxle argued.

"There is more to House Oblodra than we know, regarding their relationship with the Spider Queen," Dab'nay argued. "Who can know what they really think or believe? All we can know is that Matron K'yorl Odran sits in the third rank on the Ruling Council. We can safely assume that she has the blessing of Lady Lolth. Zaknafein does not, and never will, and worse, wouldn't accept it if it was offered."

Jarlaxle leaned back in his seat and eyed Dab'nay head to toe. "What is this about? A lover scorned?"

Dab'nay laughed at that absurdity. "It is about me enjoying the quietness of my respite within Bregan D'aerthe, and so wanting to preserve Bregan D'aerthe," she answered honestly. "Zaknafein has opened his heart to me, and it is not one that will accept Lolth—"

"The same could be said of many of my associates," Jarlaxle interrupted, but Dab'nay went on undeterred.

"He will never accept Lolth," she repeated, "nor excuse the behavior of those who do. Go and learn for yourself if my observation is not enough for you, Jarlaxle. You survive by knowing, and this that I tell you is easy enough for a high priestess to magically discern. You know many who would do you this favor, no doubt."

With that, Dab'nay took her leave, having said her piece, but as she departed, she was already considering where she might run if Jarlaxle did indeed allow Zaknafein back into the mercenary band. Would she betray her lover? Would she betray Jarlaxle, who had helped to spare her after the defeat of House Tr'arach?

"Yes," she told herself before she had even left the Clawrift.

She hated herself for saying it, for thinking it, even, but Dab'nay was above all else a survivor.

She had to be.

She understood what awaited her in the afterlife, and she was not ready to face the Demon Queen of Spiders and her court.

Not yet.

CHAPTER 20

The Roll of Years

"E xtract him," Dab'nay begged Jarlaxle. "Get him out of there. Drizzt is back at Matron Malice's side—she will part with Zak for the proper coin."

"You told me only tendays ago that Zaknafein was as happy as you had ever known him," Jarlaxle argued, caught off guard by the request. "His son, his protégé, is returned from the academy with all honors, with whispers that he will grow beyond even the prowess of his father."

"And now he is morose," Dab'nay said. "For now he knows that Drizzt is drow, truly drow, wet in the blood of *darthiir*."

Jarlaxle heaved a great sigh and shook his head. *Darthiir.* An elf. The details of the war party surface raid were out.

The year was young, Dalereckoning 1329, the Year of the Lost Helm, but already it was proving more eventful than the past decade.

As with many of the swirling rumors and whispers in Menzoberranzan these past decades, the center of that swirl was D'aermon N'a'chezbaernon, House Do'Urden, the Ninth House of Menzoberranzan. Matron

Malice's treasured son Drizzt had returned to her home after completing his training at Melee-Magthere. It was little surprise to many, and none at all to Jarlaxle, that Drizzt, the son of Zaknafein, had dominated his class and was already being compared to his father, who was considered one of the top three weapon masters in all of Menzoberranzan, if not the greatest of them all.

So many other whispers had Jarlaxle heard, as well. That was why he had urged Dab'nay to increase her trysts with Zaknafein, which had been few and far between of late.

"The raid," Dab'nay explained, and Jarlaxle made himself appear surprised—always better to hear varying voices even regarding the same tale, and always better still if the source thought she was breaking the news.

"Dinin Do'Urden led the war party to the surface and there they found the elves at their frivolous play, exactly as Matron Mother Baenre had predicted," Dab'nay explained.

"Dinin led well, I am sure," Jarlaxle said, feigning his ignorance, understating both what he had heard of the excursion and the complete success it had achieved, to the glory of both Do'Urden sons. It had been a complete success in the eyes of the Ruling Council, and no doubt in the eyes of the Spider Queen.

To Jarlaxle, it had been just another atrocity in millennia of atrocities, another waste of life and energy for ethereal ends that had never made any sense to him. Why kill someone when you can sell things to her? Or learn things from her?

"House Do'Urden basks in the favor of the Spider Queen," Dab'nay said. "Zaknafein has never been pleased with such favor."

"True enough," Jarlaxle admitted, for it was an undeniable assertion. The weapon master, after all, always took such glee in murdering priestesses of Lolth.

"And now it shines on his son," Dab'nay went on. "It would seem that Drizzt is not so much like Zaknafein in that regard. More like his zealot mother, perhaps. His blades were wet with blood and I have heard no words of remorse."

"That wouldn't please Zak," Jarlaxle said, more to himself than to Dab'nay, who nodded. "And so you think Matron Malice would be willing to elevate Drizzt to serve as Do'Urden Weapon Master, and be rid of Zaknafein?"

"If she does not, it will not end well for Zak or for Drizzt. Of that, I am sure."

Jarlaxle considered that for a while, yet again finding it hard to disagree. When Dab'nay had claimed that Zak was morose, Jarlaxle had thought her exaggerating—Jarlaxle had seen Zak at his highs and lows for centuries, and if anything, the man had become more balanced of late, resigned and carving out what little peace of mind he could find in his studies and training.

And hopes for his son.

Jarlaxle knew more about the surface raid than Dab'nay, of course, and more than Zaknafein, likely. Without Zak's knowledge, but with more than a passing interest, Jarlaxle had planted a scout from his band among that war party: Nav Rayan Dyrr.

Jarlaxle knew all about Dinin's exploits.

Jarlaxle knew that Drizzt had killed a helpless elven child.

Apparently Zak knew, too.

"Go back to him this night," Jarlaxle instructed. "Go to him often now, as many nights as you can manage. Comfort him. Coax his thoughts."

"I do not wish to spy on Zaknafein."

"Any spying you are doing, any information you are bringing back to me, is for his sake, not mine," Jarlaxle told her. "Once, long ago, Zaknafein Simfray spared you. Now you can possibly return that debt, and do so in a way that brings comfort to a man you just described to me as morose."

Dab'nay considered that for a few moments, then nodded.

"SO SOON?" JARLAXLE ASKED BENIAGO WHEN THE BAENRE informed him that Dinin and Drizzt were out again on a raiding party, and only months after the surface raid. This time, they were hunting a group of adventurous svirfnebli who had ventured too near to Menzoberranzan for the comfort of the Ruling Council.

Jarlaxle shook his head and blew out a sigh, thinking a lot more than he was speaking. The target of this new raid had thrown Jarlaxle's thoughts back to that day more than fifteen years before, his last great adventure with Zak.

The rogue gave a snort, half chortle, half chuckle. Helpless chuckle. Now Zak's son would possibly kill the same deep gnome Jarlaxle, Zaknafein, and Kimmuriel had gone to such great lengths to save.

Sometimes it seemed to Jarlaxle as if nothing really mattered at all. He was mostly an optimist—look at all that he had survived, after all! Moments like this, when he could only sigh, almost always led to that one source: Lolth, the great sword hanging over the heads of every drow in Menzoberranzan and neighboring Ched Nesad. What might a drow city without the influence of the goddess look like, Jarlaxle often wondered.

He hoped that he would live long enough to find out—silently hoped, of course.

He turned back to the matters at hand. This new mission would do little to brighten Zak's mood, Jarlaxle realized, and according to Dab'nay, the weapon master's mood hadn't improved much since her visit with Zak that same day he had learned of Drizzt's murderous actions against the surface elves. But while that mood hadn't improved, it had shifted, according to Dab'nay. She wasn't calling him morose any longer.

Now she spoke of a simmer, one building to an explosion.

Jarlaxle silently cursed himself for not taking Dab'nay's advice those months before and attempting to purchase Zak from House Do'Urden.

"I am surprised that Matron Malice is being so cavalier with her sons," Jarlaxle said. "Deep gnomes are no easy opponents. Even victory here will likely prove costly."

"She may lose Dinin, but I have come to believe that she thinks the younger son blessed and protected by the Spider Queen," Beniago replied. "This young Drizzt is as fine a warrior as Melee-Magthere has ever graduated, true, but that means nothing unless it is proven often in battle. My cousin Dantrag was not the highest-ranked in his class. It took him a decade of battles, many battles, before his true skill became obvious. Uthegentel Armgo was a hulking beast, of course, overwhelming the other students, but few expected him to survive his first years after Melee-Magthere. There had been others like him, so promising, and then, so dead."

"And that is the point," Jarlaxle said. "Those first months and years after the academy are often the most dangerous. Yes, they can build a great reputation, but if a weapon master is to die in battle it is usually when he is very young or when he grows old and slow. Either way, it always happens in his last year, yes?"

Beniago chuckled at that.

"Matron Malice has so much riding on the promise of Drizzt," Jarlaxle explained. "He is her second weapon master—he and his father will prove an enormous advantage to her in her quest to sit on the Ruling Council. She likely already has Lolth's favor from the successful surface raid, so yes, it surprises me that she would risk them, particularly Drizzt, again so quickly."

"Surprises?" Beniago said slyly.

"Intrigues me," Jarlaxle corrected.

"Do you suspect that she is plotting her next move?" Beniago asked. "Perhaps she is eager to bring Lolth's favor to a crescendo to aid in her ambitions."

Jarlaxle grinned and cocked his head, sizing up his Bregan D'aerthe soldier. "So now you have decided to do some spying for House Baenre?" he asked slyly.

Beniago shrugged, not denying the point. "Matron Mother Baenre allows me my service to you with a price," he reminded. "A price to both of us."

"I have heard nothing, but it wouldn't surprise me," Jarlaxle replied honestly.

"Have you ever known Matron Malice to be so silent as she neared a move?"

"I've never known Matron Malice to attack a Ruling House before," Jarlaxle answered. "There is no house ranked below House Do'Urden threatening them, surely, particularly not at this time with House Hunzrin still in disarray, or at least in transition. If Matron Malice is plotting a war, it will be one that sits her on the Ruling Council. I would not expect her to signal that, no. Those eight matrons ranked above her sit together often. Who knows what tendrils they have tied to each other? Who knows their alliances? I don't doubt that Matron Malice is planning her move, but I wonder if she even knows at this time who she will move against. I would expect that she will announce her move when she next speaks with Matron Mother Baenre, seeking hints as to which of the eight houses would be considered the least costly loss."

Beniago was no child, and surely not sheltered within the luxury of his house. He understood the reasoning, of course.

"You said it yourself," Jarlaxle offered. "She is building the music, the favor of Lolth. This will be an eventful year."

"Indeed," Beniago answered, wearing a grin Jarlaxle could not quite decipher.

"Do tell," he prompted.

"Perhaps Lolth's favor does not shine on House Do'Urden as brightly as Matron Malice believes," he said. "And so, perhaps another house will be the one initiating the events of the coming months."

"What do you know?" Jarlaxle demanded, trying not to give away just how surprised he was at that news.

"Less than you believe and more than I can tell," Beniago replied.

Jarlaxle had no answer to that, and no follow-up question. Beniago was a soldier in his band, but Beniago was also a Baenre, after all.

ANOTHER PIECE OF THE STRANGE PUZZLE FELL TO JARL-axle not long after, when Dab'nay came to him yet again, this time to inform him that Zak's mood had shifted once more.

"Happy?" Jarlaxle asked incredulously, after Dab'nay had reported the abrupt shift from the weapon master.

"As happy as I have ever seen him."

Jarlaxle searched for some answer to this unexpected turn. When Dab'nay came to him this day, he had almost expected her to tell him that Zak had murdered his son, or that the weapon master had fled House Do'Urden and Menzoberranzan altogether.

But no, he was still there, and Drizzt was very much alive, battling svirfneblin-summoned elementals in the corridors of the Underdark, or on whatever new adventure Malice had sent her sons.

Had the news of Drizzt's ethical failure completely broken his friend? Had Zak simply gone mad?

"He gave you no clue as to why?" Jarlaxle asked.

"He only said that he was no longer alone," she replied. "He has found an ally and a friend."

"Who?"

Dab'nay shrugged and held up her hands helplessly.

Jarlaxle thought back to his conversation with Beniago. The pieces almost fit, but Jarlaxle knew that he was missing something here, something important.

Something that would probably get some drow killed.

JARLAXLE DROPPED HIS FACE INTO HIS HAND, SHAKING HIS head. On one level, he was sorry his curiosity had led him to the chambers of Triel Baenre. Jarlaxle hated coming here—Triel was among the most dangerous and intelligent of the drow priestesses he dealt with. She was very short, less than five feet, shorter even than most men, and perhaps because of that, she always operated as if she was determined to stand atop anyone who dealt with her. With the Baenre imprimatur behind her every move and her own tremendous divine powers, she was usually successful in her attempts.

"You know what Matron Malice will do, of course," she said, only to twist the knife and cause more pain. Triel had just informed Jarlaxle of Drizzt's betrayal, or cowardice, during the surface raid on the *darthiir* clan.

"Matron Malice knows?"

"She does. She had an unfortunate encounter with a handmaiden, and there learned that D'aermon N'a'chezbaernon was not in Lolth's favor. Matron Malice is no fool—I give her that much. She looked, and looked hard, and so she discovered the truth. Her prized son did not kill the elven child. Quite the opposite. He covered the child in her mother's blood and thus saved it from the blades of those who had accompanied him on the raid. An amazing betrayal."

"Cowardice, as you said," Jarlaxle quickly added, trying to shape the opinion of this very powerful priestess. If Drizzt had failed because of cowardice, he would be punished, of course, but cowardice was something that could be corrected.

Blasphemy was not.

"The weapon master, your friend and sometimes associate, knows the truth, as well," Triel told him.

Jarlaxle was not surprised by that as the pieces began to fall into line, all perfectly explaining the dramatic shifts Dab'nay had been describing in Zaknafein's mood.

"Drizzt told him," Triel went on. "And Matron Malice had invisible ears."

Invisible ears, a phrase priestesses often reserved for Lolth and her handmaidens. "If you behave badly," every drow was taught from her or his earliest days, "Lady Lolth will know. Her ears are all about you, invisible, hovering, waiting to catch your transgressions."

Malice had magically spied on Zak and Drizzt.

"That evidence is weak," Jarlaxle said, and he knew he was flailing here, but he had to do something. He had to try. "Perhaps Drizzt was simply telling the weapon master what he thought Zaknafein wanted to hear."

"Lady Lolth's disfavor clouded House Do'Urden before the second-boy told the weapon master," Triel reminded him, before Jarlaxle could find any wiggle room in whatever wild theory he might concoct to throw her down a different path.

"The disfavor was not from Drizzt's words, but from his actions during that raid." Triel's obvious glee had Jarlaxle grinding his teeth. "You know what Matron Malice will do, of course," she said again, openly smiling—and more about Jarlaxle's discomfort than any feelings regarding Drizzt or Zaknafein or House Do'Urden she might hold. It was all just a game to her, to all of them, and now her play was bringing pain to Jarlaxle.

Which she enjoyed immensely.

Jarlaxle did know what Malice would do, what she had to do. She would sacrifice Drizzt to Lolth. However much she prized her promising secondboy, however much she thought Drizzt might bring to House Do'Urden, none of it was possible—in fact, quite the opposite—if Malice and her family were under the cloud of Lolth's disfavor.

One of the houses ranked behind Do'Urden could use this to ascend, or more likely and more devastating to House Do'Urden, any of the eight Ruling Houses who saw the ninth house as a threat could use this to eliminate that threat with finality.

Jarlaxle played it out further in his thoughts. It wouldn't end with Drizzt, he realized. Malice would be rid of the boy, though she didn't want to, and then Malice would have to deal with the person Drizzt had told of his crime, a person who had certainly not gone to her with the news of Drizzt's admission of guilt.

Zak's mood swings filled in all the holes for Jarlaxle.

Zak, too, was surely doomed. Not right away, of course. Vicious Malice would make him suffer the pain of losing Drizzt for a while—perhaps she would even allow Zaknafein some chance at redemption, since she might well need his blades in upcoming struggles.

But he wouldn't take it. Jarlaxle knew that.

He wondered if he might somehow extract Zak then, perhaps even find a way to pull Drizzt from Malice's grasp.

He dismissed the notion immediately, particularly given the woman standing before him. The Baenres knew the truth. The Matron Mother herself knew the truth.

Jarlaxle and Bregan D'aerthe would never get close to Zak or Drizzt at this time, and this time was all the time they—Drizzt, at least—had left.

"You do not much like the die that have been rolled out before you," Triel remarked, drawing him from his contemplations.

"I find the whole incident unfortunate and sad," he admitted. "A tremendous waste of great talent and promise."

"Of course it is," the first priestess agreed. "And what does Jarlaxle do when he does not like the die roll but cannot change the numbers? How does Jarlaxle mitigate his losses?"

"My losses?"

Triel laughed at him.

Jarlaxle had never felt more naked.

"What does Jarlaxle do?" she asked again.

Jarlaxle just looked at her.

"You don't know," Triel said. "It does my heart good to see Jarlaxle at a loss. Here, I will offer just a bit more: this will be a momentous night, I expect."

She stopped there, and Jarlaxle had to consciously keep himself from leaning toward her.

"How so?"

"I have much to do, many prayers yet to recite," came the answer, one delivered with that wicked smile. "I will be here for many hours. You know the way in, so please, do come and tell me what you mean to do. In fact, I insist upon it."

Jarlaxle left House Baenre then, making for the Clawrift and House Oblodra, thinking that Kimmuriel might help him sort things out more clearly in this desperate time. He changed his mind, though, and went instead to the Oozing Myconid, and soon after that, he sat in a room upstairs at the tavern, across the table from Dab'nay Tr'arach.

The woman waited patiently for Jarlaxle to tell her why he had summoned her. Jarlaxle saw that clearly but simply wasn't sure how much to divulge.

"Drizzt Do'Urden did not kill the elven child," Jarlaxle said finally. "He protected her."

Dab'nay gave an audible gasp.

"Mali—Matron Malice knows," Jarlaxle went on. "And she knows that Zaknafein knows."

"Zaknafein knows?"

"Why do you think his mood brightened?"

Even as Jarlaxle asked that question, though, Dab'nay seemed to catch on, sighing at her own question, which seemed ridiculous in the face of this evidence.

Jarlaxle stood up and began pacing. "What will Matron Malice do?" he asked, as much to himself as to Dab'nay.

"She'll give Drizzt to the Spider Queen at the end of her sacrificial dagger," Dab'nay answered without hesitation. "Would any matron do differently?"

"But what will Zak do?"

Dab'nay held up her hands. "What does Zaknafein always do? He will fight, and take pleasure in killing every priestess in House Do'Ur—"

"No," Jarlaxle interrupted. "No. Malice knows him better than any of us."

"Matron Malice," Dab'nay corrected, but Jarlaxle brushed it off.

"She knows how dangerous he is, better than any of us. He'll never get the chance. He is cornered and caught."

"She'll kill him, too," Dab'nay whispered in horror.

"Eventually. She'll make him suffer the loss of Drizzt first. She'll blame it on him, make his heart heavy with guilt. That is her evil way, like all of them."

He looked to Dab'nay, expecting her to scold him, but she had nothing to say.

"She'll blame the disfavor of Lolth on Zaknafein to make it worse!" Jarlaxle said with flair, and his own words stopped him cold.

"The disfavor of Lolth," he whispered again.

"Where are you going?" Dab'nay asked, when Jarlaxle headed for the door.

"To play the die that have been rolled out before me," he answered.

There was no bravado in his reply or in his heart. There was nothing good to be found here, but perhaps, just perhaps, he had found something less bad.

He was back with First Priestess Triel Baenre soon after.

"You interrupt my prayers," the diminutive woman greeted him sourly.

"Do not pretend that you're not enjoying this as much as any prayer you've ever uttered," Jarlaxle replied.

Triel laughed, and it was one full of joy, wicked and evil joy.

"The disfavor of Lolth on House Do'Urden isn't just because of what Drizzt did," Jarlaxle told her, eliciting a curious look.

"Zaknafein, too, has erred, years ago, in the tunnels outside of the city."

Triel's expression did not change.

"The details are not important," Jarlaxle added. "But tell me this one thing: would Lolth's disfavor be mitigated if Matron Malice claimed only one sacrifice?"

"If she sacrificed the weapon master instead of the secondboy?"

"Can you discern the answer?"

"Are you asking me to convince Matron Malice to sacrifice your friend, Jarlaxle?"

"No!" he said reflexively, fighting revulsion. "I am asking if that would be enough."

"That the secondboy might be saved and redeemed?"

That is not how I would put it, Jarlaxle thought, but did not say, and it didn't matter anyway, for certainly Triel understood that her own version and "redeemed" would never align with Jarlaxle's understanding of the word.

A moment later, Triel laughed again. "I see," she replied. "Matron Malice will kill them both, you fear."

"It wouldn't matter," Jarlaxle admitted. "I know Zaknafein Do'Urden well. When Matron Malice gives her secondboy to Lolth, it will destroy him, and he will fight her."

"Do you not understand that I might enjoy such a spectacle as that?"

"I ask you to do me a favor," Jarlaxle explained. "I will be in your debt and will repay it many times over."

"This is important to you," Triel said.

"And profitable to you."

"Name it, but take great care before you utter a request I might find blasphemous."

"Get word to Matron Malice that the sacrifice of Zaknafein alone would suffice in this, alleviating the cloud that hovers about House Do'Urden. If that is the truth, of course. If that sacrifice would make proper amends."

"It will be easy enough for me to discern from a handmaiden," Triel replied.

"You know of Zaknafein's transgression?"

"I speak to handmaidens all the time, foolish man," said Triel. "Of course I know. Of course we all know."

"We were out in the tunnels in service to Matron Mother Baenre those many years ago," Jarlaxle felt he had to remind her.

"Which is the only reason Zaknafein survived the ramifications of his actions."

Jarlaxle shut up then, his lips going tight. They knew everything. They always knew everything. They saw the fall, they anticipated the fall, they relished the fall.

He wanted to stab Triel in the eye, then and there. He felt like Zaknafein, he realized, and never before had he so appreciated the unrelenting rage of his friend.

"Go home, Jarlaxle," Triel told him. "Go to your tavern or to the Clawrift and do nothing more this night or in the days to come. Do nothing more regarding this at all. That is not my advice, it is my warning to you, and one that comes with no caveats at all."

The walk across the city was long and terrible for Jarlaxle. He opted for the Clawrift, not the Oozing Myconid. He didn't want to talk to Dab'nay or Kimmuriel. He didn't want to talk to anyone. The die had been rolled before him and he had made his play.

He tried to envision the unfolding scene in the Do'Urden compound in the West Wall of the city. Malice would tell Zaknafein that Drizzt's life was forfeit, and Zak would be helpless, so utterly helpless.

Zak had only one play, and Jarlaxle was confident that he'd take it. He'd offer himself in his son's stead.

It had to play that way, the only way.

Many times in that long walk did Jarlaxle consider alternative courses he might take. He could assault House Do'Urden with Bregan D'aerthe and extract both Zak and his son!

But no, of course he could not.

The Baenres would crush him if Malice did not. They would destroy him and Zak and Drizzt and anything and everything Jarlaxle had ever built with his mercenary band. For to interfere in this instance would put Jarlaxle against Lolth, openly.

There was nothing more he could do.

He felt helpless, indeed, but he knew that dear Zak would likely soon know a helplessness and despair beyond anything Jarlaxle had ever experienced.

IT HAPPENED THAT VERY NIGHT, AS TRIEL HAD PREDICTED, and happened as Jarlaxle had anticipated, except that he didn't know that Drizzt Do'Urden was not in House Do'Urden that night, but was instead out in the city, settling a score.

Triel had performed her favor and Malice had accepted Zaknafein's offer.

Jarlaxle's friend was dead, given to Lolth, whom he hated above all others.

Jarlaxle could only hope that Zak went to his grave with hope that his action would save his son.

What Zak hadn't known, however, and Jarlaxle only then the next day discovered, was that Drizzt was gone, from House Do'Urden and from Menzoberranzan altogether.

The young fool, outraged by the death of Zaknafein, had cursed his matron and fled into the wilds of the Underdark, by all reports Jarlaxle could gather over the next few days.

That left Jarlaxle in roiling turmoil, wondering if he should go and try to help Drizzt.

But soon after, Drizzt was openly declared an apostate, leaving Jarlaxle helpless yet again.

He sat on the roof of the Oozing Myconid one night soon after, staring in the direction of the northern exit of Menzoberranzan, thinking of Zak's son, a true blade master, a young man cut from the cloth of Zaknafein in so many ways.

That Zak hadn't failed in raising his son to his own image brought comfort to Jarlaxle, whatever fate Drizzt might find out there (which Jarlaxle presumed would be an early death).

For Drizzt had done what Zak had always wanted to do. Drizzt had seen the corruption, the evilness, the ugly weight of Lolthian edicts, and Drizzt had rejected it more fully than Zaknafein had ever found the courage to do, more fully than Jarlaxle had ever found the courage to do.

"Run free, Drizzt Do'Urden," Jarlaxle whispered into the Menzoberranzan night. "Find your way with untainted heart and die with honor and integrity. Do something your father was never able to do."

Satisfied, Jarlaxle stood up and turned for the door, adding under his breath an admission that weighted his every step, "Something *I* never had the courage to do."

PART 4

Without
the Middle

I am empty.

I have been given a great gift, so I believed, in being returned to life again, and in a world full of changes both hopeful and desperate—and in the latter, I feel as if I can make a significant difference.

On the surface, it is everything I wanted. It is an open fight against Lolth and her evil minions, a chance to strike back for all of the suffering that I and my people, and indeed the whole world, have endured at the Spider Queen's hands.

But I am empty.

In the last moments of my previous life, I gave myself that my son might live. That was the deal and the deal held, though only because Malice failed in trying to kill Drizzt. Because of that bargain, Drizzt was given a good life, one in which he found a better way, found an escape.

He found love.

All of this should lighten my heart, but how can it? I gave my life for Drizzt, and now, in what is to me only a few tendays of time, my deal was unwound, both ways. I am alive and he is lost to me—and that makes me wonder if I even want to be alive!

I know that I cannot think this way, particularly now. I will fend my grief with anger and determination—anger at my loss and determination that the product of Drizzt's love to this human woman will live the promise I wish I might have given to my son . . . or to my lost daughter.

Drizzt's child will grow up in the arms and care of a loving mother, and with many worthy and wonderful friends.

If she or he can survive this onslaught now faced in this place called Gauntlgrym.

The child will survive.

If I have to kill every demon, every drow, every enemy in all the world, this child will survive.

That is my promise to you, my lost son Drizzt.

And to you, my lost daughter Vierna.

Would that I had been better to both of you.

Zaknafein Do'Urden

CHAPTER 21

THE YEAR OF DWARVENKIND REBORN
DALERECKONING 1488

The Danger, the Thrill

The retrievers are indestructible?" Brother Afafrenfere said to Yvonnel. He had coaxed her out alone, asking more about the end of Drizzt.

"Almost," the drow woman answered. "The dwarves here dumped one into the chasm with the fire primordial. I know not if it is thus destroyed, but that was some time ago and they have not seen it. That one was targeted for Zaknafein, we are certain, and he remains within the complex. If it was still surviving, it would be trying to climb out."

"So it was destroyed?"

"That would be my guess."

"And the one chasing Drizzt? Is it possible that he destroyed it?"

The woman shook her head, but answered, "Anything is possible. But where is Drizzt, then?"

"You think him dead or taken to the Abyss with the golem."

"That seems most likely." Yvonnel cocked her head a bit to study the monk. "What are you thinking, monk?"

Now it was Afafrenfere's turn to shake his head. "I do not know. But I must find this place."

"Thornhold?"

"The fortress of Drizzt's apparent last stand, yes."

"It is a long way," Yvonnel replied, "Perhaps hundreds of miles, and none will be more difficult than the first."

"Get me out of here, just past the demons and the drow on the surface, I beg of you," Afafrenfere said.

"Tell me why."

"I do not know that you would understand."

"Brother, my memories date back millennia, to the founding of Menzoberranzan," the drow explained. "I have been to the Abyss and the Nine Hells. I have roamed Tartarus and battled celestials. I am the reincarnation of all the lessons learned by Matron Mother Yvonnel the Eternal, her memories gifted to me by an illithid when I was still in my mother's womb. More recently, on my own, I led the defeat and destruction of the corporeal form of Demogorgon.

There is much about the multiverse I do not understand—it is a nearly infinitely wide place, after all—but I assure you that there is more I could tell to you that *you* would not understand than this issue now before us. You ask me for help, and so, as I am friend to the dwarves here and to the man you sought, I will help you—as soon as you convince me that you are deserving of my help and that there may be some gain to my efforts."

Brother Afafrenfere thought it over for a few moments, then nodded. "Let me tell you of Grandmaster of Flowers Kane," he said. "Let me tell you of a fight I shared with him, he within me in a willing co-possession of my physical being, against a white dragon above the mountains of the Silver Marches."

"THIS IS UNTENABLE," YICCARDARIA SAID TO MATRON Zhindia. The two handmaidens and the drow commanders had gathered in the house in Bleeding Vines that Matron Zhindia had taken as her command post, to evaluate the situation and plot their next moves.

Surprising the mortal drow, Yiccardaria and Eskavidne had come in once more intent on rehashing the past: the disposition of the retrievers, the apparent success of one, the miserable failure of the other.

"These valued weapons were given to you with the expectation of care, Matron," Yiccardaria said, and her tone sounded as a great threat to all around the table.

"They were given to me as indestructible weapons with singular purpose," Zhindia replied, trying to sound equally as aggressive for reasons obvious to all.

"Under your command!" Yiccardaria silenced her.

"It was always assumed that Matron Zhindia would exercise wisdom and temperance in deploying the constructs," Eskavidne added.

Zhindia stuttered over her words for some time, flabbergasted that they were even talking about this again. Immediately following the handmaidens' explanation of the retrievers' outcomes the last time, after all, Eskavidne and Yiccardaria had then opened the magical gate to bring back the many long-dead driders, putting them at Zhindia's disposal.

So, why now? Why were these two, particularly Yiccardaria, determined to replay the conversation about the retrievers and this time point fingers of blame?

Matron Zhindia wasn't sure of the answer to that, but she certainly understood the potential implications if the accusation gained any traction.

She took a deep breath and said calmly, "I brought the retrievers to the surface in my march, as instructed, and turned them loose to fulfill their destiny—one determined by others. You two? Lady Lolth herself? Could I have stopped them from pursuing their targets had I tried? Would that not have made me, and those I assigned to the task, obstacles to the retrievers' sole and compelled goal? And we all know what retrievers do to those who impede their mission."

"But did you *aid* their mission?" Yiccardaria pressed.

"What would you have had me do? Send my forces deep into Gauntlgrym or spread them far and wide to the Sword Coast to chase the construct pursuing the heretic Drizzt? They had singular goals. I have a war to win."

"At least she admits her tactics, and thus her failing," Eskavidne said to her peer, and Yiccardaria nodded.

Matron Zhindia barely contained her snarl.

"It is not so terrible an ordeal for you, Matron Zhindia, and surely you can repair the damage you have wrought," Eskavidne told the woman.

Zhindia's eyes narrowed. Her jaw clenched. It took all of her will-power then, and a constant inner reminder that these were representatives of the Spider Queen, whose blessing was all that really mattered to her, to hold back her curses and her orders to her companions to properly send these two back to the swirling mists of the Abyss.

"A retriever is destroyed after its mission is complete, in any case," Eskavidne went on. "The loss is not important. It is the loss without the gain of the target that matters and reflects badly. Drizzt Do'Urden is removed, but Zaknafein Do'Urden remains. Correct that and this conversation will be forgotten, of course."

"Of course," Yiccardaria echoed, "it would also be best if you capture Zaknafein and bring us to your side, that we may more fully bless the ritual as you give him to Lolth."

Zhindia couldn't hide her curiosity from her expression here, she knew, but so be it. It made sense that the handmaidens would wish to be around to witness such a grand gift to Lolth, of course, but there was something about the way Yiccardaria had issued her demand, some extra bit of enthusiasm perhaps, that made the perceptive and always suspicious matron wonder if there was more to this than the simple execution of a heretic.

As far as Matron Zhindia knew, it remained a mystery of how Zaknafein had returned to life, of which divine being had for some reason thought it wise to bring the him back from a well-deserved grave.

What was she missing here? What motivation beyond this way and Matron Zhindia's campaign to destroy the heretics had brought her the two handmaidens and their generous offers, first the retrievers and then the driders? There were always webs of intrigue with the drow, more so with those demons surrounding Lolth, and most so with Lolth herself. It was their way, and therefore, Zhindia could still take heart that her victory here was greatly desired, and it would be one realized with the full blessing of Lolth.

There was something more, though, probably many things, and one in particular concerning Zaknafein Do'Urden. It was likely irrelevant to her—or would have been, had not the handmaidens just blamed the loss of the retriever on Zhindia to compel her to handle Zaknafein as they had demanded—but even so, it was always wise for a drow to search as deeply into the webbing as was possible.

"I would like nothing more than to plunge the sacrificial dagger into the chest of Zaknafein Do'Urden, handmaiden," she answered—and honestly. "And when I do, having Yiccardaria and Eskavidne beside me, sharing in the prayers to Lady Lolth, would make it all the more glorious."

"You need to press them, Matron," Yiccardaria said. "Harder. Take the halls and hold the halls. Catch and kill their leaders. Secure this place, and while doing so, eliminate the heretic Zaknafein to repent your failure with the retriever."

Matron Zhindia bit back her retort, but neither did she verbally, openly, before these other witnesses, agree with the advice. "You would have me send in the driders?"

"No," Eskavidne blurted before Yiccardaria could answer. "No! The driders are for maintaining that which you win. You have demons. Use them. Even the major fiends. A great and magnificent push to purge this place of the dwarven plague. Go and claim the first part of your kingdom."

Around the table, other drow cheered, and Zhindia joined in. In her thoughts, though, she wasn't so thrilled with the command. Holding back the major demons had been a wise course, one that ensured victory, even though it delayed the outcome. The major demons were doing no more than using their energies and magical powers to open gates to the Abyss, to bring in reinforcements to throw against the battle-weary dwarves. They were getting very restless—so much so that more than one had gone into the fray anyway. But it was working.

"Time is our greatest ally," she reminded.

"Not so," Eskavidne replied. "To an extent, yes, and until the time to fully engage was at hand, it surely was. But we are in the realm of humans, and they may soon wake to the truth of that which is happening here and come against you in great numbers. And I do not discount the resourcefulness of King Bruenor and his companions. Perhaps they will find a way to open their gates, as they intended, and in that event, dwarven armies will come against you. Thousands of shield dwarves, armed in the east and ready to do battle."

Zhindia nodded. What choice did she have? This wasn't an argument she wanted to wage—especially knowing that to lose it could mean losing the favor of Lolth.

Aloud, at least.

Because there was more to it all, she knew. She wanted to uncover that. She needed to see the lower strands of this still-weaving web, to figure out a way to make it take the shape *she* wanted.

FROM THE MOMENT HE HAD COME OUT OF THE WIND-LIKE state of Yvonnel's spell and bid farewell to the remarkable drow, Brother Afafrenfere had begun his run. It had been a weave over those first few hours as he cleared the outer perimeter of the occupying drow force, zigzagging about encampments and patrols of those huge half-drow, half-spider abominations.

He had been seen only once, a drider calling out the alarm and launching its spear at him, a missile Afafrenfere had caught and thrown back in one single, fluid motion, even scoring a hit on the original thrower, though not enough to dispatch the monstrous beast.

It had given chase, its companions had joined in, and the monk, having no desire to engage out here, had fled with all speed.

Driders were swift creatures, and tireless. A normal human would have little chance of outrunning one.

Afafrenfere, though, was not normal in this regard. He was a monk of the Order of St. Sollars, an aesthetic dedicating his entire life to wholeness of body and mind, a man who had learned through endless training to channel the energy of his very spirit into the honed muscles and joints of his physical being. Afafrenfere was Master of the East Wind, a very high title, a very high rank, a testament to his dedication, his skill, his discipline.

Few could outrun a monk, fewer still one as skilled as Brother Afafrenfere.

He sped away from the driders, moving swiftly beyond their reach, and unlike a normal man, he did not quickly tire in his sprint.

Brother Afafrenfere had put many miles between himself and Gauntlgrym before pausing to take a brief rest, with no sign of the pursuing monsters anywhere to be found.

After only that short rest, he went on his way again, moving deep into the night, climbing the tallest nearby crag to gain some perspective, he hoped, on the journey before and behind. On the eastern side of that tall mound, he found a sheer drop to a rocky ravine.

Afafrenfere nodded at his good fortune.

He jumped from the cliff.

Hands and feet working miraculously, the monk descended hundreds of feet in short order, touching down in a rolling landing that absorbed most of the shock of the fall, leaving him with only a few bruises down a descent that no one who did not understand the ways of the monk would believe a human could survive.

There, confident that he had shaken any chance of pursuit, Afafrenfere took his first rest.

He awakened with the dawn and began his run once more, straight now into the rising sun.

He didn't know exactly how far he had gone, but Afafrenfere guessed it was well more than two hundred miles from the gates of Gauntlgrym to Thornhold, as Yvonnel had warned.

Brother Afafrenfere approached the ruins only five days from his departure.

He went through the gate and found the scar of the retriever easily enough. He did a quick scan before dropping to a cross-legged sitting position, hands on his knees, palms facing upward, where he fell into a deep, deep meditation, a joining of all that was around him on a level something more than his physical senses could tell him.

He searched for a ghost.

Several times, he thought he had found some measure of one, a wayward thought, a momentary inspiration or observation that seemed exterior to him.

Perhaps the remnants of Drizzt?

He desperately wanted Grandmaster Kane's observations of transcendence to prove true, and to prove the work of his drow friend. Even so, however, Afafrenfere knew that it had been a while since that occurrence Kane had sensed.

Too long, almost certainly.

Still, he had to know the truth of it, to offer peace to Catti-brie and the other Companions of the Hall, if nothing more.

Determined, he sat there, and he opened his mind, his heart, his spirit and became a being of pure receptiveness, hearing every sound, smell, whisper, sensation of the region about Thornhold. It was hard to discern the physical from the spiritual in such a state, and thus was Afafrenfere caught off his guard when at last he opened his eyes to find himself surrounded by a group of armed, armored, and indisputably angry dwarves.

"Kill 'im" was the first thing Afafrenfere heard clearly from one of them.

And the last.

"THAT WAS A DANGEROUS PLOY, SISTER," ESKAVIDNE SAID to Yiccardaria when they were alone, though still on the material plane. They were in their natural, roper-like state, their voices bubbling and popping like hot mud, their language that of the yochlol so that if they were overheard, they would not likely be understood.

"Zhindia tarries too long now," Yiccardaria returned. "I fear that the gains will be short-lived."

"Gains? Sister, what gains concern us, or Lady Lolth?"

Yiccardaria spun about, her appendages waving in protest.

"There was only one gain here for you, and it is done or it is not. As of now, it is not," said Eskavidne.

Yiccardaria's growl popped and grumbled like bubbling water.

"A dangerous ploy," Eskavidne insisted, not backing down. "Zhindia will likely soon commune with Lolth, and Lolth might not be pleased to learn of all we have done."

"Everything we have done is for chaos, and chaos serves Lolth," Yiccardaria retorted. It was true enough—mostly. And wasn't that at the heart of chaos anyway?

"It is not just the what, but the way," the other handmaiden replied. "Will Lolth be pleased to learn that we were granted two retrievers from Malcanthet, Queen of the Succubi and consort of Demogorgon?"

"She will take pleasure that such constructs were given at Demogorgon's expense," reasoned Yiccardaria, "and for reasons that support Lolth and not Demogorgon."

"*Do* they support Lolth? How do you know?"

"Sister!"

"We do not know Lolth's feelings for Drizzt Do'Urden," Eskavidne said. "Ever has she been coy about that particularly minor player in her grand game."

"She lost him to the goddess Mielikki."

"No, she lost him to himself. That is not the same thing. Her strife with Mielikki was decided in the cavern of the primordial, the proxy battle of two women, Catti-brie and Dahlia. As for Drizzt, she made her play in the tunnels far to the east and was denied."

"And so he deserved to die."

"You do not know this. Perhaps Lady Lolth saw that he would weaken and submit in time."

"With Zaknafein his father returned?" Yiccardaria's sarcasm ended with a roll of popping mud bubbles deep in her throat, as if her physical being itself was mocking Eskavidne's claim.

"Returned by whom?" Eskavidne promptly stopped her. "We do not know."

The two faced each other silently for a long while.

"The Spider Queen cannot be angry," Yiccardaria at last offered. "Heretics both!"

"Do you really want to find out?"

"My memory is long, sister," an emboldened Yiccardaria insisted. "I have not forgotten the insult."

"He thought you a rival drow."

"No, he knew! When he continued his assault, he knew. Zaknafein the heretic murdered a handmaiden of Lolth, and she, I, do not quickly forget, and never forgive. I will have Zaknafein, sister. He cannot be rewarded. He cannot be redeemed to Lolth. I will have him in the Abyss, and there I will torment him for eternity."

"The rest of the powers of Menzoberranzan have come," Eskavidne reminded. "Do you think Quenthel will side with Zhindia or battle her?"

"We settled that question by giving Zhindia the driders. Quenthel will recognize them as the futility of any resistance she might offer."

"Only if she thinks them Lolth-bestowed."

"Who else could have done it?"

"An angry handmaiden who had the keys to their abyssal cages, of course."

The yochlol Yiccardaria smiled, the ends of her maw turning up, then dripping back down her melted form. "A possibility even Quenthel Baenre cannot understand," she said confidently.

Eskavidne said no more, but neither was she fully convinced. The two had been having grand fun at the beginning of this all, urging on Zhindia Melarn while teasing the Baenres, even in supporting Zhindia's threat against Archmage Gromph. It was all chaos, all play.

Except for the retrievers, an offer that Yiccardaria had leaped at without consulting her companion in the game. Malcanthet was a clever one with a long memory and knew exactly how to approach angry Yiccardaria with just the right bait.

But why? Yiccardaria was convinced that Malcanthet thought she would be hurting Lolth by killing the two heretics, or possibly, in a completely different direction of motivation, perhaps it was a peace offering to the Spider Queen after her drow minions had so fully dis-embodied Demogorgon at the gates of Menzoberranzan.

A peace offering or a misaimed attempt at payback?

Did it matter?

Perhaps it did matter, was Eskavidne's fear now, and seeing Yic-cardaria, who was usually so clever and calculating, beginning to take this entire game so personally was beginning to unnerve her. Yes, part of the impetus for initiating the play was Yiccardaria's desire to pay back Zaknafein for a long-ago injustice—that had always been true. But now that the game had advanced, now that the retriever had failed, it seemed to Eskavidne that the stakes had been raised, and that Yiccardaria was now taking the defeat of the retriever as yet another personal affront against her by Zaknafein Do'Urden.

That was the thrill of chaos, she told herself to calm down. Un-leashed, it would lead to unforeseen outcomes, sometimes minor, sometimes, as seemed quite possible now, quite major.

That was the thrill.

That was the danger.

Eskavidne looked at her sister and smiled, letting the thrill over-come her fears.

CHAPTER 22

The Absence of Compromise

A rtemis Entreri stood at the edge of the chasm that held the primordial of fire, his jeweled dagger laying loosely atop his open and up-facing palm. He stared at the weapon, hatred in his eyes, but only because that dagger was a reflection on him. He understood that now. He realized now, after his stint in the cocoon of conscience, that his worst crimes were those when he had put this evil weapon to use.

Entreri had killed many foes, both in battle and in secret. He had lived as a hired assassin. Always had he justified his work by telling himself that he had never killed anyone who hadn't deserved it—the world was a brutal place, after all. He still believed that to some extent . . . except when it came to the work he did with this particular weapon. He hadn't just killed people with it; he had obliterated their souls and stolen whatever afterlife might have awaited them.

How many of his victims had deserved that?

Even the most heinous? The most villainous?

He couldn't justify it, not ever.

He stood there staring, contemplating, and the biggest question twisting his thoughts in that dark moment was whether he should simply toss the weapon to its destruction or jump in beside it.

A fall, a flash of intense pain, and it would be over.

The man winced. Nay, it was not a fear of death that kept him on that ledge, but the fear now of what awaited him when he crossed that final river.

Perhaps that was the true torture of Sharon, he considered. She had shown him what awaited him, making him fear death more than he hated life.

"Damn it all," the broken man whispered, his words disappearing under the continual hiss of the dripping water falling to the heat below. "Damn that I was ever born."

"Once I might have agreed with you," came an unexpected response, and the assassin spun about to see Catti-brie and Yvonnel walking up behind him.

"There was an Artemis Entreri I thought worthless," Catti-brie continued. "That is not the man standing before me now."

"We have already had this discussion," Yvonnel reminded the man. "You have been given a great gift."

"A gift," Entreri echoed with a snort.

"A message, then, and clearly a powerful one," the drow restated, staring at his open hand and the dagger. "You wish to destroy that weapon?"

"Perhaps I'll drop it in and it will eat the primordial," Entreri mused.

"Not hardly," said Yvonnel.

"If you wish, I'll bring it down for you," Catti-brie offered. She paused and smiled. "Didn't you try to do the same with the sword you still carry?" It was a rhetorical question, of course, for Entreri had indeed thrown Charon's Claw into the chasm, only to have it retrieved by this very same Catti-brie.

Entreri laughed at the reminder. "It would seem that I have been long cursed with evil weapons."

"Weapons are merely tools," Yvonnel said. "The intent is in the heart of the wielder, not the blade."

294 R. A. SALVATORE

"One could argue that the dirk Regis carries is equally vile," Catti-brie reminded. "Or the sword I once carried."

"The sword that nearly drove you insane, if I recall," Entreri said dryly.

"Because I was not nearly experienced enough and skilled enough to control the base instincts it teased," Catti-brie said. "Such is not the case now, as with you and your sword."

"Is death at the hands of simple iron any less death than that with your dagger?" Yvonnel asked.

"Yes," said Entreri. "That is the point."

Yvonnel looked at him doubtfully.

"The magic of this dagger obliterates the soul," Entreri said. "And gives me their physical health."

"Yes, yes," Yvonnel said. "This is why Zhindia Melarn was so outraged at the loss of her daughter to your dagger. I remember now. The girl could not be resurrected because of the manner of her death."

"Exactly," he muttered.

"But that cannot be," Yvonnel replied, giving him pause. He looked at her curiously.

"One cannot 'obliterate' a soul," Yvonnel explained. "Such energy is eternal, beyond the gods, even, and surely beyond the power of a simple dagger."

"You just said that Zhindia was outraged because—"

"Because her daughter could not be brought back from the after-life," said Yvonnel.

"Because she had no afterlife," Entreri reasoned.

Catti-brie looked to Yvonnel, who was shaking her head.

"If the souls are not destroyed, then is it possible that they have instead been absorbed and trapped in the dagger?" Catti-brie said. "Is it a phylactery of sorts?"

"That is possible," said Yvonnel, who looked from Catti-brie to Entreri. "Or perhaps they reside in another person now."

"In me?"

"You just said that the dagger grants you your victim's physical health. Perhaps there is more to it."

Entreri blanched at the thought, and then thought once more that he should accompany the dagger to the fiery maw of the primordial!

"If that is true, either case, then they can be exorcised," Catti-brie put in. "Set free."

"Then I should throw the damned thing into the pit," said Entreri bitterly, but Catti-brie was shaking her head.

"I know a better way." She smiled and nodded as the first hints of some plan began to formulate in her thoughts.

"Do you intend to share?" Entreri asked after a few moments.

"Patience," Catti-brie said. "Make no final decisions until I have considered our course, I beg. For now, though, I have something else I must see to." She stepped up past Entreri, pulling him back from the ledge and replacing him on the lip of the chasm.

"I still do not agree," Yvonnel said to her. "There must be a safer choice."

"Maybe, but what time do we have?" Catti-brie replied.

"Then give to me your ring and let me do this."

Catti-brie shook her head. "You said you would help me. I welcome your enchantments."

"What are you doing?" Entreri asked, but they didn't seem to be listening.

"You risk your child," Yvonnel said.

"How much do we risk if I do not do this?"

"You don't even know if the primordial will hear you. Nor can you predict its response if it does! It is a creature of long-past millennia. Its way in the world is not ours, is not known to us, more foreign even than the beings we name as gods. Please, child, my experience is vast in such matters. Lend me your ring that I might go and speak with the creature instead."

Catti-brie seemed to be considering it, even put the thumb and finger of her other hand upon the ring, as if to pull it off.

"It knows me," she said at length, speaking as much to herself as to her companions, bolstering herself, obviously, for this task ahead.

"It cares nothing for you or any of us," Yvonnel countered. "We cannot even know what brings it pleasure, what dreams or desires . . ."

"It knows me, and I know it," Catti-brie said with finality, holding up her hand to ward away the woman, who was leaning toward her. "I've been down there before in communion with the creature."

Yvonnel considered the words, then finally surrendered with a nod. She held up a finger, bidding Catti-brie to pause, then cast a powerful dweomer over Catti-brie, one that the pregnant woman had to accept and allow to take hold upon her. Then Yvonnel began casting more mundane enchantments, throwing wards against heat and flame over Catti-brie, to bolster her in the face of such a beast as awaited her in the pit.

"Promise me that when this is done, that when we have won the day, you will grant me that ring that I, too, might experience a communion with this most magnificent creature."

"It's a damned volcano!" Entreri said loudly, but the two women just replied with smiles.

On a sudden thought, Catti-brie took out the onyx figurine of Guenhwyvar and held it out toward Yvonnel. She pulled it back, though, and couldn't help but shake her head at her instinct. She intended to protect the panther by handing the figurine off, while still going down into the chasm with her child in her womb?

Catti-brie laughed aloud at the seeming absurdity and shook her head, and for a moment, the woman was unsure of . . . everything!

What was this madness? Why wasn't she just forcing her friends to teleport to safety, or at least, taking her unborn child to safety, instead of trying to parlay with a godlike being that was indeed, as Entreri just said, more a volcano than anything sentient to which she could relate?

After another moment, though, she sorted it all out. She was doing this because it was what she and her friends, particularly her husband, had always done. She wouldn't shy in the face of danger, even in the face of danger to her child. No, because the cost of cautiousness was too high. They had to win here, for all the goodly folk of the region, including the child in her womb.

They had to win.

They all needed her to be a part of that.

Catti-brie started to extend her arm once more, but then changed her mind and instead called Guenhwyvar to her side. The gray mist formed into the great panther, and Catti-brie bent low and whispered instructions into the panther's ear.

Guen leaped away, darting out of the room.

Catti-brie tossed the figurine to Artemis Entreri, not Yvonnel. "If I don't return, give it to Zaknafein," she instructed.

The stunned man looked at her.

"Yes," she said. "I trust you in this. Do not betray that trust, and do not insult us all in this moment of need by worrying about yourself above others."

That brought a scowl from Entreri, but one that only lasted a moment, replaced by a helpless laugh and a nod.

"Drizzt believed in you," Catti-brie told him.

Catti-brie cast her own warding spell then, and stepped off the cliff.

THEY BROUGHT THE BIG BOYS, JARLAXLE SIGNED, COMING back around the corner of the corridor and putting his back against the wall. *A glabrezu, some large bear-like demon, and a group of manes.*

Good, Zak silently replied. He began tightening the bracers on his wrists, the speed-enhancing bracers his son had worn as anklets. Someday soon, Zak would try that, but not now, not with such powerful enemies so near.

We can fetch a dwarf patrol. Four or five should be enough.

You go get them, Zak's fingers answered.

Jarlaxle looked at him curiously. *And you will wait here?*

Zaknafein nodded, but his smirk somewhat belied his intentions.

Too close. Come with me, Jarlaxle answered.

Zak shook his head. *Be quick.*

Zak . . .

Go! Zak implored his companion.

Jarlaxle stared at him hard for a short while, then started off down the corridor. He had barely rounded the next corner back toward the

298 R. A. SALVATORE

secure dwarven positions, though, when Zaknafein went around the one toward the demons.

The weapon master held fast to a basic truism when battling a group: pick off the weakest members first. Even an unskilled fighter could be deadly when defending against multiple attackers.

He sprinted straight for the six-limbed glabrezu, its pincer arms snapping hungrily. At the last moment, the bear-like demon moving up beside the glabrezu, Zak darted and rolled to the side, coming up in the midst of a trio of zombie-like manes.

His swords had always worked as a blur, but now, with the bracers secured on his wrists, Zak had taken out the third of the trio—Icingdeath taking its head from its shoulders, before even consciously registering the strike of the first or second mane. He hopped away from the three demonic corpses as the smoke began to rise from them, telling himself repeatedly to trust in his muscle memory, his movements honed by centuries of training.

"Don't think," he admonished himself aloud, for his movements in the moment of combat, enhanced by the magical bracers, were faster than any plotting he could do. He knew his first move and his second—after that, having experienced the speed of these marvelous bracers, would have to be pure reaction.

He leaped aside, feeling the pressure coming at his back, and spun in midair to land facing his glabrezu opponent.

Left, right, left, and left again went his scimitars, keeping the two pincer arms and grasping, clawed hand of the huge fiend away—and he even managed a fifth movement, not a block, but a stab, that got in a small wound on the hulking demon.

In that moment, Zaknafein realized another unexpected advantage, as he felt the scimitar named Icingdeath bite harder into that fiend than it should have. He knew it was a frostbrand and understood the properties of such an enchanted blade in theory, but this was the first time he had experienced Icingdeath feasting on the fiery core of a creature of the lower planes.

The glabrezu knew it, too, clearly, for it didn't follow through with its ferocious attack, instead going back on its heels.

To the side, the bear-like demon charged in with a feral roar, a shambling mane to either side of it.

Zak charged, too, right for it, moving low. And when the bear went low to tackle him, the weapon master leaped and rolled right over its back, breaking his tuck as he came over, legs straightening, scimitars going out wide and powerfully to either side. The manes collapsed, and he landed and kept running a few steps before spinning about once more.

Suddenly, it was just him and the two demons.

Full of confidence, Zak met the second charge of the ursine demon with a wall of cutting blades, striking it repeatedly, cutting its huge paw-like hands, cracking *Vidrinath* upon its nose as it tried to bite at him.

The glabrezu moved in, but Zak wasn't overly concerned. He was faster than either, so much so that he could block and counter repeatedly. And even a parry with Icingdeath, he knew now, would bring pain to the fiends.

He was facing back the way he had come initially, though, and so sounds behind the weapon master brought some concern. He angled to get a view at the corridor behind, expecting a horde of manes, but found instead a group of vrock demons, powerful birdlike monsters. Even with the bracers, even with the frostbrand scimitar, Zak knew that he was outmatched here, and so he turned to find his way back to ally lines.

But the glabrezu and the bear-like demon knew it, too, he realized.

He went at them anyway, a wild flourish, and only a last-moment downward strike with Icingdeath forced the glabrezu to retract a pincer that had gotten dangerously close to encircling Zak's waist.

Zak knew enough about demons to realize that had the glabrezu's pincer gotten around him in such a manner, it would have likely snipped him in half—and he had no desire to die such an ignoble death.

The vrocks were not quiet now, howling and cawing as they charged in at Zak's back.

The weapon master continued to slash and stab at the two fiends before him until the last moment, then spun and met the charge with a charge of his own. He took several hits—the thrumming of heavy winglike arms on either side, even a peck of a vrock beak on his shoulder that left his arm tingling and numb, as he crossed between a pair to barrel into a third.

That one, too, struck at him wildly, but Zak bore on, and with Icingdeath leading the way, biting hard at the demon vrock's animating energy, the beast had no choice but to retreat with him.

It tumbled over, and Zak rolled with it and over it, plunging Icingdeath into its torso for the kill strike. He expected to tear the weapon free as he came back to his feet, but found himself being kicked hard by the fourth vrock, and the sword was torn from his hand.

Zak staggered and stumbled, skidding to a stop, one leg sliding wide to almost drop him. He heard Icingdeath clang against stone to his side and knew he had to get to it.

Forcing himself up through the pain and out of the awkward position, Zaknafein sped across the tunnel, leaping the fallen vrock as it melted into the stone, deflecting the batting arm of the one that had kicked him. Still, from the power of its blow, Zak landed awkwardly yet again.

He didn't fight it and let himself fall into a roll, perfectly executed and aimed.

And when he came back onto his feet, he had Icingdeath in hand.

But his back was to the wide tunnel's wall, and worse, these were not manes he was fighting anymore. Before Zak could even congratulate himself on the magnificent execution of his roll and retrieval, he saw that part of his success was because the three remaining vrock demons had run past him instead of at him, now blocking the backside of the tunnel, while the glabrezu and ursine demon had moved forward to hem him in from the front.

They were working together.

Zak knew then that he had no chance.

"Come on, then," he spat, determined to do the legend of his son well.

DESPITE THE MAGICAL WARDS SHE HAD PLACED ON HER-self and the additional protections from Yvonnel, Catti-brie felt a dis-tinct discomfort as she floated down into the primordial pit. When she came below the steam, she noted immediately that there was less solid ground down here, the orange-glowing lava rolling about—it wasn't *flowing*, for the area was level, but it was certainly moving, as the surface of a pond might move with the current of a feeding stream.

No, Catti-brie thought, not like that. This was more like the wa-ters of a pond moving because of some large animal swimming about just beneath the surface.

She felt the energy here, anxious, eager.

She reached through her ring, which was enchanted to bring her sensibilities into the elemental Plane of Fire, and to give her some measure of communication with, and control over, creatures of that plane. She offered her greetings to the primordial, not with words or even focused thoughts, but rather, simply because she was there, in a manner in which they could sense each other on a sentient level . . . and found herself surprised.

The beast was happy.

No, that wasn't quite the correct descriptor, she thought. It was excited. The primordial understood the diminishing magic, the weak-ening of the elementals above which were holding it within this pit.

The beast wanted to get out, eager for release.

Catti-brie found the memory of the last such explosion flooding through her. Melded with the primordial, she at last understood the desire.

She knew then that her mission here was foolhardy.

For the anticipated, desired release wasn't anything of conscious thought—at least, not conscious thought a human might understand or experience. It was more like the demand of a physical release, the last moments of lovemaking, the uncontrollable desire.

Release was reproduction for the primordial. She saw the volcanic eruption as a spreading of the most primal fire, the seeding of the material plane.

Instinctual, not planned. Unstoppable, not negotiated.

The obvious analogy shook the woman profoundly and made her think again of Drizzt. She tried to put him out of her thoughts. She had no time for that worry now, or more importantly, though she tried to deny it, for that grief.

She tried to look for ways to bargain. Would the primordial be pleased to open the gates, to bring in more mortals to secure this place, its home?

No.

Would the primordial open the gates that those inside could leave, then?

The denial came to her with less intensity.

Remove the cursed water, Catti-brie felt in her thoughts.

If you open the gates, we leave and take the creatures of your opposed plane with us? she pointed her thoughts to ask.

Yes. Yes. Take it away. Now!

What had initially seemed to her a bargain suddenly turned into a demand, one filled with a level of power and anger Catti-brie had never before experienced. It was as if every cell in her brain and body reverberated with the command, and she felt small then, tiny and inconsequential, a speck of sand on the endless beach that was this creature, this living, godlike being.

She tried to focus, to discern a way to bring the exchange back to a bargain. Perhaps this would be the only way, to open the gates and flee, all of them, and let the volcano explode.

It seemed the best option of no other options.

But what of Neverwinter City? The last time the volcano had erupted, the place had been buried beneath a gigantic rush of ash and lava flowing as smoothly and quickly as a tidal wave.

A wall of indifference struck her the moment the consideration came to her, one that quickly turned to umbrage. That she would even harbor such a meaningless concern separated her from the primordial, she suddenly understood.

It didn't care.

They were all inconsequential, nothingness, temporary.

So temporary.

She knew then, to her horror. It was all beyond her comprehension or emotions, and she knew, too, that the primordial would never care, could never care, for any mortal being. Including her. Instinctively, from somewhere so deep within her that she wasn't even aware of her action, Catti-brie canceled the magical connection of the ring.

She realized only then where she was. She felt the heat, the sweat sprouting from her every pore.

And she saw through the mist a wall of orange, a cresting wave of lava, breaking over her.

No magic in all the world could deny the pure heat energy of the primordial of fire.

Her wards were nothing. Nothing!

Her child . . .

HE THREW HIMSELF AT THE LINE OF VROCKS, BLADES slashing and stabbing with abandon, letting his body lead, for there was no plan to be had. He felt every hit he scored, doubly so when it was Icingdeath biting hard at the demonic life energy, but he also felt the raking claws, and another hard peck on his shoulder that sent him staggering back toward the wall, stunning him momentarily.

The more dangerous enemies, the glabrezu and the ursine demon, bore in. The bear-like monster reared up and rumbled forward to simply overwhelm him and bury him beneath its bulk.

Zak tried to line up Icingdeath that the beast would impale itself. He was dead, he realized, but he was determined to take this one with him, at least.

The demonic bear went low to all fours suddenly, surprisingly, and Zak wasn't sure how to react—for it took him a long moment to recognize the massive black panther atop the fiend, as Guenhwyvar's powerful maw clamped down on the back of the demon's neck, long fangs deeply buried.

To the side and behind, the glabrezu jolted suddenly, lightning arcing all about its waving limbs.

Down went the ursine demon, skidding short of Zak, a loud crack sounding as its neck bone snapped.

It stopped struggling, and Guen leaped away, flying past Zak and into the nearest vrock, driving it backward, bulling it down the hallway.

The other two came in and Zak readied to meet the attack—and he thought a third joining from the other way, running past the gla-brezu. But no, he realized, it was no vrock. It was a diatryma, a huge flightless bird, and one Zaknafein had seen before, one produced by the large feather on Jarlaxle's outrageous hat!

Despite his predicament, despite the blood flowing over his collar from his wounds, the numbness in his battered right shoulder, the sheer heaviness of the bruise a pecking vrock had hammered through his fine mithral shirt across his chest, the weapon master nearly laughed aloud when the diatryma and the second vrock crashed together, both leaping and kicking out with clawed feet, little wings flapping furiously to give them each additional height. He had seen this type of fight before among chickens kept by drow, but now, on this scale, with each of the combatants nearly twice his height and weight, that similarity struck him as patently absurd.

He wasn't about to pause and question his good luck, though, not with a vrock so near and the glabrezu a few strides away. Back and forth worked Icingdeath, Vidrinath held in reserve. He wanted the frostbrand to intercept the flailing wings of his attacker, for each mo-ment of defense was also a bit of offense.

He felt that scimitar's satisfaction with every parry, or maybe it was the continual squawking of the vrock that showed him the wisdom of his technique. Still, the creature wouldn't give him an opening to finish, and he needed to dispatch it before the more powerful glabrezu joined in.

A glance to the side offered relief, though, for the larger demon had spun away, charging down the corridor—at Jarlaxle, he presumed.

It staggered and was driven sideways enough for Zak to see a glob of greenish goo over its upper torso and face. Another lightning bolt had hit it, then.

Zak fully focused on his own fight and pressed forward with sudden intensity, fearing that Jarlaxle would need him. Back and forth whipped Icingdeath, driving the vrock's arms low, before Zak hopped up, lowering his leading sword and cutting across up high with Vidrinath.

Too slow to hit, though, purposely so, for the vrock predictably ducked, arms rising to protect its head, and Zak, as he landed, did so in a posture to propel himself fast forward, Icingdeath stabbing powerfully. How easily did the frostbrand slide through demon flesh, devouring. The vrock hit him repeatedly, but each blow came with less power as it quickly expired.

It fell away.

Before him, Zak saw Guen finishing the vrock farther along the corridor. Ahead and to the side, the diatryma held its own with the remaining birdlike demon.

Zak turned back and saw the glabrezu charging down the corridor, moving awkwardly, one arm stuck tight against the side of its doglike head. Another lightning bolt hit it, but hardly slowed it, and from the inception point of that spark, Zak realized that the hulking monster was barely strides from Jarlaxle.

He rushed off after it, wishing then that he had put those bracers on his ankles!

But then the demon disappeared, as if it had fallen off a cliff, and there stood Jarlaxle, calmly holding two wands in one hand. The mercenary leader offered a shrug to his approaching friend.

Zak understood as he moved a bit nearer.

Jarlaxle had thrown down his portable hole in the glabrezu's path—the demon was in the pit between Zak and Jarlaxle. For good measure, Jarlaxle had then used his innate drow abilities to fill that pit with magical darkness, obviously disorienting the wounded and struggling behemoth.

Zak glanced back, noting that Guen was now with the diatryma, overwhelming the remaining vrock.

He looked back to Jarlaxle and returned the mercenary's shrug.

"A moment, please," Zaknafein said, and he jumped into the pit.

The sounds that came forth—howling, shrieking, roaring, though muffled by goo—still echoed off the walls of the corridor for a long, long way.

Perhaps signaling to other demons to come to the glabrezu's aid.

But it didn't matter.

For they ended quickly.

Zaknafein jumped back out. "Let's go."

SHE DUCKED.

She screamed.

She tried to cover herself, hoping against hope that the redundant wards and protections against fire would shield her—but of course, even if they did, the sheer weight of the wave would crush her and drive her into the creature's bubbling fire maw.

Still, instinctively, Catti-brie braced, and her scream became a strange cry of surprise as she overbalanced when the wave did not hit.

When a hand grasped her by the arm, helping to ease her down onto the stone.

Wet stone.

Cool stone.

Catti-brie looked up to see Yvonnel bending low over her.

"I don't . . ." Catti-brie stammered, trying to collect her thoughts, trying to remember the telepathic conversation with the primordial. She was too stupefied at the moment, however, too stunned to be here. Too shocked that she was still alive. "How?"

"I heard it all," Yvonnel said.

"Heard it? We weren't speaking."

"Telepathy is words, floating freely, and those who know how can catch them," Yvonnel explained. "Maegera was not possessing you."

"Maegera?"

"The primordial."

Catti-brie paused and considered the primordial. Maegera. Yes, that was its name.

"Your exchange was free-floating," said Yvonnel. "I heard."

"Then you heard the bargain the pri—Maegera, offered? We can get out, some of us, at least," Catti-brie said, accepting Yvonnel's hand to help her shakily to her feet.

"Yes."

"It's too high a price. I cannot condemn a city."

"Do you think you can stop it?" Yvonnel asked.

Catti-brie scoffed at the thought. Of course she could not. No one could deny the power of a primordial.

"The creature was lying, in any case," said Yvonnel.

"Lying? I don't think there is such a thing in the conscience or consciousness of the primordial."

"Well reasoned," Yvonnel congratulated. "Its thoughts are not as ours. Its wants and needs are unknown to us. What we consider a promise could mean nothing to it. All we know is that the beast craves release."

"And that it will find it soon enough."

As if on cue, the chamber shook suddenly and violently, nearly throwing Yvonnel from her feet and causing a stumbling Catti-brie to nearly pitch headlong back into the chasm!

Artemis Entreri was there at once, however, grabbing both of them, pulling them back—and just in time, for high into the mist of the water elementals leaped a lava appendage of Maegera. Most of it hardened fast in the grip of the elementals to fall back down, but some splashes escaped the pit, splattering about the floor.

A waft of warm steam washed over the three.

Yvonnel stepped forward then, chanting, her voice strong and unwavering. Catti-brie and Entreri watched as the moments slipped past.

The drow woman stopped her chant and lifted her hands, palms together before her. A final word, shouted with power as she swept her arms out to either side, brought forth a great geyser of water, appearing in the air, rushing out and over the lip of the chasm—not like a river, but more a blob of water.

A giant elemental, Catti-brie realized.

It rolled over the ledge and fell from sight, and the chamber rumbled again in protest.

A second creature from the Plane of Water followed from Yvonnel's opened gate, then a third and a fourth.

The cavern rumbled and shook again, but in a diminishing manner. Combined with the residual powers of the swirling elementals from the Hosttower, the primordial Maegera was contained again for the time being.

"There is no reasoning with it," Yvonnel said.

"It is not evil," Catti-brie said, as much to herself as to the drow woman.

"Definitely not. It does not even understand the concepts of good and evil," Yvonnel replied, and Catti-brie knew it was true. "It does not matter. Maegera does what it must to do, what it is compelled to do. Like a lover desperate, beyond reason."

"To destroy and to create," Catti-brie whispered. "That's all it does. That's what it will do unless we hold it. We are nothing to it."

"Not even you and your ring. Not a city. Not even your child. It does not care."

"There is no sympathy, no empathy, no emotion." She looked at Entreri and noted the man blanching at her words as if they reflected on more than the beast in the pit.

"You saved me," she said to Yvonnel.

"That was the plan."

"You saved my child. I'll not forget that. I'll never forget that." She breathed heavily, then, feeling flush, her face warm, uncomfortably so. Thinking she was simply overcome by the powerful experience, Catti-brie brushed it off—no time for such weakness.

Yvonnel nodded and put a hand on the woman's shoulder. She started to say that she was certain Catti-brie would return the favor, but stopped short and pointed a curious look at the woman. "What?"

"It needs release more because its powers are not being well used," Catti-brie said on a sudden insight. She looked to Yvonnel, then to her hand and the ring, rolling it about her finger. "This is a ring of great power, but it gives me no power over the primordial."

"Of course not," said Yvonnel.

Catti-brie looked back up, her lips turned up in a wicked smirk, her blue eyes sparkling in the orange glow. "But over its seed?"

"What are you thinking?"

Catti-brie narrowed her eyes, her face, normally so innocent and generous, taking on a very different affect then.

"Nothing good for our enemies," Artemis Entreri whispered.

"I'm not sure yet," Catti-brie said to Yvonnel. "Let us discuss it when I have sorted my thoughts more clearly."

CHAPTER 23

That Nagging Discomfort

O ne thing stayed with Kimmuriel over the next few days, one nagging implication from his time with the illithid hive mind. Not from what he had learned, but from what he had *not* learned.

Ouwoonivisc? The memories that particular illithid had added had struck him as odd at the time—or not odd, perhaps, but somehow out of place.

He knew what he had to do regarding Brevindon Margaster. He had to engage the man and force Asbeel to the surface, then somehow destroy the phylactery and intervene in the battle over the man's physical body.

But there remained a problem, and one that could put him right in the face of a powerful demon if he could not resolve it and find an answer to a pressing question:

Why had Wulfgar missed?

The inescapable conclusion, particularly to a skilled psionicist, was that the barbarian's thoughts were being scoured, for surely

Wulfgar was too fine a warrior to reveal the coming attack. How could that be, though, for Kimmuriel was connected to Wulfgar at that time, maintaining his kinetic barrier. He should have sensed any such intrusion. He had learned much about Asbeel in the hive mind. Asbeel was not really a demon, not a demonic incarnation, at least, but rather, an elf—or he once had been. There was no indica- tion of psionic powers, and even if there were, how could Kimmuriel not have sensed any such magic upon Wulfgar?

There was an answer, one answer, but though it was glaringly ob- vious, Kimmuriel couldn't quite come to accept it.

But he had to. He considered again the last memories imparted to him by Ouwoonivisc, images accompanied by sentiment and words that were not unfamiliar to Kimmuriel Oblodra of Lolth's Menzoberranzan.

Familiar thoughts in an unexpected place. Shocking, even. Ou- woonivisc's contributions at the hive mind were nothing Kimmuriel had felt there—ever—even when the communal joining of the illithid community had been focused on Menzoberranzan, House Oblodra, or Lady Lolth. Ouwoonivisc's manner of thought, a hint of the joy of not just chaos, but destructive chaos, was nothing Kimmuriel would have ever expected of the disciplined, always-in-control mind flayers.

It reminded him of other experiences, Torilian experiences. The words, the cadence, of Ouwoonivisc's memory had come straight from the Fane of the Goddess, the most holy altar to Lady Lolth in Menzoberranzan.

That alone wouldn't have bothered Kimmuriel so much, except that this particular memory wasn't related to Asbeel—he now under- stood that after taking so many hours in separating things out. No, this was an aside, an offered memory.

No, that wasn't right, either. Not a *memory*.

As he finally worked through it all, Kimmuriel had his answer. He put this in perspective to his own memories, ones barely shared with the hive mind. Terrible memories of the fall of House Oblodra.

That, too, now made more sense to him.

He went to Wulfgar, in his quarters with Bonnie Charlie and Dab'nay.

"Now?" the barbarian asked eagerly. He rose from his chair and took a step toward Aegis-fang, which was leaning against the wall.

"Not yet," Kimmuriel told him. "But soon. This day, if I return."

"Where are you going?" Dab'nay asked.

"Nowhere that concerns you, priestess," he replied, his voice edged with more than a little animosity, particularly with the memories of the fall of House Oblodra so close in mind. He softened his visage almost immediately, though, and considered the possibility that, indeed, he would not return from his dangerous journey. In that event, Dab'nay might prove to be his best option.

If I do not return, deliver this message, Kimmuriel telepathically instructed her. He considered the best persons to whom he might offer such revelations. To Jarlaxle, he decided, then knew that this was not time for caution and changed his mind. *To Matron Mother Quenthel, to Yvonnel Baenre—yes, to them, and only to them. But privately, and speak nothing to Matron Zhindia Melarn or High Priestess Sos'Umptu Baenre.*

Dab'nay stared at him in confusion, an expression that only amplified as the moments passed, as Kimmuriel revealed his epiphany. He walked closer to her and lifted his hand, resting it gently on her forehead as he gave to her some memories and his explanation in tying them all together.

He found the woman a willing vessel for such heresy, and only in that exchange did Kimmuriel understand the depth of Dab'nay's apostasy.

Good. Very good, he thought.

"You would have me tell these things to the Matron Mother of Menzoberranzan?" Dab'nay asked him incredulously. "That way lies doom! She will make a drider of me before I have uttered a hint that will resonate . . ."

"You know that I am correct in my beliefs here," Kimmuriel said.

"It matters not!"

"Indeed, nothing else matters," said Kimmuriel.

"What are you two jawing about?" Bonnie Charlee demanded.

"Nothing you would begin to understand," Kimmuriel retorted, without ever bothering to look at her.

"Perhaps you could persuade them—by showing them, as you showed me," Dab'nay said.

"That would be preferable," Kimmuriel admitted. "But first, I must confirm my suspicions."

"I thought we were going for Brevindon this day?" Wulfgar asked, but Kimmuriel ignored him.

"You have not even confirmed this, yet you ask me to speak with the Matron Mother?" Dab'nay remarked, shaking her head.

"If I do not return, consider it confirmed," the psionicist told her.

"I do not understand," the priestess argued. "What? Where?"

"It is not your concern. Do as I instructed if I do not return this day. Tell Matron Mother Quenthel and Yvonnel alone. No one else."

"I will need the assistance of those here to even find them, I am sure."

"And they will give it," Kimmuriel replied.

"But if they ask . . ."

"They will not." He looked hard at Wulfgar and at Bonnie Charlee. "Bregan D'aerthe will know that these orders came from me alone, and so they will aid you unquestionably and unquestioningly."

"And Jarlaxle?"

"He will learn when he needs to know," Kimmuriel answered. "Matron Mother Baenre and Yvonnel alone. Do you understand?"

Dab'nay nodded and Kimmuriel took his leave.

THE EXCHANGE BETWEEN PESCATAWAV AND KIMMURIEL was rapid and complete, for the drow psionicist accepted the great risk in allowing the Most Endeared illithid into his deepest thoughts and reasoning. If he was wrong, if he had missed some obvious flaw in his reasoning, Kimmuriel understood that he would be destroyed without hesitation, for to make such an accusation against another illithid was no minor charge, after all. Other races spoke of the value of family, but in the hive mind, such a notion went far deeper. Illithids were more than brothers, or sisters, or whatever—if any—gender they might hold at any given time, as they defined such things far differently than any of the other races. As with everything among the mind flayers, the desires of the mind overwrote the limitations of the body.

In the final note, however, the community was one. One. So to levy a charge against an illithid, in this case Ouwoonivisc, was to point out a flaw in the entire mind flayer community. In a way, Kimmuriel had just privately called Pescatawav a traitor.

I offer only my observations and memories of the fall of my house, he pointedly imparted when he felt Pescatawav pulling away from him.

I know what you offer.

"It is her, Lolth, not Ouwoonivisc," he said aloud, thinking that they were less likely to be overheard audibly than telepathically in this particular place.

"Your reasoning is not proven, but is sound," replied the illithid in its scratchy voice, picking up on his cue. "But why?"

In his mind, Kimmuriel sensed the addition of *House Oblodra* to the question.

"Matron K'yorl went too far in the Time of Troubles," Kimmuriel said. "She threatened the order of the Lolthian drow. The ever-hungry infection that is Lady Lolth craved domination of the illithids, but the drow were her base of power in the place she most coveted, the material plane," he answered out loud, though of course Pescatawav had already felt that same reasoning within him.

Kimmuriel sensed his doubt—this was the critical point: *Drow above illithid. How could that be?*

"She could not have both at that time, but now she can," Kimmuriel answered, a response that was an epiphany both to him and to Pescatawav in that very moment.

Engage Ouwoonivisc now, the drow was told.

Kimmuriel took a deep breath and followed the Most Endeared out of the quiet side chamber to the main area of the illithid castle, wherein rested the great brain of the community. Slaves of all races were in there, gently massaging the delicate and all important brain, and many illithids moved about, some going to the brain to see what memories had been recently left for them, or to leave their own. Others were off to the sides, typically in pairs or threes, close together and facing each other, their tentacles entwined in something that Kimmuriel had come to understand was either lovemaking or psionic battle, or perhaps a bit of both.

Pescatawav sent out a thrumming wave of energy, one that sent the slaves scurrying away and brought the illithids rushing to meld with the brain, the mind flayer equivalent of a ship's boatswain's call for all hands on deck. The Most Endeared held Kimmuriel back for a moment while all of the others settled in.

"Are you certain you wish to proceed now?" Pescatawav asked quietly, for any telepathy now would be akin to shouting.

"More time will not help," the drow replied. "It will not help either my predicament or yours."

His framing stiffened the back of the Most Endeared, reminding him pointedly that, if he was right, the hive mind was in dire trouble here.

Pescatawav and Kimmuriel took their places, side by side and with Kimmuriel right next to Ouwoonivisc. The Most Endeared was in Kimmuriel's mind immediately, using the power of the central brain to silence Kimmuriel to all others. Then, through the brain once more, the Most Endeared silenced all, except for Kimmuriel and Ouwoonivisc.

The drow poured forth his thoughts, as he had privately to Pescatawav, and with the speed of the telepathic transmission came the wall of denial and outrage from Ouwoonivisc.

You work with the agents of Lolth, he accused. *You were there with the attackers in Luskan, in the thoughts of Asbeel the demon, aiding him. You carry the desires of Lolth in yourself, and bring them here to the community of illithids.*

Ouwoonivisc's protests continued, but without conviction. One could not hide here, and could not lie.

It all happened in a matter of heartbeats, and then Pescatawav opened up the floor to all.

Kimmuriel had engaged in this communal expression of the hive mind many times in the past, but never like this.

Never anything remotely like this.

Swirls of anger and denial came at him, mixed with horror at the thought that what he had imparted could be true. He felt as if he were in a tornado, not a physical wind of course, but a spinning of so many viewpoints that it left him dizzy and so terrified that he wanted to lift his hand and flee from this place forever.

But he didn't. Kimmuriel Oblodra had spent his life engaged in discipline, and he needed all of it now. He focused on one thing, long in the past, and showed the illithid hive mind in a running loop, the fall of House Oblodra and the drow woman standing before the great house as it tumbled into the Clawrift, her face a mask of ecstasy.

Matron Mother Yvonnel Baenre. Yvonnel the Eternal. The virtual avatar of Lady Lolth.

The thoughts of the entire colligate continued to swirl about him, jumbled, opposing, battling.

The drow kept his focus, and focused, too, on the illithid right beside him, Ouwoonivisc, who had no defense against the memory, indeed, who seemed appalled by it.

Gradually, the swirl seemed smoother, one side growing louder.

Kimmuriel knew the truth, and the illithids were confirming it: Lady Lolth was not a goddess, was not a demon queen. No, in this matter, to the perspective of creatures chasing the truth of pure thought, Lady Lolth was an infection. Ouwoonivisc was infected, diseased. The illithid had, almost certainly unwittingly, become the conduit of Lolth's newest attempt on the hive mind, one that was now ongoing. Before, it had been House Oblodra acting as the conduit to bring the infection of Lolthian chaos to this place, perhaps even Matron K'yorl herself.

That attempt had failed because during the Time of Troubles, when Lolth's minion drow, her beloved priestesses and even the wizards of Menzoberranzan, had lost their magical powers both divine and arcane, the ambitious Oblodrans had threatened the entire structure Lolth had spent millennia creating.

Thus had Lolth failed.

But the Spider Queen hadn't given up. Quite the opposite. Now the clever malevolence—with the infinite patience of the immortal—

had found an even more direct organism to come here and infect the central brain and, thus, the entire hive mind.

All of the thoughts coalesced, the spinning tornado now a roaring hurricane, denying Ouwoonivisc's attempt, denying the physical being of Ouwoonivisc itself.

Kimmuriel felt the doomed illithid's protestations—not a denial, but simply a plea for mercy. He understood it all now. Lolth was a goddess, perhaps, but also perhaps a demon, *and* a being with physical form. But she was much more than all that. A bit of Lolth was inside every reasoning being, usually dormant, but like a disease or an infection, it could awaken. That should never have happened within the brain of a disciplined illithid. It seemed utterly impossible.

But it was not.

Clearly not.

There was little conviction in Ouwoonivisc's protestations, for even the illithid now understood the truth.

For the sake of the hive mind, Ouwoonivisc was there and then wasn't, driven mad, every synaptic pathway twisting and killed. From madness came emptiness, a continuing shutdown of the illithid's mind.

One last telepathic howl of horror, a silent shriek that shuddered Kimmuriel to his very core, escaped the illithid.

The central brain cried out in sorrow so powerfully that Kimmuriel was pushed back, his hand forcibly coming from the fleshy membrane, the contact sundered. He saw that he was not alone, that all the illithids were standing as he was, dumbfounded, confused, trying to find some balance against the shock Kimmuriel had given them, the horror Ouwoonivisc had been forced to reveal to them, and the overwhelming emotions of a central brain so suddenly made vulnerable that it had to destroy a part of itself, as if a drow were to bite off his own finger.

Right beside Kimmuriel lay the lifeless body of Ouwoonivisc, propped against the arching side of the central brain.

So it must be, Pescatawav imparted to all.

And that was it. It was over, other than the slaves being brought forth to destroy the body of the inadvertent traitor.

Kimmuriel's work here was done. He offered that thought to Pescatawav, and the Most Endeared excused him to go and tend to the
more pressing problems he faced on his home plane, among his own
inferior people.

There was no sense of gratitude, no thoughts of hope that Kimmuriel would succeed.

It just was.

There were a few moments like this for Kimmuriel Oblodra, when
he almost reconsidered his life's journey, when he saw so plainly the
difference between the sensibilities of the hive mind and those of
Jarlaxle.

His only friend.

"COME AT ONCE," KIMMURIEL TOLD WULFGAR. "IT IS TIME
to meet Brevindon Margaster and be done with this."

"Now?" asked the surprised barbarian.

"Now," Kimmuriel demanded. "Our enemy is vulnerable, but he
likely does not yet know that one of his great advantages has been
stolen from him."

"I don't understand."

"Aye, nor do I," Bonnie Charlie added.

Kimmuriel sighed. "Of course you don't. It matters not. If you were
only included in things you truly understand, the two of you would
spend your days doing nothing but drinking and rutting."

Bonnie Charlee scowled at that, but Wulfgar laughed.

"Kimmuriel told a joke. I thought I'd never live long enough to
witness such a thing."

"If you tarry now, you'll likely not live long enough to tell anyone
else about it," said the drow. "Now come along, and quickly."

He held out his hand toward Wulfgar, then, as both humans approached, reluctantly held out his other one for Bonnie Charlee. She
had no role here, Kimmuriel knew, but perhaps Asbeel would kill her
and thus waste a swing.

The two took the offered hands.

"He is in Ship Kurth, a place I know well, and there is a room not far from the seat of power with which I am quite familiar—one I have prepared for instances like that before us now."

"Aye, like a wizard's glyph for teleports," Bonnie Charlee said.

"To put it in crude terms, yes," Kimmuriel replied. "I know not what we'll find there in this moment, so weapons in hand and ready. I do not wish to waste my skills on mere underlings."

That brought a snicker from Wulfgar.

"You understand your role?" Kimmuriel asked him.

The barbarian nodded. "One of them."

"That is all you will need to do."

"We'll see."

Kimmuriel wasn't thrilled with the man's evasiveness here. He had told Wulfgar of his plans, of specifically what he would need from the man in order to perhaps decapitate the new order in the City of Sails. He knew that Wulfgar wanted more—Kimmuriel had read that thought clearly during his explanation of how he intended the fight to go.

Telepathically, he gave them a visual image of the room where they would arrive in Ship Kurth and another more pointed warning that the place was likely occupied, perhaps even guarded.

Barely had Wulfgar nodded to those imparted thoughts than Kimmuriel focused his mind keenly on that room, and in that focus, he pictured himself and these two humans in that room.

And so they were.

And, as expected, they were not alone.

SHE WAS BLUFFING. SHE KNEW THAT AS MATRON MOTHER, she couldn't show doubt—she was the voice of Lolth, after all. But Quenthel was full of doubt at that time. She wanted nothing more than to retire privately for a long rest, one in which she might yet again search the memories of her dead mother. Her previous meditation had led her to the one inescapable notion that she could not stop Zhindia's victory, and thus, she had to find a way to share in it.

But could she?

And worse, and more baffling, did she really want to?

Her alliance was falling apart—she knew that without doubt. She had strong-armed the others to join her in this campaign, but as a foil to Matron Zhindia Melarn. Her impetus was to make sure that Zhindia did not gain enough to threaten the order of the city. Few matrons would enjoy serving under the zealotry and viciousness of Zhindia Melarn, after all.

But now Zhindia had been given an army of driders, brought back into existence by Lady Lolth. The retrievers had been a difficult enough sign for Quenthel to overcome—how could Zhindia have been given those if not for the favor of Lolth, after all—but this development had all the others, even her two closest allies on the Ruling Council, Matrons Byrtyn Fey and Zeerith Xorlarrin, glancing about nervously.

The best Quenthel could hope for now, so it seemed, was to get them all in on a piece of the glory of this magnificent conquest. And it was indeed magnificent. As much as Quenthel wanted to deny that, she could not.

There would be a reshuffling of powers back in Menzoberranzan when this was finished, she knew. If she was lucky, Matron Zhindia and House Melarn would leap to the third house of the city. That would outrage Matron Zeerith, of course, and it would shake those others loyal (or at least sufficiently cowed) toward House Baenre. Matron Mez'Barris would then no doubt quickly plot with Zhindia to build a new and formidable alliance, one intent on displacing House Baenre once and for all. Because if Zhindia Melarn became the most favored of Lady Lolth, how could Quenthel continue to claim the mantle of Matron Mother of Menzoberranzan?

And that scenario was if Quenthel was lucky.

If not, she would be the matron of the city's second house the moment the drow returned to Menzoberranzan, simply because the other seven matrons on the Ruling Council would unanimously agree that Matron Zhindia's successes, so beautifully blessed by the Spider Queen, had to be recognized with Zhindia seated at the head of the table.

Could House Baenre withstand that demand?

And could they remain as second house much longer after that?

All of that was the reason Quenthel now led the army, some fifteen thousand drow soldiers, priestesses, wizards, and thrice that number of goblinkin slaves, to the highest levels of the Underdark, to a cave that opened on the wide world above.

They waited until that infernal fiery ball set far below the ground before coming out from under the sheltering stone.

"How far?" Quenthel asked Saribel Xorlarrin Do'Urden. She was keeping the two noble children of Matron Zeerith close to her side, and indeed, had put the whole of Zeerith's house within the ranks of House Baenre. Zeerith had dozens of powerful wizards, after all, including the current archmage of Menzoberranzan, and Quenthel thought they might be needed, if for no other reason than to help expedite a hasty retreat for the two houses via teleport spells back into the city.

Right behind that lead force came House Barrison Del'Armgo, with Matron Mez'Barris wearing a sour expression the whole way. For behind her came the other Baenre allies. She knew the truth, Quenthel understood: Quenthel was putting her in a box that could create havoc upon her ranks in the first exchange if things here turned into a civil war.

But there was nothing she could do to protest it, and that meant Quenthel still held the power.

For now.

Such a scenario was Quenthel's desperation play, though, and only in such dire need. She wasn't even sure if those matrons behind the Armgos would join in such an ambush—she wasn't even sure if Zeerith would.

If she was being truthful, she wasn't even sure if many of her own forces, particularly those under her sister Sos'Umptu would! Sos'Umptu, above all else, was devout to the Spider Queen, her loyalties more aligned with Lolth than with House Baenre.

She was a true believer.

Just like Zhindia Melarn.

Saribel conferred with her brother Ravel for a moment before pointing to the southwest. "The destroyed village is less than a day's easy march," she replied. "We could make it before the dawn if we hurry."

Quenthel nodded but gave no such order. She needed to buy time here, to sort it all out, to weigh the mood of so many of her fellow matrons, women who had spent their lives perfecting deception and duplicity.

"Go to Matron Zeerith," she instructed the two nobles. "And to Matron Mez'Barris. Tell them that we will set a wide perimeter out on the surface. They can choose among their ranks no more than fifty soldiers, two priestesses, and one wizard. The rest of the sentry force will come from the other ruling houses."

The two bowed and rushed away, and were replaced almost immediately by Sos'Umptu, Minolin Fey, and Myrineyl.

"Matron Mez'Barris will send her weapon master," Sos'Umptu said.

"No," Quenthel disagreed. "Not here. She doesn't fear for Malagdorl in battle, but he is too dim-witted to be the one to represent her if Matron Zhindia learns of our position and comes to parlay."

"Perhaps," High Priestess Sos'Umptu conceded. "I am to represent House Baenre on the front line?"

"No," Quenthel said, and Sos'Umptu stiffened as if she had been slapped.

Quenthel quickly continued, diverting the truth of her denial of such an honor. "No, I need you now. You speak with Lolth as clearly as any, save myself, and your counsel will be greatly valued as we walk the webs that have been woven here."

"Perhaps Matron Zhindia speaks to Lolth most clearly of all," Sos'Umptu returned, and it was Quenthel's turn to be startled.

This was the first hint of her fears coming to fruition.

Quenthel tightened her face into a determined scowl and stared at her, trying to back her down, but Sos'Umptu was no minor player here, not even in the face of the Matron Mother of House Baenre and of all Menzoberranzan. Sos'Umptu was mistress of Arach-Tinilith, high priestess of the Fane of the Goddess, and held a seat on the Ruling Council. Quenthel had given her that seat, adding a ninth to the table, to bolster the power of House Baenre.

But now?

Matron Zhindia had been given two retrievers and hundreds of mighty drider abominations.

Did Quenthel dare to force the most devout Sos'Umptu to choose between her and the Spider Queen, the secular and the divine?

Was blood thicker than soul?

THE ROOM THEY APPEARED IN REVEALED TO WULFGAR how very confident Kimmuriel had been in Bregan D'aerthe's hold on Luskan. Normally, wizards (and Wulfgar assumed the same for Kimmuriel) would set their prepared magical teleports, rooms speckled with dweomers to make the journey more secure, off to the side. Small rooms, from which they could come forth from the disorienting instant transportation in private and in safety.

Not here, though. Despite some recent remodeling, Wulfgar knew this room, the large side hall of the main ballroom of the great Ship Kurth. Now it was a bedroom, a barracks, and the three intruders hardly arrived in private.

A table upended and a trio of gnolls leaped to their feet, reaching for their weapons. On beds lining the perimeter of the place, more dog-faced villains stirred.

Without hesitation, Wulfgar rushed toward the table. A small dagger flew past him, embedding into a gnoll's hand as the creature reacted to block. It howled and ran for the door.

A second missile chased it, a much larger missile, and the gnoll, even had it been looking, would find no defense against spinning Aegis-fang. It struck the fleeing gnoll square in the back, lifting it from its feet and throwing it forward and to the floor, where it lay groaning.

The two at the table lifted their weapons, short sword and cudgel, and grinned wickedly at the suddenly unarmed human charging in at them, any feeling they might have had for their friend behind them inconsequential in the face of what seemed an easy kill.

Wulfgar didn't slow.

He also grinned back at them, which startled the gnolls.

He went for the one with the sword, calling Aegis-fang back into his hands just before he reached his target.

The gnoll stabbed ahead, not even realizing that its attacker had produced another warhammer.

Wulfgar stabbed ahead, as well, punching out with the top of his hammer, the heavy weapon easily intercepting the sword and driving it aside. The barbarian took a long step forward, right foot leading, turning his right shoulder ahead, to further extend as he continued to stab, sending the gnoll skidding backward.

He ducked his head in time, lifting his front shoulder to deflect the cudgel from the gnoll on his right. His arm went numb from the blow, but he fought through it and held on with that right hand, dropping his left as he turned behind the blow. As he went, he sent his numb right arm up and over the gnoll's extended arms, sweeping Aegis-fang up and over as well. Wulfgar spun about, reversing his feet and hips with a short leap, then burrowing ahead before the gnoll could fully extract its arms from his clench.

He hit the creature on the side of its snout with a vicious left hook and let go as it stumbled backward, enough to buy him enough room to finish the rotation with his right arm, bringing it up before him and letting fly the hammer in a short throw that caught the sword-wielder right in the chest as it finally managed to turn back to the fight.

Wulfgar didn't watch the impact and had to hope it bought him enough time. He leaped on the gnoll he had stunned with the punch, again wrapping it, more completely this time, with his right arm.

His left hand went to work, jabbing and hooking, cracking the dog-faced monster's jaw.

It tried to pull back again, and Wulfgar let it, but only a bit, putting a clamp on its left wrist, the hand that held the cudgel. With a tug to pull the creature back at him—and as strong as it was, it couldn't resist the power of that pull—Wulfgar rolled to his right, slamming the gnoll in the chest with his left shoulder. He knew he was vulnerable to a bite if that jaw still worked, but he was confident that he would be quicker here. He continued to tug the wrist, straightening the arm, and drove his left arm powerfully over the upper arm, hooking it, locking it.

With a suddenness, a brutality, and sheer strength the gnoll could not comprehend from a human, Wulfgar turned farther to the right and punched out with the hand clamped on the gnoll's wrist, bending the arm in a manner that arms simply shouldn't bend.

The gnoll's elbow exploded. The gnoll howled in pain. The cudgel flew across the room.

Before it even landed, Wulfgar released with his left arm, leaped high as he turned about, and came down from on high with a driving right hand, pounding the gnoll just under its left eye with such force that the creature seemed to shrink suddenly, as if its entire body simply contracted, and as Wulfgar landed and jumped back a step, that energy seemed to rebound weirdly, as if rising from the gnoll's ankles.

It hopped from the ground and tumbled backward, inadvertently, unconsciously, falling just out of reach of Wulfgar's ensuing left hook.

It hardly mattered. The gnoll wasn't about to get back up anyway.

But the other one proved a stubborn foe, and in it came again at the seemingly unarmed man. Obviously too stupid to expect the same trick twice, the gnoll came straight in for the kill, and if it became aware that the big man was once more holding his magical warhammer, it was only after it was too late to do anything about it.

Both hands grasping the large hammer, Wulfgar brought it down from on high, cutting diagonally downward, crushing the gnoll's shoulder and driving through to flip the beast into a weird roll. It barely hit the floor before Wulfgar clamped a hand on the collar of its tunic, and up into the air it went, but limply, already quite dead.

Wulfgar dropped Aegis-fang to the floor and cupped his hand hard against the gnoll's groin, then hoisted the heavy creature up over his head with ease as he turned, seeking a target.

He noted a gnoll coming off its bunk—so fast and furious was his dispatching of the gnoll pair that this one had barely reacted to the unexpected intruders!

Three strides toward it, Wulfgar used its companion as a missile, launching it hard, both target and missile tumbling back onto the cot.

Wulfgar saw yet another gnoll coming in his direction. He thought to call his warhammer to his hand, but hesitated, noting Bonnie Charlee on this one's back, one arm wrapped about its neck, the other pumping her dagger into the side of the bleating creature's neck, covering it in red liquid and filling the air with its blood.

Off to the side, another fight raged, gnoll against gnoll, which confused Wulfgar only for a moment until he noted Kimmuriel off to the side, calmly watching, controlling his dominated puppet.

Bonnie Charlee and her impromptu mount went past him, then crashed to the ground, and Wulfgar turned and nodded approvingly as his companion pulled herself from the dying beast. Good fortune had pulled him from the mesmerizing dance of Kimmuriel's surrogate fighter, he realized, for there was one more gnoll that he had not noted. It rushed out from behind a large footlocker, nearer to Bonnie Charlee than to Wulfgar, and charged at the woman, scooping up Aegis-fang as it went.

Wulfgar yelled a warning and rushed to intercept, knowing he couldn't get there in time.

Knowing he didn't have to.

He waited until the very last moment, the aggressive gnoll bearing down on Bonnie Charlee, lifting the heavy warhammer over its head, then recalled Aegis-fang from the brute's hand.

The gnoll swung, suddenly empty-handed, and stumbled. To its credit, it rebalanced quickly enough to backpedal out of the reach of Bonnie Charlee's slashing knife.

Wulfgar roared when the gnoll started back at the woman, and it glanced his way and threw up its arms in panic.

As if that would help.

Aegis-fang hit it squarely in the face, throwing the gnoll high and far through the air, and leaving more of the creature's head on the end of the warhammer than still on the gnoll.

A yelp from behind told Wulfgar and Bonnie Charlee that Kimmuriel's surrogate battle was over. They realized that the psionicist's proxy had won, likely in no small part through the surprise its companion must have felt, for that victorious gnoll was limping back toward Kimmuriel, arms by its side.

Wulfgar thought to hit it with a thrown warhammer, both because it was a gnoll, after all, and because the psionicist's enslavement of it offended him profoundly.

He didn't make the throw, though, for the room's door burst in at that moment, and there stood Brevindon.

Or more accurately, Asbeel's contortion of the Margaster's body, muscles bulging, skin deep red, bat-like wings sprouting from its back.

BRAELIN HAND-SIGNALED A COMPANION DOWN A SIDE tunnel, confirming that he had seen the report of all clear along the way. It had been like that since they had run out of Illusk, moving through the same tunnels that carried the tendrils of the Hosttower to Gauntlgrym. They hadn't encountered a single enemy, or anything else for that matter, and so they were making great progress to the south—progress aided by the enhancements of Bi'anza Dossouin, a wizard from a long-dead minor Menzoberranzan house, and the lone spellcaster in the group of four. The journey would normally take about five to seven days at a swift pace, but because of the clear surroundings and the magical aid, Braelin's band was more than two-thirds of the way there before the second day.

He should have been thrilled by that, but the idea that these tunnels were so empty concerned the veteran scout as much as it pleased him. There had to be a reason.

And so there was, as Braelin learned soon after when Bi'anza Dossouin caught up to him at a crossroad.

"The tunnels ahead are thick with drow," the wizard informed him. "I have cast my vision ahead."

"All the way to Gauntlgrym?"

The wizard shrugged. "I know not where the Underdark ends and Gauntlgrym begins."

"It doesn't matter," said Braelin. "It is Matron Zhindia, and her, we must avoid. Find a way for us to get up to the surf—"

He paused, for Bi'anza was waving his hands and shaking his head, trying to interrupt.

"It is not House Melarn," he said. "Nor House Hunzrin, their allies. I saw the banners."

"Which house, then?"

"Far easier for me to name the major houses who were *not* represented by the banners."

"Name them," a confused Braelin said.

"Melarn and Hunzrin," Bi'anza replied. "The others are all there, in full force."

"Baenre?"

"Most prominent of all."

"Has the matron mother come forth?" Braelin asked, nearly choking from shock.

"Do you think me fool enough to loiter, or to move closer in any form with that possibility?"

"Of course not," Braelin said, collecting himself. "No, you did well. Gather the others and let us keep close together now."

"To the surface?"

Braelin paused, unsure. "We shall see" was all that he could answer at that time.

Braelin's hand reflexively moved to the magical whistle Kimmuriel had given to him. He dropped it almost immediately, though, for Kimmuriel unnerved him, truly, and he understood that he should learn more of the situation to avoid prematurely summoning the frightening psionicist.

"Prepare more spells of clairvoyance and clairaudience," he instructed. "And any others you may have that can help us learn more of why the drow have come."

"Isn't it obvious?"

Braelin almost agreed, but as he considered it, he found that it wasn't obvious at all. Jarlaxle's conquest of Luskan and King Bruenor's position in Gauntlgrym had all been accomplished without scorn from House Baenre, and indeed, Matron Mother Quenthel served to gain from the new arrangement.

Thus, he had no idea of what was going on here, of why the tunnels were full of forces that should have remained in Menzoberranzan. This disturbed him.

Braelin was a disciple of Jarlaxle. He didn't like having no idea.

KIMMURIEL CALLED UPON EVERYTHING HE HAD LEARNED at the hive mind in that critical first moment all the while rushing behind a bunk bed to try to shield himself and not give Asbeel or Brevindon a clear enough view to recognize him. He focused particularly on the deepest thoughts of Ouwoonivisc the Infected.

. Yes, he had understood that mind flayer and its fall, for it had been lured by the same pattern of lies and descending stairway of little sins for personal gains into a hole of no return and no redemption.

He used that now—as a drow who had grown up in Menzoberranzan, he was well suited for the task.

But this was a demon, an incarnation of evil. There would be no remorse within Asbeel, and no doubt, and so Kimmuriel understood that he had to be near-perfect.

He reached out telepathically to Wulfgar, the man already rushing in to engage the demonic creature.

Let me in! he implored the man.

If Wulfgar had hesitated in that instant, he would have been in desperate straits, but to his credit, he trusted Kimmuriel in that critical moment.

Immediately Kimmuriel sensed his plans, his movements, and now reached out, too, to the demon possessing the body of Brevindon Margaster, and did so in the thought identity of Ouwoonivisc.

Wulfgar hadn't missed with his swing on the boat; nay, Asbeel had dodged because the infected illithid had acted just as Kimmuriel was acting now, relaying the movements of Asbeel's opponent so that the monster could move with perfect anticipation.

So now did Kimmuriel, offering Asbeel an advantage. He could feel the pleasure of the beast.

You have been missed, he felt in response, confirmation that he had been right in all of this.

Kimmuriel projected a series of false movements from Wulfgar, but aggressive ones that would keep Asbeel on defense and thus not offer him a chance to put that huge, wavy sword through Wulfgar's skull.

Wulfgar's next swing missed as the demon backed up and moved deeper into the room.

"The door!" Wulfgar said to Bonnie Charlee. He charged at Asbeel, forcing the beast farther from the entrance, as Bonnie Charlee ran behind him to close the room's door.

The barbarian pressed on, and the momentary confusion Asbeel signaled to the being he thought Ouwoonivisc was answered by the demon itself, silently congratulating the human on changing his tactics in order to prevent reinforcements from coming in.

Who is this drow? Asbeel did ask.

A witness from the powers of Menzoberranzan to judge the battle of Luskan, Kimmuriel answered, thinking quickly.

But the demon didn't believe him.

The demon had seen him too clearly.

The demon remembered him from the boat.

The demon, no doubt through the vile work of the traitorous Ouwoonivisc, understood the kinetic barrier Kimmuriel had offered to Wulfgar in that previous encounter.

Kimmuriel had planned to goad Asbeel with half-truths about Wulfgar's intended movements, coming just close enough to elicit confidence before blowing the whole thing up and forcing the demon to turn left when it should have turned right.

But now he felt the wall of denial, severing his influence over the body of Asbeel's slave, and Asbeel was no minor enemy.

Wulfgar and the demon squared off on a level battlefield.

And for the first time in forever, Kimmuriel felt doubt.

"STAY BACK!" WULFGAR ORDERED BONNIE CHARLEE. HE admired her courage, but her small knife wasn't going to do much against this demon with that huge sword.

The woman backed from Wulfgar's side, and not a moment too soon as Asbeel leaped across the room, lifted by his wings so that he covered the distance easily.

Wulfgar rushed sidelong to intercept, Aegis-fang and the demon's sword ringing loudly as they crashed together. A slight turn of Asbeel's wrist hooked the blade under the hammer's head, the powerful creature giving a sudden jerk then to try to disarm the man.

Wulfgar tugged back, his great strength more than enough to match that of his adversary. He silently cursed himself even as he won that embedded match, though, thinking that he might have used the opportunity to appear unarmed, the trick that so often worked to his benefit.

He let the thought go, concerned with the moment, and tugged again violently to break Aegis-fang free, then immediately sent the hammer into a series of short chops, back and forth before him as he advanced.

Asbeel backed from the first, struck the second (and nearly lost his sword), and surprisingly came forward for the third, accepting the brutal hit on the side to get up close to the man.

Wulfgar was quicker than most assumed for a man of his size, and that saved him then as he let go of Aegis-fang with his left hand, and shot his arm out and up to tangle Asbeel's lifted arm and prevent the demon from bringing his sword to bear.

Now they clenched and struggled, Asbeel biting at Wulfgar, Wulfgar jerking the demon back and forth like a wolf snapping a rabbit's spine.

He felt the sharp teeth of the fiend sinking into his cheek and howled, tearing his head back, then flashing forward with his forehead, slamming Asbeel in the face with tremendous force.

The demon staggered backward, lifted his sword in both hands, and started to bring it straight down, but Wulfgar stabbed Aegis-fang first, the top of the hammer head thumping Asbeel's face and driving him back too far for his downward slash to connect.

On came Wulfgar, leaping, swinging, following through so that the warhammer came up and around over his head and right back across, one, two, three, and more.

Asbeel continued its staggered retreat, Wulfgar barely missing with every swing.

Wulfgar watched the demon's feet—that remained the most important lesson of fighting Drizzt Do'Urden had ever taught him. Watch your opponent's feet.

Because of that lesson, he saw and reacted to the intended counter coming before it had ever begun, Asbeel balancing himself to dart in high behind the next swing.

Across came Aegis-fang and down went Wulfgar to his knees, with a spin that brought the hammer across yet again even as Asbeel's stab went right above him. He clipped the demon across the legs, flinging Asbeel over sideways. Wulfgar scrambled ahead and now had to let go with his top hand to press Asbeel back and keep the demon from re-angling the sword.

He had hurt the demon, he knew, and badly, but now Asbeel surprised him by letting go of the sword and punching Wulfgar on the side of the head instead.

There was magic in that punch, which hit the big man more like the charge of a ram than any fist.

Wulfgar fell to the side and crunched his own fingers under the handle of Aegis-fang in a desperate attempt to prevent him from falling fully prone, which would have been the end of him. He planted his trailing foot immediately and sprang away—and heard the cut of Asbeel's sword right behind him.

Scrambling, stumbling, he forced himself to his feet and around to face Asbeel, expecting the demon to be coming hard and fast.

But no, Asbeel had barely moved and was now standing up very straight.

With Bonnie Charlee on his back.

The woman put her dagger to work, but not on Asbeel's neck.

Not on Asbeel at all.

With admiration and fear for her safety, Wulfgar watched as she broke the chain holding the pendant, and flung it toward Wulfgar, even as she kicked off the demon's back, lessening the punch of a spinning Asbeel—one that still sent her slamming into the wall, where she crumpled and lay very still.

Wulfgar set himself, glancing at the fallen pendant and back at the demon, trying to gauge his next best move.

"Huh?" escaped his lips as he watched the demon, red-skinned and then not, horned and then not. Asbeel did take a step forward, but then fell back one.

Wulfgar recognized an internal battle here, the human and the demon fighting for control with the phylactery thrown aside. He knew that he could run in and land a devastating blow on his enemy, but he remembered vividly Kimmuriel's instructions to him, and the most important role he had to play.

He lifted his warhammer and roared, then spun to the side and brought Aegis-fang down hard with tremendous force, shattering the gemstone.

FROM THE MOMENT BONNIE CHARLEE DISLODGED THE phylactery, Kimmuriel knew that the fight was his to win or lose.

He threw his mental energy into the body of Brevindon Margaster like a javelin, jolting the man and the demon possessing him as surely as any physical weapon ever could. He had one objective with his initial attack: to separate the two warring spirits within that one body.

As soon as that was accomplished, the moment he felt the struggle between Brevindon Margaster and Asbeel, Kimmuriel turned his attention to Wulfgar—and breathed a sigh of relief that the violent man had followed instructions instead of his vicious and crass human instincts. In that intangible realm of the spirit, Kimmuriel sensed the destruction of the phylactery keenly. He knew that Asbeel would, as well.

So he went right back in, inserting himself into the fight between the two entities possessing the one body.

And pointedly imparting to Brevindon Margaster the future awaiting him if he lost this struggle.

There was nowhere for him to go, no phylactery to hold a spirit that it might fight another day.

For Asbeel, to lose was banishment. For Brevindon, to lose was to die.

Asbeel knew it and attacked the man with all of his willpower, hammering him, confusing him, driving him out once and for all. The demon did not want banishment any more than the human would welcome death. And because of that desire, Brevindon hadn't a chance of winning . . . except for the chance named Kimmuriel Oblodra.

Kimmuriel bolstered the man. Kimmuriel led the counterattack, assailing Asbeel. It held for heartbeats, which seemed an eternity in the realm of pure thought. Kimmuriel knew that he was at a disadvantage here and now, because Asbeel was already within the corporeal form and Kimmuriel was an outside attacker.

He fought defensively, then, bolstering Brevindon more than trying to weaken Asbeel, but he did throw one other possibility out there, hoping that Asbeel would grab it.

Their spiritual battle was a spiritual connection, and so one that Asbeel could use to move swiftly behind Kimmuriel, into Kimmuriel's body instead. While Kimmuriel could join with Brevindon here in this body, Brevindon could not join with Kimmuriel in Kimmuriel's body!

With no ground being gained and the expectation that the barbarian would soon destroy this body anyway, Asbeel made his move.

And found Kimmuriel moving just ahead of him, waiting for him, letting him take the fight to Kimmuriel's body.

As soon as he fully broke his lifeline to Brevindon's body, Asbeel realized his mistake, and Kimmuriel smiled.

Now Kimmuriel had the upper hand.

Asbeel was no minor foe, to be sure, but Kimmuriel had spent a life learning the hive mind. To him, being surrounded by other minds was natural. To be overwhelmed by those minds would have meant madness or, more likely, death.

Clearly he had survived those minds. Had thrived among them.

And this was just *one* mind he now contended with.

The spirit of Asbeel was a spirit unhoused, with only two options: banishment or possessing Kimmuriel.

Thus, in truth, Asbeel had only one option.

The fiend's time on the material plane came to a swift and prolonged end.

WULFGAR APPROACHED WITH THE INTENT TO OBLITER-ate the struggling form, but he was given pause, for the creature continued to shift color and details as the internal struggle continued.

Then, suddenly, it was a human, fully so.

Brevindon Margaster howled in pain, grabbed at his broken ribs, and tumbled as his wounded legs would not support him. On the floor he writhed and yelled and squirmed.

Wulfgar looked to Kimmuriel for guidance, looked across at Bonnie Charlee for hope.

Neither offered what he desired.

He turned back to Brevindon, to see the man calmed, lying on his side, his right arm extended up in the air, palm out to fend off Wulfgar.

"Please, please," he begged.

Bonnie Charlee stirred and sat up. That alone stayed Wulfgar's killing strike.

There came a flash, then a last, primal scream accompanying a ghostly image of a red-skinned demonic elven form, and then all three dissipated fast to nothingness.

"Gather him," Kimmuriel said from behind Wulfgar. "We need him and we must leave this place now."

CHAPTER 24

Echoes of Memory

Snapping his right hand out like a viper's strike, Afafrenfere caught a swinging axe by the handle just under the head, only a finger's breadth from his face, and so strong was his determined armlock that he stopped the swing cold. Up came Afafrenfere's right foot, going high and across to the left, then swinging back to the right over the dwarf's caught arms and down.

The stubborn dwarf was strong enough to prevent the monk from yanking the axe from his hands, but he should have simply let go, for as he was driven forward and down by the monk's pressing leg, his arms bent awkwardly, and Afafrenfere punched out with his right, driving the pointed back of the axe into the dwarf's forehead.

The dwarf howled in pain and fell away, leaving its axe behind in the monk's grasp.

Feeling pressure closing, the monk flipped the weapon back over his shoulder, spinning it through the air, and turned fast to see it clip off a second attacker's shoulder, doing no real damage as the dwarf spun to the left to bat it aside.

But it was enough, for the charging dwarf never got fully back around, and as he neared, Afafrenfere's foot hit him squarely in the face, snapping back his head. He staggered and Afafrenfere came on furiously, battering him about the head, sending him sprawling away.

Afafrenfere turned again at the last moment, snatching a thrown spear right out of the air, bringing it around, reversing his grip, and launching it right back at the dwarf who had thrown it.

That dwarf, too, fell away, grabbing at the spear that stuck from her shoulder.

The monk felt a punch in the side and spun back, but no one was there.

It wasn't a punch, he only then realized, but a crossbow quarrel, for he saw yet another dwarf and a fifth beside it—the one who had shot him reloading his crossbow, the other one leveling hers.

Afafrenfere set himself, feeling the tug in his side from the deeply embedded crossbow bolt.

The dwarf woman fired.

Afafrenfere's hand snapped up and out, deflecting the quarrel high, but the movement brought a great wince of pain as the embedded bolt tore at his insides. Instinctively, he reached down to grab at it, then he threw his left arm up defensively as the one he had clipped with the thrown axe came charging in, warhammer swinging.

The monk took the blow, his arm going numb under the weight of it, and returned a stunning open palm into the dwarf's face.

But now two crossbows were leveled his way.

He started to set, then arched suddenly as a spear drove hard into his back.

The dwarf drove in with all her strength.

Afafrenfere looked down to see the spear tip poking out from his belly. He tasted blood in his mouth. He looked up just in time to see two crossbow quarrels flying for his chest.

His arms would not answer his call. He couldn't catch these missiles, or deflect them, or block them.

He was only slightly aware of the spear being ripped out of his back, only distantly cognizant that he was then staring up at the sky, lying on his back, fighting for his breath.

He knew that he had to get up immediately.

But . . .

BREVINDON MARGASTER HAD SPENT MANY LICENTIOUS nights in Waterdeep, surrounded by too many women and far too many drinks. As he had grown older, he always shook his head after he came out of near-unconsciousness the next morning and cradled his face, which felt many sizes too large for his body, and swore that he would never again imbibe that much alcohol.

He felt that way now on an unimaginable scale—as if he had swallowed the contents of every bottle at a raucous party, then been kicked repeatedly on the side of his head, then had fingers jabbing his eyes without pause.

"Just kill the fool and be done with it," he heard a woman's voice.

Brevindon opened his eyes—it took him several attempts—and took in the unfamiliar room. He felt the mustiness about him, the ancient dust. Where was he? He couldn't make sense of any of this, except that he certainly recognized three of the five of the people in the room with him. The woman, the huge man, the small drow man . . . they had all been on the boat in the harbor fight. That warhammer carried by the giant man had broken the mast with an incredible strike.

"Wulfgar, son of Beornegar," Brevindon mumbled, for who else might it be?

"See, he knows ye, and sure that he'll be finding a way to pay you back," the woman said. "Just kill him."

"If you say another word, someone in this room may well die," said the drow man, "but it won't be him."

Brevindon felt a hand on his shoulder and turned his head to see a drow woman, eyes closed, casting. He tensed, wondering if this was the end of him, but then relaxed as waves of healing magic swept through him.

"Sit up," the small drow man said, and when Brevindon didn't immediately respond, the woman beside him grabbed him by the shoulder and hauled him upright.

"Do you know what happened to you?" the drow man asked, moving very close. "The phylactery necklace . . ."

"Asbeel," Brevindon said, and the name shocked him, as did the fact that he felt free suddenly, as he hadn't in many tendays.

"Asbeel is destroyed," the drow explained. "He'll bother you no more."

"But we will," said yet another drow, a taller man, and Brevindon blinked and for a moment thought that maybe he had indeed imbibed too much alcohol as the man transformed before his eyes, becoming a tall and lanky, red-haired human.

"I am High Captain Kurth," he said.

"Or he was before you decided to attack our city," the other drow man said.

Brevindon spent a long moment trying to digest all of that, whispering as much to himself as to them, "Why am I alive?"

"Because you are going to help us rid Luskan of your filthy gnolls and the other mercenaries you brought here," the drow who went by Kurth answered. "You are going to help us restore the order of the city properly."

"The gnolls," Brevindon said. He shook his head, not in denial of them, but in denial of all that had transpired. How had he been so foolish? So vile? He had sided with gnolls—with a demon!—as had the other nobles of his house.

His house . . . House Margaster, once so glorious . . .

What had become of it?

What had he done?

"You were coerced by a demon," the smaller drow said, and it took Brevindon a moment to wonder if he had spoken his terrible thoughts aloud.

Then he remembered more and knew that he hadn't needed to—not for this one.

"Kimmuriel?" he whispered under his breath. He thought it a name, the name of a drow, this drow, who had been in his thoughts as Asbeel had assailed his very soul.

"The demon is purged," Kimmuriel said flatly. "Asbeel will bother you no more."

"Only to be replaced by you in my head?" Brevindon argued.

The drow snickered. "Only when I choose to be. But that will not be the case in the deal you have just been offered."

"What deal?"

"You do as we ask, and you will remain in some position of power here in this city," High Captain Kurth told him. "You will find it a lucrative offer."

"And one that will allow Brevindon Margaster to restore some bit of his reputation if he is wise in his decisions," said the big man he knew to be Wulfgar.

"Should've just killed him," said the woman.

"So I should choose?" Brevindon asked again, simply to clarify all of this shocking information in his own thoughts.

"You already made your choice," Kimmuriel told him. "And now you will do as you have been told."

"Because if I don't you will kill me."

Another snicker from Kimmuriel. "Your imagination fails you if you think that."

Brevindon Margaster felt a wave of foul thoughts filtering through his mind, turning his every observation and reflexive response into an image of utter horror. He closed his eyes, slapped his fists against them. He screamed as loudly as he could, trying to deny the suggestions, the images, the emotions.

Finally they subsided, but only because of Kimmuriel and nothing to do with Brevindon's denials or mental response, and the drow left him then with the complete understanding that he would be begging for death for a long while before the drow ever offered him the mercy of it.

YOU DO NOT UNDERSTAND WHAT IT IS TO BE AN ELF, DO YOU?

Brother Afafrenfere heard the woman's voice, but it was not the voice of a dwarf, more melodious . . . distant.

He felt his blood pumping.

No, I would not want to live in a world without dragons.

This time it was a male voice, elven . . . no, drow. A voice he recognized.

Drizzt!

Are ye more trapped by the way the world sees ye or by the way ye see the world seein' ye?

Madness . . . a woman . . . an image of Catti-brie, but different, younger perhaps, her hair styled in a manner as Afafrenfere had never seen. But those deep-blue eyes. Yes, it was Catti-brie.

Suddenly, Afafrenfere saw a child, elven, beneath the torn body of an elf woman—was this the first voice her had heard? Blood, blood everywhere.

His blood?

He saw her again, but she was not a child, and oh, how he recognized her! And it was the same bloodied child, he knew.

He just knew.

But who was she? How did he know her?

A profound sadness overwhelmed him. The words came as emotions, came as images, came as experiences.

Their deaths usually come from the front.

Drizzt's voice again.

Afafrenfere's thoughts spun. He found an image of Parbid, then, so clear and close that he felt as if he could reach out and touch him once more. Images of his own life flickered about him, his loves, his fears, his father denying him and throwing him out of their home, the last look on his mother's face.

But other images intermingled, as if his own memories were mixing with those of another.

With those of Drizzt, of course.

It was only the sound of dwarves laughing that brought him back to the present and the physical. He opened his eyes and realized his pain.

The dwarves were all around him, four now, showing one another the wounds they had suffered in the fight.

"He killed him to death!" one woman roared. "Me husband's dead, and I'm payin' that one back."

He saw the dwarf woman approaching, spear in hand.

It made sense now, though. Afafrenfere understood. Drizzt had transcended here, and bits of the drow's memory remained, the echoes of a ghost. Afafrenfere was near death, had nearly slipped to the nether realm, and thus had he heard those memories, felt them keenly.

And he felt, most of all, the joy of Drizzt.

Oh, how he wanted to go and tell Catti-brie and the others! Drizzt was gone, but the retriever hadn't killed him or taken him, no! He had escaped through transcendence. He had stepped from this life willingly.

To fool the retriever and save them.

The demons didn't have him. He was forever beyond them now, and in a place of beauty and peace and oneness.

A place Afafrenfere hoped to soon join.

He felt peace at that. Drizzt's friends should not cry for him, nay, for he was in the harmony of the universe now, in the place of purest joy. Afafrenfere desperately wanted to tell them, but he knew he would not leave this place. He was broken, and even if that approaching dwarf didn't stab him, he was already mortally wounded.

She leaned over him, staring down at him with hateful eyes, lifting the spear to plunge it into his chest.

Brother Afafrenfere smiled at her, giving her pause.

It was time, he knew.

Grandmaster Kane had been right. And now, he was ready.

The monk felt his physical body come apart, bursting into bits of light, into scattering memories, the torn and flittering pages of the book that had been Brother Afafrenfere.

He kept his physical presence just long enough to see the startled look on the face of the dwarf. He wanted to tell her that he forgave her, but he had no voice with which to speak.

The dwarf's expression shifted from curiosity to fear to sheer outrage. She lifted her spear suddenly and stabbed it down.

But she didn't hit Brother Afafrenfere, for he was already gone.

She didn't hit anything, except perhaps punching a hole in the monk's empty robes.

"THAT ONE CHANGED HIS MIND QUICK," BONNIE CHARLEE said to Wulfgar, soon after the encounter with Brevindon. "I'd've thought a Waterdeep lord would have a bit more spunk than that in him."

Wulfgar sighed. "Kimmuriel," he explained. "Do not underestimate the power—and danger—of that one. I'm sure that he let Brevindon Margaster understand exactly what would befall him if he did not play along."

"Bah!" Bonnie Charlee snorted, sounding so much like Bruenor at that moment that Wulfgar almost laughed aloud.

"Trust me on this," he told her. "Kimmuriel is the most dangerous creature you have ever encountered. *Ever.*"

His tone left no room for debate, and stole the grin from Bonnie Charlee's face.

"If you ever forget that, there is nothing I will be able to do to save you," Wulfgar added.

"Damned drow elves," she said. "And why're ye making o' them friends, then?"

"One of them," Wulfgar corrected. "Perhaps someday I'll get the chance to tell you all about Drizzt Do'Urden. Perhaps I'll introduce you, and you will understand."

She didn't seem convinced.

"Or maybe there are two drow I would name as friends," Wulfgar went on. "Jarlaxle . . ."

He stopped when Kimmuriel came back into the room. He noted that Bonnie Charlee took a step away from the approaching drow. Yes, she had heard his warning.

"You will both do as Beniago instructs," the psionicist told them. "I am off to the south."

"Gauntlgrym?" Wulfgar asked eagerly.

"Eventually, perhaps, but no."

"Take me."

"I would possibly be taking you to your death, fool."

"You just had me fight a demon. This is a chance I'm willing to take. Take me, Kimmuriel, I beg. Have I not earned that much from you, at least?"

Kimmuriel started to respond, but stopped and considered Wulfgar for a long moment. "Are you so desperate to find your friends that you would risk your—"

"Yes!" he interrupted. "Of course."

Kimmuriel considered it for a moment.

"Very well. You might prove of value to me." He turned to Bonnie Charlee. "Do as Beniago instructs."

"No. If he's going, I'm going," she said.

"No, you're not," Kimmuriel replied simply.

She started to argue, but looked to Wulfgar, who shook his head at her. "Do as Beniago instructs," Wulfgar told her. "Please. I'll be back for you. You have my word."

"I've not e'er been stupid enough to take a man at his word," the clearly despondent woman replied.

"Then you'll be pleasantly surprised," Wulfgar assured her. He walked over and kissed her on the forehead and whispered in her ear, "I will come find you. Stay safe and do as Beniago . . ."

"Yeah, I heard ya," she grumbled.

CHAPTER 25

Firestorm

On her way to speak with Catti-brie later that day, Yvonnel inadvertently intercepted Penelope Harpell and Donnola Topolino.

"Quite a chance she took with a bairn in her belly," Donnola remarked after a greeting. "Are you going to see her, then?"

"I wish she had spoken with me before she went down into that hellish chasm," Penelope added.

Their concerns, and their aiming those fears at Yvonnel, were not lost on the drow woman.

"She consulted me and I begged her not to go," Yvonnel replied. "I even offered to go in her place. She is quite determined."

"Headstrong," Penelope corrected.

"Stubborn as any dwarf I've ever met," Donnola insisted. "And as you might know, I've met a few."

"I got her out of there as soon as she needed to be extracted," Yvonnel assured them.

346 R. A. SALVATORE

"She's a bit . . . warm, from the experience, we're hearing," Donnola said. "You think it worth it?"

Yvonnel considered that as they neared Catti-brie's door. "I do," she decided. "We had to know and we learned a lot. More than Catti-brie and the baby are at risk here. If Maegera finds its way free, there won't be much left of Gauntlgrym or anyone in here."

"And you think that Catti going down into that pit might help prevent that?" Penelope asked.

Yvonnel paused a moment, then nodded. "She gained insight. She has an idea, so she claims. That's why I'm here." She looked from one woman to the other. "And you?"

"Just checking on her," Donnola answered, moving up to the door.

"But we heard that she might have some trick formulating," Penelope conceded, and she and Yvonnel joined Donnola, who had paused.

Before Yvonnel could ask about that, she understood, for here, close, they could hear the sobs coming from inside the room.

"Every night," Penelope quietly explained. "Perhaps we should go." And she turned away.

"No," Donnola surprised her by saying. "She's trying to be strong for everyone and so taking it all on herself." The halfling shook her head resolutely. "I'm not for letting that happen."

Donnola pushed through the door, and after a quick exchange of glances, Penelope and Yvonnel followed her in.

Catti-brie was crying, indeed, but as soon as she noted the intruders, she sucked in her breath. Donnola went for her with arms wide, but Catti-brie held up her hand and managed to say, "Don't."

"But my friend . . ."

Catti-brie shook her head, her jaw clenched as she held back further sobs.

"Aye, if I touch you, then you'll melt, I know," Donnola said. "But I can't stand seeing you . . ."

She stopped when Penelope rushed past her, moving aside Catti-brie's upraised hand and wrapped the woman in a great hug. Immediately, as Donnola had just predicted, Catti-brie melted into great sobs, her shoulders shuddering, tears pouring down her face.

Donnola joined in the hug, and even Yvonnel, so unsure of her place here, moved closer and put a comforting hand on Catti-brie's shoulder.

"You'll be strong," Penelope whispered to the woman. "You are strong. But get it out now. You've been dealt a bad hand, my love. Nothing fair about it."

Rarely in her young life had Yvonnel felt so uncomfortable or so out of place. She wanted to be a part of this—she felt all the sympathy Donnola and Penelope were showing to the woman, and indeed, felt in her very pores the pain exuding from Catti-brie. The woman had lost her beloved, and indeed, part of the reason Yvonnel had come to care so much for this human woman was because she, too, had felt the love between her and Drizzt.

Early on, Yvonnel had found Drizzt quite attractive and interesting, and had even fancied that she might become his partner at some point, but once she had seen Drizzt with Catti-brie, she knew that her desires would certainly have to wait. There was something so tangible between them, so intermeshed and beautiful, that in a very atypical stance for a drow, Yvonnel hadn't even tried to interrupt that and instead celebrated it.

The emotion between them was so foreign to her! But not entirely, she knew, though she had to look far, far back in the memories of her namesake to better understand it.

So, too, with this encounter. The shared hug.

What drow would do that?

None, Yvonnel knew. Nor would any cry over a lost lover, replacing tears with sneers and growls of revenge.

And that, Yvonnel understood in that very moment, was the weakness.

Not of these people, nay, but of the drow.

Catti-brie soon settled, Donnola and then Penelope pulling back from her. Yvonnel removed her hand from the woman's shoulder but

Catti-brie caught it with her own. As she held Yvonnel's gaze, Catti-brie offered a little nod of gratitude.

Now composed, Catti-brie took a deep and steadying breath.

"We're here for whatever you're needing," Penelope said to her.

"I'm just being silly," Catti-brie said, and it sounded ridiculous to them all, even to Catti-brie. "How is Regis?" she quickly asked Donnola.

"Madder than I ever knew he could be," she replied. "He says he knows, though, after his own journey to the afterlife, and that's keeping him."

Catti-brie nodded and managed a smile, but she didn't seem as convinced, Yvonnel thought.

"I'm just crying for my own loss, not for Drizzt," Catti-brie said. "If . . ." She paused. "There's divine justice, I know, and none are more deserving of heaven than my love."

The conversation went on from there, and despite the urgency of their mission regarding Maegera, whatever it might be that Catti-brie had thought of, Yvonnel didn't interrupt. She just listened to the banter, sharing memories of Drizzt, sharing hopes for the child, Donnola and Penelope promising they'd be there every step of the way to help her with the babe.

Yes, Yvonnel waited and listened, and patience wasn't at play here. She didn't want it to end. This simple moment of shared pain and shared love and shared hope so suddenly seemed more important to her.

This, she understood finally and fully, was what they were fighting for. It was what Drizzt had sacrificed himself to preserve.

It was worth it, the drow decided.

"YE CAN'T BE THINKING THIS WILL WORK," BRUENOR SAID, hands on hips, as Yvonnel and Catti-brie went over their final plans, revealing the desperate ploy. The dwarf king shook his head. Preparations had been going on for days, but Bruenor still couldn't seem to believe in the plan.

"But we do," Yvonnel told him. "The drow are formidable even without the press here. We can't simply hunker and hold ground."

"Hold ground?" Bruenor asked. "We been givin' ground, as ye asked."

"We'll push them back," Catti-brie assured him.

"Aye, we," Athrogate interjected and held up his fist. The dwarf, full of anger, raving vengeance for his dear lost Ambergris, had never stopped arguing against the plan. "We! Dwarves and halflings," he looked to Regis and Donnola. "And even some stinkin' drow elfs. What's makin' ye think we're needin' . . ."

"If you stay quiet, you can hear the baying of doglike demons," Yvonnel stopped him. "They are near. Too near. Even aside from this fighting, all of Menzoberranzan has risen now, and if those drow forces become one fist, they will be near enough to us for the matrons to strike with their magic."

Athrogate's shoulders slumped.

"We're going to push them back, all the way back," Catti-brie told him, told them. "But we need to do this first for it to work."

"I want the entry cavern," Bruenor said with the same conviction as his daughter. "Let's see 'em fight through it when we know they're coming."

"Then we are agreed?"

Bruenor looked to Donnola and Regis, then to his queens, Fist and Fury. All nodded their agreement.

"You've no choice, anyway," Catti-brie said, drawing a scowl from her father. "You've felt the rumbling, eh? The ground's been shaking beneath your feet because the beast is getting restless and the magic is fast fading, the water elementals diminishing and longing for their home. We've got to do this or we'll all be riding a volcano soon enough."

"This'll stop it?" Bruenor asked.

Catti-brie looked to Yvonnel, and the two of them could only shrug.

"It's the best idea we've got," Catti-brie said. "Both against our enemies and to take the urgency from the primordial."

"Then it'll have to work," Bruenor declared, as if being king meant he could proclaim such a thing and make it so. He stepped back from the huddle and began barking orders to his under-commanders, including his battle-seasoned queens. Word spread fast for final preparations in the assigned tunnels, and for locking down those which would not be used. Blacksmiths took their positions in the forge room, putting on their heavy gloves to man the great valves controlling the forges, particularly the Great Forge itself. Other smiths and engineers collected the many bellow from the forges that would not be needed, gathering them and speeding away to their determined destinations.

A third group, warriors all, including the Gutbusters, scrambled into the kitchens to collect even more baskets of wood chips, then went out to meet the dwarves carrying the bellows.

"Bellows? Ye're sure?" Bruenor asked Catti-brie as the teams went about their work, moving with such precision and discipline that it bolstered the hopes of all defenders. The strength of Gauntlgrym, of Clan Battlehammer, of Delzoun dwarves in general, lay in their dedication to the common good. They each accepted their role and stayed within it, trusting in the dwarves on either side to do the same, to do their job.

"We're sure," Yvonnel answered. She tapped her finger on the determined spots on the map of Gauntlgrym spread before them. "Put a dozen dwarves in a circular pool of water and have them walk the perimeter in the same direction. Then try to reverse your step and you'll find the current overwhelming. Close these doors, open these, as we planned. Channel our enemies against the hot winds, channel our unexpected allies with the winds at their back and the fuel running before them."

"Whoosh," Catti-brie added with an evil little smile, one Bruenor knew all too well.

"Ye thinked this all up, did ye?" Bruenor asked Yvonnel.

The drow pointed to Catti-brie. "She did, all of it."

"Whoosh," Catti-brie said.

"Aye, whoosh," the dwarf king echoed, shaking his hairy head.

A short while later, after word came back from the readied positions,

Catti-brie moved before the Great Forge. She felt the ring on her finger, connecting her to the plane of fire. She felt the rush of heat—welcoming heat, this time—as the furnace door was cranked open.

Catti-brie stared into the hot white-orange flames within, a tendril of Maegera, like one of the primordial's fiery fingers poking at her. She tore her gaze away and nodded to the dwarves working the main valves behind the furnace, then fell through the power of the ring as they opened them wider.

The woman called to the primordial, bidding it to come forth.

Catti-brie heard clearly the song of the fire, the voice of living, sentient beings forming within that heat.

A gout of flame shot from the furnace, roaring out and roiling in the air.

On a nod from Catti-brie, then a motion from Yvonnel, the dwarf working the oven shut the door, cutting off the source of fiery energy. The roiling ball of flame already out of the furnace did not wink away, though, but continued to burn, falling to the floor before the forge, taking shape, becoming bipedal, a living being, like a giant, flame-shrouded bear. It was a piece of Maegera, or it had been, for now it was its own entity, as if cutting this tendril from the energy of the primordial had given birth, and now the progeny stood independently.

Catti-brie heard the new elemental's name—she couldn't pronounce it, but she could think it, and that was all she needed to coax control of the fiery beast. She waited for the signal from the opened doorway, then sent the monster along its journey of devastation.

The furnace door opened and Maegera stabbed forth its fiery power once more, and another tendril was cut off, another elemental birthed. This time, Yvonnel used her magic to compel this one into obedience, to show it the enemies awaiting it and send it sweeping along.

And so it went, back and forth between the two women. Fire elementals, fiery salamanders, living balls of flame, small but roiling white-hot with their tremendous proportion of energy. All of these creatures of fire, bits of Maegera, rushed along the prescribed path, the only tunnels open to them, hungry, even for living fuel.

She found her breathing hard to come by, but she knew she couldn't falter here. With her connection to the creatures of the plane of fire, Catti-brie was sending them along with ease, one after the other, giving them that which they wanted: things to consume, to burn, to spread their fiery wings.

When the oven door slammed closed for the last time—Yvonnel having reached her limit and Catti-brie agreeing with an upraised hand as she, too, grew weary—the woman fell into different spells alongside the drow and dwarven priestesses and a trio of halfling wizards. Yvonnel led the ritual of her next spell, creating a great wind, combining their magical energies to focus the continuing gust, wind at the backs of the creatures of fire, adding to their strength, speeding their intended catastrophe.

Howling winds whistled down the corridors, urging and feeding and pushing the living flames along.

"RECKLESS DOES NOT BEGIN TO DESCRIBE YOUR CHARGE," Jarlaxle scolded Zaknafein, who sat on a stone table, his wounds being treated by a pair of dwarven clerics.

"Five major fiends sent home to the Abyss," Zaknafein replied. "You think that not worth the risk?"

"I think our friends—your daughter-by-law in particular—have suffered one great loss. I don't want to pile another atop it."

"Do you think they'd see me as such?" Zak replied. "They . . . she hardly knows me, and I'm not so sure she likes what she knows."

"Probably not," Jarlaxle deadpanned. "But let's not risk it."

"Never a risk," the weapon master answered. "Just some big birds and a six-legged dog."

Jarlaxle managed a chuckle at that.

The door banged open then and a young dwarf poked her head in. "It's coming," she said. "Like a wave."

Jarlaxle nodded, having felt the warmth as soon as the door was opened.

"Bear witness?" he asked Zak.

"Witness? I mean to chase the fire beasts down the hall. They won't kill everything," Zak replied. He brushed back the attending dwarves and hopped from the table, pulling on the mithral shirt Cattibrie had given to him, then gathering his sword belt and strapping it on. "At least, I hope they won't. And this blade is hungrier than I!" he finished, drawing Icingdeath from its sheath.

Down a short corridor, through a pair of rooms, then down another longer passageway, the pair came to an angled door as the corridor ended, the wall reaching farther on the right-hand side. This selected section of Gauntlgrym had many angled intersections, the side corridors meeting the main hallway like the low-hanging limbs of an evergreen. There the pair paused, for they could feel the intense heat on the other side, could see the flickering brightness of the living flames.

The door, heavy petrified wood, iron-banded, was smoking.

"Pull it open and move fast behind me," Jarlaxle instructed, pulling the giant feather from the band on his hat.

"Planning to cook some bird?" a surprised Zak asked. "The firestorm hasn't swept past."

"You don't think this feather has only one use, do you?" the rogue replied. "Trust me," Jarlaxle added, when Zak stood staring.

"The last words heard by so many of your old friends," said Zak.

"The door, please," Jarlaxle returned.

Zak stared a bit longer, then wrapped his hand with the edge of his heavy *piwafwi* and gingerly reached for the bolts holding the portal shut. He threw them open, then grabbed the pull ring and tugged the door open.

Or tried to, for the rushing wind on the other side was so strong, the living flames eating all the air, that the portal was truly stuck.

"Bah, but what're ye about, then, ye bald-headed maker of chaos?" came a voice from behind, and the two turned to see Athrogate rushing up, accompanied by some other dwarves.

"Get that door opened," Jarlaxle told him.

"Not a good idea," said the black-haired dwarf.

"Trust me," Jarlaxle said, and Athrogate snorted loudly.

"Quite the reputation you've crafted," said Zak.

"The bellows, the fires, th'embers be flyin'," Athrogate crooned. "Open the door and ye're sure to be fryin'!"

"Just . . ." Jarlaxle sighed and put his face in his hand.

Athrogate roared at his successful rhyme, then rushed past the mercenary. "Get ye back," he told Zak, and he grabbed the door ring with a heavily gloved hand.

"So you trust him, then?" Zak asked the dwarf.

"He lights like a candle and it's 'is own doin'," the dwarf answered.

Zaknafein ran back to join the other dwarves, noting that one was dragging a large basket full of wood chips.

Athrogate looked to Jarlaxle and nodded, then tugged on the ring. The door didn't budge.

The dwarf turned to it, puzzled.

"The air on the other side," Jarlaxle started to explain, but then just shook his head and called the dwarf back. Catti-brie and Yvonnel must have cooked up a tremendous storm, he thought, if Athrogate, with his girdle of giant strength, couldn't open the door!

Athrogate took up the door in both hands and tugged mightily, but it wouldn't move. He let go and kicked the heavy portal, grumbling, "Come on, then. I know another way."

He rushed back past Jarlaxle, who was removing his hat and shaking his head. When Athrogate was safely behind him, Jarlaxle pulled his portable hole out from the hat and sent it spinning and widening at the portal. It hit flat against the door, immediately creating a wide hole in it, revealing the maelstrom beyond.

Orange flame light brightened the tunnel. Beyond the door, the windstorm, the firestorm, raged, rushing left to right before the startled onlookers. They noted individual elementals, salamanders of flame, and sweeping waves of burning embers.

Jarlaxle shook himself from his awe, whispered to his feather implement, and began waving it before him.

"He think he's goin' to fly?" Athrogate asked Zak.

"A wind fan?" Zak asked, more to himself or to Jarlaxle than to the dwarf. "That's new."

"That one's always got a trick," Athrogate said, yelled—because now Jarlaxle, too, was creating a loud wind of his own, billowing out from him and distorting the flames weirdly as it joined the conflagration in the tunnel beyond.

Athrogate and his dwarf companions hoisted the large basket and rushed up beside the drow, heaving their payload into Jarlaxle's windstorm. The embers flew forth, blown into the corridor, into the flames, where they ignited immediately and were swept away.

"Not new," Jarlaxle replied to Zak's observation. "Only new to you."

Zak could only shake his head, no longer surprised by anything regarding Jarlaxle.

AT THE BASE OF THE LONG HALLWAY, A FEW STEPS BACK OF the side corridor through which the creatures of the plane of fire were entering, teams of dwarves worked bellows of various sizes, spewing their gusts into the main tunnel to join with Catti-brie and Yvonnel's maelstrom, fanning the flames as the fire monsters charged into the main hallway, boosting them on their way with powerful tailwinds.

Far away along the same passage, the demons were coming, large and small, but mostly small, the fodder of this attack force, leading the major fiends in a charge that had already brought them much farther into the complex than they had known before.

The leading fiends, manes, mostly, felt the rising heat, but it meant nothing to the barely thinking shock troops. Their lead groups rambled around a long bend right as the living permutations of the vomit of the Great Forge swept forward from the other direction.

More like a flood of water rolling through a forest than stones striking a solid barrier, the fire elementals washed right past the manes, sweeping all about them, igniting them, turning them into animated torches. In the passing wave of fire, those lesser fiends melted and fell, desiccated skin curling and burning. Shrieks of protest filled the corridor, diminishing as the manes fast fell to the hot stone floor into piles of charred bone and ash, blowing about as smoke in the wind of the firestorm.

The elementals fed and grew and raged and charged on.

IT KNEW.

Maegera understood the deception of Catti-brie. She heard it in her mind, for as she had reached into the primordial's being to coax it forth, the brilliant godlike creature had quietly reached back.

Now as the spellcasters about her continued their wind ritual, Catti-brie faltered, stumbling in the cacophony of thoughts and protests from the beast. She understood the true power of Maegera then, brilliant and horrifying. And the anger. If her time in the pit had shown her the physical strength of the primordial, this new event revealed to her something even more terrifying. This was no circus bear performing.

No, Catti-brie realized then that *she* was the performing animal against the likes of Maegera.

Compulsions came swirling about her—to open the oven fully, to close the levers in the adjoining chasm room and dismiss the water elementals, to side with Maegera, only Maegera, and share in the beauty of fiery destruction and thus, fiery creation. In only a brief moment, Catti-brie saw the multiverse through the eyes and desires of Maegera and that mere instant wobbled her knees and sent her determined spellcasting to gibberish.

She was just a human, after all, a mortal being who could not begin to comprehend the truth of Maegera.

In her failure, she revealed her limitations, and those limitations brought new sensations from the primordial.

It was disappointed in her.

It had no use for her.

It was angry at her for teasing forth its tendrils for her own use.

Now Maegera promised retribution.

Catti-brie had taken a piece from it, and so it would take a piece from her.

Catti-brie had stolen Maegera's children, the birthed elementals, and so Maegera . . .

She grew hot and began to shiver. She knew that her face was turning red . . . the heat within.

The woman felt a sting in her mind, in her heart, in her womb.

She heard a splatter below, and looked down, her head spinning, to see blood between her feet.

Curiously, she never lost focus on that blood as she went down hard onto the stone floor, all strength flying from her, all hope flying with it.

THE WHIRLING FIRE SWEPT ALONG THE CORRIDORS, MELT-ing the lesser fiends, wounding the greater demons, and behind the maelstrom came a second, this one of muscle and mithral, of mortal flesh and singing voices.

With the wind at their backs and King Bruenor in the lead, the sweating dwarves charged down tunnels still glowing with residual heat. Soles melting on their heavy boots, the dwarves nevertheless kept up their run. They fought for their home, for their kin, for their king.

Few demons remained alive in the wake of the firestorm, and under heavy boots, the dwarves stamped into smoke those fiends still clinging to their tethers to the material plane.

But as they moved farther along, the corridors grew cooler. The numbers of charred demons diminished, with more living fiends remaining to take up the fight.

Bruenor, or more accurately, Bruenor's many-notched axe, led the way willingly, cracking the skull of a glabrezu, shearing the bill from a vrock.

When they came to intersections or forks, the dwarven force tidily separated, predetermined strike teams running their routes in corridors Clan Battlehammer called home.

They were fighting, every step, but they were climbing higher in the complex, blasting through demons half killed by the living primordial vomit.

"Grabbers!" Bruenor yelled when his lead team came to the middle of a large, high-ceilinged room whose ladders were all up or missing altogether. Teams of dwarves with grappling hooks let fly, catching their barbs on the circular stairwell some twenty feet up.

Bruenor was the first to a rope, tugging himself skyward powerfully, hand over hand. When he got to the ladder and stair platform high above, he was surprised—even as he was not—to see Jarlaxle and Zaknafein already looking down at him from on high, urging him and his fellows on.

More dead demons, several major fiends among them, greeted Bruenor when he arrived in the corridor of the next level. The walls and floor here were cool. If the fire elementals had made it this far, they had little left to offer, for the skin of the fallen fiends was not burned.

Slashed and stabbed, but not burned.

"How long ye been up here?" the dwarf king asked Jarlaxle.

"Fine plan," the drow answered. "The living flame stole the fodder from our enemy."

"Ye didn't answer my question."

"Not long," Jarlaxle replied.

"That one fights like his son," Athrogate explained, coming out of a room, a large and misshapen husk of a melting demon on the floor of the side chamber behind him.

Bruenor looked across the wide room and down the hallway beyond, all of it strewn with dead demons, the air filling with smoke as their corpses melted away to nothingness, Jarlaxle's huge diatryma bird walking among the dissipating corpses, pecking at them.

On the far end, he spotted the black form of Guenhwyvar, crouched and looking farther along, her back hunched, rear legs tamping.

The dwarf shook his head and harrumphed.

"To the throne room?" Jarlaxle asked.

"Can't think of a better place for me to be," Bruenor answered. On they charged, now led by Guen. Overrunning pockets of demons. Soon enough, they were met by more and more dwarf strike teams coming out of the side corridors, almost all showing signs of recent battle.

For all of their success, it had not been easy. Clan Battlehammer had more than a few fallen heroes that day, and a lot more than a few wounded, but now the goal was in sight and the dwarven army rolled on eagerly, accepting the losses knowing they were for the greater good.

There were fewer side chambers up here, fewer alternate corridor routes, and the progress increased into a focused, roaring, shield-thumping charge.

The dwarves banged their swords, their axes, their maces, their hammers, and stomped their boots, many with soles misshapen from the heat of the lower corridors.

They sang, they banged, they cheered, they fought, they died.

But on they rolled.

Into the throne room, they rolled, right into the arms of a demon horde.

But they did not waver and they did not falter.

And as dawn broke on the surface, now not so far above, King Bruenor Battlehammer once more sat on the Throne of the Dwarven Gods.

"Give me yer strength, Clanggedin Silverbeard," he called to the god of war.

"Give me your whispers of hidden truths," he implored Dumathoin, the Keeper of Secrets Under the Mountain.

"Give me your heart and let me boys know ye're with me," he prayed to Moradin, the All-Father.

The great entry hall loomed right outside.

The drow and demons and abominable driders held it.

Bruenor wanted it back.

He felt the answer of his gods, all three, in the form of strength flowing into his limbs, and the dwarf king who leaped from the Throne of the Dwarven Gods was much larger than the one who had sat upon it.

"Forward!" Bruenor yelled in a voice blessed by his gods.

The others knew it, and how they cheered, and how they charged, swarming out into the entry cavern of Gauntlgrym, taking the beach on the near side of the pond, taking the bridge in short order, driving the demons back, back.

Back.

HE HAD TO TELL BRUENOR OF THE HAPPENINGS OUTSIDE of Gauntlgrym. Thibbledorf Pwent focused on that thought, that duty, as he floated back among the corridors held by dwarves, a gaseous cloud hiding in cracks and staying flat against the ceiling, seeming no more than some residual smoke of the burning furnaces or of the perpetual steam from the primordial chasm.

Many times did the dwarf pause on his journey, or retreat or throw himself through a crack into another side chamber, for nearly every dwarf he saw, and surely those he recognized, called to him, to his loneliness, to his hunger. It would be so easy for him to create companions.

He had to tell Bruenor of the happenings outside of Gauntlgrym, of the gathering drow!

In the forge room at last, Pwent was glad to see Catti-brie, thinking he was must therefore be close to Bruenor. He looked around, noting the dwarven priests and priestesses, noting the drow woman, Yvonnel.

One priestess in particular caught his eye, a striking woman named Copetta.

Copperhead, the vampire thought, for that was the nickname Pwent had given her years before because of her long and thick golden-red hair, and also because she could strike as swiftly as a snake whenever the battlerager got out of line with her. The other dwarves called her Penny, a common old Delzoun name for the copper bit coins. To Pwent, though, she would always be Copperhead. Long had Pwent fancied this lass. Seeing her now was almost more than he could take . . . nay, perhaps it was more than he could take, and the vampire began plotting. If she walked out of the room, or even out of sight of the main gathering, he would transform and sink his fangs into her neck.

He would take her hand and fly away.

She would be like him.

They would be together forevermore.

Copperhead.

Pwent could feel her soft touch, could hear again her sharp wit, could smell the blood—yes, most of all he could smell the blood. Her blood, he believed, waiting for his kiss.

He felt himself descending from the ceiling, out of the smoke of the forges. The smell of blood grew thicker, calling to him, telling him that it was time for him to surrender at long last, to accept his fate, to take a companion.

Or many companions.

The blood . . . so sweet . . .

Then he saw. No, it was not Copperhead's blood at all. It was Catti-brie's, between her feet, running down the insides of her legs!

Catti-brie fell to the floor. Blood soaked into her gown about her crotch.

The drow ran to her. The dwarves ran to her.

Yvonnel began yelling orders, but Pwent couldn't hear. Not then. Not watching his dear princess of Mithral Hall falling.

Not smelling the blood.

The blood.

They carried Catti-brie away.

Pwent hovered there above the red puddle, not knowing what to do, not knowing right from wrong. Perhaps he should go to Catti-brie and take her into undeath, to save her. Yes, to save her!

But no, that could not be right, the confused dwarf insisted. Did he even know right from wrong anymore? Did he know where Pwent ended and the vampire began? Where duty and honor ended and desire demanded?

The notion that he had even truly considered inflicting his curse upon dear Catti-brie shamed the dwarf. He flew from the forge room, down the small side corridor and into the great steamy chamber that held the primordial chasm. Once before, he had thrown himself into that chasm along with the giant spider construct, thinking to save his beloved King Bruenor and end his torment all at once. But he had flown back out, and now again, he failed.

The vampire curse would not let him destroy himself.

Every passing day made it stronger.

He had thought to bite Catti-brie! The daughter of King Bruenor!

He flew from the chamber, through the forge room and along the halls. He knew where they were going, knew Catti-brie's chambers, and there he found the woman in her bed, surrounded by clerics, Copperhead among them, the drow Yvonnel among them.

He watched as they worked frantically, many casting spells upon the woman, who seemed so near to death. Yvonnel, too, cast, but it wasn't a spell of healing, more of divination, and the vampire Pwent could sense the strength of her magic and he recoiled, fearing that she was magically searching for him.

But no, she rushed to Catti-brie and took up the woman's hand and began tugging insistently, violently even. She fell back a step, holding up a ring, Catti-brie's ring, which she slipped upon her own finger.

Yvonnel closed her eyes and began chanting insistently in a language the vampire dwarf did not know, and one, judging from the looks of those around, foreign to the dwarven clerics, as well.

When she finished, she moved through them back to Catti-brie and began spellcasting once more, waggling her fingers above the woman's face, creating water that fell and splashed upon her, then leaning low and blowing a frosty breath behind the magical rain, as if she was trying to physically cool Catti-brie.

Pwent didn't understand, nor did those other dwarves about, clearly, but soon enough, the princess of Mithral Hall seemed to be resting more comfortably, and the dwarves sighed and nodded one after the other.

Pwent simply hovered, fighting his compulsions, trying not to smell the blood, trying to not look at Copperhead, beautiful Copperhead.

She could be like he was.

Eternal.

The vampire slipped out of the room.

He had to tell Bruenor of the happenings outside of Gauntlgrym.

But where was Bruenor?

Pwent didn't fly away. He couldn't fly away.

Catti-brie . . . Copperhead . . . sweet, sweet blood.

THE MALEVOLENCE SHE FELT THROUGH THE RING SUR-prised Yvonnel, not because of the strength of it, but because of the manner. It wasn't anger, but simply annoyance, a person slapping a bug that had stung it and nothing more. There was no sense of remorse, not a whit of conscience or regret.

Maegera had slapped Catti-brie back for her trick. The beast had somehow put some of its very essence into the woman and created with that a fever of dramatic proportions. A fever strong enough to harm her child, perhaps, or to permanently damage Catti-brie. To kill them both, likely.

Maegera was feeding it through the ring, and now, too, Yvonnel could feel herself growing warm.

Yvonnel didn't remove the ring, however, for she, unlike Catti-brie, was forewarned. She battled back and cooled the primordial warmth.

"Will she live?" one of the dwarves asked Yvonnel.

"Aye, and what of the baby, then?" asked another, a dwarf woman with striking reddish-brown hair.

"Keep working over her" was all that Yvonnel could offer, for she really didn't know.

"I think the muffin's still kickin'!" said the priestess Copetta. Yvonnel offered a hopeful grin at that, and put her hand beside Copetta's on the woman's belly. Indeed, she felt a kick, and could only hope it was not one of distress.

"I need to study more powerful spells of healing," Yvonnel told the dwarf. "I wasn't expecting anything like this today."

"Aye, just a bunch o' livin' flame balls to send rushing through the tunnels, eh?"

"Eh," Yvonnel answered.

"We'll be givin' her plenty of the healing," Copetta told her. "Good thinking on the water and cold. Seems her fever's a lot down."

"Down, but not gone," Yvonnel added, moving her hand up to Catti-brie's sweaty and clammy forehead.

"We might be needin' to take the babe," Copetta said.

Yvonnel only had experience with such things through the memories of Matron Mother Yvonnel the Eternal, but she took some solace in the apparent confidence and competence of these very capable dwarves. She looked about the room for a place to take some rest, to regenerate her magical energy and to prepare some powerful spells.

She had thought to go off in pursuit of the fight she and Catti-brie had started, to aid in driving the demons as far back as possible, but that wouldn't take her from this woman right now.

She moved into the anteroom and was surprised to find Artemis Entreri and Dahlia coming into the room through the opposite door.

"The blood," Entreri said, rushing up to the drow. "They say it was Catti-brie's."

Yvonnel nodded. "She is resting." She stepped back and took a long look at the human and his half-elven companion. Bother were battered, covered in demon gore and blood, likely their own. "You seem as if resting would do you some good, as well," Yvonnel said.

"We just left the upper corridors for exactly that," Dahlia answered. "The demons are in retreat, the dwarves pressing for the throne room, perhaps already there."

"We were fighting through the day, before the firestorm," Entreri explained. "Our enemies are infinite."

"We nearly walked into that firestorm," Dahlia added. "We were returning through other tunnels and were not forewarned."

"The heat was enough of a warning," Entreri quickly added. "Pray give me some healing," he added. "And some magic to bolster my weary arms, I beg. I want to be with them when the fiends are driven from Gauntlgrym."

"With *them?*" Yvonnel asked.

"With Jarlaxle and Zaknafein," Entreri answered. "With Bruenor and Regis. With Catti-brie, too, so I thought."

"With your friends," Yvonnel said.

Entreri looked at her curiously.

"Are you afraid to admit the truth of the word?" Yvonnel teased. "Or do you not understand the meaning?"

That brought a laugh from Entreri, but a scowl from his companion.

"It is a good word, Artemis Entreri," Yvonnel said. "The more familiar you become with it, the greater the chances for you to escape the fate you were shown. More than that, familiarity with the word will enhance your life—something you deserve more than you're ready to admit." His face looked pained at that, but also held a sense of wonder, as if the thought had never dawned on him. Smiling gently, Yvonnel said, "If you will excuse me now, I must rest and prepare more spells to help Catti-brie. She is in distress. The primordial struck at her and brought a fever."

"How bad?" Entreri asked with obvious concern.

"She is comfortable now. We don't know the damage, but the priests are working tirelessly, as will I."

Entreri nodded. Yvonnel returned it, then moved for a cot in the far corner of the room, but paused, noting a strange steam-like cloud up in the corner rim of the ceiling, sliding through a crack from this anteroom into Catti-brie's bedchamber. Most might have mistaken it for simple smoke or mist—certainly there was much of that floating about these reaches of Gauntlgrym, particularly after the efforts in the forge room.

A quick minor dweomer, though, confirmed Yvonnel's suspicions. She rushed past the two in the room with her and charged back through the door, Entreri and Dahlia close behind.

"What is it? Catti-brie?" Entreri asked, nearly running over Yvonnel just inside the room.

"Take form, vampire Pwent," Yvonnel called up to the cloud.

It shifted, then began to drift back toward the crack in the ceiling from which it had emerged.

Yvonnel threw a spell at it, one to steal the magic of the shape-shifting, and sure enough, the cloud coalesced and Thibbledorf Pwent materialized in midair. He dropped like a stone halfway to the floor, before magically catching himself and slowing, turning weirdly in the air so that he touched down lightly upon the floor facing the drow woman.

The others in the room all gasped, some calling to their old friend, one in particular even coming forward a step, until another warned her back with "Penny, no!"

"Ye're not wantin' me here, lady," Pwent warned, grinding his teeth with every word and displaying his long fangs prominently. "Not now, I tell ye."

"You came here uninvited," Yvonnel reminded.

"Got to see me king," Pwent said to Yvonnel, but his eyes were not on the drow, she noted. No, he was staring across the room to the dwarf lass name Copetta.

"Got to tell him," Pwent went on, his voice fading in and out around several low growls, part feral, part pure desire.

"Thibbledorf Pwent!" Yvonnel said, trying to make him focus.

And he did focus, but not on her, launching himself across the room in a great spring, half leap and half flight, descending over poor Copetta and bearing her to the ground beneath him.

The other dwarves presented their holy symbols, denying the vampire, trying to drive him off with their divine energy. But most prominent among those presentations was the simple force of Yvonnel. As much to her own surprise as to any other who might notice, Yvonnel did not lift the spider-shaped symbol of Lolth, but simply stabbed her pointed finger at the cursed, undead thing.

Pwent looked over his shoulder at her, hissed, and showed his fangs, then spun back and opened wide his mouth, descending upon the neck of his helpless victim.

No, not his victim! His lover!

He noted Entreri drawing his red-bladed sword and that jeweled dagger, charging at him. Up he leaped to face the threat, but before Entreri got near, the drow priestess struck.

"I deny you!" Yvonnel said. "You were not invited here!"

If she had launched Pwent from a side-slinger catapult, he would not have flown more forcefully. He was thrown from his intended victim, smashing hard against the side wall of the room, halfway up.

And there he held as if stuck, as if Yvonnel's pointing finger was some kind of energy ray pressing him in place.

Yvonnel recognized the magic she was enacting here, for it was the same as that of the dwarves. She was using the power of divinity to turn the undead creature.

Yet she wasn't.

Because she wasn't invoking the name or symbol of the Lady Lolth. She almost questioned that, given the effect on the vampire, paralyzed and being seared by holy energy against that wall.

"Yield!" she demanded.

Pwent growled at her.

"Yield!" Yvonnel answered a continuing growl by reminding him, "You had news for your king. Your king, Thibbledorf Pwent!"

The dwarf's snarl melted. He turned his head and let Yvonnel's divine power press it against the stone. "Aye," he gasped, gaining some measure of control.

Yvonnel let him go and he dropped hard to the floor, bouncing right back into a crouch and growling at her with unmasked hatred. But it was mixed with profound embarrassment, everyone in the room understood.

"Thibbledorf Pwent," she said to him, "remember where you are. Remember *who* you are!"

The dwarf's expression softened even more.

"You need to see King Bruenor," Yvonnel reminded.

Pwent growled and gasped. "Me . . . king," he managed to fight out through his wild desires and anger.

"Why?" Yvonnel demanded. "Why do you need to see him? You must tell me."

"Me . . . king."

"The dark elves?" Yvonnel asked. "Is it about the dark elves?"

Even Yvonnel was surprised of the effect of her guess, as if the reminder hit the mark perfectly on Pwent. He went from his crouch to a sitting position against the wall, lowered his arms and his gaze.

"They're outside, all o' them," a thoroughly defeated Pwent said. "They're meanin' to join together."

Yvonnel took a deep breath. This was her worst fear coming true. The battered dwarves would have no chance against the combined might of Menzoberranzan, not after the energy and blood they had already expended in battling the demons.

Yvonnel had no idea of why the news surprised her, though. Of course Quenthel and the others had come to join in the glory Matron Zhindia Melarn was beginning to realize. What else could it have been?

"Show me," she told the vampire. "You will take me out there and show me."

"Is that what ye're thinkin' then?" Pwent asked skeptically.

"For your king Bruenor, Thibbledorf Pwent," Yvonnel replied flatly. "I might be able to stop this, and if I cannot, then woe to Gauntlgrym and woe to King Bruenor." She glanced at the bed. "And woe to Catti-brie and the child of Drizzt Do'Urden," she added. "For the power of Gauntlgrym alone will not win the day here. You know it. You've seen them. How many drow soldiers? How many slave fodder?"

Pwent growled at that.

"Show me!" Yvonnel demanded.

Copetta moved up beside the drow, stealing the bluster from the vampire.

"Thibbledorf Pwent," she said. "My old Thibble, it's me, Penny."

Copperhead, Pwent mouthed, and the dwarf lass smiled.

"Aye, yer own Copperhead," she answered sweetly. "Ye must do as the drow asks. For all yer kith 'n' kin."

The vampire's face softened even more as he stared at the woman. At long last, he turned his gaze to Yvonnel and offered a slight nod of agreement.

"I'm going with you," Artemis Entreri told Yvonnel.

"No," said Dahlia in surprise.

"I cannot guarantee your safety, or my own," Yvonnel told him.

"No one ever has," Entreri answered. "But I'm coming with you."

Yvonnel considered it a moment, then nodded.

The room began to shake then, so violently that more than one of the gathering stumbled and one of the dwarves even fell over.

"We've not much time," Yvonnel warned. "We have stolen the explosive pressure from Maegera, but it will build again and quickly. Maegera knows that it will soon escape."

Her words, meant to rouse the others, particularly Pwent, to action, sounded hollow to her. They were true enough, of course. She could feel it keenly through her ring. Catti-brie's ploy had bought them a bit of time, perhaps, but little more.

Maegera would escape.

And there was nothing Yvonnel Baenre could do to stop it.

CHAPTER 26

Between the Living and
Those Who Have Crossed

I t took Brother Afafrenfere a long while to even realize what he had done. He had melted from the physical world, become an entity of pure spirit—and had done so just ahead of the plunging blade.

Or had it been *after* the blade had driven through him? the monk wondered.

It didn't matter. If this was death, then so be it, and at the moment, he saw his life's journey. He sat in the small cottage with his mother and his father—who would turn on him years later when the truth of Afafrenfere became known to him. He remembered—no, "remember" was not the right word! He *lived* again his journey to the monastic life, his acceptance into the order.

He saw again the first time he had met Parbid. He walked again his travels to the shadow realm.

So many memories. Separating. Scattering. Becoming a living part of the multiverse around him, unbound and shared.

It was beauty.

He understood now Grandmaster Kane's warning that he wasn't ready to transcend, that he hadn't the discipline or the desire to reverse the journey and return to finish his days.

That warning rang hollow now, though.

Of course, he didn't want to go back!

He existed in the moment, his senses widening, losing focus, becoming all and everything.

It was beauty, yes, but it was veiled beauty. The monk felt as if he was swimming in a thick cloud, his senses filtered to all that was around him. Or in a fugue state, a malleable reality, a malleable identity and sense of self even.

It was only when Afafrenfere encountered another untethered memory that he even remembered what had brought him to Thornhold in the first place, for he knew it to be the residual life force and identity composition of Drizzt Do'Urden.

He looked more closely, found focus in that sense of duty. How clearly he could see the drow's journey now, finding bits of scattered memories and piecing them together. Drizzt's entire journey, and not just this last one, which had brought him from the realm of the living.

The intimacy overwhelmed him, as intimate a joining as he had known with Parbid—and as joyous.

But this was different. Afafrenfere felt almost like a voyeur, peeking in on the deepest thoughts and secrets of another who did not know he was watching and listening.

His last sensibilities of decorum—and truly, they seemed petty now—made him reach out to Drizzt reciprocally, to let the drow know that he was there now, too.

And yes, he could see Drizzt so much more clearly now that he, too, was in that thin time-space between the living and those who had crossed over, between the physical and the spiritual.

Between life and death?

Afafrenfere wasn't sure those terms applied anymore.

He reached out to Drizzt. He called to the drow. He told Drizzt to return, to reform to the physical world.

You are needed.

Your wife.
Your child.

Drizzt couldn't hear him, or at least, offered no response, no sensation of being affected by Afafrenfere's calls at all. Deeper went the monk, trying to coax the drow back, but the deeper he went, the further he, Afafrenfere, fell from the physical world and any notions of his body. He was surely losing himself as much, if not more, than he was rescuing Drizzt.

So be it.

For the being who had been Brother Afafrenfere could not view his accelerating journey as a loss, not with this beauty and truth all about him.

He reached further for Drizzt.

But Drizzt Do'Urden, gone so long, could not hear.

THIS IS MADNESS, DAB'NAY'S FINGERS SIGNED TO BRAELIN Janquay.

The forest around them was alive with driders, packs of them roaming wildly, hacking at trees, throwing enormous spears at squirrels and birds—anything to vent their unending rage.

Braelin couldn't disagree. He motioned for the woman to follow and led her to a deep hollow beneath a spreading oak tree, a place they had huddled the previous night.

"We knew that Matron Zhindia had brought driders alone with her," Braelin reminded her when they were out of earshot.

"Not like that!" Dab'nay insisted. "You saw them. They were different—I don't even know how to explain it. Somehow bigger, more feral even than what we have seen of the abominations. That was . . . I don't know . . ."

"You may be right, but we still must find our way to Matron Mother Quenthel or Yvonnel," Braelin replied, but Dab'nay was shaking her head with almost every word.

"You cannot expect this of me," Dab'nay protested. "This is larger than my powers, larger than Kimmuriel's demand, larger than Bregan D'aerthe, even."

"We survive because we each do our part."

"My part puts me in the face of Matron Mother Quenthel Baenre, and with this chaos about us," Dab'nay argued. "It is not a path to survival. No." She shook her head resolutely. "I need to know more before I begin to go deeper into this forest, let alone deliver Kimmuriel's message to the Matron Mother. These driders unsettle me. Something huge is afoot and it seems likely to me that merely uttering that which Kimmuriel has claimed will mark me as an apostate. I do not wish to join this drider force."

"If it is Matron Zhindia's force, then it is at odds with Matron Mother Quenthel."

"Before, perhaps. We do not know that now."

Braelin blew out a sigh and lowered his gaze, trying to find an answer. "Then we look magically," he decided, glancing up at Dab'nay. He pointed to the back of the hollow, where some water had collected from a recent rain.

"You would ask me to magically look in on Matron Mother Baenre? On any Baenres?" an incredulous Dab'nay asked.

"No, we'll look over the forest and Bleeding Vines. We'll find Matron Zhindia. She's not known for divination, and is usually too consumed by her anger at everything around her to even note any magical eavesdropping."

Dab'nay didn't look convinced.

"It is this or we trek through the forest and try to avoid the driders as best as we can," said Braelin.

"No."

"You would not like Kimmuriel when he is angry," Braelin warned. As Dab'nay hesitated, he turned and motioned his hand out toward the pool.

She followed.

"YOU WILL TAKE ME TO MATRON ZHINDIA," THE PRIESTESS told the enormous drider.

"Will I?" Malfoosh answered slyly. The woman was out in the

forest with a handful of attendants, now fully surrounded by dozens of driders, weaving in and out of the shadows all about.

"I am Taayrul Armgo, first priestess of the Second House of Menzoberranzan," the woman replied.

"The second house?" asked Malfoosh. "Where is the Baenre, then?"

Taayrul chuckled. "The Baenres would not be pleased with the message I offer to Matron Zhindia. It is clear that Lolth shines upon her. We all know it, but Matron Mother Baenre isn't sure that she can bring herself to admit it yet. Matron Zhindia should learn all of this before she makes a rash move. Time is on her side, not Matron Mother Baenre's."

Malfoosh glanced about, nodding to her minions. "You may come," she told Taayrul. "You alone."

"That is not accep—"

"That is all you get," Malfoosh interrupted. "You alone."

A drider rushed up beside Taayrul and held out his hands to her.

"You will ride," Malfoosh instructed.

Taayrul looked around at her guards, then nodded. "Wait here," she instructed, and as she did, she looked to Malfoosh, who agreed that this would be the place for them to remain. The priestess took the drider's hand and was hauled up and swung around to take an uncomfortable seat behind her mount.

Malfoosh skittered up right beside her, and before Taayrul could stop it, plopped a heavy bag over Taayrul's head. Before the priestess could begin to protest, the driders set off at a tremendous pace, rushing through the forest, arriving at last in the ruins of Bleeding Vines, at the court of Matron Zhindia Melarn.

"IT GROWS EVER MORE CURIOUS," BRAELIN SAID, AS THEY watched the journey of the drow priestess riding the drider.

"That is Taayrul, first priestess of House Barrison Del'Armgo," Dab'nay told him.

"Sent to meet with Matron Zhindia? Matron Mother Quenthel would never agree to such a thing."

Dab'nay smirked at him for stating the obvious.

"Do it," he ordered her.

Dab'nay took a deep breath. She had thus far refused to cast clairaudience to go along with her clairvoyance dweomer, as the former was often more easily detected. Now, though, it seemed rather obvious that they needed to know exactly what was going on. As they watched Taayrul Armgo walking forward to speak with Zhindia, Dab'nay cast the spell.

She was not detected during that conversation, but that did little to assuage her—or her companion's, she noted with some satisfaction—nervousness.

As she had earlier insisted—and as it quickly became obvious as they listened in—the scene here was much bigger than her. Taayrul, the voice of powerful Matron Mez'Barris Armgo, was all but offering Matron Zhindia the second seat on the Ruling Council. The drow often spoke quietly about interhouse wars, but the idea here was well beyond that. The two women, a matron and a first priestess of another house, were openly discussing a civil war in Menzoberranzan, a war against House Baenre. And they were doing so brashly, apparently without concern.

"The way is clear now," Taayrul said. "The way is Lolth, of course, and Lolth has shown us the glory before us."

"Shown *us*?" Matron Zhindia replied, her skeptical, almost mocking tone, the first hints of a crack in the asked for alliance.

"We have all seen the gifts the Spider Queen has offered."

"Offered to whom?" Zhindia asked.

"Yes, Matron Zhindia, Matron Mez'Barris does not deny that you were the vessel for Lolth's desires."

"I am Lolth's *champion*," Zhindia corrected. "Is that not obvious?"

Her question sounded like a threat to Dab'nay and Braelin—and obviously to First Priestess Taayrul, who began shifting nervously from foot to foot.

"And you will be rewarded like her champion," Taayrul finally managed to reply.

"Well, it seems clear to me that Lolth's champion should sit at the first seat of her table, not the second," Zhindia declared.

"The logic is hard to argue," Taayrul quickly replied—and the speed and smoothness of her response told the onlookers that Mez'Barris had sent her daughter here with the expectation that Matron Zhindia would demand no less. "I will take your answer to Matron Mez'Barris."

"Matron Mez'Barris desires the first seat," said Zhindia, stalling Taayrul's leaving.

"Would she be a proper high priestess of Lady Lolth if she did not?" Taayrul answered.

"True enough," Zhindia admitted with a mirthless chuckle.

Even the vicious priestess's laughter evinced a threat.

"You understand the power of the army—of *my* army?" Zhindia said. "An army granted me by the Spider Queen?"

"I have seen it, yes. Matron Mez'Barris understands it as well."

"Then understand this: I will win here. The gathering of Menzoberranzan must join in with me to finally clear the land of our enemies and restore the mighty forge and complex into the hands of Lolth's faithful. The victory is mine above all others, and that will not be forgotten. Nor will this fight be the last, obviously, unless House Baenre agrees to Lolth's obvious demands. If they do not—and I do not expect the stubborn and foolish Matron Quenthel to put Lolth above her pride—then I welcome Matron Mez'Barris's assistance in carrying out the will of Lolth, and thus her seat will be secured as it now stands, of course. But do not misunderstand anything I say to you. I will win. Lolth is with me. Her handmaidens stand beside me. Menzoberranzan will be reformed by the will of Lolth. The perversions of Matron Mother Yvonnel Baenre's foolish daughters will be corrected with extreme effect."

Taayrul nodded, and seemed to the eavesdropping Dab'nay as if she couldn't find her voice for a reply.

"The actions of Matron Mez'Barris will be properly judged. That is my promise," Zhindia concluded.

She waved her hand to Malfoosh and the other driders.

"Leave me," she ordered Taayrul. "I have a war to finish."

Braelin Janquay slapped his hand into the water of the scrying pool, breaking the connection.

"This is madness," he told Dab'nay.

"This is *chaos*. But then again, what hasn't been so of late?" the priestess answered. "The demon surge in Menzoberranzan, the fight with Demogorgon. Matron Mother Baenre using Drizzt Do'Urden as the sword to cleave Lolth's greatest demon rival—it is all madness. Are we really so surprised now to learn that Menzoberranzan's very structure and identity is tearing asunder?"

"We have to get to Matron Mother Baenre, or to Yvonnel, at least."

Dab'nay shook her head. "You are welcomed to try."

"Kimmuriel gave you your orders," Braelin reminded her, but again, the priestess shook her head.

"Our lives—nay, more than our lives, our very existence—rests upon the choices we make in this moment," Dab'nay explained. "You heard Matron Zhindia, and even Matron Mez'Barris does not refute the ascension of House Melarn under the glory of Lolth. Now you would think to side *against* that?"

"And you would think to side against the Baenres?" Braelin returned skeptically.

"No, I would deign to stay removed from this altogether. There is nothing here that lowly Dab'nay can truly influence. I am less than a speck to them, my voice less than a whisper. I would go to Matron Mother Baenre, and perhaps she would declare me a heretic and turn me into an abominable drider. And would she be wrong if I was delivering to her words against Lady Lolth?"

"Matron Mother Baenre needs to see the truth Kimmuriel has revealed to be able to decide . . ."

"And if she decides not to fight Matron Zhindia and her growing allies, one of whom might well be Lolth, then what am I?"

Braelin stared at her but didn't respond.

"I am then a drider," Dab'nay answered her own question. "And so are you."

"Jarlaxle would not allow that," Braelin said.

Dab'nay's laugh answered it all, reflecting the absurdity of Braelin's protest. Still, she felt the need to say, "Jarlaxle? Jarlaxle, too, is a dust mote against the shifting powers battling before us."

"Perhaps you are correct," Braelin conceded. "It is bigger than the voice of Dab'nay, and of Braelin." He reached under his shirt and produced the whistle. "Perhaps Kimmuriel, too, will have second thoughts with this new information."

"If he survived his journey to the hive mind," Dab'nay said. "What if he did not?"

"What would Dab'nay suggest?"

This time the woman just stared and shook her head.

So Braelin blew hard into the whistle. No sound came forth, but the scout wasn't expecting any, for he had seen Jarlaxle use this item of communication with the strange Kimmuriel Oblodra before.

Only a few moments later, Braelin was indeed surprised, though, for he found Kimmuriel right outside the hollow of the tree, with Wulfgar the barbarian standing beside him.

"I was already on my way to this place," the psionicist answered their obvious surprise. "Your call was most welcomed, given the task before us. Have you found Matron Mother Baenre?"

"She's not hard to find," Braelin replied, pointing to the southeast. "The whole of Menzoberranzan surrounds her."

"Then come along," Kimmuriel instructed.

"We also found Matron Zhindia," Dab'nay said, stopping him in his tracks. "And First Priestess Taayrul Armgo."

Kimmuriel looked at her curiously. "Open your mind to me, child, and do tell."

Despite his dismissive pejorative, Dab'nay did let him into her thoughts as she recounted their scrying, for she wanted Kimmuriel to see all of it, every terrifying bit. To her surprise and with Kimmuriel's power, both Wulfgar and Braelin joined the telepathic discussion.

"So what do we do now?" Wulfgar asked when she was done.

Kimmuriel cast a sidelong glance at him.

"I would go to find King Bruenor," Wulfgar decided. "If the drow are going to go to war against one another, that isn't my concern."

"They'll slaughter everyone you hold dear before they do so," Kimmuriel assured him. "Is *that* your concern?"

Wulfgar didn't shrink back from the unnerving diminutive drow.

"Let us go. Matron Mother Baenre awaits," Kimmuriel said, hardly intimidated. He started away, but Dab'nay and Braelin exchanged looks and did not follow.

Kimmuriel turned back to regard them. "Yes, I understand," he told them, then specifically to Dab'nay, he added, "I saw your plans in the midst of your storytelling. You wish to go and hide, to see how it all plays out."

"I won't deny it," Dab'nay said.

"Denying with words does not override clear thoughts."

"I know not what you expect of me, but I'll not serve myself up to Matron Mother Baenre or to Matron Zhindia Melarn," Dab'nay resolutely replied.

"And you would not have carried out my orders had I been killed or detained in my journeys," Kimmuriel bluntly stated.

"No," Braelin answered before Dab'nay could.

Kimmuriel considered that for a moment, then nodded. "In light of what you divined, that is perhaps the best choice for you, I admit. Go, then. Scurry to a dark hole and hide. This will be decided quickly, I expect, and if not, then you will at least know better the drawn lines."

"And if Matron Mother Baenre prevails, then so will Bregan D'aerthe," Dab'nay said. "In that event, what for us?"

"Jarlaxle values you both."

"But you will tell him of our cowardice here?" Braelin asked.

"I will tell him that you behaved exactly as Jarlaxle would behave in your place," Kimmuriel answered.

Dab'nay and Braelin exchanged looks that were both surprised and relieved.

"Oh, he has done similar before, I assure you," Kimmuriel told them. "Many times. It is how he survives. It is how we all survive." He ended with a snort and quietly added, "Perhaps to our everlasting damnation."

With a shrug, Kimmuriel turned, bidding Wulfgar to follow, and started away.

"Kimmuriel," Braelin called after he had gone a few steps, turning him back once more.

"I wish you well in this journey, and not just for my own good fortune," Braelin told him.

For all of us, then, Kimmuriel telepathically imparted to both Braelin and Dab'nay.

CHAPTER 27

Malevolent Infection

W hy are we out here?" Dahlia whispered to Entreri. Along with Yvonnel and Pwent, the two lay atop the ridge of a wooded hillock, looking down at the vast gathering of drow. Nearest them was the largest contingent, one bearing the banners of House Baenre—banners well-known to Entreri, who had once found himself in the dungeons of that most powerful drow house.

"There is too much at stake," Entreri whispered back. "Maybe we can find a way to help."

"Against that?" Dahlia asked incredulously. She held her hand out, sweeping it over the vast army of deadly drow.

"What would you have me do?"

"Waterdeep," she answered. "Let us go back and spread the word of the happenings here. Rouse the lords against this invasion. That might be Gauntlgrym's only hope."

Entreri held up his hand to silence her, shaking his head and turning his attention to their two companions.

Pwent was very near to Yvonnel, who seemed unconcerned about the presence of the vampire.

"Kill me, then," the dwarf pleaded. "But cure me o' this curse, I beg. Yerself's the most powerful, so I been told. Avatar o' Lolth herself. Surely . . ."

"I have told you already, Thibbledorf Pwent," Yvonnel interrupted. "There is no known cure for your affliction. If there were, I'd find it for you, I promise. But no, there is none."

"Then kill me to death for real."

"You told me that you were able to sit in the Throne of the Dwarven Gods," Yvonnel replied. "Does that offer you no hope?"

"I was thinking that I'd found a way to control it," the dwarf admitted. "Might that I had. Aye, but this curse, lady, this curse . . . It won't e'er leave me, and the hunger returns. I might hold it back a hunnerd times, but the hunnerd-an'-one'll have me puttin' me teeth into the neck o' Copperhead."

"There is a great fight before your king Bruenor," Yvonnel reminded him. "You will sate your hunger on his enemies."

"For now," the despondent dwarf said.

"And when it is done, if you feel the same, I will end your . . . affliction."

"What then for poor Pwent?" Pwent asked.

"You won't be blamed," Artemis Entreri interjected. "I've seen. Losing to your curse isn't malevolence. You will find, in the end, that only those things in which you can truly blame yourself will wound you."

"What happened to you?" Dahlia whispered into Entreri's ear, and her tone wasn't of concern, but more of distaste.

Entreri looked at her and shrugged helplessly.

"Stay about and find your place, Thibbledorf Pwent," Yvonnel told him. "Be gone from us now. If you cannot find your way, if you think I am wrong in presenting the duty before you, then attack King Bruenor's enemies. There are many hundred drow before us capable of bringing your end. But I say again, this is not the time for that. We have a war to fight, I fear."

After Pwent took his leave, becoming a large bat and flying off, Yvonnel led the other two down the slope, moving ever closer to the banners of House Baenre. Dahlia grew more uneasy with every step, and kept tugging on Entreri's sleeve, motioning to him with her head whenever he looked at her that they should be long away from this area.

Finally, drawing very near to the drow camp, Entreri slowed.

"Do you mean to present us before the Matron Mother?" he whispered to Yvonnel.

"I want you to bear witness," she explained. "I know not what I will find there, or that my aunt will allow me to leave. In that case, you must inform King Bruenor." She paused, then pulled of a ring and handed it to the assassin. "And return this to Catti-brie, I beg."

"If they won't let you leave, what makes you believe that we will get out?" Dahlia snapped at her.

Yvonnel smiled at the intended slight, for that of course is what it was: a clear intimation that Dahlia expected that Yvonnel would betray her and Artemis to save herself. Yvonnel stood up tall and looked all around. "I believe we are close enough now," she explained, not answering Dahlia, then produced a pair of small circular stones disks. She held one up to her lips and whispered into it, and the sound came out of the second one.

"These are akin to sending stones, or more appropriately, clairaudience stones," she explained. "Much more limited by distance, but more complete while the magic I have placed in them holds. It will not be long, but you should hear enough of the conversation to understand what King Bruenor needs to know."

"While we sit here and wait for them to catch us?" came Dahlia's next sarcastic question.

Yvonnel shook her head helplessly and took out a length of rope. She whispered the mystical sequence to enact a spell and tossed the end of the rope upward, where it stuck in midair as if attached to some invisible grapnel. Yvonnel stepped back and motioned for them to ascend.

Entreri was familiar with the spell and so leaped upon the rope and scrambled up. When he reached the top, he pulled himself into Yvonnel's extradimensional creation.

How strange he looked from below, as if he were passing into nothingness, vanishing inch by inch as his form slipped from the material plane into the extra dimension.

Dahlia had lived most of her life among the Red Wizards of Thay. She was not surprised, or much comforted, but she, too, went up and entered the pocket dimension, pulling the rope up behind her to further conceal the place.

Yvonnel didn't even wait for her to get up there before she ran off. She had limited time for her sending stone dweomer to hold.

More than that, the drow woman was truly terrified now. She knew that the moment before her was critical, and to more than her own safety. Everything rested on this.

Mostly, though, she just wanted to get it over with, because she knew that she would lose her nerve altogether if she did not.

It would be so much easier and personally beneficial for her to just go along with whatever Quenthel was doing.

"WE CAN STILL GET AWAY," DAHLIA TOLD ENTRERI, THE two sitting in the bland extradimensional chamber. "Yvonnel won't stop us. She probably won't even blame us. And the vampire dwarf will care not, unless he intends to bite us."

"We've already had this discussion," Entreri sourly replied.

"No, we haven't had a *discussion*. You've just kept pressing on, as if it's not madness for us to be here. Look at them!" Dahlia said. She noted that Entreri was tightly grasping the stone disk Yvonnel had given him, as if trying to muffle their conversation.

"You don't trust her, either," Dahlia said, nodding to his hand. "She told you it was clairaudience, but you fear that she lied and is spying on us."

"Trust doesn't come easy to me," the assassin replied.

"Exactly my point. Look at them. A vast army, any three of which would likely be enough to defeat us. We sit here within a league of not one, but two monstrous forces, both of which could, and likely would, destroy us if they found us. This is madness, all of it, and it is our madness to participate in it. You cannot believe that we will truly make a difference here."

"You're probably correct in that."

"Then let us be gone!"

"No."

"Why?"

"Because I cannot. I'm not leaving them."

"Them? Your *friends?*" Her tone with that last word was hardly complimentary.

Entreri stared at her in disappointment.

"What about me?" Dahlia insisted. "I stood beside you. I went to the end of the world to save you! Right into House Margaster. I faced down demons and those stinging wasps. All for you. Doesn't that matter?"

"So did Regis," Entreri replied, stealing her bluster. He added, "Don't doubt my gratitude—"

"Maybe it's not that that I'm doubting."

"My love?"

"Do you even know what the word means? I wish to be out of this hopeless predicament. If you loved me . . ."

"Loyalty, then?"

"Yes!"

"What about my loyalty to them? To Regis for helping you every step. To Catti-brie . . ."

"To Drizzt, you mean."

"Him, too, even if he is dead."

Dahlia fell suddenly silent, and Entreri couldn't read the look on her face. But it frightened him.

They heard calls then through the clairaudience stone. Yvonnel had arrived at the drow perimeter, demanding to be brought before Matron Mother Quenthel's court.

Entreri moved his hand and took a deep breath.

Dahlia turned away from him and looked out the small window to the material plane afforded by such spells as this rope trick. She started almost immediately, seeing movement in the trees.

She reached back and touched Entreri's leg, and he moved up fast, noticing the movement as well.

Then noting two forms, two men, drow and human, walking through the trees.

He knew them both, quite well. He moved for the window. Dahlia grabbed him by the arm.

"Do not," she said.

"That's Wulfgar."

"And Kimmuriel," Dahlia said. "A drow. A most dangerous drow in the face of a drow army."

That did give Entreri pause, but just for a moment. Then he shook his head and pulled away from her, tossing the rope out from the window and sliding down to the ground, literally appearing in midair before Kimmuriel and Wulfgar.

Entreri went back up that rope soon after, Wulfgar climbing up behind him, while Kimmuriel, informed by Entreri of Yvonnel's actions, continued on to meet with the Matron Mother.

Entreri and Wulfgar did not find a happy Dahlia waiting for them.

"Great—now Kimmuriel knows where we are," she said. "Perhaps it is time for us to be gone."

Entreri gave her a skeptical look.

"Listen," she said, holding forth the clairaudience disk. "Yvonnel has only just arrived, and now they are discussing an alliance with Matron Zhindia."

Entreri's jaw dropped open, as he had no response to that.

Nor did Wulfgar.

"We must be out of here, and quickly," Dahlia said. "Far, far away."

"IT SEEMS OUR ONLY COURSE," MATRON MOTHER QUEN-thel told Yvonnel when the latter unexpectedly joined the ranks of the Baenre priestesses, who were joined by the priestesses of House Do'Urden and House Fey-Branche in a shallow cave protecting them from the infernal ball in the sky.

"Do you think that even with her driders, Matron Zhindia can defeat the combined power of Menzoberranzan?" Yvonnel asked. "Or even defeat House Baenre alone?"

"Do you believe we will *have* the combined power of Menzoberranzan?" Sos'Umptu countered, and her looks toward Yvonnel told the younger drow that Sos'Umptu wasn't much enamored of her at this time, and that she was most certainly advising Quenthel strongly on this. "Or that House Baenre would survive such a conflict strong enough to fend Matron Mez'Barris in the aftermath?"

Yvonnel had no answer. Perhaps they were right. Perhaps Matron Zhindia was in Lolth's highest favor and the only chance for House Baenre to survive this dangerous time was to admit such and join in the glory of Zhindia's conquest.

So much of Yvonnel's reasoning argued against this, however, both because of the confusion given the previous actions regarding the destruction of Demogorgon, and the Spider Queen's own treatment of Drizzt, face-to-face. It didn't make sense. Not much was making sense to her at that critical moment. She felt lost, as if something wasn't right.

More than even that logic and those feelings, though, Yvonnel's heart screamed against the move. She had come to know Drizzt and his friends. They did not deserve this. But the drow in her sneered at this moral conscience, decrying her weaknesses, and she honestly considered giving in and betraying these new friends she had known.

Because what other path lay before her?

What was she missing?

"We did Lolth's bidding in filling Menzoberranzan with demons," she reminded her aunt after some pause. "We did Lolth's great service in destroying the physical form of great Demogorgon. House Baenre led that, and against Matron Zhindia and House Melarn's desires and actions." She looked to Matron Zeerith Xorlarrin Do'Urden for support here, as their actions against the Melarni had been when Zhindia had dared to attack the fledgling House Do'Urden. "Why would Lolth abandon us now, after all that has so recently transpired?"

"Perhaps because we failed her test," Sos'Umptu answered. "She showed us Zaknafein, stolen from her grasp, and showed us that Drizzt would not succumb to her will. The test was to gather them and destroy them, obviously, as Matron Zhindia saw, and as we foolishly ignored."

"You do not know that," said Yvonnel.

"And you don't know it's *not* true," Sos'Umptu snapped. "What I do know is that Matron Zhindia and not Matron Mother Baenre was gifted with two retrievers to do the task, and now with a drider army to finish it all, and likely to finish us."

Again, it was hard to argue that point.

Again, to Yvonnel, it made no sense.

Or maybe, she feared, her heart made her want to believe that it made no sense, and so that was all she could see.

A commotion outside the cave interrupted the conversation, and then all eyes widened indeed as a dark elf, well known mostly because of his unusual talents and associations, was hauled into the cave by several Baenre guards.

"Well met," Kimmuriel greeted them, when the guards dropped him from their grasp. He twisted himself to straighten his robes and added, "Again," as he noted Yvonnel.

"What are you doing here?" Sos'Umptu demanded at the same time Quenthel asked, "Where is Jarlaxle?"

"Inside Gauntlgrym, I expect," Kimmuriel answered the Matron Mother. "I have not seen him in some time."

"Then, yes," Quenthel asked, "why are you here?"

"I have information I thought you might find valuable," Kimmuriel answered. "Both about this current situation you face, and about something far more important. You are right to fear Matron Zhindia and even those about you. Matron Mez'Barris's First Priestess Taayrul only now returns from her meeting with Matron Zhindia, pledging alliance and, it would seem, even fealty to the Matron of House Melarn."

That brought sneers and muttered curses, but none seemed

surprised, of course. Ever could House Baenre count on the treachery of Matron Mez'Barris Armgo.

"Our options seem thin," said Quenthel.

"Less than thin," Sos'Umptu answered. "Nonexistent. Joined with the second house, and no doubt many others, armed with demons and an army of gifted driders returned to life to serve her, Matron Zhindia's ascension is assured. We must accept the will of Lolth."

"You ask us to surrender the position House Baenre has held for millennia? To give up all that our Matron Mother Yvonnel the Eternal spent centuries building?"

"Give it up or have it taken from us, with no chance of future recourse," Sos'Umptu calmly replied.

Matron Zeerith sucked in her breath audibly, her old lips flapping in a great harrumph. Her own fate was at stake here, surely, as Zhindia Melarn positively hated her and had long accused her of heresy because of her elevation of men in her family.

"You ask us to do what is wrong," Yvonnel dared to say, for arguing against the edicts of Lolth on moral grounds was always a dare—and usually a fatal one! "When did that stop mattering to us, I wonder?"

Sos'Umptu and many of the others stared at her with abject shock.

"Our duty is to Lolth," Sos'Umptu said when she found her voice. "That is all that is right."

"Is it?" asked Kimmuriel Oblodra.

Sos'Umptu shot him a threatening glare. "You will speak when you are asked to speak, or not at all!"

"I ask you to speak," Yvonnel said, locking with Sos'Umptu's glare and not letting go. "Your simple question is shocking to many here. Tell us—tell them—what you mean."

Yvonnel knew that she was taking a great risk here in even allowing this man to speak. But what did they have to lose that wasn't already being taken from them?

"I invite you, Yvonnel, and the Matron Mother to allow me into your minds, for there I can relate much more to you both than with mere words," Kimmuriel said. "I will impart to you everything I know."

"But not the rest of us," Matron Zeerith sharply said. When all turned to her, the old matron, sitting on her summoned magical disk, added, "You would tell Yvonnel, who is not a matron, who does not sit on the Ruling Council, who is . . . what?"

"She is infused with the memories of Matron Mother Yvonnel the Eternal," Kimmuriel reminded. "Priestess Yvonnel will perhaps understand the implications of that which I have learned, as will Matron Mother Quenthel. They will be better informed and equipped to relate those implications, those truths, to the rest of you than I."

"Presumptuous," Zeerith said.

"I do not pretend to understand anything at all about you and your damned family, Oblodran," Matron Byrtyn added. "Nor do I trust you."

"Not at all," Zeerith agreed. "Take care, Matron Mother. This one has not forgotten that it was House Baenre's Matron and matriarch, your mother, Yvonnel's grandmother, who dropped the heretical Oblo-drans into the Clawrift."

"Because we were heretics," Kimmuriel echoed with a sigh. He looked to the two Baenres he had been addressing. "Perhaps in that, too, you will find some insight from that which I wish to show you."

"Speak it," demanded Sos'Umptu.

Perhaps it was that particular speaker and the insistence of her demand, both Kimmuriel and Yvonnel thought, that spurred Matron Mother Quenthel to hold up her hand and bid Sos'Umptu to silence.

"We may not trust him, but will any here deny that it was Kim-muriel more than anyone else who brought to us the power of the hive mind in our battle with Demogorgon?" Quenthel reminded. "Have we so soon forgotten?"

"Perhaps now the hive mind can offer insight to you," Kimmuriel said, and Quenthel nodded.

"We garner our insight from our prayers to Lolth," Sos'Umptu re-minded. "Is this illithid hive mind your god, Oblodran?"

Kimmuriel paused and considered that. "It is not all-knowing, but more knowing than most, for what we hide with spoken words we cannot hide within ourselves. A god? No. But it and its illithid limbs comprise a library of truth, where no lie can exist without it being known as a lie."

As all the others stood trying to decipher the unexpected answer, Quenthel nodded, led Kimmuriel and Yvonnel a bit to the side, and motioned for him to begin.

The psionicist closed his eyes and linked first with Quenthel, then with Yvonnel, and there, telepathically, he told them his truths. Both, Quenthel particularly, resisted and even recoiled, nearly breaking the connection when Kimmuriel informed them that to the illithids, Lolth was not a goddess at all. She was a manifestation of malevolence, an infection. Lolth was a bitter bit of a reasoning being promoting pride and envy, greed and power, but nothing more. She was a whispered internal lie coaxing the speaker and listener, one and the same, into a deepening gloom.

He convinced them that this was just what the illithid believed—and that he did not share that belief—and Quenthel stopped struggling against him.

He told them everything that had transpired with Ouwoonivisc at the hive mind, and emphatically bade the two women to remember the fall of House Oblodra in order to gain perspective. They had that memory, Quenthel both as perpetrator and witness, for they had all of Yvonnel the Eternal's memories and it was she, after all, who channeled the power of Lolth to take down the house.

Then he began to impart the rest, the obvious conclusions to coincide with his explanation of the illithids' beliefs, and more particularly, of what he had learned regarding Zhindia's sudden ascension. But Quenthel stopped him once more, her thoughts screaming back at him.

Kimmuriel blinked open his eyes to find the Matron Mother staring at him.

"You cannot make such claims," she said aloud.

"I only relate what I learned at the hive mind. I thought it best to tell you."

"The Matron Mother might not agree," Yvonnel remarked. "Sometimes there is innocence in ignorance."

"Surely you do not believe him!" Quenthel shouted at her.

"There are times, like now, where I no longer know what to believe," Yvonnel answered.

"Are we to be left in our ignorance?" Zeerith demanded from across the way.

"Yes, Matron Mother, I, too, demand that you have this man speak openly to us all," said Sos'Umptu.

Yvonnel looked to her, then to Kimmuriel, and nodded.

"You will not like it," the Matron Mother said.

"I'm certain of that," Sos'Umptu said, and the others nodded their agreement.

"Very well. Start with the claim of this illithid," Quenthel instructed, as the others joined them.

"Ouwoonivisc," said Kimmuriel. "He has been uncovered by the hive mind as an agent of Lolth, carrying the infection to the illithids."

"Infection?" Sos'Umptu demanded.

"That is how they see it, not I," Kimmuriel replied, and lied, for that was exactly how he had come to understand this Spider Queen creature. Lolth was within every reasoning being, that dark and selfish side of the mind. A disease, an infection, most often suppressed to a great degree. But not when Lolth got these beings under her thrall. Then the malignancy did grow, and the dark thoughts emerged. Even as he considered that, Kimmuriel better understood why Lolth had tried for the hive mind multiple times—and was probably still trying to infect the illithids now. How great might her powers become if the illithids, with their ability to tap into the thoughts of sentient beings, began to spread the infection?

"This is not the first time Lolth has tried to ensnare the illithids, as I showed you both with the memories of your mother and your namesake," Kimmuriel went on. "Then, too, in that long-ago era, lies the secret of House Oblodra, one that I did not even know until now."

He looked to Matron Zeerith. "Think back to the Time of Troubles, one hundred and thirty years ago. Your house was then ranked fifth in the city, but you knew that you were more powerful than Faen Tlabbar, immediately above you, and more deserving than House Oblodra, then ranked behind only Houses Baenre and Barrison Del'Armgo."

"I accepted the decisions of the Ruling Council," Zeerith protested.

"Of course, but truthfully, you almost certainly more readily accepted House Faen Tlabbar ahead of you than House Oblodra," Kimmuriel dared to presume. "We were hardly devout and yet Matron K'yorl sat in a higher seat than you. You thought that because of the fear our strange mind magic brought to the others."

Matron Zeerith didn't disagree.

"It was more than that," said Kimmuriel. "Matron K'yorl did indeed hold the favor of Lolth in those times, for she was acting as Lolth's agent in trying to infect the hive mind. But she was doing more than that. She could not be satisfied with that which Lolth had promised her. In the weakening of the priestesses and the wizards in the Time of Troubles, as you recall, Matron K'yorl began to place herself above the order of Menzoberranzan itself, above even the Matron Mother. And in her arrogance, K'yorl tried to enlist the hive mind in a plan of conquest."

"She wanted to conquer Menzoberranzan?" Zeerith asked.

"She wanted to conquer Lolth," Kimmuriel replied. He had their attention then, fully.

"I believe it to be true," Yvonnel said. "When I consider the memories I was given, I feel that this conclusion is true."

Quenthel agreed.

"Lolth was not conquered, of course," Kimmuriel went on. "Nor was she deterred. She has tried again . . . and has failed." His use of the name of the Spider Queen and the word "fail" in the same sentence brought a wild-eyed scowl to the face of Sos'Umptu. Kimmuriel knew he was on dangerous ground here, but he had gone too far now to reverse course.

Too, when was a male drow *not* on dangerous ground surrounded by the females of their race?

"This time, she used an illithid as her agent, one she had infected," he said.

"You keep using that term, 'infected,'" said Zeerith. "Perhaps you should choose better words regarding the blessings of our Lady Lolth."

"I am using the terminology of the illithids," he replied. "I am telling you their beliefs, to do with as you will."

"And the fact that we haven't killed you already for your blasphemy probably explains a bit why Lolth has chosen to favor Matron Zhindia," said Zeerith.

"Better that he become a drider," Sos'Umptu threatened.

"If Lolth does favor Matron Zhindia," Yvonnel interjected, backing them both a bit.

"How can we doubt that?" Sos'Umptu replied. "*Two* retrievers!"

"Kimmuriel claims that it was not Lolth who gave the magnificent constructs to Matron Zhindia," said Quenthel.

"It was her handmaiden, Yiccardaria," Kimmuriel said.

"With the blessing of Lolth, of course," said Sos'Umptu.

"I do not believe that Lolth even knows," Kimmuriel said. "Or rather, I doubt more that Lolth would even care. Yiccardaria holds an old grudge against a drow warrior who once banished her for a century, even after she had revealed her true form to him. She was with House Hunzrin back when they were challenging Bregan D'aerthe for extra-Menzoberranzan trade privileges. She posed as Priestess Iccara, creating mischief along with Priestess Bolfae."

"Handmaiden Bolifaena," Quenthel clarified for the others.

"With the prompting of Kimmuriel, I remember the incident, or the report of it," Yvonnel said, and Quenthel nodded. "Yvonnel the Eternal summoned Bolifaena to confirm the reports brought to her by Jarlaxle. Yiccardaria was banished by the blades of Zaknafein Do'Urden."

The news brought gasps but also a warning from Sos'Umptu. "You remember it with his prompting, or is it something he just imparted in your thoughts?"

"It is true," Quenthel insisted. "Yiccardaria was banished for a century by Zaknafein."

"And now she gave to Matron Zhindia the means to pay Zaknafein back."

"A handmaiden is not nearly powerful enough to create or control a retriever," Zeerith said doubtfully.

"Yiccardaria was given them by Malcanthet, queen of the Succubi, consort of Demogorgon," Kimmuriel stated.

"This is madness and foolishness!" Sos'Umptu declared. "Why would Lolth allow this? She made great gains with the destruction of Demogorgon, but she—"

"Because Lolth does not care about the details," Kimmuriel interrupted, drawing another wide-eyed scowl of utter hatred from Sos'Umptu. Kimmuriel knew then that he was certainly about to die (if he was lucky), but he pressed on. "The illithid use the terms they use, and they are not without merit. Lolth holds the motivations of an infection, a disease, not a goddess. She does not guide. Rather, she afflicts. She yearns to find that within each of us that is chaos and unleash it, and she will take whatever path she sees most clearly to inflict her glorious catastrophes."

"Execute the fool!" Sos'Umptu demanded of Matron Mother Quenthel. "We must turn him into a drider at once to let him suffer forevermore in the pain of abomination! Maybe then we will stave off the disfavor of the Spider Queen!"

"I cannot deny that Lolth would enjoy that," Kimmuriel quietly admitted, but the others were focused on Quenthel, who was shaking her head with doubt.

"Then this will be the fall of House Baenre," Quenthel answered Sos'Umptu, "whatever course we choose."

"If Lolth decrees it," Sos'Umptu insisted. "I cannot say that it is not deserved."

The room exploded in shouts, all the women looking to one another for guidance.

"Lolth isn't decreeing anything," Kimmuriel interjected, above Sos'Umptu's yelling at him to be silent.

"That's the whole point of her," Kimmuriel added, when Quenthel had silenced her devout and outraged sister. "She doesn't care. She never cared, at all. This isn't about the Baenres and never was. It isn't about any of us. It's about the infection that is Lolth, the disease of wickedness, of chaos and strife."

"You will die horribly, or beg for it for eons," Sos'Umptu promised.

Kimmuriel shrugged. "Think far back," he told Yvonnel and Quenthel. "Much further back. All the way back . . . to the beginning. You carry those memories. Think of how it all started, the founding of the city. Consider the little lies, accepted in return for something, some small gain, some little blessing, even. That is how the darkness is deepened, bit by bit: accepted lies followed by coerced actions—wrong and unjust, but not so bad at first. The darkness deepened in your heart."

"Why are you suffering this fool to speak? Matron Zhindia has the blessing of Lolth," Sos'Umptu interrupted. "All see it now, to our doom!"

"Lolth doesn't care," Kimmuriel dared reply, the chorus to the song of his own demise. "Oh, what power she has gained now because of the actions of Menzoberranzan, of those of Yvonnel and Matron Mother Quenthel against her rival, Demogorgon. Now she tries for the hive mind of the illithids—or tried, but she has failed, again discovered and defeated. Because they know the truth of her, the truth I have offered to you. She is more disease than being, more affliction than goddess. And yet for all that, *she doesn't care.* She doesn't care about Zaknafein Do'Urden—it was not she who brought him back."

"It was me," Yvonnel admitted, to loud gasps. The young purple-eyed woman shrugged helplessly. "I do not even know how I did it."

"Just that it was without Lolth," Kimmuriel reasoned. "How could you manage among the greatest of spells, resurrection itself, against the wishes of your supposed goddess?"

"Supposed?" Sos'Umptu warned.

"We are past that," Kimmuriel said to her, the dismissal causing the high priestess to growl. "Yvonnel was able to perform the spell because Lolth doesn't care. Not for Zaknafein, and surely not for Drizzt Do'Urden. He might be the biggest joke she has played on her children in centuries. We think him the ultimate heretic, yet Lolth confronted him in a tunnel and tried *again* to convert him. She could have destroyed him, but she did not. She did not!"

Kimmuriel paused . . . and offered a chuckle.

"Do you think this is funny, Obladran?"

"Of course. You just said it—it really doesn't matter who wins here in Lolth's grand scheme, because no matter the outcome, against the northland of Faerun, or within the coming storm to decide the hierarchy of Menzoberranzan, the Lady of Chaos will move on to her next game. This is what I learned at the hive mind of the illithids, and this is what I relate to you, at great risk. The judgment is yours, not mine."

"The judgment upon you will likely be decided by Lady Lolth," Quenthel said then, silencing Kimmuriel. If he had lost her, his life was over, but he didn't need to press his luck. "For now, perhaps our most prudent and easiest course will be to side with Matron Zhindia, finish this business on the surface, then fight whatever battle we find back in Menzoberranzan."

"Thank you, Matron Mother," Sos'Umptu said with a bow. "I should not have doubted your judgment."

"That is the easiest course," Yvonnel agreed, and Kimmuriel swallowed hard, expecting the blow. "But is it the right course? Or have we so fully lost our sense of guidance and conscience that such a thing as that, as simple a matter of right and wrong, matters not at all?"

"Deep is the darkness," Kimmuriel whispered, and it—like so much he'd said here—was not well received by Sos'Umptu and several of the others.

"Darkened through centuries," Quenthel reasoned.

"This is madness! Blasphemy!" Sos'Umptu shouted, having none of it. "No one will follow us—will follow *you*—if you persist in this fantasy foisted upon us by a desperate and vengeful heretic and fool."

"We will think on it, all of us," Yvonnel said.

"We will *pray* on it," Quenthel corrected her.

"We should be quick in our contemplations," Matron Zeerith warned. "Matron Zhindia is coming."

"Something is wrong with all of this," Yvonnel said. "I cannot ignore that if Lolth wanted Zaknafein dead, or Drizzt dead, it could have been accomplished much more easily. How could that be a test that we failed? We destroyed her rival—Drizzt was the spear of that destruction. And she herself met him in that tunnel far from here and did not destroy him even when he denied her. You all, even you, Mistress Sos'Umptu, believed that it was likely Lady Lolth who returned Zaknafein to Drizzt."

"And you knew better and hadn't the courage to tell us," Sos'Umptu replied.

"It is true," Yvonnel admitted. "But still, why would she turn on us?"

"Perhaps because of your act, fool," Sos'Umptu said.

"I could not have done such a thing as resurrection, true resurrection, without her, if all that we believe about her, about all the gods, is the truth," Yvonnel argued. She wasn't convincing Sos'Umptu, obviously, but just as obviously, her target audience here was Quenthel.

"Then why?" Quenthel asked, considering her theory.

"Perhaps Lady Lolth is as tired of the Baenres as so many of the other matrons," Zeerith stated openly, a remark that would have started wars in years past.

"I will have none of this," Sos'Umptu decided then. "This is heresy. I am no apostate. Will you fight me, sister?" she asked Quenthel.

Quenthel shook her head. "I ask only that you give us some time to sort through this."

"Until Matron Zhindia arrives. No longer."

Quenthel nodded. "I must pray."

"You must remember," Kimmuriel said, and now all scowled at him, except, he noted, for Yvonnel.

"To the beginning," Yvonnel said.

"The darkness is deepened very gradually," Kimmuriel offered. "Perhaps by looking back to the—shall we say, lighter and more innocent times?—will you see the starkness of where we are now compared to where we once were."

"Before we lost our sense of conscience that such a simple thing as a matter of right and wrong mattered?" Sos'Umptu asked Yvonnel, her voice dripping with sarcasm and threat.

"I beg you to remember in sequence," Kimmuriel remarked. "Consider the time frame, action by action."

"We know the sequence of the memories that were given to us by the illithid, Methil El Viddenvelp," a clearly frustrated and angry Matron Mother Quenthel assured him.

"The sequential effect, then," Kimmuriel clarified. "Remember how Yvonnel the Eternal felt with her first kill. Remember how she felt with her hundredth."

"As the infection grew?" Yvonnel asked.

Kimmuriel couldn't tell if she was asking honestly or if she, too, was stepping back from the cliff to which he had led them. He was surprised to find a strange sense of calmness spreading within him. His vengeance against House Baenre was no more—he felt as if he had properly repaid not them, but the infection that was Lolth, simply by revealing the truth of the malevolent fiend.

Truth is the best antidote—especially for those who had lived in the dark for so long.

His fate was in their hands. He knew it would not be easy to flee this place, and that he could not escape the power arrayed before him unless, perhaps, the hive mind offered him sanctuary . . .

Yes, that would be his only hope, for this was far beyond Jarlaxle!

Strangely, however, Kimmuriel didn't want to flee, whatever his fate.

He felt free, felt as if he had at long last escaped already.

"EVERYTHING WILL BE DECIDED IN THE NEXT MOMENTS," Entreri whispered to his two companions inside the extradimensional chamber.

"And if it goes against us?" Dahlia warned. "If Yvonnel sides with those who wish to support the Melarn force, then your trust in her has doomed us. We have no escape, nowhere to run or hide."

"She will not betray us, whatever her choice," said Entreri.

Dahlia argued, "She will! Because she knows that her, that their goddess will know! I never before thought you a fool."

"Have faith in her," Wulfgar suggested, drawing a sharp glare from Dahlia.

"On my life?" she shot back. "Why would I do such a thing?"

Wulfgar looked to Entreri, but that man, too, had no answer.

"We should be gone," Dahlia insisted. "Now!" She started for the window to the material world.

"No," Entreri answered, stopping her short.

"We're going to die, and horribly."

"It's a chance I'm willing to take."

"And if I'm not?"

He said nothing.

"*Why?*" Dahlia asked. She looked at Wulfgar with disgust, then back to Entreri. "For them? For your friends?"

Entreri chewed his lip but was nodding his head.

"I knew in the end you would choose them," Dahlia said.

"Choose? Why am I to choose at all?"

"Better that Drizzt had died on the hill that day we parted," Dahlia said, her voice a clarion of pure frustration.

Entreri noted Wulfgar's scowl. "You said that was unintentional," he said to Dahlia. "An accident."

"It was, but so what?" she answered. "Had Drizzt died, I would have shrugged. He deserved it."

Entreri held silent, staring at this woman.

"I came for you when you were in need," Dahlia said. "I went into House Margaster for you."

He nodded.

"Now you would choose them?"

"Now I ask that we both choose our allies," Entreri replied.

"Your friends?"

"Friends to Dahlia, too."

"I'm not going to die for them," she answered, and moved to the window. "Are you coming with me?"

Entreri stared at her for a long moment, then shook his head. He started to explain but held his tongue, for Dahlia didn't wait, dropping the rope and moving through the window.

Wulfgar sighed deeply, then turned to Entreri and offered a nod of approval.

Entreri offered nothing in return.

"SEQUENTIAL EFFECT," YVONNEL SAID QUIETLY TO QUEN-thel after the two had gone off to contemplate and, mostly, search their memories, the oldest memories given to them by the experiences of Matron Mother Yvonnel the Eternal.

Quenthel could hardly believe the revelations. Instead of experiencing the events, and more importantly the darkening feelings, that had led them to this point, she had gone back to those earliest memories, and the emotions accompanying them—hope, joy, freedom—and played them against the deepest darkness, the more recent experiences.

The contrast was too stark to be ignored. Looking at the emotions, the actions, the mind-set, of Matron Mother Yvonnel the Eternal in the latter years of her life had revealed to both Quenthel and Yvonnel a distinctly different way of looking at the world around her.

"How did this happen?" Quenthel asked. "How did we get here?"

"One lie, one bad act at a time," Yvonnel answered, reflecting Kimmuriel's earlier remarks to them.

"We must tell our people," said Quenthel.

"And they will not believe us."

"We must . . ." Quenthel started to argue, but she couldn't help but agree with the logic here.

"Sequential effect, he called it," said Yvonnel.

"And now I understand. My mother—and I could have called her that in the early days, I know now—from those early days did not resemble the Matron Mother Baenre that I knew. Even through her memories, through the emotions within those memories, you can feel it. So subtle, a hairsbreadth at a time, this deepening darkness of Lolth."

"The people we need to convince are already fully within that darkness," Yvonnel reminded. "They are comfortable in the shade."

"What do we do?"

"I do not know, but I do know that I will not fight against the dwarves of Gauntlgrym. Nor will I capture Zaknafein for the pleasure of Lolth."

The Matron Mother of Menzoberranzan stared at her for a short while, then replied, "Nor will I. Nor will House Baenre."

When the two left the back chamber of the cave, they found the others waiting for them, with Sos'Umptu and Kimmuriel nearest.

"Enlightening," Yvonnel said, mostly to Kimmuriel.

"I have prayed as well," Sos'Umptu said.

"But I have no hope that you have come to the same conclusions," Yvonnel said.

That brought a profound scowl to the face of devout Sos'Umptu. "Then you have been deceived by a trickster," she said.

"No," Yvonnel said, but at the same time, Quenthel offered to Sos'Umptu, "Perhaps. Either way, we will soon enough learn the truth. And I understand that you cannot remove that which is in your heart now to examine the past, as we have been blessed to do. All I ask of you is that you bear witness as we all learn who is right and who is wrong."

"You expect passivity in the face of sacrilege?" Sos'Umptu retorted. "I am a mistress of Arach-Tinilith, a high priestess of Lolth, the first priestess of House Baenre, the mistress of the Fane of the Quarvelsharess. I . . ."

"And I am the Matron Mother," Quenthel said. "Of House Baenre and of Menzoberranzan, who leads the Ruling Council and serves as voice of Lolth in the City of Spiders."

"Then act like it," Sos'Umptu replied, squaring her shoulders.

"Do you even know what that means?"

"I know that Matron Zhindia Melarn has been offered great gifts to carry out her war," Sos'Umptu said. "You ask me to take the lies of a mind-magic trickster above that which I can see clearly?"

"Call a handmaiden, then, that we might all speak with her," said Quenthel.

"Call Bolifaena," Kimmuriel offered.

"Shut up," Sos'Umptu growled at him. "Count your luck that Matron Mother Quenthel is here and that you have found a way to temporarily confuse her, Oblodran, else your legs would be splitting four ways each at this very moment."

Kimmuriel fell silent.

To the two women, Sos'Umptu railed, "I do not need guidance. Lady Lolth has given Matron Zhindia the driders."

"Sos'Umptu will pledge fealty to House Melarn, then?" Yvonnel said.

"Of course not!"

"As with the driders, how do we know it was Lolth?" Quenthel asked. "Are there not other demon lords who are quite angered at Menzoberranzan right now? Particularly angered at House Baenre?"

"Demon lords known to be adept with retrievers," said Yvonnel.

"Retrievers who bear the image of Lolth!" Sos'Umptu reminded.

"So much better the ruse, then."

"Matron Mother, this is easily tested," Yvonnel said. "What if we undo that which we believe was not done by Lolth?"

"Fight the driders?" a concerned Sos'Umptu asked.

"No, better than that."

Yvonnel's smile gave it away, and Sos'Umptu didn't need to be a psionicist to figure out what Yvonnel was hinting at, an action that represented the highest attempt at sacrilege to date.

"You cannot," she said with a long snarl.

"No, they cannot," Kimmuriel agreed. "What you are thinking could not be done by one not in the favor of Lolth unless one was more powerful than Lolth."

That brought gasps from all three, and Sos'Umptu would hear no more of it. She drew forth her scourge, lifting it, the living serpents rising to strike at the psionicist. As one they struck . . . but not at Kimmuriel.

Dominated by the psionicist, the living snakes bit at Sos'Umptu, tearing the flesh of her face and neck, filling her with their deadly venom.

Shrieking, horrified, the priestess threw down her weapon, though it took her several slaps to finally extract the last of the serpents from their fanged grip. She stumbled back then, shocked, trying to cast a spell.

Both Quenthel and Yvonnel did it for her, sending magic to seal her wounds, to neutralize the poison. Sos'Umptu continued to stumble.

"I did that," Quenthel announced, shocking everyone, and Kimmuriel most profoundly.

Sos'Umptu gave a sound that none had heard before, a strange, squealing, disbelieving protest, then ran off. In her wake, the other priestesses and matrons moved closer to confer with the Matron Mother.

Yvonnel glared at Kimmuriel, and the Matron Mother seemed ready to strike him down, despite her lie that she, not he, had turned the serpents.

"More proof that what I have shown you is correct," Kimmuriel explained before the others arrived.

Quenthel expression didn't soften. "Trickster?" she asked. "If so, you will come to wish that I had let First Priestess Sos'Umptu turn you into a drider, I promise."

"Did I not just do what you intend to try, on a much smaller scale?" Kimmuriel asked her. He nodded to the scourge writhing on the ground. "A creation of Lolth shown not to be as we believed? How is it even possible?"

The two, and those joining them now, had no answer.

"Because I know the truth," Kimmuriel explained. "And when the goddess is not a goddess at all, that truth is freedom and that truth is power. She is an infection."

The Baenres exchanged looks.

"Can we?" Quenthel quietly asked Yvonnel.

"I think so."

Quenthel lowered her gaze, sighing repeatedly, shrugging helplessly. They had to try, but surely it seemed an impossible task.

"Gather House Baenre," she instructed Minolin Fey Baenre.

"It is war, then, drow against drow," reasoned Matron Zeerith.

"Perhaps, perhaps not," Yvonnel offered. "But if it is, where are you?"

Zeerith spent a moment thinking, then agreed. "Gather House Xor . . . Do'Urden," she told Priestess Saribel.

"And House Fey-Branche," Matron Byrtyn Fey agreed.

"This will be the end of everything we ever believed," Quenthel warned her niece.

"But is it everything Yvonnel the Eternal ever believed?" Yvonnel answered. "Or is it simply the end of what she came to accept?"

Quenthel, who had the same memories, and now, with Kimmuriel's prodding, could access them clearly, finally, resignedly, nodded.

When all the drow of the three houses were gathered in a large clearing before the cave, Matron Mother Quenthel told the priestesses and wizards to follow the lead of her and Yvonnel. After some discussion, the two powerful women decided on a pair of sturdy oaks, pillars about the entrance to a main trail heading to the west, where Matron Zhindia's forces gathered.

The two fell into a spellcasting trance, accessing the memories of Yvonnel. This dweomer had been done before, long before, they both remembered. But done singularly, with special dispensation, and certainly never on such a scale as they intended—never anything nearly on the scale they needed.

They began to weave a web, translucent filaments flying out from their waggling fingers, stretching tree to tree.

The other priestesses tried to help, as did the wizards, but there was no known ritual for such a creation as this, and ultimately, it failed, the webbing falling apart.

Stubbornly, Quenthel and Yvonnel pressed on.

"The magic is not strong enough," a defeated Quenthel said at last, her shoulders slumping.

"We have not chosen wrong," Yvonnel insisted.

"That thought will comfort me as I am murdered, or worse," Quenthel replied.

All around them, the dark elves whispered and milled about and worried.

The earth beneath their feet shook then, a tremendous rumble and roll, the largest grumble yet from Maegera—so great a quake that Yvonnel looked to the mountaintop, expecting the volcano to explode.

When it did not, the woman found herself focused on that place, the mountain, and on the events transpiring in Gauntlgrym beneath it.

"Pray, stand strong," she told Quenthel. "I have an inspiration."

"Tell," Quenthel said.

Yvonnel shook her head. "I will return shortly. Stand strong. Hold this ground."

CHAPTER 28

The Magic of Creation

He was battered and bruised and bloody, but he knew that he had suffered far less than many of his companions here in the great antechamber or Gauntlgrym. The exhausted King Bruenor refused all aid, as did his queens, no less beaten up than he.

He needed rest, though, after a long day of fighting, but he took it at the wall, or what was left of it, out by the tram station across the pond. From there, he would direct his forces. They had secured the front half of the cavern, including three important choke points, but their enemies were pressing them once more. Too many dwarves were hurt and exhausted to take the fight to the demons, but the area they had gained was defensible, affording them some respite, that they might gather their strength, and more importantly, that they might get a couple of the stalagmite artillery stations, and stalactite archer and scout posts back in operation.

From a strictly military perspective, it had gone better than they could have hoped, but the task before them remained truly daunting, and now time seemed to be running short. For the ground was rumbling again already, the primordial threatening to break free.

Even clearing the remaining demons from this cavern was going to take too long, Bruenor feared.

But he pressed on. What choice did he have?

He rallied his dwarves, ever loyal, every one more than willing to die for Clan Battlehammer, for their king and queens, for their Delzoun heritage, and for the belief that their actions would advance the cause they thought of as good, the cause of the dwarves of Faerun.

At any point in which the situation was stabilized, Bruenor ignored the clerics calling for him to rest and went to the wounded, walking their lines, encouraging the priests to do more, to find every last gasp of magical energy they would muster.

Then he went back into the throne room to pay respect to the dead, every one, and thanked them, and kissed their cold, bloody cheeks.

On one such journey, King Bruenor was met by a cleric they called Penny.

"O, me king Bruenor, ye must be comin'," she said, gasping for breath, for she had run a long way to find him. "The babe's comin', don't ye doubt!"

Bruenor took a deep breath and tried to consider the moment, The child of his daughter, his beloved Catti-brie. The child of Catti-brie and his dearest, now lost friend. He gave a helpless chuckle, telling himself that he had to win here, or at least find a way to break out. He wasn't afraid to die—he already had once!—but the child of Drizzt and Catti-brie?

That one, Bruenor decided then and there, was not going to die before it got the chance to live up to the incredible promise of its lineage.

"Take me," he told Penny, but they had barely started when Bruenor stopped and changed his mind. "I'll go to her. Yerself's to find Zaknafein. Seen him out by the tram not long ago. Ye find him and ye tell him and ye bring him!"

"Aye, me king," she said, and ran off.

"And Rumblebelly!" Bruenor yelled after her. "Don't ye forget Rumblebelly!"

Bruenor ran off, too, but not before running to the Throne of the Dwarven Gods and hopping into it once more.

"I only ask when it's not for meself," he prayed to Moradin. "And I'm knowing that this one's not one o' yer own by blood heritage. But it's me grandchild, and know that whate'er me girl has here, it couldn't be more me own than if it was me own, or me own blood girl's own. So don't ye let the babe die in this place now, I beg."

He felt the sticky blood on his cheek when he moved to wipe his tears. "Damned I'll be if I come back here just to see this all fall down," he muttered, rambling through the halls and down the stairs—all empty except for patrols and guard posts he had ordered kept in place, and the occasional couriers heading back to the entry cavern, bearing weapons and tools and other supplies, and one group of eight carrying a side-slinger catapult.

Their determination and attention to duty and detail lifted Bruenor's heart as he made his way, but another quake from the primordial tempered his hopes.

They were going to have to leave, likely, and soon. Bruenor entertained thoughts that perhaps they could break out into the Underdark.

He only hoped that if that occurred, his enemies would take the place right behind their departure, and have the primordial blow the whole durned complex up right under their feet, and good enough for them!

Would Bruenor again soon be crowned king of Mithral Hall, far to the east?

He shook that thought away as soon as it entered his head. If they lost here, he would die here, almost certainly, and if by some strange chance he and his fellows did escape, Bruenor would take to the road, following the path of adventure.

Aye, he thought. He'd gather Rumblebelly and find Wulfgar, and they, with Catti-brie, when she was able, would go . . .

It all seemed so hollow suddenly.

The Companions of the Hall were four now, not five.

No time for such dark thoughts! Bruenor chuckled then, imagining what Guenhwyvar would have done if she'd heard him so excuse her from the companions!

Bruenor ran on, finally coming to Catti-brie's private chambers. He was surprised, but only momentarily, to find Zaknafein already there waiting for him. The drow's clothing was torn in many places, blood and demon gore splattered all over him. He had a gash on one cheek, and his eye above it was swollen nearly closed.

"What do we know, good king Bruenor?" Zaknafein asked, scrambling up to him.

"How'd ye . . . ?" Bruenor started to ask, but he understood when Zaknafein pointed to the anklets he wore.

"Thought ye was wearin' 'em on yer wrists, as they were made," Bruenor asked.

"I wanted to get here fast, so I put them on my ankles as my son does . . ."

The tense of his words, the desperate intimation that Drizzt was alive, stiffened Bruenor with discomfort.

"Ain't knowin' nothin' yet," said Bruenor. "Me girl's soon to be a ma, so I been told, but ye beat me here."

He nodded to the door.

"I haven't gone in," Zaknafein replied. "I thought it best to wait for you."

A loud groan came from the other side of that door.

Bruenor hesitated. "Ain't never seen something like this before," he admitted.

Zak managed a laugh. "Where I come from, any child's birth witnessed by a man would likely mean the immediate execution of both the child and the witness."

"Yeah, lovely place," Bruenor said, and when another, louder, cry sounded, the dwarf moved past Zak and pushed into the room.

They found Catti-brie kneeling on the bed, leaning forward, blowing out her breath powerfully. Her face was bright red.

"Aye now, good ye've come, but get ye out o' here!" said the priestess tending her. The second midwife, holding Catti-brie's hand, scowled mightily at her king.

"Aye, aye," Bruenor apologized. "Me girl . . . I'll be right outside."

"You stay," Catti-brie gasped between blows, and when the dwarf priestesses tried to argue, she said, "He stays!" with such intensity that the both of them fell silent.

"I will wait outside," Zak offered. "All my good thoughts and prayers are with you . . ." Zak paused and seemed unsure. "My daughter," he finished.

Catti-brie couldn't manage a smile, it seemed, but she did manage a nod, and with a return acknowledgment and an awkward bow, Zak went out of the room. He started to close the door behind him, but stepped aside as Penny and another drow rushed past him.

The sight of Yvonnel surprised Bruenor, but he was glad that the powerful priestess had come. When the two women crossed into the room, Bruenor saw past them to two others: Regis, who looked as battered as Bruenor had ever seen him, his fine clothes splatted with gore and bits of blood. Beside the halfling stood Jarlaxle, looking very much like he was about to attend a formal court ball, not a mark or a splatter on him.

Of course not.

"It's past," Catti-brie said then.

"Aye, lie her down," Penny said. "Poor girl's looking like she's crawled all the way from Waterdeep."

They got Catti-brie down and covered her with a blanket quickly. Yvonnel moved up and brushed the three priestesses aside. "Go away, to the other room," she told them. "I must speak with Catti-brie."

"What're ye about?" Bruenor asked, but Yvonnel ignored him. "When a king asks ye what ye're about in his house, ye're wise to tell him," Bruenor reminded.

"I have to speak with Catti-brie," Yvonnel replied. "It's about the delivery of her child, which I expect will be before the dawn."

Bruenor didn't move.

"Me da can hear whatever you've to tell me," Catti-brie said.

Bruenor looked to his daughter, then nodded to the still-open door and the drow eagerly leaning toward them, obviously nervous.

Catti-brie agreed.

"Zaknafein, get in here," Bruenor called.

He didn't have to be asked twice and stood at Bruenor's side in the span of an eyeblink.

Bruenor saw that Catti-brie appeared quite fine with Zak being there, so he turned his attention to Yvonnel, and noted her look at Zak, one that was first sour, but quickly, it seemed, accepting.

"You actually have some knowledge of this," she said to the weapon master, drawing a curious stare in reply. "Perhaps when I am done and have departed, you can help this woman make her decision."

Catti-brie grunted in pain, then puffed it away in short and determined blows. "If you want to talk, do it now," she insisted through gritted teeth.

"There is a secret among the drow, known only to a few priestesses—matrons—among us," Yvonnel began. "It concerns a magic, little used and sometimes dangerous, uncontrollable, even. In our own history, it is utilized only when available, and only in desperation."

"Birth magic," Zak whispered, nodding, for the war with House Hun'ett was a fight he would never forget.

"Magic to assist in the birth?" Catti-asked, and winced. "If you have something—"

"No, not that," Yvonnel interrupted. "Not that at all. The moment of childbirth is the most powerful moment of creation a person can know. There is nothing to rival its intensity. It is the epitome of a woman's closeness to the powers of the universe—call them gods, call it nature, call it . . . a primordial. There is a magic that can channel that intensity into a thrown spell, and send it wide across great distances."

Catti-brie's face twisted in more than the grimace from her discomfort.

"As I have told you, we did not use it often," Yvonnel said. "The last time in Menzoberranzan was to utterly stun an entire room of priestesses, many high priestesses, even a matron, as one house overtook another. Many believe that victorious house would not have had a chance in that fight, except that the matron, in the moment of giving birth, battered her enemies."

"You ask me to deliver my child in a moment of great destruction?" Catti-brie asked, her tone somewhere between disbelief and anger. "I cannot . . ."

"It does not have to be that," Yvonnel replied. "At least, I believe it does not, though with my own people, with my long memories, I admit I have no example of something other than war."

Catti-brie was sweating now, her face turning bright red. "Leave me," she ordered Yvonnel.

"I can teach the dwarves attending you the ritual easily," the drow replied. "It is similar to their other rituals—they serve as no more than the conduit for your amplification—"

"Leave me!" the woman demanded.

Yvonnel nodded and stood. "Of course," she said, and bowed. "I pray that you and your child will come through this easily, and hope that he or she will live up to the integrity and beauty of the parents."

She gave a look and shrug at Zak and walked out of the room, closing the door behind her.

Zak offered a resigned look at Catti-brie.

"You cannot agree with this," the woman growled at him. "Do not make me believe that all I have come to hope about you was folly, and that you really are a drow of Menzoberranzan in your heart and soul."

Zak offered a helpless laugh at that. "I know well the incident to which Yvonnel just referred," he said. "The last time birth magic was used in Menzoberranzan, I was the spear thrown behind the magical stun. My sword, my whip, took down the enemy priestesses. It was Matron Malice who threw . . ."

Catti-brie was already replying, angrily, and so it took her a moment to realize what Zak was saying. Then she stopped arguing, staring at him dumbfounded.

"It was the birth of your husband," Zak confirmed. "Drizzt was born in the moment of birth magic, powerfully thrown. Destructive magic, indeed. I see no proof that Drizzt was badly damaged by the act."

412   R. A. SALVATORE

"So you would have me do it?"

"I would have you do whatever you think best. My place here is merely to support you and to fight for King Bruenor and those others my son thought dear."

"Pretty words."

"If you didn't believe them, would you have given me Drizzt's scimitars?"

"And what of you, me da?" Catti-brie asked Bruenor, who was sitting perfectly silent and stone-faced.

Bruenor shook his head.

"I need a better answer."

"I can'no' know," Bruenor replied. "Could ye open the gates, then? Could ye banish a thousand demons? Suren that'd be a grand thing to make yer babe a hero even as it's born. But how am I to know, me girl?" He shook his head.

Catti-brie started to reply but stopped, fumbling for words. A moment later, it didn't matter, for a brutal contraction lifted her head right from the pillow, doubling her over.

Led by Penny, the dwarven priestesses rushed into the room. Some priests came in, as well, but Yvonnel was not to be seen.

CHAPTER 29

Of Fire Born

As with her first journey, Yvonnel had to use some spells
and pick her way carefully to get through the drow army
now flanking House Baenre. Their positioning was no
accident, she now understood more clearly, and that
only reminded her of the urgency and critical nature of these next
few hours, or perhaps minutes.

When she arrived, finally, at Matron Mother Quenthel's side, she
found the Baenre camp astir, soldiers and priestess preparing the expected battlefield—and notably, spending as many recourses securing
their flanks and rear guard as their forward positions, the west, where
they expected Matron Zhindia to be.

"What word?" Quenthel asked her. Myrineyl, Minolin Fey, and
all of the other Baenre priestesses were there with Quenthel, with the
notable exception of Sos'Umptu.

"Where is Matron Zeerith and Matron Byrtyn?"

"They are with us," Quenthel assured her, but her voice did not
relate the confidence she obviously tried to put forth.

"They will do what is best for them," Yvonnel said. "Loyalty will play only a small part."

It became obvious that Quenthel couldn't disagree with that harsh reality. "Perhaps we should reconsider," she said. "Matron Zhindia's case of Lolth's great favor is apparent to many others. Perhaps they are correct in their assessment."

"But you and I know better now," Yvonnel answered. "He showed us the truth." She pointed to Kimmuriel, who stood a short distance away, heavily and restrictively guarded, she noted, by Baenre soldiers.

"Do we?" Quenthel asked, her resignation clear. "Or does it matter? If we are hopeless here in our 'truth,' then what purpose does it serve? Do we fight half, perhaps even seven, of the ten greatest drow houses?"

"House Baenre has faced such possibilities for millennia," Yvonnel rightfully pointed out.

"But here, away from our house and defenses, and with Matron Zhindia commanding an army of a hundreds of driders and hundreds of demons? She alone is our match, I expect. With the others, with Barrison Del'Armgo . . ."

Yvonnel held up her hand, her eyes going to the distance, for she felt then a tremor beneath her feet, tiny at first, but growing.

"The primordial?" Myrineyl asked with great concern. "Is the beast breaking free?"

"Matron Zhindia," Kimmuriel Oblodra called from the side. "Her running driders are shaking the ground."

All eyes went to Yvonnel and Quenthel.

"We should try again, and immediately," Yvonnel suggested. "If we fail, then that is the will of Lolth, it would seem, and we will still have time to make our ultimate choice."

Quenthel mulled on that for a bit. Yvonnel knew what she was thinking, for they shared the pertinent memories here, recollections from a time long past, two thousand years and more, in the fledgling days of Menzoberranzan.

The stark difference could not be dismissed. Seeing that without, as Kimmuriel had noted, the "sequential effect" was so dramatic that Yvonnel and Quenthel could not ignore it, and so it was hope and not fear that drove the Matron Mother forward when she said, "All priestesses and wizards in line to support us." To some nearby sentries, she ordered, "Go to House Do'Urden and House Fey-Branche. Quickly. Tell the matrons to send us all of their wizards and priestesses. Tell them to come and join in this."

"The matrons won't come," Yvonnel told Quenthel when they headed back for their respective trees at the end of the wide trail that spilled onto the meadow. "And their aid, if any, will be thin."

"I know," Quenthel replied.

"If we fail, they can deny participation," Yvonnel warned.

"That will hardly matter if we fail," Quenthel said. "But if we succeed, they will be more wedded to House Baenre and will deign to show it to forego the wrath of the victorious Matron Mother."

They parted then, and Yvonnel gave silent approval to her aunt. Her invitation was putting Matron Byrtyn, and particularly the wavering Matron Zeerith, into a tight box.

They took their places at their respective trees, each supported by a bevy of priestesses and wizards. With a shared nod, they again began to weave.

Little seemed to come of their efforts.

The ground began to shake more noticeably under their feet.

SWEATING AND EXHAUSTED, CATTI-BRIE TRIED TO PUT aside the acute pain and her very real fears that the primordial had damaged her coming child. She tried to put aside the critical situation outside of this room, where the dwarves of Gauntlgrym fought for their very existence against seemingly overwhelming odds. She tried to sift through the confusion of Yvonnel's request and Zak's clarification—and that led her back to Drizzt, her Drizzt, the love of her life.

More than anything at all, that settled Catti-brie. The memory of her husband pushed the pain away, threw any fears aside, and gave her the strength she needed both for this birth and more.

Much more.

She whispered the words Yvonnel had given to Copetta and

Copetta to her. She whispered the incantation as she blew in short breaths to push the pain away.

And there, as the magic began to execute, she found something, something wonderful, something beautiful.

The beauty of creation, of a life coming forth.

And in that creation, power as the woman had never known before.

She sent her magical voice out far and wide, like an announcement of the birth to bolster the dwarves and their allies, to shake their enemies. She had no specifics to add to that simple message dweomer at first, unlike when Matron Malice had blasted the room in House Hun'ett to paralyze the priestesses.

Not at first.

BROTHER AFAFRENFERE KNEW THAT HE WAS LOST, DELI-ciously so. He had come to this spiritual state to escape the lethal bite of a blade, and then determined to find Drizzt, but now, all of that was gone from him, as were any thoughts of returning to his physical body, of being *alive* in any sense of the word he had ever known.

For now he was alive, more than ever. Now he knew truth and eternity and the beauty of . . . everything.

And he could be a part of it. He was a part of it, and that was good. Any grounding he had to the world he had left behind wisped away to almost nothingness.

Almost.

For then Afafrenfere heard a voice, sweet and strong. He knew it to be Catti-brie, sweet Catti-brie, powerful Catti-brie.

He heard her call, heard her announcement, felt her determination, her sheer force of will, and it beckoned him back, reminding him of his unfinished business.

Her voice found him and guided him like a beacon on a distant shore. The path to reforming his physical body and fighting with his allies was clear to him then, and the call beckoned.

YVONNEL'S FINGERS BEGAN TO MOVE AS IF NOT OF HER own accord, weaving in the air as if she was playing some unseen harp.

Across the way, Quenthel similarly fell into a rhythm that surprised her consciousness.

For there was a music in the air, but one of magic, not notes. They felt the power of Catti-brie, thrown out to them as Matron Malice had done to House Hun'ett, except to reverse effect. Where Malice had paralyzed the Hun'etts, Catti-brie now filtered her power into the two Baenres, lending them strength, giving them harmony, lifting their magic to heights they knew only from the memories of Yvonnel the Eternal, first in Matron Mother Yvonnel Baenre's own use of birth magic in the early days of Menzoberranzan and then a second time when Yvonnel the Eternal had dropped House Oblodra into the Clawrift.

Webs spewed from the fingers of the priestesses, attaching to their respective trees, climbing high and out toward each other in the highest branches, then with filaments drifting down to attach across the way.

The priestesses and wizards supporting them felt the magic, too, though they didn't understand it. Regardless, their energies filtered into the unknown ritual.

The web grew, very quickly, filling the air between the trees.

So soon after, Yvonnel and Quenthel fell back to the eastern end of the meadow, the other priestesses and wizards following them. The web was there, completed but almost fully translucent, a filament here or there shining only in those moments when the wind pushed it to align with the first rays of dawn coming into the sky behind the drow.

The ground shook now continually.

Matron Zhindia was coming.

AS SHE FELL INTO THE FULLNESS OF THE MOMENT, HER child moving from her body, the magic of the spell filling her with unbridled joy and hope and a great sense of oneness with everything— with her fellow humans, with every sentient race, with animals, with the plants, with the stones and the water and the air itself—Catti-brie knew a level of peace she had never before imagined. More than she had known in the magical forest of Mielikki in the years when she was, in some regard, dead.

This was understanding. This was beauty.

This was power.

For a brief flash, she wished that she still was wearing her ring. Perhaps she could quiet the primordial, perhaps even open the portals!

But no, she realized just as quickly. Her understanding of the multiverse was clearer now and she understood that Maegera would not be affected by this magic, by her attempts at persuasion, by anything at all. For Maegera was a wall, a literal force of nature, and no spell she might cast, even in the heightened state, would matter at all in that regard.

Her mind whirled, the pain intense but the joy sweet, so unbelievably sweet.

She sensed the moment of culmination, the moment of separation, the true power of creation, upon her. Distantly, she heard the dwarves, heard Copetta, begging her to push the child out.

She didn't need the encouragement.

This moment beckoned to her and she rushed to it with every ounce of strength, physical and emotional and mental, she could muster, and as the child passed into the world, Catti-brie threw all of that strength through the moment and out wide and far, out to the drow allies gathered near Gauntlgrym, north to Luskan and those who battled the Margaster invasion, west aiming for the ruins and the missing monk, and in the fleeting hope that there she might find a bit of Drizzt's spirit, to tell him at least that his child had arrived.

Even if he would never see the baby.

In the beauty, in the pain of the moment, Catti-brie threw forth a magical bomb, as had Malice those centuries before, but not to assault the invaders, no.

That she would not do. For all of Zaknafein's assurances, she could not so taint this moment of love and beauty with carnage.

Instead, she planted her flag, her beacon, across the northland, encouraging her allies, calling to them all, willing her thoughts and magical force to them to raise and bolster their spirits.

In the west, she heard a call back, and it was from Afafrenfere, and she reached toward the lost monk and planted in the courtyard where he had fallen that image, that moment of beauty, sticking it there like a flag of triumph that Drizzt might know.

She was out of her body. She was, in that instant, as Drizzt had gone and Afafrenfere had gone, lost in a flowing stream of connectedness and consciousness. Of oneness, truly, as everything was broken down before her into its tiniest elements, and they were all so similar. Starstuff.

There was harmony here, and eternal and universal beauty and calm, that mocked the mortal concerns, that made the wars and strife of mortal beings seem . . . stupid.

The cry of a child brought her flying back into the room, to her waiting body, and she blinked open her eyes to see Copetta holding the child.

The babe was swaddled already—she could see only the head and the white hair, and the cord, still attached, hanging down from under the blanket.

"Aye, lady, ye've a beauty here," she heard Copetta say. "She looks like you, but she's her da's eyes."

Catti-brie hardly unpacked that.

Her da.

Her da!

She had a daughter.

Her da!

Drizzt, who would not know her.

But she was okay now, for in the moment of creation, through the power of the magic, she, too, had crossed into that place between the living and eternity—she would never think of it as the living and the dead anymore.

Drizzt was there, and her heart ached for her loss keenly in this moment, particularly in this moment.

But Drizzt was okay.

It was okay.

CHAPTER 30

The Web of Past and Future

One other heard Catti-brie's call, and though he didn't immediately recognize it for what it was, Gromph Baenre understood that something huge was afoot. He moved to his crystal ball and sent his vision to Bleeding Vines—to find the place all but abandoned.

He managed to manipulate his angle and swing out to the south, then the west, then east, to locate Zhindia and her forces at long last.

And beyond them, not far and waiting, he recognized the Baenres and their allies, and he was smart enough and knowledgeable enough about the petty gyrations of the matrons to understand and recognize, too, those who seemed not to be allied with House Baenre.

Indeed, a skirmish in one small pocket broke out between soldiers of House Fey-Branche and those of House Barrison Del'Armgo.

"Lovely," the great mage muttered sarcastically. "Idiots."

He was about to dismiss the image, to let them fight it out and be done with the lot of them, when a familiar voice carried alongside this magical force he was sensing.

The beast will soon escape and no house will leave unscarred, if any house leaves at all, Kimmuriel Oblodra told him.

To the Abyss with all of them, then, Gromph thought.

Even whichever holds the blessing of Lolth?

The point was not lost on the former archmage.

Your inaction now is action, Kimmuriel warned him. *Any who survive will know that Gromph allowed the catastrophe. Lolth will know that Gromph allowed the catastrophe, the destruction of her minions.*

The moment of communication was fleeting, Kimmuriel's telepathy fading to nothingness.

Gromph sat back from his scrying device and took a deep breath, his hands going up to cover his mouth.

He nodded, sorting it out, then ran from the room, from his extradimensional chamber and down through the Hosttower of the Arcane. In the side room to the tunnel at the base of the lowest stair, he dismissed his wards and magical locks and pushed through the door, and before he could convince himself otherwise, he threw the lever, once more letting the power of the Hosttower flow down into the tendrils, the veins.

Across the leagues to the south it flowed, gathering speed and gathering ocean water, and in that magical journey, summoning elementals from the water plane.

"I ANNOUNCE THE ARRIVAL OF MATRON ZEERITH DO'URDEN," Myrineyl Baenre told Quenthel, who was standing on the eastern edge of the meadow in the shadows of the trees as the sun rose behind her. Grim-faced Baenre guards surrounded her as she conferred with Yvonnel and Kimmuriel Oblodra.

Before them, across the way, other scouts came out of the forest cover, specifically avoiding the main trail, as they had been ordered.

"Zhindia comes," Yvonnel noted, nodding off to the east.

"Matron Zhindia," Quenthel corrected, drawing a chuckle from Yvonnel.

"Does it really matter now?"

"It might. It might not" was all that Quenthel would answer.

"Matron Mother?" Minolin Fey, who had come in with Myrineyl, dared ask.

Quenthel scowled at her.

"Matron Zeerith is not patient . . ." Minolin Fey dared to press.

"Then bring her," Quenthel told her, but she needn't have, for there was Zeerith, floating in on her magical disk, Matron Byrtyn Fey beside her.

"Where are we?" Zeerith demanded before any formal greeting.

"We are already fighting, though it is just a testing by Matron Mez'Barris," Byrtyn Fey added. "If we fight here, am I to send my full force at House Barrison Del'Armgo? I will need support, else she will destroy me utterly and quickly."

"You will need more than I could give you," Zeerith said with obvious disgust. "More, likely, than the Matron Mother could share. Do not doubt that Matron Mez'Barris has other matrons behind her. Tell us, Matron Mother Baenre, what is our course?"

"You seem to have already decided yours," Quenthel replied.

"You ask me to commit suicide, and that in the disfavor of Lolth, I fear," Zeerith bluntly replied.

"Driders," came a call from the side.

"Then let us see our course," Quenthel answered. "Together."

"And quickly," Byrtyn begged.

"There!" Yvonnel said, pointing to the trees across the way. Huge shadows moved about through the underbrush, occasionally coming clear enough into the sun for the drow, whose eyes were not strong in the daylight, to make out the distinct form of a drider abomination.

"They will suspect that the open ground is a trap," Zeerith said.

"They are driders," Yvonnel replied. "They won't care."

Quenthel motioned to the side, and Baenre soldiers rushed out onto the field, forming a line quickly and presenting a shield wall.

Several huge spears flew down at them and before most had even landed, the ground began to shake more violently under the thunder of the charge, with hundreds of abominations pouring through the trees across the way, exiting the paths, even the main one strung with magical webbing.

"What will happen?" Myrineyl asked.

"I don't know," came the honest answer from both Quenthel and Yvonnel.

A group of driders led by one huge female appeared on the path beyond the translucent web. Whether they saw it or not, they didn't slow, charging onto the field.

Or trying to.

For there came a great flash of dark light, deep purple, almost black. Then another, and several more as each drider plunged through the trap.

Dark smoke lifted, leaving the abominations writhing and screaming in pain on the field. The ones behind managed to stop and looked on in horror, like everyone else, as those few who went through suffered in obvious agony.

Suffered and writhed, shrieked and tumbled, bones snapping, skin splitting—a sight inspiring the very worst memories of those who had been turned into such an abomination. The difference became stark, though, as the behemoth driders began to shrink, bloated bodies withering, eight legs becoming two.

In short order, nine drow, not nine drider abominations, sat on the meadow, confused, each tapping herself or himself all about with trembling hands to see if it was true. They wore the jerkin and battle armor still, though now that their bodies had shrunk, it was knee-length, not just to their waists.

It could not be!

But it was. Their magical web had undone that which Lolth had done, because no priestess of the Spider Queen believed herself to have the power to transform a drow into a drider. Any priestess, and there were very few, ever given that "privilege" understood herself to be a conduit to the work of Lolth and nothing more.

This before them, more powerful still, wasn't the will of Lolth. How could it be?

Yvonnel glanced around. Time had seemed to stop. Everyone around the meadow, drow and drider, even the slave goblins and bug-bears House Baenre would send into battle, stood staring, mouths hanging open in shock.

This was the highest heresy possible.

"Do you doubt me still?" Kimmuriel Oblodra shouted at the Baenre priestesses.

Before either Yvonnel or Quenthel could reply, from a hillock in the forest across the way, Matron Zhindia screamed her outrage. "For Lolth!"

She was answered, stunningly, by one of the driders-turned-drow, a broad-shouldered woman who was the first of the nine to lift herself from the ground. "Damn Lolth!"

"Mal'a'voselle Amvas Tol," Minolin Fey Baenre remarked, and Quenthel and Yvonnel nodded. "The weapon master of what most considered the very first First House of Menzoberranzan."

"Kill them all! It's a lie!" Zhindia screamed in a voice thick with magic.

"You are the lie!" Matron Mother Quenthel yelled back, her voice, too, magnified by a magical spell.

"I have handmaidens at my side."

"Do you indeed?" Quenthel replied with confidence.

The moment of hesitation shattered. Drow and slave soldiers rushed to form defensive lines on the eastern end of the meadow, while Zhindia's drow and slave soldiers formed into battle groups across the way, in the shelter of the forest shadows. Wizards and clerics alike be-gan their intended spells, and the driders rushed all about, confused and shouting, both to one another and to the nine drow remaining on the field.

Directly across from Yvonnel, a drider on the path rushed down and leaped through the magical webbing—eagerly, almost—and again came that dark, fiery flash and the screaming and writhing. That ob-vious pain did not discourage the others, though—quite the opposite! One by one or in small groups, the abominations swarmed to the web and plunged through.

The few driders of House Baenre, House Do'Urden, House Fey-Branche, and every other house in view of the spectacle didn't wait for permission but charged forward, sprinting across the field and into the forest, to the path, before turning back and plunging through the web.

The glorious web.

"Go and greet the driders, the former driders," Yvonnel told Minolin Fey, Myrineyl, and Saribel Do'Urden. "Guide them to us that we might tell them that they are free."

"Free to join House Baenre, if they wish, as family," Matron Mother Quenthel said, and more than a few gasped at that! Even after all they had just witnessed, such an offer seemed incomprehensible and utterly blasphemous.

And yet, the three priestesses rushed out onto the meadow, heading for Mal'a'voselle Amvas Tol.

"Now what?" Matron Byrtyn Fey asked.

"What have you done?" Matron Zeerith added. "What does it mean?"

"I do not know," Quenthel admitted.

"OPEN REVOLT!" ZHINDIA SNAPPED AT YICCARDARIA AND Eskavidne.

The handmaidens looked to each other, their drow faces masks of great concern.

Then, together, they broke out in mocking laughter.

"How does this amuse you?" Zhindia roared at them. "They just defied your goddess. They, the Matron Mother Baenre herself, just slapped blessed Lolth in the face!"

"Did she?" Yiccardaria gasped, clapping her hand across her heart for dramatic effect—quite the practiced move for one who was not normally a bipedal humanoid.

Eskavidne laughed even louder.

"The others will side with me," Zhindia declared—and loudly, for she knew that the Hunzrin contingent, including First Priestess Charri, were watching this unfolding wildness.

No, Zhindia thought. "Wildness" was not the right word.

"Chaos," she whispered, her correction and her epiphany.

"Sometimes it takes these inferior creatures a bit of time to understand, sister," Eskavidne said to Yiccardaria, and they laughed again, then touched their fingers together, drew a portal in the air, and stepped through it to their abyssal home.

"It's a shame about Zaknafein, though," Yiccardaria muttered as she entered the door.

Such a door was not like a physical door, of course, but Matron Zhindia Melarn started when it closed as surely as if it had been a physical portal slamming shut.

ANOTHER GROUP OF DRIDERS, WEARING THE COLORS AND insignias of several houses, rushed across the field, desperate for that magical web.

"Barrison Del'Armgo," Yvonnel noted of more than a few. "And no doubt Zhindia's own house driders join the resurrected ones as drow once more on the field."

"Matron Zhindia," Zeerith corrected.

Quenthel chuckled at that and looked to Yvonnel, who joined her. Once in Menzoberranzan—long ago—the woman chosen by each family to sit on the Conclave, before it was called the Ruling Council, only wore her title while at the table.

They didn't need to tell the others that then, however. Indeed, they both understood that they could not.

Sequential effect.

"Do not attack Matron Zhindia," Yvonnel advised her aunt.

"No," Quenthel agreed. "It is time to go home. It is time for all of us to go home."

"You don't think there will be a fight about this?" Zeerith asked.

"Of course there will," said Yvonnel. "Menzoberranzan will be a bloody battleground."

"A true civil war is quite possible," Quenthel added.

"What have you gained?" an outraged Sos'Umptu called from a short distance away.

The four, and many others, turned to regard her.

"Do you think this will stand?" Sos'Umptu yelled at them. "Lolth herself will come against you! I only pray that she will use my imperfect body as her avatar to destroy the mockery you have made of glorious House Baenre!"

Yvonnel locked the priestess's gaze with her own.

And shrugged.

Sos'Umptu ran off.

"Is she wrong?" the skeptical and clearly terrified Zeerith asked. "What has happened but a pause? What have we gained?"

Yvonnel and Quenthel together turned to regard the field. "Many hundreds"—Quenthel paused and smiled, for more and more driders were eagerly rushing through that web, desperate to try, even in the face of such agony of transformation, even against any fears that it might be a trick designed to punish them even more—"Perhaps a few thousand soldiers to our cause."

Zeerith took a deep breath, but neither it nor the assurance from the Matron Mother seemed to have any calming effect upon her.

Yvonnel understood. Their world had just turned upside down and was about to shaken by the ankles until everything they thought they knew fell to the ground below them. Sos'Umptu would likely be a problem, a big one, and would no doubt run to the side of Mez'Barris and whisper in her ear.

Zhindia Melarn, too, so zealous and vicious, wasn't finished. Perhaps it would have been expedient to turn the full force of House Baenre on her in that moment of vulnerability, to erase her and hers from the world in one swift slaughter.

But no. They had to give her the chance.

To do less would be to become exactly that which they had just rejected.

CHAPTER 31

Rebirth

A re you coming out?" the two men in the extradimensional chamber heard, from a familiar voice.

"Jarlaxle," Entreri confirmed, peering out the small window to the region immediately below. He dropped the rope and scrambled outside the pocket dimension, sliding down to the ground, Wulfgar close behind.

When he went out, Wulfgar saw that it was indeed Jarlaxle, and he was not alone, both Regis and Zaknafein beside him.

"How . . . ?" Entreri started to ask, but he shook his head and dismissed it. Was there ever any purpose in asking this one how he knew the things he knew?

"Regis told me that you had come out here," Jarlaxle answered anyway, which of course told none of them of how he had found the extradimensional chamber. He did have that eyepatch, though . . .

Jarlaxle looked to Wulfgar. "You are an uncle, my friend," he said with a grin. "Of sorts, I suppose, and yes, the daughter of Drizzt and Catti-brie is as beautiful as you would expect."

"I must get home," Wulfgar said.

"Perhaps that would be best for all of us," said another, and the foursome turned as one to see the approach of Yvonnel and Kimmuriel.

"You heard?" the priestess asked Wulfgar and Entreri.

Entreri tossed her the clairaudience disk. "We heard."

"The drow are leaving?" Wulfgar asked.

"All of them," Yvonnel confirmed. "Already on the march, or the run, depending upon which house concerns you. They flee to the corridors of the lower Underdark, and I expect that many different routes will be used as they, as we, all rush back to our guarded homes."

"Well, not all," Jarlaxle quipped.

"Where do you see Bregan D'aerthe in all of this?" Kimmuriel asked Yvonnel.

"I'm not sure that is where I see myself in all of this," Yvonnel answered. "There are no examples of that which is about to befall us all, I fear."

"Just the memories of Yvonnel," said Kimmuriel, and Yvonnel nodded.

"Return the ring to Catti-brie as I bade you," Yvonnel told Entreri. "For I must be away now to fight for my home. My real home and not the one that has been . . . infected for two millennia." She looked to Zak. "Will you join me?"

"I don't even know what you're talking about. I don't even know what just happened."

"And I don't know what just happened, either," an annoyed Jarlaxle pointed out.

"I resist telling you because I know that you cannot comprehend the magnitude of it," Yvonnel started. "But then again, perhaps you particular two, more than most others, will understand enough to appreciate it—and I'm certain that Kimmuriel here will fill in more details in short order.

"The truth is, you don't know Menzoberranzan. Not even you, Jarlaxle, who has spent your life trying to figure it out. You cannot understand the hope that brought us to the great cavern those millennia removed. Yes, *hope*. It was not anger that brought us there, nor fear. It was hope. We fled a world of tyrant queens and insane kings, a place of unending war and injustice. We found a sanctuary, a deep cave, full of Faezress magic—though we did not understand that at the time—and easily defended. A sanctuary, I say, and indeed that is what the word 'Menzoberranzan' then meant in the ancient tongue of the drow.

"A hundred families," she continued. "Ten thousand dark elves. And each had a say in their family, and each family had a voice in the Plenum, and the largest families spoke those concerns in the Conclave, which you now—and only—know as the Ruling Council. We were not rulers then as much as servants, heeding the words of all the drow. And it was Lady Lolth that led us there, before she was called the Spider Queen."

Yvonnel gave a little laugh and shake of her head.

"I remember well now that I—my namesake, I mean—thought spiders ugly little things, and quite terrifying back then," she added. "But like many things I thought ugly and wrong, I and all the others came to see them as normal and good, even exalted, as the years passed."

"Were men on this . . . Conclave?" Jarlaxle asked. "This Plenum, even?"

Another helpless laugh came from the woman. "No, sadly," Yvonnel replied. "I do not pretend that it was idyllic, nor that we were far removed from the barbary and injustice we tried to escape. Even so, I insist, this was not the Menzoberranzan you have ever known. When I see our city as it is against the vision of what it was, I am appalled and almost without hope.

"Almost.

"But I will hold that hope tightly to my heart. Because the struggle is worth it."

Zak looked confused, as did Jarlaxle, but Wulfgar was nodding.

"I just told you, but I do not expect you to understand," Yvonnel said to them. "Just hope. And my aunt Quenthel cannot tell the others . . ."

"Your aunt Quenthel?" Jarlaxle asked, drawing a wide grin from Yvonnel.

"She is, after all. She cannot tell the others, particularly not the other matrons, for they do not have the gift that she and I have been given."

"The memories of Yvonnel the Eternal," Jarlaxle reasoned.

"And the ability, because of your lieutenant here, to view those memories separately and from afar, without the emotional, visceral attachment to them that led my namesake—indeed, I have to say that led me, for in this context her actions truly become a part of me!—to do the things she's, I've, done."

Jarlaxle and Zak exchanged helplessly puzzled looks.

"To see the beginning and the end without the middle," Yvonnel told them. "To see the effect starkly, without the steps of the cause."

Jarlaxle gave a little gasp and nod.

"The hole is dug one handful at a time," said Zak, catching on as well.

"The darkness is deepened one lie, one act, at a time," Kimmuriel agreed.

"Wish me well, my friends, for your stake in this is no less than my own," Yvonnel finished. "King Bruenor will win here now—the battle is almost over."

"Luskan is soon reclaimed," Kimmuriel added.

Yvonnel bowed to them all and took her leave, disappearing into the forest.

"I expect that you will shed light on this," Jarlaxle said to Kimmuriel.

"Yvonnel explained it quite well," the psionicist replied.

"And you weren't surprised at all. How could you know?"

"The hive mind of the illithids is a vast repertory of knowledge," Kimmuriel answered. "A great library—the greatest library—full of musty thoughts in unknown places."

"So you told Yvonnel and Quenthel?" a startled Jarlaxle asked.

"I led them to their own memories, nothing more," Kimmuriel explained. "I did not know exactly the end of that path, but it had become clear to me that the path would show them the truth of Lolth, and that revelation would—so I hoped and so I bet with my very life—turn them away from the Spider Queen."

Jarlaxle answered with an uncustomary "Hmm."

"At least that," Zaknafein agreed.

"So you learned this from the illithids," Jarlaxle reasoned, speaking very slowly and following his developing thoughts carefully, "and the memories of Yvonnel the Eternal taught the truth to Yvonnel and the Matron Mother of Menzoberranzan."

"Yes."

"And the memories of Yvonnel the Eternal were given to Yvonnel and to Quenthel by . . . ?"

"By Methil El Vidden—" Kimmuriel stopped short.

"By an illithid," Jarlaxle remarked. "It all goes back to the mind flayers."

It wasn't often that Jarlaxle saw Kimmuriel Oblodra flustered, but he was then, obviously so.

"Or maybe even further," the clever mercenary added, stabbing a finger into the air as if in epiphany. "By Methil El Viddenvelp, who was instructed to do so by . . . ?"

Kimmuriel started to answer, but stopped short again and merely laughed at the deepening absurdity.

"By Gromph Baenre," Jarlaxle answered his own question. "It makes one wonder who it was that inspired Gromph to begin such a tale as this."

"Unwittingly," Kimmuriel said.

"Probably," Jarlaxle agreed. "But Gromph is often in the company of . . . demons? Handmaidens? He was until recently, after all, the archmage of Menzoberranzan."

"Perhaps there is no deeper cause, or greater force behind this change, or revelation, or whatever else you might consider it," Artemis Entreri offered. "Maybe it just happened."

"Or maybe it was an unforeseen result of a demonic inspiration," Kimmuriel added. "Or a miscalculation by Lolth."

"Or exactly what Lolth wanted to happen?" Jarlaxle suggested.

"Or maybe," Jarlaxle started to add, then stopped and smiled rather wickedly at Kimmuriel. *Yes* . . . he mouthed cryptically.

Kimmuriel narrowed a glare at him. He knew what was coming.

"My friend here knows the illithids well," Jarlaxle told Wulfgar, Zak, and Entreri. "And this one, Kimmuriel, he has for centuries wanted revenge on Menzoberranzan for the fall of House Oblodra."

"By rescuing the Matron Mother Baenre?" Kimmuriel replied with as much sarcasm as the psionicist had ever managed.

"Ah, yes, true that," Jarlaxle agreed, feigning defeat. "It escaped me that you are without the strong sense of irony to go that delicious route." Jarlaxle turned to the others. "So we have it, then," he declared. "It was the illithids, a grand and brilliant plan! Or it was Lolth herself, ever making chaos for her enjoyment. Or it was one of her great rivals, then—perhaps Demogorgon!—blowing up the whole damned Lolthian world on Faerun."

"Or it was nothing at all beyond the epiphany of two women in position to make a difference," Entreri said dryly. He sighed and shook his head, then looked up at Wulfgar, who stood beside him. "You see, my friend?" he asked with sarcasm exceeding that of the others. "This is why we can't have good things, good thoughts, simple joy, or hope."

Jarlaxle laughed loudly at that, amused. But there really was a nagging doubt here, about all of it. The most important lesson he had learned in his desperate struggle to survive in Menzoberranzan was that nothing—nothing!—was as it seemed.

Not ever.

But how he wanted to believe that this time would be different.

HE SAW THAT MAGICAL ENERGY THERE AS CLEARLY AS IF Catti-brie had planted a beacon on the ground where lay his skewered robe.

The robe of the Monastery of the Yellow Rose. The robe of a master, given to him by Grandmaster Kane, who had warned him about this transcendence.

A pang of remorse filled Afafrenfere commonly throughout his scattering thoughts, and that regret pulled at his dispersing consciousness like a great ocean whirlpool, moving them around and around, and inward, coalescing once more.

Now he heard the magical call more clearly still, Catti-brie announcing the birth of her child. Her daughter! Drizzt's daughter!

Afafrenfere was about to reconstitute his mortal body. Anyone looking on the courtyard of Thornhold would have seen it as bits of magical light, cascading across the ground like a knot of baby toads hopping to a common point.

Drizzt's daughter!

He had to relay that message. How could he become a mere man again and not tell the scattered remnants of this drow he had come to love as a brother?

The knot of toads unwound once more, a determined monk reaching out to those fleeting bits of Drizzt Do'Urden yet again, this time with the power of certainty behind them.

Afafrenfere felt the residual magical energy keenly and understood that it was already fading, that he hadn't much time.

And understood, too, that it wasn't strong enough for him to take Drizzt Do'Urden back to the courtyard of Thornhold with him.

Alas.

ARTEMIS ENTRERI GAVE THE RING TO WULFGAR TO RE-turn to Catti-brie. He wasn't ready to go back to Gauntlgrym, then. He wondered if he would ever return to that place.

"You will go find Dahlia?" Wulfgar asked.

The assassin shrugged, even shook his head a little bit. Too much had happened to him here this day. He couldn't deny that Dahlia had indeed come for him at great personal risk or that he cared for her on so many levels.

But the only thing that Artemis Entreri knew in that moment was that he didn't know . . . anything! His encounter with Sharon, with the physical manifestation of conscience, his own conscience, was not diminishing. The power of it hung over him, frightening him, giving him hope.

He just didn't know.

Anything.

He suspected that Dahlia wouldn't support the changes that had come over him. He could explain his epiphany over and over to her, but could he really? Could anyone understand such a thing as the cocoon Sharon had put around him without experiencing it?

Or perhaps it was part of Entreri's own redemption to *make* Dahlia understand. She was another lost soul, of course, and had been for a long, long time. Dahlia had been scarred in more than her body. Her heart was crossed, no doubt, with dark lines of mistrust and anger.

Even that last notion overwhelmed him. He was to be her teacher? He? The prized assassin of Calimport?

He almost laughed out loud, but instead just walked away.

Into the forest a short distance, he heard Jarlaxle coming quickly behind him. The mercenary said not a word—the tormented Entreri was truly glad of that!—but just walked up beside and matched his every step. Soon after, Jarlaxle draped an arm across Entreri's shoulders, and the assassin hadn't the strength to shove it aside.

He was kidding himself again, he knew. He didn't *want* to shove it aside.

He wasn't sure of where he was going until he was almost there, turning onto the path that led into the meadow.

All was strangely quiet now, and remarkably empty of drow and driders and goblinkin. Indeed, only a solitary figure remained, one the two walking companions recognized.

They joined Thibbledorf Pwent as he stood before the web, hands on hips.

"Ye see it?" the dwarven vampire asked when they arrived. "Ye see what it did?"

"I did," Entreri answered before Jarlaxle could.

"Turned them spidery drow things back into elfs!" Pwent exclaimed.

Jarlaxle gasped.

"All of them," Entreri confirmed. "Yvonnel and Quenthel weaved this . . . I don't even know what to call it."

"The driders went through it and became drow once more?" Jarlaxle asked, his voice shaky. "You cannot . . ."

"They did," said Entreri.

"Hunnerds and hunnerds o' the damned things," Pwent agreed.

Jarlaxle fell to the side a step and stood as the dwarf had been, hands on hips, shaking his head. "I see that I have a lot to learn about what happened out here."

"Kimmuriel will tell you," Entreri answered.

On a sudden impulse, the assassin pulled a weapon from his belt. He didn't know why, and had no idea of what might happen, but he threw his jeweled dagger right at the web. It passed through with a great flash of purple-black energy, then fell to the ground beyond. There it sparked and flipped about, smoke pouring from it.

No, not smoke.

Spirits!

Souls trapped within the foul thing, coming out in droves. Souls taken over the course of a millennia and more of deadly, evil use, flying free into the multiverse at last, leaping and spreading, climbing into the sunlight and fading fast to eternity.

"Aye!" Thibbledorf Pwent howled, and with no more thought, he followed the dagger, leaping through the web.

Another flash of that deep purple light exploded, and the dwarf stumbled and tumbled onto the meadow grass beyond. He tried to bounce up to stand, but could not, and fell forward onto his hands and knees and began vomiting violently, black mucus pouring from his mouth.

Jarlaxle ran to the left to go around the oak that anchored one end of the web.

Artemis Entreri took a more direct route and did not slow despite Jarlaxle's cry of "No!"

He walked right through the web.

But there was no flash and Entreri wasn't thrown to the ground or slowed in any way. He got to Pwent before Jarlaxle arrived and put his hand on the dwarf's back.

"Free," Pwent managed to proclaim, before another gout of black fluid fell from his mouth.

Entreri held him through the vomiting and convulsing, and when it was over, Pwent laughed, and there was such joy in it! Such . . . freedom.

"Free," he said again, and he tumbled to the side and rolled onto his back. "It took the curse," he said, Jarlaxle and Entreri leaning over him. "Aye, and to be sure but it killed me to death."

"Pwent," Jarlaxle said.

"Ye tell me king," Pwent gasped, choking forth another splash of the foul liquid. "Ye tell him that his Pwent died happy . . .

"That he died free . . ."

His voice trailed off.

"No!" Artemis Entreri declared, and he slipped one arm under the dwarf's back, the other under Pwent's hips, and hoisted him into his arms, carrying the heavy, armored dwarf as if he was a child.

"No!" Artemis Entreri declared again, and he started off for Gauntlgrym.

"The whole world's gone mad," Jarlaxle said, standing alone on the field, hands on hips once more. He noted a glimmer to the side and laughed, then walked over and plucked the jeweled dagger from where it had stuck in the ground.

"This could be fun," the rogue said, following the path Entreri had taken. "And profitable."

Jarlaxle regarded Entreri again, carrying the heavy Pwent, almost staggering under the weight but determinedly pressing on. Jarlaxle had several magical items that could lessen that burden, or could indeed cart Thibbledorf all the way. He shook his head at the thought, though.

Artemis Entreri needed to do this.

LED BY MAL'A'VOSELLE AMVAS TOL, AS MOST OF THEM HAD been in the Abyss for many years, the vast army of reformed drow elves—driders returned from the grave and the many driders who had come to the surface in the service of the various houses—marched as one behind the banners of House Baenre. None had pledged allegiance yet, but the course seemed obvious to all of them—they understood the truth of Lolth because they had seen the awfulness of her worst wrath. The unspeakable torment had burned into them a hopelessness that only now lifted to see a glimmer of hope.

That glimmer shone from the woman who should have been among the most hated of the group, but it was indeed the very same Matron Mother Baenre who had given them hope and who now promised them a very different future.

Baenre soldiers and Mal'a'voselle's closest advisors filtered among the long lines, identifying the new recruits and organizing them into battle groups in case they encountered another drow house on the long journey.

One former drider watched with trepidation as a trio of soldiers approached.

"Welcome," one greeted him. "Are you returned from the Abyss or have you come from another house?"

"Or from House Baenre?" a second asked.

The man shrugged. "I was dead, long dead."

"What is your name?"

"Dini . . ." he started, and quickly added, "nae."

"Dini Nay?" the Baenre soldier asked.

"Dininae," he corrected, trying to hide his nervousness, for he had heard enough of the events that had precipitated this still-unfathomable event to understand that his real name, Dinin Do'Urden, might bring him a fair amount of grief and trouble.

"Of what house?"

"No house," he lied. "I lived in the Stenchstreets."

The soldiers noted his name and moved on. Dinin didn't know what to think or what to do.

THEIR SPIRITS SHARED IN KNOWLEDGE. CATTI-BRIE'S MESsage was delivered.

Again the knot of magical lights hopped across the courtyard, and this time coalesced, and the naked man scooped up the robes and donned them, then used those memories to go inside the keep of Thornhold, to a crack in one wall.

Fishing fingers found a chain.

He held it in his hand, staring at the whistle, the summoning call to the unicorn that had carried Drizzt Do'Urden for many years.

EPILOGUE

They were all gathered there, for Catti-brie had promised them the name of the child: Bruenor and his queens Tannabritches and Mallabritches, Regis and Donnola, Wulfgar, Penelope Harpell, Athrogate, Jarlaxle, and Zaknafein and Artemis Entreri. Even Guenhwyvar was there, for Entreri had thought it fitting to bring the panther forth for this event.

And Thibbledorf Pwent, fast recovering from his ordeal, alive once more, hungry for mutton and thirsty for beer, ready to serve his beloved king Bruenor. He kept glancing at Entreri, tossing him a nod and hoisting his flagon. Entreri had carried him all the way to this very room, where the clerics of Gauntlgrym had found enough remaining magic to bring his ravaged body through the ordeal of shrugging off his vampiric curse.

So much had been cleansed or healed. Or contained! The magic of the Host Tower had arrived, finally, the primordial caught fast once more, and they had even managed to reopen the portals to Luskan and Longsaddle, and now those to the Silver Marches and the other dwarven strongholds.

Indeed, Queen Dagnabet Waybeard of Mithral Hall sat beside Bruenor. Her army was out in the grand entry hall now, finishing the cleansing beside the ferocious dwarves of Clan Battlehammer and the determined halflings of Bleeding Vines. The armies of Citadel Adbar and Citadel Felbarr awaited a call should they be needed, but no one expected that they would. Not now. The drow were gone, the demons destroyed or dispersed.

Finally, the door to the private chamber opened and Catti-brie entered, carrying her daughter, the priestess Copetta beside her, as she had been the three days since the child had come into the world. The baby's eyes were more open now, and as Penny had said, she had her father's eyes—somewhat.

They were purple, yes, but not the light lavender of Drizzt's eyes. They were purple, as rich and deep as Catti-brie's blue eyes, so striking against her skin, which carried the hue of a pink rose at twilight, and peeking out below her somewhat startling shock of reddish hair, so much like her mother's thick auburn mane.

"Drizzt and I spoke of this for a long while soon after we learned I was with child," Catti-brie told them, her voice somewhat shaky but holding strong. "We knew from the beginning that this child belonged to more than we two parents, that it . . . she was a child born into love from many who would help us make sure that her life was blessed."

"I'll harden her head!" Pwent promised, and all laughed.

"She was conceived in love and in the spirit of tolerance and trust," Catti-brie went on. "It could not have been—none of this could have been, had not her grandfather looked past the color of my beloved Drizzt's skin and looked instead to the man he was." She turned to Wulfgar. "You would not be here if not for that same generous spirit and belief in the goodness of all."

"That's something Bruenor will never admit," Wulfgar agreed.

All eyes went to the dwarf king, who was blushing fiercely, tears welling in his eyes.

"And so, in the spirit of what blessed us and in the hopes of what might come, four names did we pick. Two if it was a boy and two if it, if she, was a girl. First, I tell you my own name. It was not always Catti-brie."

"You were given a different name in your rebirth from Mielikki's garden," Wulfgar remarked.

Catti-brie shook her head. "That is true, but I speak of my first name, my name as a child before I came to be the daughter of Bruenor Battlehammer."

That brought curious looks, particularly from Wulfgar, but Regis smiled knowingly and Bruenor could only nod.

"Cataline," Catti-brie went on, "though I know not my first surname. It was changed to Catti, and the name Brienne added."

"Brienne, or Briennelle, is the woman's version of Bruenor," Dagnabet explained, for a certain dwarf king was not able to speak at that moment.

"Catti-brie," Catti-brie said. "And so I give to you, my dearest friends, Briennelle."

They started to cheer, but Catti-brie stopped them short with an upraised hand. "Brienne in the spirt of that which blessed us, and Zaharina in the hopes of what might be."

Zaknafein nearly fell off his chair.

"Zaharina is the feminine of Zaknafein," Jarlaxle explained. "Brie-Zara, then!"

"Breezy!" Thibbledorf Pwent shouted.

They all cheered, or started to, but then the other door to the room burst open and a man rushed in.

All in the room recognized the robes of a master of St. Sollars and the Monastery of the Yellow Rose, and recognized even more the man wearing them.

The lavender-eyed, white-haired drow ranger wearing them.

ABOUT THE AUTHOR

Thirty years ago, R. A. Salvatore created the character of Drizzt Do'Urden, the dark elf who has withstood the test of time to stand today as an icon in the fantasy genre. With his work in the Forgotten Realms, the Crimson Shadow, the DemonWars Saga, and other series, Salvatore has sold more than thirty million books worldwide and has appeared on the *New York Times* bestseller list more than two dozen times. He considers writing to be his personal journey, but still, he's quite pleased that so many are walking the road beside him! R.A. lives in Massachusetts with his wife, Diane, and their three dogs, Ivan, Pikel, and Dexter. He still plays softball for his team, Clan Battlehammer, and enjoys his weekly *DemonWars: Reformation* RPG game. Salvatore can be found on Facebook at https://www.facebook.com/RA-Salvatore-54142479810/, on Twitter at @r_a_salvatore, and at RASalvaStore.com.